6-29-18

6-29-18-RD

D1047117

DETROIT
PUBLIC
LIBRARY

Detroit Library for the Blind and Physically Handicapped
If you can only read Large Print, you may be eligible to borrow audio books through the mail at no cost to you.
For more information or to apply for service:
Phone: 313-481-1702
Email: lbph@detroitpubliclibrary.org
Web: www.detroitpubliclibrary.org

DETROIT
PUBLIC
LIBRARY
Library on Wheels
3666 Grand River Ave.
Detroit, Michigan 48208
313-481-1706

AUG -- 2004

Low
cont

To Tame
a Rebel

*Also by Georgina Gentry
in Large Print:*

To Tame a Savage
To Tame a Texan
Cheyenne Song
Warrior's Heart

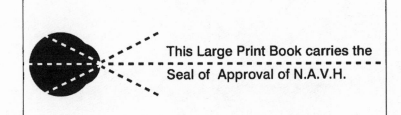

This Large Print Book carries the
Seal of Approval of N.A.V.H.

To Tame a Rebel

Georgina Gentry

Library On Wheels
3666 Grand River
Detroit, MI 48208
313-833-5686

WHEELER
PUBLISHING

0376997423

Copyright © 2004 by Lynne Murphy

All rights reserved.

Published in 2004 by arrangement with Zebra Books, an imprint of Kensington Publishing Corp.

Wheeler Large Print Compass.

The text of this Large Print edition is unabridged. Other aspects of the book may vary from the original edition.

Set in 16 pt. Plantin by Elena Picard.

Printed in the United States on permanent paper.

Library of Congress Cataloging-in-Publication Data

Gentry, Georgina.
    To tame a rebel / Georgina Gentry.
      p. cm.
    ISBN 1-58724-762-3 (lg. print : hc : alk. paper)
    1. United States — History — Civil War, 1861–1865 —
Participation, Indian — Fiction. 2. United States — History
— Civil War, 1861–1865 — Fiction. 3. Indian captivities —
Fiction. 4. Cherokee Indians — Fiction. 5. Creek Indians —
Fiction. 6. Women spies — Fiction. 7. Nurses — Fiction.
8. Large type books. I. Title.
PS3557.E4616T58 2004
813´.54—dc22   2004043082

This story is dedicated to the people of the Five Civilized Tribes: the Cherokee, Creek (Muskogee), Seminole, Choctaw, and Chickasaw. They fought valiantly on both sides of the Civil War in Indian Territory, suffered and endured much, and after all that, saw their tribal lands taken by the U.S. government a few years after the war ended, to be given to white settlers in the land runs.

National Association for Visually Handicapped
------------------------ *serving the partially seeing*

As the Founder/CEO of NAVH, the only national health agency solely devoted to those who, although not totally blind, have an eye disease which could lead to serious visual impairment, I am pleased to recognize Thorndike Press* as one of the leading publishers in the large print field.

Founded in 1954 in San Francisco to prepare large print textbooks for partially seeing children, NAVH became the pioneer and standard setting agency in the preparation of large type.

Today, those publishers who meet our standards carry the prestigious "Seal of Approval" indicating high quality large print. We are delighted that Thorndike Press is one of the publishers whose titles meet these standards. We are also pleased to recognize the significant contribution Thorndike Press is making in this important and growing field.

Lorraine H. Marchi, L.H.D.
Founder/CEO
NAVH

* Thorndike Press encompasses the following imprints: Thorndike, Wheeler, Walker and Large Print Press.

Prologue

You said . . . no white people in the world should ever molest us . . . and should we be injured by anybody you would come with your soldiers and punish them. But now the wolf has come, men who are strangers tread our soil, our children are frightened and the mothers cannot sleep for fear. . . . We want you to send us word what to do . . . My ears are open and my memory is good.

— Creek leader *Opothleyahola*
to Abraham Lincoln,
Summer 1861

Unfortunately, the president is busy with more pressing matters with his Civil War farther to the east. No one is answering the old Creek leader. No soldiers are en route to aid the tribe in fighting off its invaders. The wolves are coming, and only a handful of brave warriors stand between the attackers and their helpless prey. One such warrior is Yellow Jacket. Once this great warrior and the Cherokee Jim Eagle were friends; now they must face each other and kill or be killed. Two very different women love these two braves, thus complicating this saga of the Indian Territory.

Find a comfortable chair, and escape with me now back to that long-ago time when the West was uncivilized and set ablaze as the Civil War spread like wildfire across the Indian lands. . . .

PART ONE

Yellow Jacket's
(Matt Folane's) Story

Chapter 1

Twilight Dumont was both desperate and scared, but at least now she wouldn't have to make a decision. It was being made for her.

She held Harvey's letter and stared out the shack's window at the smoldering ruins of her Virginia plantation. Damned Yankee renegades had burned the place to the ground two days ago while she hid in terror. The slaves had run away weeks ago, headed north.

Twilight ran her hand through her tangled brown hair and sighed, feeling guilty because she didn't really like her stepbrother, Harvey, even though they'd been raised together. She reread the letter she'd gotten two days ago:

> *Dear Twilight,*
> *I know things must be dreadful for you with your dear husband killed in the war.*

Dear husband. It had been a disastrous marriage, but Pierre had been a friend of her stepbrother, and Harvey had encouraged the

11

match. Certainly Harvey had thought Pierre's money would give her an easy life, and she hadn't argued over it. Genteel Southern ladies usually did what they were told.

. . .Twilight, do come out here to Indian Territory and join me. I have a flourishing sutler's store near the fort and there's a good chance to make a fresh start. I'm enclosing money for the stagecoach.

Warm regards,
Harvey

Indian Territory. Twilight's petite form shuddered at the thought of savages. Everyone knew that faraway place was wild and uncivilized. Well, at least there was no war there. Twilight sighed and looked out at the smoldering ruins again. Yes, the decision had been made for her. She would throw her few things in a valise and journey to Indian Territory.

Indian Territory, mid-October 1861

Yellow Jacket frowned as he watched his niece comb her hair. "Heruse, where do you think you are going?"

She stopped humming and turned to face him. Her name meant *Pretty* in the Muskogee language, and it suited her. "Uncle, must you question my every move?"

12

He rubbed his chin and frowned. His dead brother's child was so lovely and so naive. "You're only sixteen, and I feel responsibility to your father."

Her beautiful face saddened; then she shrugged. "I can look out for myself."

"Stay away from the soldiers," he ordered. "They will tell an Indian girl anything to get them into their blankets. Remember, they killed your father."

She played with the blue beaded bracelet her uncle had given her, and didn't look at him. "I swear I'm not seeing any soldier. I'm merely going over to visit a friend."

Yellow Jacket shook his head. "I think you'd better stay here. It'll be dark soon, and with rebel soldiers camped all around, I don't like you being out alone."

Her dark eyes flashed fire. "I'm not a child. You can't tell me what to do."

"Yes, I can," he answered patiently. "I owe that to my dead brother."

She whirled on him. "That was an accident. At the fort, they say they mistook him for a hostile in the dark."

"He was hunting for food for us all," Yellow Jacket reminded her. "Now, stay here and get ready for bed. I've got a meeting with the council."

"All the council does is talk, talk, talk," she complained, pouting.

"That's because there's so much riding on

their decision." Yellow Jacket sighed. "The leaders are meeting with our leader, Opothleyahola, tonight to decide what to do. There's talk our people might go to Kansas to join the Union forces there."

She blinked, askance. "Kansas? That's crazy. I'd just as soon stay right here."

"It's not your decision to make. Now, do as I say. I'll be back late."

"I hate you!" she yelled after him.

Yellow Jacket didn't bother to answer as he went out into the dusk and shut the door behind him. His brother's death weighed heavily on his soul, and he hated the rebel soldiers for it. If he learned which one was responsible, he would kill that man very slowly. Yet, he had no time for personal revenge. Events were in upheaval for all the Five Civilized Tribes of the eastern Indian Territory because of the white man's Civil War raging to the east of them, far, far away.

As he slipped through the night to the meeting place, he fingered the big knife in his belt. It was dangerous to be out after dark, but Yellow Jacket, named for the aggressive stinging wasp, was a seasoned warrior who was afraid of nothing . . . except that he might let his dead brother down in rearing the wild, pretty Heruse.

The weather had a chill to it. The coming winter might be a bad one with snow and cold winds. That would not be good for the tribes in their temporary shacks and tents who had gathered around their old leader, Opothleyahola.

Yellow Jacket crept through the grove of blackjack oak, his moccasins as soundless as a bobcat moving through the forest. Now he saw the silhouette of a sentry and paused in the shadows, scarcely breathing.

"Halt! Who goes there?" The rebel soldier sounded young and scared.

Yellow Jacket did not move or answer. He could easily slip up on the green youth and cut his throat, but it would only bring trouble to his people when they found the body tomorrow.

After a time the soldier resumed his march, and Yellow Jacket continued his trek through the trees until he came to an old tent deep in the woods. Outside, Smoke, the mixed-blood black-Muskogee former slave stood guard. "Yellow Jacket?"

"Yes, Ekkuce." He came up to the big man and smiled. The black people had been slaves and then comrades. There were many with black blood mixed into their tribe. "Is everyone here?"

The other nodded. "Waiting for you."

Yellow Jacket's big frame stooped and entered nodding to the many tribal leaders gathered around the small fire. "I was dealing with my niece. Sometimes dealing with women is worse than fighting ten warriors."

The others laughed, and he sat down cross-legged.

"She is not satisfied to be a Muskogee girl?" Alligator, the Seminole chief asked.

Yellow Jacket shook his head regretfully. "Now that we have all been uprooted, she sees the easy life of the white girls and envies it."

Ancient Opothleyahola sighed. "Once we were a proud people; now that they have marched us to this land at gunpoint, we are not much better than beggars."

The leader was very old and frail. Everyone knew he had fought on the side of the British many, many years ago in the War of 1812. Yellow Jacket said with great politeness, "O great one, we will tame this new land yet and be prosperous, once the bluecoats and the graycoats stop fighting each other and go away."

Alligator said, "We all must now drink the black drink, *vsse-passv,* and purge the impurities from our bodies before we meet in council."

They all went outside into the darkness and passed the ceremonial drink among them. The powerful herbal drink soon made them all vomit, and now they were cleansed and ready to make momentous decisions.

They returned to the ragged tent, and someone lit a pipe and passed it around. The Seminole chief, Billy Bowlegs, took a puff. "I think they will never go away. The whites will not be satisfied until they have every inch of every bit of land."

It was true; Yellow Jacket was certain of it. "Tell us, oh, ancient leader, if you have reached a decision." He accepted the pipe and took a puff of the fragrant tobacco.

Opothleyahola's rheumy eyes surveyed the gathered men. "Yellow Jacket, you are one of the leaders of my people, the warrior the others will follow."

Yellow Jacket ducked his head modestly. "Our people follow you, great leader."

The old one stared into the sacred fire that had been brought all the way from their old homeland in the South. The original ashes had been buried with ceremony here in Indian Territory at Tulsey Town. "I am old and frail. Soon the Indian Territory will become a battleground as the gray ones from Texas fight the bluecoats from Kansas. We are unlucky enough to be in the middle of this land they both want."

The others looked at each other. One of the mixed-black braves said, "Which side shall we go with, great leader?"

He shook his gray head. "I do not know if, in the long run, it matters. Whichever we choose means disaster for our tribe and our relatives, the Seminole."

The others considered his words. Yellow Jacket looked around. There were leaders from almost twenty tribes sitting around the fire. One of them said, "Both sides promise us much to join them."

"And both sides lie," Yellow Jacket snapped. "Can we not ignore this white man's war and stay neutral?"

Opothleyahola considered. "The western tribes like the Comanche and Kiowa are doing that, but here in the eastern part of the Nations, the whites will pull us into their war whether we like it or not. We must be on the winning side for the sake of our people."

Yellow Jacket nodded. "I say that will be the bluecoats."

The old leader considered. "Perhaps, perhaps not. The graycoats have won several battles lately in their faraway country to the east, if gossip is to be believed. The graycoats offer us much — rifles and food and blankets — if we side with them. They say that when they win, they will make Indian Territory a separate state, and no white man will ever be allowed to trespass here again."

Yellow Jacket could not stop himself from snorting in derision. "It is the Southern whites who have run us out of Alabama and Georgia, stolen our land there. Have any of you forgotten how many of our people died on the Trail of Tears? There is not a man sitting here who did not lose many ancestors on that long forced march. I am only here because my older brother carried me on his back most of the way."

"We are all sorry for the death of your brother at the hands of the rebel soldiers." Opothleyahola took the pipe and smoked it. For a moment there was no sound save the crackle of the fire and the chill autumn wind blowing outside the tent. "Yes, Yellow Jacket, we hate the Southerners as much as you, and yes, we all remember how they stole our land and sent us here to this hostile place."

"Will we be any better with the North?" Alligator asked.

The Muskogee leader nodded. "I have had a message from the great white chief, Abraham Lincoln, this past summer. He promises that he will provide us with the supplies we need and protect us if we will stay loyal to the bluecoats."

Yellow Jacket shook his head. "I trust them no more than the graycoats."

Smoke took the pipe. "So great leader, what would you have us do?"

He considered. "I have been stalling the rebels as they press me for an answer about joining their cause, but they grow impatient. They are insisting on an answer."

"Maybe we can remain neutral," Smoke suggested. "This is, after all, a white man's war."

The Seminole Billy Bowlegs shook his head. "No one will be allowed to remain neutral; the whites will not allow it. Like my friend Yellow Jacket, I trust the Southerners the least."

Old Opothleyahola nodded. "Yes, I agree. We must gather our people and head north. If we can make it to this place called Kansas, the bluecoats there will protect our women and children."

"Kansas?" The others looked at each other askance.

"Old One," Yellow Jacket reminded him gently, "Kansas is hundreds of miles away, and the snows are coming."

"Would you have us sit here and be harried by the graycoats or be caught in the middle of the white man's battles?"

Another warrior cleared his throat. "But we have thousands of people gathered here; old ones, women, children. There are even some of the other Union tribes coming, to say nothing of all our livestock."

"I am aware of that," the ancient one said. "Did not the white man's Good Book speak of God's chosen people escaping from their enemy and marching toward the promised land with old people, women, children, and livestock?"

Alligator chewed his lip. "We are surrounded by the graycoats. They will try to stop us from leaving."

"Then we will fight our way through," Yellow Jacket said.

"We will lose many," said another.

"Better to die trying to join the Union forces than remain here and be killed by the graycoats, whom we know we cannot trust," Yellow Jacket said.

"Well spoken," said the ancient one. "I have prayed to the Master of Breath and feel there is no other answer."

The others looked to Yellow Jacket, and he turned the alternatives over in his mind. It would be like the Trail of Tears all over again, marching thousands of people through the cold, with not even time to bury their dead if they fell.

"Opothleyahola is right," Yellow Jacket said, "we must do this. We need to leave as soon as possible to beat the snows."

Now the ancient leader shook his head. "We cannot leave right away. Tribal members are still arriving from all over the Indian Territory and driving their cattle with them. It will take careful planning and an element of surprise. If we could be on the trail a few days before the graycoats know we are gone, we have a better chance."

"Then we are sworn to secrecy," Yellow Jacket whispered, "and we will wait for the signal from you, great leader."

"Maybe the Master of Breath will be with us," the old man murmured. "We will head northwest and pick up reinforcements among the Union Cherokee, then turn due north.

Now, let us depart this meeting with care. We do not want the graycoat colonel or his aide, Captain Wellsley, to suspect anything."

They had been in council for several hours. Now they went out into the night, nodding to the faithful giant, Smoke, who would stay to guard the ancient leader.

Pretty had hatched a plan as she watched her uncle, Yellow Jacket, leave for his meeting. He might be a big, respected warrior, but because he idolized her, she figured she could bring him around. Tonight, though, she had plans to meet her lover. She waited a few minutes after Yellow Jacket left; then she put pillows under her blankets to make her bed look as if she slept. She took one last look in her little mirror, adjusted the blue bracelet on her arm, then sneaked out the door and through the woods toward the sutler's store. Her lover would be waiting there, and she had something very important to tell him: She was now certain she was expecting his child.

Harvey Leland looked up from his bookwork as Pretty entered the store, and frowned. "I didn't send for you."

"Dear one, you hadn't sent me a message in such a long time . . ."

"It's been no more than a few days." He was gruff and out of sorts as he slammed his ledger shut. In truth, he was tired of the silly Injun girl. Besides, now he was scared. "Why didn't you tell me Matt Folane was your uncle?"

Matt Folane. The white man's name for her uncle. She walked around the store, fingering ribbons and trinkets, the blue beaded bracelet on her delicate wrist gleaming in the light of the kerosene lamp. "It never came up."

"No, you deliberately didn't tell me." He got up from his chair and limped across the store to confront her. "You knew I'd think twice —"

"Would you have?" She threw her arms around him, looking up at him coyly with her big, dark eyes.

His body reacted to the warmth of her full curves; then he regained control and pushed her away. "Anyone with any sense would tread lightly around that big warrior. They say he used to be a Lighthorseman and has killed a dozen men."

"Or maybe more," she laughed. "You know what *folane* means in our language? *Folane* is a Yellow Jacket, a kind of wasp that will sting — and sting hard."

Harvey shuddered. "You know what your uncle thinks of whites and particularly Southerners. You should have warned me." He looked about anxiously. "Where is he, anyway?"

She shrugged and played with her bracelet. "Gone to some silly meeting. He won't be back for hours." She reached to kiss him, molding the full curves of her body against him, her lips opening against his.

Damn, he wanted her, even knowing the risk of messing with Matt Folane's niece. Harvey put his arms around her and deepened the kiss. "If he won't miss you for hours, maybe we could . . ."

"Maybe we could," she murmured, taking his hand and leading him toward the room at the back of the little store.

Damn, he was taking a chance, but she was so nubile and exciting. "Just a minute — let me turn off the light and lock the front door. Can't be too careful."

He did that, then took her hand, leading her back to his room and closing the door. A small kerosene lamp burned on the bedside table, illuminating her pretty brown face as she lay down on the bed.

"Dear one," she whispered, "we have to talk."

"Not now," he replied in a hoarse whisper, hurriedly beginning to remove his clothes. He'd take her one more time and then tell her good-bye forever. His stepsister should be arriving by stage soon, and he didn't want to have to explain Pretty to Twilight.

"Yes, now," she protested even as he lay down on the bed naked and began to fumble

24

with the top of her faded calico dress. "I have something I have to tell you —"

He cut off her words with his mouth, kissing her feverishly, running his soft, pink hands over her lithe brown body. He was all over her, enjoying her as much tonight as he had the night he had first taken her virginity, in July. "Save it, beautiful," he gasped. "Let's make love first."

But she was pushing him away, scrambling out from under him to the other side of the bed. "No, we talk now."

He was breathing hard, annoyed and angry. "You little tease. Get me all hot and then —"

"Remember that first night?" she smiled at him.

"Oh, honey, do I? Let's do it again like we did that night. Let's —"

"You remember you promised to marry me?"

Had he? What did it matter? He would have promised anything to get the voluptuous little redskin under him. "Maybe someday," he drawled, and tried to pull her to him, but she resisted.

She put a stiff arm on his hairy chest to hold him back. "No, Harvey, we need to talk about that now."

"Oh, hell. All right, I'll marry you. Now let's make love." He tried to pull her into his fervent embrace, but she refused.

"Harvey, I — I think I'm going to have a baby."

"What?" The mood was gone now. He sat up on the edge of the bed and began to curse.

Behind him, the girl started to cry. "I thought you'd be pleased."

"Pleased? I don't want no half-breed Injun brat. . . ."

"But we could be married, and I'd help run the store —"

"Look, you Injun tart, I got someone comin' to help with the store. She's comin' on the stage —"

"A white woman?" She sounded angry and jealous. "There's a white woman?"

He sighed, not bothering to explain. "You'll just have to find some Injun buck to marry you if you've gotten yourself in trouble."

"Harvey, there was never anyone but you."

A horrible thought came to him. He turned to her. "You told anybody about us or the baby?"

Pretty shook her head, burying her face in her hands. "You — you told me not to tell about us."

Relief washed over him. He didn't want to face her vengeful uncle. Everyone around the camp said Matt Folane could cut a man's throat or break his back without a second thought.

"But if you don't keep your promise to

marry me, I'll tell my uncle."

A cold chill swept over him as he turned on the bed to face the hysterical girl. "You can't do that. You'll be disgraced if word gets out."

"I don't care!" She rose up on her knees, screaming at him. "My uncle will make you marry me! I'll tell him! I swear I will!" She was hysterical now, sobbing and screaming, beating him on the chest.

"Hush! Hush!" he ordered. "Someone will hear you!"

"I don't care! You hear? I don't care if everyone knows!" Her voice increased to a shriek.

"Shut up! You hear me? Shut up!" Harvey was terrified now, scared some of the Confederate officers camped nearby or some of the Injuns might hear her and go for her uncle. Harvey didn't want the half-naked crying girl to be found in his bed. He'd placate her somehow — anything to make her hush. Harvey put his hand over her mouth, and they struggled. "Be quiet, you little slut! Stop that screaming now!"

They fought on the bed, but she was no match for his strength. He muffled her voice, but then she bit his fingers and he pulled back, cursing as she began to scream again. He had to shut her up. Harvey grabbed her by her throat — anything to stop that noise. She battled him, and he grabbed her arm as

27

she scratched his face. The bracelet she wore broke, and blue beads flew everywhere.

"Shut up!" he shouted in panic. "Shut up!" He tightened the grip on her throat as her small fingers clawed at his hands. He was terrified that someone might have heard the uproar. In his mind, he saw the big Creek warrior bursting through the door, slamming him against the wall and then reaching for that huge knife he wore in his belt.

He tightened his grip on Pretty's throat. If he could only shut her up until he had time to reason with her . . . He'd promise to marry her to buy time — anything to keep the secret until he had time to think what to do next. His lust had caused him to toss all good sense aside, and now it was coming back to haunt him. "Hush," he pleaded as his fingers tightened, "Hush up!"

Her screams had become a mere whimper now as her eyes bulged and she gasped for air. Her small hands still clawed at his fingers, and she bucked and tried to twist out of his grasp, but she was powerless against him. He was past reason, past anything but sweating fear and anger. Yellow Jacket must not find out. He must not.

Pretty's voice was only a gasp, and her struggles grew weaker. All Harvey Leland could feel was relief that he might make her stop screaming, figure a way out of this mess without having to marry this Injun slut. All he wanted to do was save his own hide — the same reason he had fled to Indian Territory to avoid the war. "Shut up, girl," he gasped. "Oh, please shut up!"

Pretty stopped struggling, her breath coming in gasps as he tightened his hold on her throat. Her eyes rolled back. His cold sweat ran down his balding head and dripped on her brown face. What had he done?

Very slowly, Harvey loosened his grip. Why was Pretty so silent? His fingers had left blue marks on her slender neck. "Pretty?"

No answer. Her silence was even more terrifying than her screams had been. "Pretty? I'm sorry, I didn't mean to grab you so hard — it's just that I panicked when you said you'd tell your uncle. Everyone's afraid of that warrior."

Still no answer. He shook her thin shoulder. "Damn it, I'm tired of your pretending, you hear me? Now you open your eyes and we'll talk about this."

She didn't open her eyes. The girl lay very still and limp, looking small and brown against the sheets. A terror began to grow in Harvey's heart, a terror even worse than the fear of her vengeful uncle's finding out he'd seduced the girl with a few ribbons and trinkets. He was more scared than he'd ever been of fighting the war. "Pretty, you wake up, now." He grabbed her shoulders and began to shake her, shouting at her, "Stop playactin' on me, girl." He shook her hard, but she did not answer. Her head shook from side to side, her eyes half open, long black hair a tangle around them.

Oh, my God. Harvey began to cry, not for the dead girl but for himself. He was a marked man. There was no telling what kind of torture that big Injun brave would mete out to his niece's killer. Or maybe the rebel army would hang him. And all this with Twilight on her way to him, and his future so carefully planned.

Maybe it wasn't too late. Maybe he could hide the body, or at least get it out of his store. Yes, that was what he would do. Anything to keep the secret. With those marks on her neck, they'd know she'd been strangled. How long would it take people to track it to him? Had anyone ever known he was her lover? Had anyone ever seen her coming and going from the store? He didn't know. All that mattered now was getting rid of the body.

Hurriedly Harvey began to dress. The pebbles that he kept in his left boot to give himself a pronounced limp rolled out, and he didn't bother to gather them up. No one would see him in the darkness, so no one would know about his fake limp.

He opened the outside door cautiously and was greeted by an icy blast. Shivering, he hurried to get his heavy coat. As he put it on, he glanced at the floor. *The blue bracelet.* Those damn beads had gone everywhere when it broke. He must pick them up.

The girl lay so still, he didn't want to look at her as he went to his knees and began to gather the beads. The dim lamp made them hard to see in the shadows, but he picked up all he saw. A sound outside. Was that a sentry, or Yellow Jacket sneaking up on him? Harvey slipped the beads into the pocket of his coat and turned to the dead girl. He must get her out of his bed, no matter what he did with her. Maybe he could make it look like an accident. Yes, that was what he would do. No one would ever know.

He didn't want to touch the body that was already so cool and limp, but he had to. Harvey had whipped many slaves, slaughtered a few chickens, and kicked a cat or dog or two in his forty years, but he had never killed a human. He didn't have the courage for that. Taking a deep breath, he swung the slight body up in his arms. Her head dangled back, so that the marks on her throat showed almost black now. Her long hair swept the worn wooden floor. Where to go? What to do? He was so scared, his hands shook. Maybe he could make it look like an accident. Harvey grabbed a coil of rope off a nail. Then he headed out the back door and into the cold night toward the forest. The ground was damp and muddy beneath his small boots. His heart beat so hard, he was certain it would wake up everyone over at the sleeping rebel camp and the Indian settlement.

Suppose he ran into someone along the way? How would he explain his carrying a dead, half-naked Injun girl? The thought was so scary, he thought he would vomit, but he must not do that right now. There'd be time for the shakes later, when he was safely back at the store having a stiff drink. All that mattered now was making sure no one could track Pretty's dead body back to Harvey Leland. If he was lucky, no one need ever know. Twilight should arrive in a few days, and he already had plans for his widowed stepsister. All he needed was a little luck and things would turn out fine, but first he had to get rid of this damned Injun slut's body.

Chapter 2

It was very late, the moon gone and the night grown chill, as Yellow Jacket slipped through the darkness to his log cabin. He didn't bother to light a lamp, because he didn't want to wake his niece. He could see the outline of her slim form under her blankets. Yellow Jacket wished his older brother were still alive. He felt helpless in trying to discipline his beautiful, silly niece.

Yet there were bigger worries now that Opothleyahola and the council had just decided to take thousands of people and hundreds of animals on the road, marching through hostile forces and bad weather all the way to Kansas. Were the people up to it? They'd have to be, or be slaughtered where they camped by the increasing number of rebel soldiers. Yellow Jacket said a silent prayer to the Master of Breath and then dropped off to sleep.

It was almost dawn when he awakened. He sat up on the edge of his cot and stretched, sniffed the air for the welcome smell of coffee. Pretty must not be up yet. He got up, hunting for his shirt, and walked quietly to her room. She still lay motionless under the blankets. Well, let her sleep. There was a lot of misery and hard work ahead of the tribe, and there was no way he could spare her from it.

Yellow Jacket went into the kitchen, poked up the fire in the old stone fireplace. He'd have to bring in some wood. Grabbing a ragged buckskin jacket and his moccasins, he stepped outside. Frost had left delicate patterns on the ground and bushes. He grinned and took a deep breath of the cold air. Life had been good up until the Muskogee had been forced out of Alabama by the hated Southerners, but he and his brother had flourished in this new land, with fat herds of cattle and good crops. He picked up an ax and strode out into the woods. As dawn broke over the autumn landscape, he put his energy into cutting timber, the muscles of his great back rippling as he worked.

"Yellow Jacket! Yellow Jacket!"

Puzzled, he turned at the shouting. Smoke, the mixed-black Muskogee, ran through the woods toward him. "Come quick! Something terrible has happened!"

Yellow Jacket ceased chopping and leaned on the handle of his ax. "Come, now, Smoke, catch your breath. What is so terrible that —"

"It's Pretty," the black man gasped. "It's Pretty."

"Pretty? Don't be foolish. She's safe in bed."

34

The other shook his head, still gasping for air. "No, my friend — oh, it's bad!"

In the distance, Yellow Jacket heard screams and shouts, sounds of confusion. Dropping the ax, he turned and ran back into the cabin, jerked the blankets from Pretty's bed. Pillows. Only pillows under those blankets. His heart began to hammer hard, and he whirled to face his friend. "She's not here, Smoke; what — ?"

"Come." Smoke gestured. "I found her myself. I'm sorry. I'm so sorry."

Yellow Jacket hardly heard the other man's words. He grabbed Smoke's arm so hard, the man winced. "What's happened? Tell me! Take me there."

"This way." Smoke gestured as he turned and took off at a ground-eating lope. Yellow Jacket's heart was in his mouth as he followed. In the distance, he heard wails and shouts. He followed blindly, running through the woods until they met other curious people, all gathering at the noise.

Yellow Jacket slammed to a stop at the sight that awaited them. For a moment, his brain refused to recognize the sight. He blinked, hoping it would disappear, but it did not. His precious niece hung by the neck from a tree, gently swaying in the cold dawn air. "No," he whispered, shaking his head. "Oh, no! Let's get her down, get her some air!"

Men rushed forward to help him, but even as someone cut the rope and Yellow Jacket caught the limp body, gently lowering her to the ground, he knew it was too late. The body was very cold and already stiff. He knelt there on the frosty ground, holding her close and looking down into her dear face. "Pretty? Pretty, speak to me! Pretty?"

The gathering tribal members grew quiet.

Yellow Jacket put his face against her cold cheek, felt the tears drip on her flesh as he gathered her closer. He must not cry. He was a warrior and had endured pain and suffering and hunger, but no pain like this . . . never like this. Old Opothleyahola came through the crowd, the others stepping back respectfully. Yellow Jacket looked up slowly, numbly.

"O my son, I share your grief. Did your niece have any reason to kill herself?"

Did she? He shook his head, still in shock. "I — I can't believe she did this," Yellow Jacket whispered, and pulled her closer still. "No, someone did this to her. Someone killed my niece."

He heard murmuring and saw the others exchange glances. They did not believe that. He hugged her closer as if he thought he could bring warmth and life back into the cold body. He wanted to scream and shout and hit someone. He had vowed to his older brother, as the man lay dying from a bullet wound, that he would look after Pretty, and he had failed. Someone had to be responsible for his dear niece's death. Yellow Jacket had lost all his family now, all.

The old leader came over, touched Yellow Jacket's broad shoulder. "Let the women take her and get her ready for burial."

Yellow Jacket shook his head and held her close. "Maybe if the medicine man or the post doctor —"

"My son, the girl is dead," Opothleyahola whispered.

Very slowly Yellow Jacket looked up at him, his eyes blurring with the hot burning tears a warrior must not shed. Then he looked down into Pretty's waxen face. Yes, she was dead, her lovely features distorted as if she had not died an easy death. He took his knife and cut the rope that dug into the flesh of her neck. The skin beneath it was almost black. "Yes, I must turn her over to the women," he murmured, and stood up, still holding her. Little Pretty was so very light in his big arms. His friend Smoke gestured, and a path opened up in the silent crowd. Swaying slightly, Yellow Jacket began to walk toward his cabin, where he knew the women would be gathering to take care of the body.

Reaching the cabin, he laid her very gently on the rough-hewn table and nodded to the silent women who stood there. As he laid her on the table, he noticed that Pretty was not wearing the blue bracelet. What could have happened to it? The bracelet was precious to her. He must find it so it could be buried with her. "Take care of her," he said to the eldest woman, and then he turned and went out.

His friend Smoke put his hand on his shoulder. "I am much sorry, good friend. Can I do anything?"

Yellow Jacket shook his head. "I — I want to be alone for a while; that's all. Tell the others to leave me be."

Smoke nodded in understanding, and Yellow Jacket turned blindly and walked toward where they'd found the body. He stood a long time under the barren branches of the oak, staring up at it. Pretty had seemed happy last night as she brushed her hair. Even then maybe she was only waiting for him to leave so she could meet someone, but who? A girlfriend? A young warrior? Some white soldier? That thought made him grit his teeth in rage. Now he began to search the area around the tree for some sign of the blue bracelet.

He found nothing. Had she met someone here under this tree? He was an excellent tracker, but too many people had walked this soft ground this morning. For the first time he noted the footprints of a white man's small boots, but when he tried to follow them, they disappeared in a dry patch of grass and went no farther.

Now he went to hunt up her friends, but none of those girls seemed to know anything. One said Pretty had hinted that she had a lover, but the girl did not know who it might be. Yellow Jacket ground his teeth in frustration. It had to be a white man. If it had been an acceptable Muskogee boy, Pretty would not have been trying to keep the secret. A white man. Who among these young rebel soldiers could it be? And what part had he played in Pretty's death? When Yellow Jacket found out, he would kill that man very slowly and painfully, as only a red-stick warrior knew how to do.

They buried Pretty that afternoon near her father, wrapped in the ceremonial way and sitting up, facing the sunrise. Yellow Jacket vowed in his grief and anger that he would seek out and kill the man who had done this.

The tribe was increasingly surrounded by white rebel soldiers, and a soldier in a uniform with bright brass buttons could easily turn a young girl's head with lies. Yellow Jacket watched dirt being shoveled into her grave and hated white Southerners as he had never hated anything or anyone in his life. They had stolen the tribal lands and forced all the Five Tribes onto the Trail of Tears. One of their soldiers had killed his beloved brother. Now another must have something to do with his niece's death.

He vowed he would take his revenge, but it

must wait. Now there was no time for grief; there was too much to be done to get his people out of Indian Territory and safely to Kansas before the rebels realized the plan.

The Muskogee began to scatter after the burial, following old Opothleyahola's orders to make ready for the trip. There was much planning to be done to move six thousand people north. Kansas would be their promised land, far away from the hated Southerners who were slowly encircling all the Union Indians.

Indian Territory, early November 1861

Twilight Dumont took a deep breath as the stage halted and the driver climbed down and came around to open her door. She took his hand and lifted the hem of her black dress, paused on the step, looking about, chagrined. The fort with its few cabins looked so much poorer than she'd expected, and there were Indians everywhere, silently watching her. For a split second, she wanted to jump back in the stage and ask the driver to drive away, but just then her stepbrother came out of the big cabin with the hitching post out front and limped down the steps toward her, extending his hands with a smile.

"My dear, so glad you made it. How was your trip?"

Harvey was plumper and more balding

than she remembered. "Rather uneventful," she said, and stepped forward to let Harvey hug her. Now she felt guilty that she had never really liked him. "It was so kind of you to send for me."

"Not at all." He tried to kiss her mouth, but she turned her cheek to him. "I can use some help at the trading post. I hope you brought your medicine bag?"

She nodded, then froze, staring past his shoulder at the biggest Indian she had ever seen. His hair was long, and he wore buckskins. He was virile and savage-looking, but it was the pure hatred on his dark, rugged face that mesmerized her. "Who — who is that?"

Harvey turned to look. His face changed. Was that fear in his watery eyes? "Come on in and I'll tell you about him. There was a tragedy a few days ago; Creek girl committed suicide."

"How terrible." She shuddered at the way the Indian looked at her, then took Harvey's arm and went inside.

Yellow Jacket stared after the white girl. She was the most beautiful woman he had ever seen. She was petite and wasp-waisted, wearing one of those foolish hoopskirts white women favored, in the somber black dress that was the signature of mourning. Under the wide-brimmed hat, her hair was pale brown, streaked light by the sun. However, it

41

was her eyes that mesmerized him most. They were a smoky gray, almost a pale lavender, just the color of dusk after the sun set — that time whites called twilight.

She was a Southerner; there was no doubt about that. Yellow Jacket had caught the soft drawl when she spoke to the greedy shopkeeper who must be a relative. When she had looked at Yellow Jacket, she had shuddered in revulsion and looked away, almost as if the sight of an Indian made her ill . . . or afraid.

Grinding his teeth, Yellow Jacket turned and stalked away, hating the woman. What he disliked most about her was the familiar way the hated store owner had greeted her. Yellow Jacket did not like Harvey Leland. The trading post owner cheated the Indians every chance he got. No doubt this was his woman, arriving to share Leland's ill-gotten gains.

Yellow Jacket's grief over the loss of his niece was still a painful thing. He could not believe Pretty had taken her own life, no matter the evidence. Somehow, he was certain a white lover must be at fault in her death.

Whites. White people, especially Southerners, seemed to be at the root of all the Indians' problems. More rebel soldiers were coming to the Territory as weeks passed. Soon there would be too many to deal with. His people would have to make their move very soon, or it would be too late. Yellow Jacket tore his attention away from the lovely white woman who had gone into the trading post. Now he went to seek out old Opothleyahola to discuss further plans.

Inside the trading post, Twilight looked around. The rough-hewn place was pleasant enough, with tools, farm implements, bolts of cheap fabric, rolls of ribbon, small trinkets. A myriad of scents greeted her from the big barrels of pickles to the dried leaves of tobacco hanging from the exposed beams. "Well, Harvey, it's much nicer than what I was dealing with back in Virginia."

He smiled and took her valise. "My dear, I think you will be very happy here. Sooner or later, you know, this land is bound to be opened up to white settlement, and it's rich land — lots of opportunities."

Twilight took off her hat and sighed. "So many Indians. That big one who watched me made me shiver — just the way he stared."

Her stepbrother frowned. "Oh, that's Matt Folane. Lately, he's gone to calling himself Yellow Jacket. He's a heap-big warrior among the Creeks. He's been on a tear lately since his niece died."

"Oh?"

"It's not important." The balding man dismissed it with a shrug as he tried to take her hand. "I'm so glad you came, my dear. Sorry

43

to hear about all your trouble."

His hand was clammy, and she pulled away from him and walked about, looking over the place. She'd always had an uneasy feeling that Harvey would like to bed her. But if that were the truth, why had he introduced her to Pierre Dumont and played match-maker? "Your offer was a godsend, Harvey. I had reached the end of my rope and didn't know what to do next."

He made a sympathetic clucking sound. "Well, now, what else is a helpless woman supposed to do except depend on gallant men to help her? Especially a widow whose brave husband died for the cause."

She brushed back a stray wisp of hair. "Frankly, I hate to admit it, but it didn't seem like Pierre at all, to go and become a hero. He never struck me as having a lot of courage."

"Oh, now, now, I'm sure he was very brave." Harvey watched her, trying to appear reassuring. To be honest, he thought Pierre Dumont was the yellowest varmint he'd ever met. There must have been some financial angle in it for him to join up. Well, what did it matter? Harvey now had the lovely Twilight here and under his control.

"To tell you the truth, Harvey, I feel like a hypocrite for wearing mourning black. It wasn't a very good marriage. I don't know why you urged me to marry him."

Because I owed him a bunch of gambling debts, Harvey thought, *and Pierre would forgive them for a relative.* He feigned a mournful expression. "I'm sorry about that, my dear. I really thought he'd make you a good husband. With our father giving all our slaves their freedom and then going off to help the wounded, we were both left rather penniless, you know."

Her beautiful dusky lavender-gray eyes filled with tears. "Dear Daddy, I miss him so."

The old rascal, Harvey thought, *giving away all that human wealth.* Owning twenty-five slaves would have made Harvey exempt from the Confederate army. Instead, he'd had to fake a limp and flee to the Indian Territory. Now the damned war seemed about to follow him here. "Yes, dear Barton. He was like a real father to me, too, after dear Mummy died." He must not appear too curious. "Uh, didn't Pierre leave you anything?"

Twilight shook her head and turned to look out the window at the trees that were dropping red and golden leaves. "I found out the bank was about to repossess the plantation about the time he was killed. He had debts, Harvey." She turned and looked at him intently. "Did you know Pierre was a gambler?"

He feigned shock. "Why, how terrible! I had no idea. Well, that's all behind you now.

45

Let's get you settled. I'll take your luggage into the back room, my dear."

"Oh, I hadn't noticed your limp." Her tone was so sympathetic. "What happened?"

He turned and gave her his most pitiful look. She need never know he got that limp from putting pebbles in his boot. "Oh, I did a brief stint in the Alabama Volunteers after you moved to Virginia. A minor wound during the height of a battle, and now I'm useless for our great and glorious cause."

"Well, I'll look after you and help you run the store."

"I was counting on that."

"What?" she looked up. Was she suspicious?

"I merely meant that with your soft heart, I knew you'd be a major comfort to me." If he could only get her in his bed. "I'll take the loft, and you can have the back room."

"I do hate to put you out. Perhaps I could find a room to board —"

"I wouldn't hear of it." Harvey made a dismissing gesture. "After all, we are family. Oh, the major's wife has invited us for tea tomorrow."

Twilight frowned. "Must we? I'm afraid I'm not feeling very sociable."

"But of course we must," Harvey said. "Young Captain Wellsley's mother is visiting from Texas. They're quite wealthy — lots of land and cattle."

46

"All right." She shrugged. "Whatever you think."

"Good." She was a spineless jellyfish, Harvey thought. She'd do anything he said. As much as he'd like to sleep with his beautiful widowed stepsister, he had something bigger planned. He would love to get his hands on Captain Franklin Wellsley's wealth. "Now, you just settle yourself in, my dear."

Carrying her luggage, Harvey led her into the back room, where there was a chest of drawers and a bed. "Sorry if it's not quite as nice as what you had back home. Things are pretty crude out here on the frontier, and these Indian girls just don't know how to be proper maids."

"It's just fine," she reassured him, looking around. "Later I'll start doing a little cleaning and dusting, help around the store."

"My dear, I really don't expect maid's work from a well-brought-up Southern lady."

"I reckon I should learn to stand on my own feet and make my own decisions."

"Southern ladies can't be expected to do that," he hastened to assure her. "Now, you just leave everything to me. I'll take care of you; just don't worry your pretty little head about it."

The bell at the store's entry jangled.

"Here," he said as he put her valise by the bed, "sounds like I've got a customer. I'll close the door, and you rest awhile. Later

47

we'll have supper and I'll show you around the fort."

She nodded and watched him leave the room. Then she walked over and collapsed on the bed. What had she gotten herself into? This country looked wild and untamed and full of savages. How she longed to be back in the security of the old homestead, the Alabama plantation where she'd been raised, where Daddy had always taken care of her after Mother had died. She wouldn't admit it for the world, but she had never really liked her stepmother, who seemed too interested in what Daddy owned. However, Daddy had outlived the greedy, unloving woman and then been killed himself, out in the field doing surgery on wounded troops during the first few weeks of the war.

The next day, with Harvey insisting, Twilight made ready to go to tea at the major's home. Harvey helped her into his buggy. "You look lovely, my dear. I'm sure every young officer out here will be wanting to meet you."

Uh-oh. Twilight frowned at him as he clucked to the horse and they pulled away. "Harvey, I really don't think I want to marry again . . ."

"Oh, but you will," he insisted as he looked at the road ahead. "Of course, you'll have to pass a proper mourning period first.

Some of these young men are very comfortably well off."

Twilight didn't say anything, but she had a sinking feeling. Perhaps Harvey's offer hadn't been so generous after all. Perhaps he hoped to better himself by making a good match for his widowed stepsister. Then she bit her lip for thinking such unkind thoughts about him.

As they drove down the rutted road, she heard a sound and looked to one side. Just riding out of the woods on a fine paint stallion was that same big Indian she had seen when she arrived. He reined in and watched them, anger in his dark eyes.

"Oh, dear," she whispered, "there's that savage again, Harvey."

"I know. Pretend you don't see him." Harvey sounded apprehensive. She looked over at her stepbrother. Sweat had broken out on his round face.

The savage was too mesmerizing to ignore. She turned on the seat and looked back. "Are — are we in any danger?"

The Indian was looking at her as if he couldn't decide whether he wanted to pull her clothes off and ravish her or maybe kill them both.

Harvey urged the bay horse to go a little faster. "I don't think so, but who knows with him? They say he hates all whites, especially Southerners."

She glanced back over her shoulder again

and wished Harvey would whip the horse into a gallop. The Indian was still glaring at her in a way that sent a shiver through her slight body. "Why does he hate Southerners?"

"He's Creek, one of the tribes run out of the South a few years ago so respectable, civilized whites could have their land."

She thought about that. "Oh, yes, I do remember reading something about it. Why are they called Creeks?"

"I don't know. They call themselves Muskogee. They're distantly related to the Seminoles, or so I hear. But enough about Injuns." He shrugged. "I've met the nicest young captain . . ."

"The Creeks were from our home state, weren't they?" She hardly heard Harvey, feeling the savage's angry eyes boring into her back as they drove on.

"That's right, Alabama and Georgia. I wouldn't tell any of them you're from Alabama, if I were you. Now, can't we talk about something else besides Injuns?"

She had annoyed him, and Southern ladies never annoyed anyone. "I'm so sorry, Harvey; that one unnerved me, is all. And don't worry, I don't intend to get close enough to any of them to exchange even one word. I'm terrified of savages."

"Hmm," Harvey said, and didn't look at her.

They drove the rest of the way in silence

through the gold and red trees of autumn. Falling leaves swirled around the horse's hooves, and she found herself enjoying the wild, beautiful country. Soon they came to a cluster of the fort's buildings and pulled up before a large log cabin.

Harvey came around to help her down. "We must stay on very cordial terms with the officers. It helps my business. Besides, I'll need good connections when they start dividing up this Injun land."

"But doesn't it belong to the Indians?" Twilight said, and she allowed him to help her down, noting that his sweaty hands lingered just a bit too long on her waist.

He guffawed. "For now. It's too good land to waste on savages. Sooner or later the whites will get it, and I want my share."

It didn't sound very just, but Twilight swallowed back her misgivings. After all, what did she care about a bunch of wild savages who went about killing and scalping people?

They went up the steps and were met at the door by an Indian girl who ushered them into the parlor as she took their coats.

Two elderly women were seated on scarlet horsehair Victorian settees, and the one dressed in the pale gray-green color known as reseda green got up and came forward with a smile. "Ah, the delightful Mr. Leland. And this must be your dear sister?"

Harvey took her hand and kissed it. "So

51

pleased to have been invited, dear lady. May I present my sister, Mrs. Dumont?"

Twilight curtsied. "So pleased to make your acquaintance," she drawled.

"Such a brave girl." The old lady took her hand and clucked sympathetically. "Your dear brother has told us how your heroic husband fell for the cause. Do come meet Mrs. Wellsley."

The white-haired old lady on the settee wore a pale dove gray dress that signified light mourning. She nodded as Twilight curtsied. "So sorry to hear you've been widowed, but after all, it was for the cause."

"Isn't it too bad?" Harvey said, "but she's bearing up well."

Twilight and Harvey took seats, and Twilight bit her lip and looked away, guilty that she had felt so little when news of Pierre's death had come. "We are all making sacrifices, after all."

The two older ladies nodded.

Mrs. Wellsley sighed. "I hear you're from Virginia. My son, Franklin, was there for a while before he was transferred to this god-awful place. I know he's quite disappointed not to be in the thick of the fray. It would have been so important to his late father. Franklin feels so useless stuck out here in Indian Territory, with no big battles to give him a chance to move up the ladder in rank."

The major's wife frowned. "Now my husband says the Yankees are going to try to capture this land, so there may be a good fight here sooner or later."

Harvey smiled. "So young Wellsley may get his share of medals after all under the superb leadership of the major."

Both older ladies beamed at her brother, and Twilight tried to look interested. She was so very tired of war, and what good were medals to a dead man? But of course, she dare not say that. Instead, she looked around the room, furnished in the height of Victorian fashion with lots of knickknacks and ornate furniture. "This is very nice," she murmured, hoping to change the subject from war.

"It's not nearly as nice as what I had in Charleston," the major's wife drawled, and looked about. "Where is that girl with the tea? I swear these stupid Injuns can't be taught much of anything."

"I could have told you that." Mrs. Wellsley nodded, quite smug. "Of course, we Texans have been dealing with savages for many, many years. Annihilation seems to be the only answer. You can't civilize them."

"Isn't that a bit harsh?" Twilight said before she thought, and was immediately sorry because Harvey glared at her. Southern ladies never offered opinions, especially controversial ones.

Mrs. Wellsley blinked. "Well, it's not as if we're dealing with real people."

"They're almost as primitive as slaves back home," the major's wife put in. "Don't seem to realize they'd be better off on our side."

Twilight asked, "We're attempting to get Indians to join the cause?"

"Of course," the major's wife said. "They may be primitive and uncivilized, but I hear they're deadly warriors."

The Indian girl brought the tea, and the major's wife poured while the girl passed a plate of sweets before she disappeared into the kitchen.

Twilight was grateful to be able to change the subject. "Such good cookies."

"Aren't they, though?" The major's wife beamed at Harvey. "Your brother has been so good about getting things that are in short supply out here, like white flour."

Harvey ducked his balding head modestly. "Well, there are ways if one knows how."

Bribery, Twilight thought, and suddenly the cookies didn't taste quite so delicious.

When she looked up, Mrs. Wellsley was looking her over curiously. "I do hope you get a chance to meet my Franklin. We've been so picky about selecting a wife for him."

"Can't he select his own?" Twilight spoke without thinking.

She saw Harvey shoot her a warning glance, and the old lady frowned with her teacup halfway to her pursed mouth. "Certainly not. Dear Franklin is waiting for his mother's approval."

"As he should." The major's wife nodded.

Twilight wanted to say something, then decided it was not her place to create a disagreeable atmosphere. "I — I'll be looking forward to meeting the captain," she murmured as she sipped her tea, her eyes properly downcast.

The old lady seemed mollified. "And I'm sure he'll be pleased to meet you; a pretty widow whose brave husband has died for the cause."

"Hear! Hear!" Harvey said. "The captain is a fine young man."

Now Twilight knew why she'd been invited to come to Indian Territory. It had nothing to do with generosity. Harvey was hoping to marry her into wealth, as he had with Pierre Dumont. Of course, Twilight would acquiesce as she had done before — or would she?

The major's wife put down her cup. "You know, Mrs. Dumont, we're afraid some of these Indians are going to go over to the Yankees' side."

"Too stupid for words," Mrs. Wellsley snapped. "After all, we've promised to make Indian Territory an Indian state when the South wins."

"Maybe they don't trust you," Twilight said without thinking, and Harvey glared at her over his teacup. "I — I mean . . ." She let her voice trail off, uncertain how to retreat gracefully.

"But that's where you come in, my dear," the major's wife hastened to say.

"Oh?"

She nodded. "We're awfully short on medical help out here on the frontier, and we understand you have some training —"

"But I'm not a doctor," Twilight protested. "I just assisted my father some."

"That'll be enough maybe to please the savages," the major's wife said, and smiled, apparently pleased.

"The savages?" Twilight's mouth went suddenly dry.

"Oh, Harvey, you naughty boy, haven't you told her?" The old lady scolded.

Harvey looked sheepish. "Well, you know, she just arrived, and we haven't had time to discuss much."

Twilight's hand was suddenly shaking so badly, she had to set her cup down. "I'm afraid I don't quite understand."

"Twilight," Harvey said, and he almost purred as he said it, "the savages have a lot of sickness in their tribes, and we thought if we could offer them some medical help, they might decide to stay with our side."

"Minister to savages?" Twilight's mouth dropped in horror. "Oh, my, I really don't think so."

"But it's for the cause," the major's wife protested.

The three of them stared at her expectantly.

Twilight looked about, uncertain what to say. They wanted her to provide medical help to the savages merely to bring them to the Confederate side. Twilight felt perspiration break out between her breasts in spite of the cool room. How could a dutiful Southern lady refuse? Abruptly, she wished she were back scrapping for a living on her burned-out plantation. Dealing with savages was more than her worst nightmare, and she was not dreaming!

Chapter 3

"I — I don't know quite what to say," Twilight stammered. "I do believe I'm getting a bad case of the vapors."

"Then I must take you home, my dear." Harvey's voice was sympathetic, but his blue eyes glared like frozen ice.

Both older ladies made sympathetic sounds.

Twilight stood up, and Harvey took her arm. "I'm sure once my dear sister has had time to think about it, she'll be happy to help win the savages over for the cause."

"Of course," said both older ladies in unison.

Twilight gritted her teeth, wondering if anyone cared what she thought, then remembered she was a dutiful Southern lady. No matter her fear, she'd be obligated. "It was a lovely tea," she murmured. "I do hope to see you again."

Mrs. Wellsley said, "Well, I'll be returning to Austin soon, but if you and my Franklin should like each other . . ." Her voice trailed off.

What a dragon of a mother-in-law she would be, Twilight thought, and headed for the entry, where the silent Indian girl waited with the wraps.

The major's wife and Mrs. Wellsley followed her into the entry.

"I do hope you'll be feeling better later," said the major's wife.

"My Franklin will be so sorry he missed meeting you," said the elderly Texan.

"Perhaps later," Twilight said, and hurried out the door and toward the buggy with Harvey trailing in her wake. He helped her up to the seat, and the ladies waved farewell from the doorway.

On the way home, Harvey drove the buggy at a fast clip, not looking at Twilight. "Honestly, you were quite rude."

"I didn't mean to be," Twilight murmured, "but I think you might have been more honest with me, Harvey, about why I was being invited to come out."

"I thought I was being quite generous," he said in a strained, self-righteous tone, "offering my protection and room and board to a destitute, widowed relative. Otherwise, I don't know what you would have done."

I would have had to make some decisions all alone, Twilight thought. She had never had to be independent before. The thought scared her. "You're right, Harvey, it was thoughtless of me. I merely thought you wanted me to help around the store —"

"You can do that, too." Her apology

seemed to have mellowed him. "Have I told you Captain Wellsley is quite handsome?"

"Who?" She'd already forgotten about the officer.

"We just had tea with his mother," Harvey reminded her as he cracked his whip at the horse. "He's not married."

She could see why, she thought, remembering his stern mother, but of course she didn't say that. It would upset Harvey. She kept watching the woods as they drove through the late afternoon. She was afraid that big warrior would appear out of nowhere and block their path. "Perhaps if we are going to travel in this area, we ought to ask for an escort of soldiers."

"I doubt we'd get them," Harvey said. "The army seems to have a lot on its mind these days. Anyway, I carry a pistol. You're perfectly safe with me if we're attacked."

She bit her lip and didn't answer. Somehow, she didn't feel secure with Harvey's protection. Not that she thought a patrol of soldiers could protect her if that big warrior decided to lift her scalp. She remembered how he had looked at her, and she shivered. "Yellow Jacket."

Harvey glanced over at her. "Yes, he's dangerous-looking, isn't he? You know, a yellow jacket is a type of aggressive wasp."

"I know. I'll wager the name suits him."

Harvey swore under his breath. "He's been

on a tear ever since his brother was shot accidentally by one of the Confederate sentries."

"What? How awful!" Twilight jerked to look at her stepbrother.

"It was an accident. The savage was out in the night, and the sentry thought he was up to no good."

"Couldn't he have investigated before he pulled the trigger?" She was appalled at the useless death, even if it was an Indian.

"You don't hesitate when dealing with savages," Harvey said. "The Indians said he was just hunting game, but who knows what he was really up to? Can't trust Injuns. And now the dead man's daughter has hanged herself. I reckon Yellow Jacket holds both deaths against white people, but it really isn't our fault."

Twilight had a scared, sinking feeling. "You want me to go out with my small medical bag and minister to these people?"

"I'm sure the major will provide you an escort," Harvey said. "Maybe Captain Wellsley. Did I tell you he's rich?"

"Yes, you did." Twilight bit her lip. "I — I really don't want to have to deal with savages, Harvey."

He glanced sideways at her as he drove. "But you must. We really need to influence the savages to keep them from going over to the Union side."

"They can't be so stupid as not to see through that ploy."

"But of course they are." Harvey sounded annoyed. "Now, do behave yourself, Twilight. You've never been one to be disagreeable."

She took a deep breath. Southern ladies did as they were told. "I — I'm sorry," she murmured.

Harvey smiled. "Now, that's more like it. I understand the major will be sending you out to the Creek camp tomorrow."

She said nothing the rest of the way back to the store, but she had nightmares all night in which the big savage called Yellow Jacket chased her down, ripped her dress off, and had his way with her, his hot mouth on her breasts, his hands stroking her writhing body. She came awake suddenly, gasping for air, her body bathed in perspiration even though the autumn night was cool. She got no sleep the rest of the night, remembering the way the warrior had looked at her when they'd driven past him in the buggy.

The next morning was warmer but still cool and crisp. Twilight put on her black dress and, with trembling hands, checked her medical bag. At nine o'clock, Captain Wellsley entered the trading post, took off his hat, and made a sweeping bow as Harvey introduced him. "I'm very pleased to meet you, Mrs. Dumont."

Twilight nodded and tried to smile. He was a handsome, yellow-haired young man with watery blue eyes, a weak chin, and a pronounced Texas drawl. "Dumont?" he asked. "Sounds familiar somehow."

"Perhaps you met my husband, Pierre? I understand you served in Virginia. He was killed in action there."

"Well, I — probably not. I — I extend my heartfelt condolences." The captain licked his lips and glanced away.

What on earth was wrong with him? Then it occurred to Twilight that Pierre might have done the young man out of money in a game of cards and the captain was too much of a Southern gentleman to say so. He looked uncomfortable, took out a handkerchief and wiped his suddenly perspiring face.

She hurried to fill the awkward silence. "I'm afraid I'm not looking forward to going among the savages."

His expression betrayed the fact that he wasn't, either. "We'll have a squad of soldiers with us," he said.

Harvey nodded his approval. "Young Wellsley here is quite ambitious. He intends to end up as a general."

Franklin Wellsley played with the brim of his hat. "Well, actually, it would please my mother. She has big plans for her only child. I'd be just as happy in Austin."

Harvey stuck his thumbs in his flowered

silk vest. "And Mrs. Wellsley's thinking, after the war, the Indian Territory will be opened to whites. Lots of opportunities for ambitious folks."

"But I thought this land was promised to Indians as long as rivers flow and grass grows," Twilight said.

Harvey and the young officer exchanged glances.

Harvey shrugged. "Now, what are a bunch of savages going to do with such good land? Good ranch land is wasted on them, while a white man with a family could put it to use."

Captain Wellsley colored. "I think so, too," he drawled, "but of course, I'm not married."

Harvey grinned. "Just hasn't met the right girl yet."

The captain nodded. "Mama says thirty is a good age for me to choose a bride."

Or for Mama to choose one for you, Twilight thought. She frowned at Harvey. Her step-brother was surely scheming to get his hands on the wealthy Texan's money. "Harvey, you aren't going out to the Indian camp with us?"

"Uh, I've got a lot to do this morning." Harvey avoided her gaze. "Inventory and all."

She'd always thought Harvey a coward, and yet here he had this bad limp from having served with the Alabama Volunteers. Twilight took a deep breath. "Well, Captain, let us be off, then."

"Ma'am." He smiled and made a sweeping bow to escort her out the door, then took her arm. "May I carry your medicine bag, ma'am?"

"Of course." She handed it over, and they went out to the buggy, where he helped her up. A squad of gray-clad cavalry waited patiently behind the buggy. They all gave a polite nod to her as she settled herself into the seat, and the captain got in and snapped the little whip at the bay horse. The whole procession started off at a leisurely clip. Twilight didn't quite know what to say to this callow youth. Why, he looked barely old enough to grow whiskers.

Her curiosity got the better of her. "Captain, are you sure you didn't know my husband?"

There was a long silence except for the jingle of harness and the rhythmic clop-clop of horses' hooves.

"I don't think so," he answered, and watched the road ahead. She wondered if he was hiding something.

"If you did, you don't need to protect me," she said softly. "I know Pierre was a rogue, but of course, I didn't know that when I married him."

Still no answer. The captain cleared his throat, and it sounded loud in the silence. "So what was your husband doing in the army? Everyone knows, as a major slaveholder he'd be exempt from the war."

"I suppose I should be embarrassed to say this, but Pierre was so cruel to our slaves, they all ran off when the war started, and the plantation fell into major disrepair."

"Oh. You have no other relatives except Mr. Leland?"

Twilight nodded. "Father was serving as a battlefield surgeon and was killed in action, and I'm afraid Harvey wasn't too good at managing our Alabama plantation."

"Too bad." He took a deep breath as if summoning courage. "Mrs. Dumont, you may think it forward of me since you've been widowed less than a year, but your brother was right: You're quite attractive."

She felt the blood rush to her face. "Why, thank you, Captain, but how did you know how long I'd been widowed?"

He stammered a moment, keeping his pale eyes on the road ahead. "Why, uh, I believe your stepbrother told me."

The captain was hiding something, but Twilight shrugged it off. Probably the gossipy Harvey had told the young captain what a rogue Pierre had been. Well, it didn't matter now. Too bad Harvey hadn't told her before she married the gambler, but then, maybe Harvey hadn't known.

"Mama was quite pleased to meet you," the captain drawled, and colored shyly. "Even Mama said you were a perfect Southern lady."

She was weary of being a perfect Southern lady but unsure how to escape the restraints of convention that seemed to bind her like a whalebone corset. "That was kind of her." Twilight remembered the iron-willed old harridan. "Your mother's opinion is quite important to you, isn't it?"

"Certainly. Doesn't every Southerner care what his mama thinks?"

Twilight sighed. She had no interest in another marriage after the disastrous one she'd just endured, but evidently Captain Wellsley was playing a big part in Harvey's plans. She decided to change the subject. "Captain, can't the post doctor deal with these Indians?"

"There's just too many of them." The captain lowered his voice as he glanced behind him at the cavalry. "Besides, ma'am, he, uh, he drinks."

"Oh, I see." She suddenly felt sorry for everyone who had to depend on the physician for medical care. "How are the relationships between our forces and the Indians?"

"Depends on which Indians, ma'am. The Choctaws and the Chickasaws are mostly on our side. The other three of the Civilized Tribes are mostly split down the middle: some for the North, some for the South."

"And your troops are caught in the middle?"

He chewed his lip. "We're a little outnum-

67

bered, but we've got more troops arriving every day. We're hoping to bring more of those wavering on the fence over to our side."

"So that's where I come in?"

He nodded. "There's a lot of sickness with winter coming on. If we can treat them kindly, convince them that they've got a better future siding with us —"

"And do they?"

He shook his head and looked ahead. "I don't rightly know, ma'am. There's talk the Confederacy might offer to turn this Territory into an Indian state, protect the tribes from white encroachment."

"Can that happen?" Twilight asked.

He shook his head. "I doubt it, ma'am," he said again. "Anyway, if we can't get the undecideds to throw in with us, we're to try to keep them from joining up with the other side. Some of these Injuns are mighty good warriors, and I wouldn't want to come up against them in battle."

"Yellow Jacket," she thought aloud.

The young man next to her paled visibly. "He's one of the toughest, and he trusts no one."

Twilight snorted without thinking. "Can you blame him?"

Captain Wellsley thought about it a long time. "I reckon not," he said finally.

About that time, a big pinto horse came

out of the underbrush near the road and blocked their buggy. Captain Wellsley reined in, and the troops following them stopped.

Twilight took a deep breath. It was Yellow Jacket, clad in buckskins, with feathers in his black hair. He said nothing, only sat his horse with a natural grace as if he and the brown and white stallion were one.

She flinched a little as the big Indian looked her over with cold, dark eyes. "Where are you going?"

The young officer cleared his throat. "We are bringing medical help to your people."

Yellow Jacket spit to one side contemptuously. "With a soldier escort?"

"I thought the lady would feel safer," the captain's voice quivered.

She didn't feel safer. With the stern warrior glaring down at her, she felt very vulnerable. As far as Yellow Jacket was concerned, she didn't think she'd feel protected with a whole regiment of soldiers escorting her.

"Safe?" Yellow Jacket snorted, and signaled with his hand. Immediately, a dozen heavily armed braves came out of the underbrush on both sides of the road. Twilight saw the sweat break out on the captain's sallow face. Behind them, she heard the movement as soldiers reached for weapons.

"Hold on, men!" the officer ordered. He acted as if uncertain what to do next.

There is about to be a massacre here! Twilight

thought in horror. "I — I'm sure Yellow Jacket has brought his men to escort us to the camp," she blurted.

Yellow Jacket smiled slowly. "The dusky-eyed one has more nerve than she first appeared to. It pleases me to have the lady doctor come to our camp."

"I am not a doctor," Twilight stammered. "I'm only a nurse." She couldn't believe she had the nerve to correct the savage.

Yellow Jacket looked at her, and he didn't smile. "I will escort you anyway." He wheeled his stallion and led off as if daring the soldiers to shoot him in the back.

"Of all the arrogant . . ." the old sergeant behind them muttered.

"Be quiet, O'Brien, before you create more trouble," young Wellsley ordered. He snapped the reins, and the buggy started off again, following Yellow Jacket down the trail.

Twilight glanced back. The warriors had fallen in behind the mounted squad, who looked ill at ease and nervous at this turn of events. She was as frightened as the captain. She could see the sweat on his pale face, even though the morning was cool. In her mind she cursed Harvey Leland for getting her into this mess.

They wound their way through the woods and drew to a halt in the center of a make-shift camp. Indians came out of cabins, tents, and lean-tos to stare at them. Twilight glanced around at the ring of dark, closed faces. She was afraid, and it must have shown in her face, because Yellow Jacket looked down at her from his big horse and smiled. "Do not be afraid. My people will not scalp you or eat you, no matter what you have heard about 'savages.'"

Captain Wellsley cleared his throat as he stepped down from the buggy. "Now, see here, don't get forward with the lady; she comes to help."

"Oh?" Yellow Jacket leaned on the neck of his horse and watched her in an arrogant manner.

"That's right." Twilight licked her dry lips. "I — I've come to see what I can do."

In the meantime, Captain Wellsley came around the buggy to help her down. "We have your leader's permission to be here." He sounded as uncertain and fearful as Twilight felt.

"And so you do." Yellow Jacket swung down off his horse and faced them. "I will escort the white lady to our worst cases."

She glanced at Wellsley, hoping he would object. He appeared as if he knew he should but was fearful of crossing the big warrior. The soldiers stirred uneasily in their saddles and glanced at the warriors surrounding them, then at the captain, as if waiting for him to take action. There was a long moment of silence. No one moved. The only sound was the crackle of the big campfire, and somewhere in the camp a dog barked and a baby cried. "All right." She took a deep breath and reached for her medical bag.

"I'll carry that." Before she could object, Yellow Jacket took it from her hand. His brown fingers brushed hers, and it was if electricity passed between them. She jerked away.

He frowned down at her. "Don't worry, Mrs. Dumont, my hands are clean." His voice dripped bitter sarcasm.

"See here —" the captain began.

"Never mind." Twilight waved the captain to silence. Looking about at the hostile faces, she was certain that if the officer and his men tried to interfere, they could all be overrun and killed. "I — I can take care of this."

She was stunned at her own words as she turned to follow Yellow Jacket. She who had always been uncertain, afraid of almost everything, had spoken out to calm a tense situation.

The Indian grinned at her, white, even teeth flashing in his dark face. "After you, Mrs. Dumont." He made a wide, exaggerated bow.

She began to walk through the row of tents, too aware that he walked behind her, no doubt watching the way her wide hoopskirts swept along the dirt. She seemed to feel his eyes burning into her back and wondered why he should hate her so. Was he insulted that she was so afraid of Indians?

"Here, this way," he said behind her, and she turned and stopped in front of a ragged tent. "Many of our people are sick, and our healers can do nothing for them."

She paused and looked up at him. "You don't think I can, either, do you?"

He shook his head.

"Then, why was I sent for?"

He grinned without mirth. "Because our old leader has more faith in the whites than I do. I hear the drawl in your voice, Mrs. Dumont. Where in the South are you from?"

She didn't like what she was feeling as he towered over her. "I — originally, I am from Alabama."

He snorted in disgust. "I thought so. The very state that ran our people out so whites could steal it."

"I wouldn't know about that." She took a step backward.

"Of course not. Every white is innocent, yet you all have our land."

She was increasingly aware that she was out of view of the soldier escort if there should be any trouble. "I'm not here for political discussion. I came to help." She reached out and tried to take her medical bag from his hand, but he held on to it, and for a moment their hands touched as she tugged in vain, feeling foolish.

He let go of it suddenly, so suddenly that she stumbled backward, and he reached out and caught her arm to keep her from falling.

"Unhand me before I scream for the captain." She jerked away, completely unnerved at the strength of his grip.

Yellow Jacket threw back his head and laughed. "I don't know what good that would do, white girl. The officer is as scared as a girl."

"Well, I'm not," she lied.

"But of course you are." He took a step closer, evidently enjoying her discomfort. "I know why you come. The whites don't care if my people die or starve; they only want them to join up with their side to fight the Northern bluecoats."

She felt a flush creep to her face and was ashamed suddenly of her people. "That may be what some have in mind, but I've come only to minister to the sick."

"Then there's plenty for you to do," he said, and she saw the dislike and distrust in his rugged face. "In this tent and that one over there" — he pointed — "and the two down the row, there is sickness."

At that, he turned on his heel and left her standing in the chill wind as he walked away. Abruptly Twilight felt very much alone. She wasn't certain if these unsmiling brown faces peering out of tents and lean-tos could speak

74

English. Pasting a smile on her face, she bent to go through the flaps of the ragged tent. A woman and a small girl lay on the blankets, coughing and staring back at her. They were both thin. Twilight's heart went out to them. Forgetting her fear, she took the woman's hand. "I am here to help you," she said slowly.

She had no way to know if the gaunt woman understood her or not, but perhaps her tone was comforting, because the woman smiled. Twilight opened her medical bag. She had very little to offer — a little homemade cough syrup and some alcohol to bathe their foreheads and bring down the fever — but the woman and little girl seemed apprecia-tive. Twilight wished she had more to offer. "You will get better," she told the woman and wasn't certain whether she lied.

She went to the next tent where an old woman lay on blankets, shivering in the cold. "I shall get someone to build up your fire," she said as she knelt by her side.

The old woman shook her head. "Not waste medicine or fuel on the old," she said in broken English. "Save the young — they are the hope of our tribe."

"Nonsense." Twilight held a little flask of brandy to her lips, "you must all get better."

The old woman lay back against her blan-kets and sighed. "They will go soon, and the old will have to die. We must not slow them down."

"Go?" Twilight paused in wiping the wrinkled old face. "No one's going anywhere."

The old woman looked as if she would protest, seemed to think it over, and said nothing else. "The bluecoats will save us, maybe," she whispered.

The old woman must be delirious, Twilight thought, but she didn't discuss anything more. She stepped outside to find Yellow Jacket standing there. "I thought you'd gone."

"I did, but then I thought you might be in danger, so I returned."

The way he was looking at her made her uneasy. "This old woman needs more wood on her fire, and some broth."

Yellow Jacket shook his head. "The wood I can provide, but she won't eat."

"Why not?"

He looked saddened. "Many of the old will refuse food. They fear there will not be enough to go around."

"That's ridiculous," Twilight said. "Doesn't the Indian agent give you supplies?"

"He's your brother; why don't you ask him?" the man challenged.

"I certainly will! Now, get out of my way and let me finish my rounds." Shocked at her own sudden spunk, she brushed past him and was relieved that he did not challenge her as she went on to the next smoky hut. There, three little boys had croup, and she instructed their mother to put water on to boil, knowing the steam would ease their breathing.

When she came out, Yellow Jacket was waiting for her. "I'll have to go now," she said. "I don't have any more medicine."

"That's what the white doctor always says," Yellow Jacket said.

"Are you not getting any supplies out here?" She couldn't believe it.

He shook his head. "Not much. It's better lately since the rebels fear we might join up with the bluecoats."

She had a sudden vision of all these muscular warriors fighting for the other side. They would be formidable opponents. "I'm sure your people don't want to support the Yankees."

He was stoic again, his face hostile and closed. "Why should we side with the ones who have run us off our land in the South?"

He had a point. Lifting her black skirts, she began walking back toward the buggy, Yellow Jacket following along behind her. When she came within sight of the soldiers, the captain smiled. "I was just about to come searching for you, Mrs. Dumont."

"She was safe enough," Yellow Jacket snapped.

Twilight waved the captain off. "There's no problem, Captain, except that these people seem to be short on food and supplies. I hope you'll be able to do something about it."

"I'll try," said the officer.

"I doubt that," the Indian said.

"Let's go now," Twilight said, and caught the officer's arm. He took her bag from her hand and helped her up into the buggy.

Then Captain Wellsley climbed in. The buggy was ringed by brown, hostile faces. For a moment, Twilight was not certain they would be allowed to leave. After a long minute, Yellow Jacket nodded to the people, and they moved back to allow the buggy to move.

The Confederate officer cracked his little whip, and the buggy pulled out, followed by the small squad of soldiers.

Twilight could still feel Yellow Jacket's dark eyes boring into her back as they drove away.

Yellow Jacket watched her go, angry with her and with himself for feeling attracted to the white woman. Behind those smoky, twilight-colored eyes, he sensed a fire and passion that was being carefully held in check, waiting for the right man to release her emotions. A hundred years ago, he might have taken a woman like that captive on the eastern frontier, made her his woman. Now women like that one belonged to rich white men like the captain. However, he sensed that the small female was more woman than

78

that high-class, weak male could handle.

His giant mixed-blood friend, Smoke, came across the circle and watched with him until the buggy and its escort were out of sight. "Forget about her," Smoke said. "I used to see women like that on plantations. If you even looked their way, the white master would have you flailed until your skin was in shreds."

Yellow Jacket snorted in disgust. "She's the crooked storekeeper's sister. Does that tell you what I think of her?" He spit on the ground in disgust.

"But she's beautiful," Smoke said.

"To hell with her. She's from Alabama; her plantation was probably built on some of our stolen land."

"The ancient one wants to see us," Smoke said.

"What about?" Reluctantly Yellow Jacket tore his gaze away from the disappearing buggy.

"You know what about," Smoke said. "Just three or four of us are going, and we might not make it back."

"You mean . . . ?"

"Yes. We've got to ride north and see if we can bring the bluecoats back to help."

Yellow Jacket shook his head. "We haven't a chance of getting through the rebel lines."

"But we must try," said the big mixed-blood. "Our people will be slaughtered here if we don't get help."

He would be riding to his death to try to get through rebel lines, but Smoke was right — they must try — and they had both faced death before. "May the Master of Breath protect us," Yellow Jacket said, and turned to go to meet with their ancient leader.

Chapter 4

Yellow Jacket felt annoyance and anger as he and Smoke strode to meet with Opothleyahola. He had not taken a woman of his own although he was almost thirty winter counts old. Many Muskogee girls had flirted and hinted that they would be pleased and honored to share his blanket, but none of them attracted him. Now he was furious with himself that the only woman who had made his blood run hot was an enemy white girl who was as far out of his reach as the ancient stars where the Master of Breath resided. He hated the haughty Southern widow because she occupied his mind and emotions when he should be concentrating on the fate of his tribe and revenge for the deaths of his brother and niece.

Smoke put his brown hand on Yellow Jacket's broad shoulder as they walked. "You need to take a woman — a Muskogee woman, as I have. That white girl will bring you nothing but trouble."

"You think I don't know that?" Yellow Jacket snapped, and then was immediately sorry. Last night he had dreamed he had the forbidden Twilight in his blankets, writhing beneath him, her white, white skin shiny with perspiration as she urged him to take her, put his hot mouth on her breasts, tangle his fingers in that pale, sun-streaked hair. "I am sorry, old friend; the deaths in my family have driven me almost to madness with hatred."

"Which accomplishes nothing," his friend said softly. "Better you should pick a girl who will give you sons and be pleasant enough, even though there is no wild passion."

Yellow Jacket did not answer. Yes, his common sense told him that was what he should do, but in his mind he remembered Twilight's soft mouth and imagined it caressing his body. Everything in him ached to put his child in that delicate body and make wild love to her until she cried out and clawed his back as he took her.

He must forget about the white woman. There were important events about to happen to his tribe. Yellow Jacket sighed and turned to follow his black-Indian friend to the old man's ragged tent. Inside, two noted warriors sat by the fire and nodded as the two newcomers sat down cross-legged.

Opothleyahola nodded to them. "We cannot hold out much longer. I have been stalling the rebels, letting them think we might be willing to join them to keep their

82

soldiers from attacking us. I am beginning to wonder if the bluecoats that Chief Lincoln promised will ever come."

Yellow Jacket stared into the fire. "Old one, what is it you would have us do?"

The old man hesitated. "It will be dangerous."

Yellow Jacket snorted. "Life is dangerous. Has not the Master of Breath told us that in many ways?"

The others murmured agreement.

"I wish your brother was here to help," old Opothleyahola said.

Yellow Jacket flinched at the thought of his lost brother — and the lovely niece, so newly dead. "With him in mind, I will do whatever needs to be done to protect us from the rebels."

"Good." The ancient one nodded. "We are surrounded by the graycoats. Sooner or later they will attack us, and many women and children will die."

In the silence no one spoke. Of these four men, only Smoke had loved ones in the camp. It occurred to Yellow Jacket then that this was a very dangerous task indeed, for the ancient one to choose noted warriors who had no women and children to protect.

The Muskogee leader said, "This is what must be done. Someone must ride to this place called Kansas to alert the bluecoats about what is happening here. Chief Lincoln has promised that if we are loyal to the Union, he will send soldiers to protect and help us."

Yellow Jacket considered. "Is Chief Lincoln in this place named Kansas?"

The old one shook his head. "I do not think so. I hear he is in that place called Washington, but he has chiefs at the fort in Kansas. They can send him messages over the singing wires, reminding him of his promise."

Yellow Jacket looked around the circle at the others and chewed his lip in thought. "You are right, old one. It is a long way to Kansas, and we will have to avoid the graycoat rebels who will try to stop us from getting through."

Opothleyahola nodded. "Some or all of you may not make it back. The rebels will shoot to kill, and the weather will soon be turning cold. Any man whose heart tells him he should not go will not be blamed."

He seemed to wait for his warning to sink in. Outside, the wind picked up and whipped the ragged tent as if reminding the warriors just how chill and hostile the weather and the terrain would soon be.

Yellow Jacket stood up. "With my brother and niece dead, no one would weep if I did not return. I have no woman, no child; no one depends on me now. I will take the message through."

Smoke, the big mixed-blood stood up, his head brushing against the top of the old tent. "I have a woman and children, but if the bluecoats do not win, we will be thrown back into slavery — and I would die to protect them from that."

The other two got to their feet. "We, too, will go."

"Good," the leader said. "I would go myself, but I am old and ill. My people depend on some young, strong man getting to Kansas with the message."

Yellow Jacket turned to leave. "I can write, old one. If you will write the message down —"

"No" — the old one shook his head — "there must be nothing on paper the rebels can use against our tribe. I will tell you what to tell the bluecoat chief, my son."

Yellow Jacket nodded. "We will leave at dark. Riding at night is a better way to slip away from the rebels."

"It may snow soon," Smoke said. "They will be able to track us."

"But if it keeps snowing, our tracks will be covered," Yellow Jacket answered. "Now, let us gather our things, pray to the Master of Breath, and make offerings to the sacred fire. When darkness falls, we will ride out."

They rode out at dark, each of the four keenly aware of the seriousness of the task with which they were entrusted. None of them really expected to return, but it was only important that they get through to the bluecoat chief so that he would bring troops to protect the thousands of loyal Indians who were ringed in by graycoats.

The wind had picked up, blowing from the north with the promise of snow, as the four rode their horses through the stark, bare oak and walnut trees. The ground looked black and frozen and sounded hard under the horses' hooves. At least there was no moon, Yellow Jacket thought as he grasped his rifle and hunched his wide shoulders against the cold wind that seemed to steal the breath from the riders' lips.

Once as they picked their way single file through the brush near the soldier encampment, a guard stopped and yelled, "Who goes there?"

Yellow Jacket reined his horse in, motioned the others to be silent. They dismounted, each holding his horse's muzzle so it would not whinny. He was not close enough to the sentry to sneak up and cut the man's throat, and a shot would alert the whole rebel camp. The sentry paused, looking their way in the darkness. Yellow Jacket's heart seemed to pound so loudly that he could hear it. He did not fear for himself — he had faced death many times as a Lighthorseman for the Muskogee nation. What he feared was the failure of his mission. The fate of the loyal Muskogee, Cherokee, Seminole, and other tribes hung in the balance.

After what seemed like an eternity, the sentry shrugged and began walking his post again. Yellow Jacket motioned to the others, and they led their horses through the night, wanting to put as much distance as possible between them and this soldier encampment before morning. At any moment, he expected to feel a bullet tearing into his back, but the only sound was the wind, whining like a complaining old woman. Finally, he motioned the others to mount up, and they took off again at a ground-eating lope.

As they rode north, the night seemed endless, and Yellow Jacket felt numb and half-frozen by the time the first pale light of dawn came up over the eastern hills. "We will camp," he said to the others, "and wait for night to go on."

Smoke frowned. "We could make good time in daylight."

"And risk running into a rebel patrol," Yellow Jacket pointed out. "The woods are full of them."

The others nodded agreement. Yellow Jacket knew this country well. For many years before the white man's war started, he had ridden with the Lighthorse, the law enforcement of his tribe. All the five Civilized Tribes had a Lighthorse patrol that kept the peace and caught and punished lawbreakers. It was ironic, he thought, that some of his old Lighthorse comrades from other tribes now rode for the Confederates and would try to kill him if they met. Yellow Jacket sighed as he thought of these good friends. He knew that Wohali, of the Cherokee, had sided with the rebels. Wohali sometimes went by a white name, Jim Eagle. Yellow Jacket was not certain what had happened to his Choctaw Lighthorse friend Talako.

They found a draw that was overgrown with brush and out of the wind. They unsaddled their horses and hobbled them so that the animals might graze. The gray, leaden sky was now spitting snow.

One of the younger warriors looked at Yellow Jacket. "Do we dare risk a fire?"

Yellow Jacket started to say no, then noted that the others were rubbing their hands together and shivering. If anyone got frostbite or grew sick, their mission would be endangered. "Smoke, make us a tiny fire so we can boil some coffee and warm ourselves. We will rest until nightfall."

He had not realized how cold he was himself until he clutched that tin cup of strong coffee in his hands and felt the warmth. He took a deep breath of the strong scent and drank the brew gratefully. The others had already wrapped themselves in buffalo robes and curled up by the fire to sleep.

Someone had to stand guard, and Yellow Jacket took the first watch. He had never felt as lonely or sad in his life as he did now, staring out at the frozen, barren landscape. He was chilled to the bone, but that did not matter. Many times he had been hungry or cold, but it had not kept him from doing his duty as a warrior should. He closed his eyes and saw the white woman with the smoky gray eyes just the color of twilight. Her mouth had looked soft, but her eyes, when she looked at him, had been hard. If he had her curled up naked in his blankets, she would be very warm, and he would put his face against her breasts and sleep.

He laughed without mirth. Harvey Leland's sister would not want to be embraced and lie naked and warm with him under his blankets. If she belonged to him, he would make her want to sleep in his arms and kiss his mouth while he stroked her full breasts. His groin ached, thinking about taking her and putting his seed in her belly in a spasm of ecstasy. Yellow Jacket awoke with a start, realizing that he had dozed off. The white woman hated Indians and was as far out of his reach as the frosty stars above him. He shook himself awake and returned to watching the stark skeletons of trees.

After a while, Smoke awoke and took a watch. Yellow Jacket curled up and slept, and in his sleep, the white girl came to him and held out her arms.

At dark they rode on. The cold wind had not let up, but the quartet hunched their shoulders against the chill, watched the North Star, and kept riding. Now the wintry blast was beginning in earnest. Once, Yellow Jacket smelled smoke and signaled the others to halt. He dismounted and crept to the top of a nearby ridge. From that spot, he could see a cozy log cabin. Lantern light glowed dimly through the windows, and he smelled food cooking and saw smoke curling up against the cold sky from the chimney. White settlers. More and more whites were trespassing in the Indian Territory. It could only be a sign of what was to come, Yellow Jacket thought bitterly. Perhaps he should attack the cabin, kill the trespassers, and take the warm food.

He crept up and looked in the window. There were a woman and small children inside. The woman was not as pretty as Twilight Dumont. The realization that he thought of the white woman back at the fort annoyed him, and he crept away, back to the waiting men. "It's white settlers."

"Are there many men?" asked one of the others.

Yellow Jacket shook his head. "I saw none. There was a woman and children."

One of the younger warriors frowned. "I say we attack them, kill them all, and take their food and ammunition."

"Warriors do not kill women and children," Yellow Jacket admonished.

"My friend is right," Smoke said.

"They kill ours," the young warrior said.

It was true, oh, so true, Yellow Jacket thought bitterly, remembering the Trail of Tears from his childhood.

"Besides," Yellow Jacket said, "If we attack and one should escape, they would find the rebel soldiers and put them on our trail. It is most important that we get through to the white chiefs in Kansas with our message. We do not have time to try for war honors."

The others grudgingly admitted this was true. Again they rode though the night and took cover in the daylight. Yellow Jacket had no idea how far they had ridden or just how far it was to this place called Kansas. He decided they must ride until they ran across blue-coated soldiers.

The next several days passed uneventfully as they rode north, except that they were always hungry and cold. The snow had begun in earnest, dusting the barren landscape. Their horses were getting thin. Yellow Jacket put his face against that of his beloved paint stallion. "I promise you, boy, that when we reach the fort, you will have hay and grain."

The horse nickered as if he understood.

Several days later, about the time Yellow Jacket thought they were safe, they ran across a rebel patrol. The quartet had ridden past daylight because there seemed to be no good place on the rolling prairie ahead of them to bed down and rest. They were strung out single file along the trail when they rounded a great cedar tree and saw graycoat cavalry riding in the distance. Smoke hardly had time to shout a warning before the rebels began the chase.

"There's a forest ahead and rough ground," Yellow Jacket shouted. "Maybe we can lose them."

Even as he said that, a shot echoed, and one of the young warriors fell from his saddle with a cry. There was no time to stop to help him; it was only important that at least one of them survive to get the message through. "Scatter!" Yellow Jacket shouted. "Let's lose them in the woods!"

Each headed in a different direction, the graycoats shouting and shooting behind them. The three were outnumbered, Yellow Jacket thought, and wondered if this was where he would die. He said a prayer to the Master of Breath. "It does not matter if I go to join my ancestors this day," he whispered as he rode hard. "It only matters that one of us survive to get the message to Chief Lincoln."

At that precise moment, a shot rang out, and the other young brave screamed in agony and fell from his horse, tumbling over and over.

He must not stop to make a stand, Yellow Jacket reminded himself. He rounded a curve on the trail and headed for a gulch ahead of him. At that moment, his horse stumbled and went down. Yellow Jacket pitched forward, his rifle flying from his hands even as his forehead struck a rock.

He did not know how much time had passed when he came to, his head throbbing. His horse had wandered up the trail and stood grazing. He could not see his rifle. Somewhere in the distance, he could hear men yelling at each other in English as they searched for the pair of riders.

Had Smoke escaped? There was no way to know. Yellow Jacket reached up and touched his throbbing head, and came away with fingers smeared with blood. What to do? He hadn't a chance of catching his horse and outriding the rebel patrol. The best he could do was to hide in the brush and hope they didn't find him.

Somewhere out there, he heard a horse coming through the brush. A white man yelled, "Jim, you go down that draw; see what you can find."

"Yes, sir." The rider came toward Yellow Jacket, twigs snapping under his horse's hooves.

What to do? Yellow Jacket grabbed for the

big knife in his belt — no good against a rifle. Besides, even if he could find his rifle, a shot would bring the whole rebel patrol down on him. He hunkered down as flat on the dead grass as he could, and waited. Up ahead, a tall, handsome Indian wearing the gray uniform of rebel cavalry pushed through the dead brush and dismounted. In one hand the man carried a rifle; in the other, a pistol. He came on now carefully and silently as a man skilled in tracking human game.

Wohali. Jim Eagle. Yellow Jacket recognized the Cherokee Lighthorseman immediately. Was it only a cruel twist of fate that Yellow Jacket and a man who had once been his friend were about to engage in mortal combat? Yellow Jacket clutched his knife and waited, hardly daring to breathe. He was not sure he could kill his old friend if he had to, and the Cherokee rebel had the advantage of weapons.

At that moment, Jim Eagle seemed to see Yellow Jacket for the first time. He froze in place, staring as though he could not quite believe what he saw. Yellow Jacket only looked back at him, awaiting the shot that would end his life. In the distance a white commander yelled, "Jim, you see anything?"

For a heart-stopping moment, Jim Eagle stared at the trapped, bloody man while the other held his breath. Once they had been friends. Now they were enemies because of a white man's war.

"Jim Eagle?" drawled the white officer again, "you see anything? You need any help?"

The Cherokee looked at Yellow Jacket a moment longer. He still clutched his rifle, and at this distance he could not miss. Then he turned his head and yelled back over his shoulder. "No, Lieutenant, there's nobody down this trail. He must have taken another route."

In the distance the white commander swore and ordered the Cherokee to return.

Yellow Jacket took a deep breath. Jim Eagle smiled at him and saluted him. Yellow Jacket saluted him back and whispered, "Thank you, old friend."

The other nodded, mounted his palomino horse, wheeled, and rode back along the trail. "Let's get out of here, men; they've all gotten away."

Yellow Jacket lay there, hardly daring to breathe as the gray-clad Cherokee rode out of sight. He heard the patrol ride away, the leader still cursing their luck at letting some of their prey escape.

Sometimes friendship was more important than war, Yellow Jacket thought. The event renewed his faith in men. He wasn't certain what he would have done in Jim Eagle's moccasins. He crept from his hiding place, the snow blowing harder now, and found his horse and his rifle. Then he gave the call of a bobwhite quail. After a moment, Smoke came out of a ravine to the east. "That you, Yellow Jacket?"

"Yes, I'm alive, just scratched up a bit." Yellow Jacket walked out to meet him, leading his horse. "What about the others?"

"Dead, I think. We'll look and make sure." Smoke stared at him. "I would have sworn you were a goner when I saw that Cherokee go down that trail."

Yellow Jacket smiled in remembrance. "A long time ago we were friends. He didn't give me away."

Smoke nodded. "I'd say you were still friends. Some things, war don't change."

They found the two young warriors sprawled along the trail, dead with the snow blowing about them, stark and white against brown skin. Yellow Jacket knelt and put his hand on the cold face. "We should do ceremonies."

"We have no time," Smoke said. "We've got to get that message to Chief Lincoln."

"It doesn't seem right to leave them here for the wolves," Yellow Jacket answered.

"They would understand," Smoke said softly.

He was right, of course. Thousands of loyal Indians were awaiting help from Union forces. They must bring that help. The snow began to fall faster. Soon the brown, dead bodies would be buried by the Master of Breath in a white, soft blanket. With a sigh, Yellow Jacket mounted up. "Yes, we must ride on. The graycoats might send a patrol out for another look."

So they rode until they were so weary and frozen, they were about to fall from their saddles, and their horses stumbled in the snow. They lost all track of time as they rode north, but finally, they ran across a bluecoat patrol.

The soldiers cocked their rifles. "Who are you?"

Yellow Jacket was so frozen, he could barely speak. "L-loyal Muskogee, the tribe the whites call Creeks. We have come far. Take us to your commander."

Within an hour, they were ushered into the Union colonel's office by a wiry sergeant. "Good Lord, Sergeant," the old man growled, and came to his feet. "What the hell . . . ?"

"We are sent from the loyal Creek leader Opothleyahola," Yellow Jacket gasped, and grabbed on to the desk to keep from falling. "Come to ask for soldiers."

The colonel gestured. "Quick, Sergeant, get chairs for these men, and some coffee."

Yellow Jacket shook his head, even though he was on the verge of fainting. "We — we must deliver our message first."

In minutes he had explained their mission, even as an orderly came in with steaming cups of coffee.

The old colonel pulled at his gray whiskers and peered at them through his spectacles. "Hmm. How many loyal Indians are there?"

Gratefully, Yellow Jacket wrapped his cold hands around the cup. "There's no way to know for sure — maybe six to nine or ten thousand, of many tribes."

"And how many fighting men?" the colonel asked.

"Not many, maybe a couple of thousand." Yellow Jacket gulped the hot, strong brew.

"You two came through enemy lines? That's impossible."

Smoke nodded. "There were four of us. The other two didn't make it."

"I insist that you rest up for a couple of days and —"

"No." Yellow Jacket emptied his cup and stood up. "We've got to return with your message to our leader. What shall I tell him? Are you sending soldiers to help us, as Chief Lincoln promised?"

Now the colonel clasped his hands behind his back, pacing his office and pausing to look out at the snow outside. "I — I'll see what I can do."

"Good." Yellow Jacket smiled at Smoke. "Now, sir, if you'll give us a little food for us and our horses, we've got to get back."

"But it's several hundred miles," the officer protested. "Why don't you remain here and —"

"The ancient one is waiting for an answer," Yellow Jacket said. "He must decide what to do next, ringed in as he is by rebels."

The officer nodded, not looking at him. "All right, Sergeant," he ordered, "get these men the supplies they need and send them on their way."

Yellow Jacket glanced at Smoke, and they both smiled. Things would be good for their people now, just as Chief Lincoln had promised. They both saluted the elderly officer and went out.

Later the old colonel went to his window and watched the pair riding away from the fort, headed south. The wiry sergeant came into the room and stood beside him. "Poor devils," the colonel murmured.

"I beg your pardon, sir?"

He watched the pair growing smaller and smaller as they rode across the white prairie until they disappeared into the blowing snow. "I couldn't bear to tell them the truth."

"Nobody blames you for that, sir," the other man said.

"But I lied to them, knowing that with the rebels threatening to overrun Kansas and Missouri, I have no extra troops to send to Indian Territory to help these poor loyal devils, even if President Lincoln did make them promises."

"Sir, maybe if you wired the president —"

"No." The colonel turned from the window, shaking his head. "The president hasn't got the extra troops anywhere, not with the way the war is going in the eastern states. I'm afraid a few thousand loyal Indians trying to escape from the rebels is a low priority."

The sergeant blinked. "This pair may not make it back through enemy lines anyway."

"Brave men," the colonel murmured, "to come this far — and it's all such a waste. Those Indians are waiting for help that won't come. The rebels will probably slaughter all six thousand of them." He sat down at his desk with a sigh. "Poor devils. Poor, poor devils."

Chapter 5

Twilight had settled into a routine at the store in the few days since she had arrived, clerking behind the counter and helping Harvey with his bookwork. This cold morning, two small girls came through the front door very hesitantly. When Twilight looked at them, she was puzzled as to their background. They appeared to be a mixture of black and Indian.

Twilight loved children. She smiled and beckoned them in, but Harvey, who was up on a ladder stocking shelves, yelled at them, "Get out of here, you little devils! I'm tired of your beggin'!"

The two turned and fled.

Twilight came around the counter and looked up at him. "Now was that really necessary? They were just children, and they looked hungry."

Harvey came down off the ladder. "Now, Twilight, dear," he said in a soothing tone, "you don't understand that those thievin' savages come in here and steal supplies —"

"Why should they have to steal?" She was really puzzled. "Haven't you got a big gov-

ernment contract to buy them food and supplies?"

"Don't you worry your pretty little head
about that." Harvey walked across the floor
to her.

His tone set Twilight's teeth on edge. She
ached to ask questions, but of course, it
would not be polite to doubt her stepbrother
on this. "I just thought, if I gave them some
candy, it would encourage the adults to buy
more."

"With what?" Harvey sneered. "They don't
have any extra money."

She realized suddenly that Harvey had
walked across the floor with no noticeable
limp. "Has your leg gotten better? You aren't
limping today."

He appeared taken aback. "Uh, some days
it's better than others."

A thought crossed her mind — a thought
so awful and disloyal, she couldn't put it into
words. *Can Harvey be faking his limp?* Of
course she dare not even think such a thing.
"Well, I'm glad your leg's improving."

He nodded. "Damned Yankee minié ball. If
my leg was good, I'd still be right in the
front line with our other brave boys."

She'd never thought of Harvey as brave,
but she didn't say so. "Anyway, I didn't think
it would hurt anything to give those children
a candy stick."

"I'm not running a charity here." Harvey

paused, and his voice had a decided edge. "Remember, dear sister, that this store is supporting two now."

If she had any gumption, she would go into the back room and pack her bags. Instead, she swallowed back a retort. "I — I'm sorry, Harvey. I don't want to appear ungrateful for your generosity."

That appeared to mollify him. He smiled and patted her shoulder. "Never mind, I'm happy to have you here. As your older brother, of course I am pleased to offer you bed and board. Of course, if you should make a good marriage, I'm sure you won't forget how I helped you when you needed it."

She hated taking his charity and, worse yet, being reminded of it. "Of course, Harvey." Her mind returned to the little girls. "Those children don't quite look like Indians."

He was limping again as he crossed the floor, climbed the ladder, and returned to stocking shelves. "Smoke's kids — part black, part Creek."

"Smoke?"

"He's Matt Folane's friend. That tribe has intermingled with black freed slaves; so have many of the Five Civilized Tribes."

"Matt Folane?"

"You know, Yellow Jacket, that damned dangerous brave."

"Oh, yes." She remembered the hostile

103

warrior. "He doesn't look like he should have a white name. He's rather uncivilized."

"Ain't he, though? He was a Lighthorseman before the War started, he and his brother both."

She began straightening a display of fabric. "What's a Lighthorseman?"

"The Five Civilized Tribes have their own law enforcement, the Lighthorse. Believe me, no one wants to get crosswise with them; they're judge, jury, and executioner to law-breaking Indians."

"But not to whites?" She paused, picturing Yellow Jacket as a lawman.

"Naw. Whites in the Territory have to be taken over to Fort Smith for trial. That makes the Territory a good place for white bandits to hide out. White deputies don't want to come into the Nations looking for lawbreakers. If they do, most of them are never seen again. 'Course, all that will change when Indian Territory becomes a state."

"Anyone ask the Indians what they think about that?" She looked up at him.

"Of course not, Twilight; why would they? By the way, tomorrow I've got to take a wagon and go over to the railyard to pick up new supplies — be gone about ten days."

"You want me to go with you?" Twilight asked politely. She didn't relish being left here alone with all these savages. On the other hand, she really didn't enjoy Harvey's company.

"Now, if you went, I'd have to close the store, and we'd lose money. Don't worry, I'll ask our young captain to check on you. I think his mother has already left for Austin."

"I'll be fine," she answered, realizing that Harvey was again pushing romance, but somehow, a mama's boy didn't appeal to her. *Who did?* In her mind, abruptly, she saw the big, virile savage, and the thought both horrified her and made her heart beat faster.

She shook her head. Frankly, she'd be relieved for her stepbrother to be gone. "The place is a little dusty," she said. "I might do some cleaning while you're gone."

Harvey grinned, showing crooked teeth. "Now, that would be nice. Place hasn't really been cleaned up in a while. Those Injun girls tried to overcharge me to do it."

Twilight didn't believe that anyone could overcharge her greedy stepbrother and get away with it, but she didn't say so.

"Oh, by the way," Harvey said a little too casually, "Captain Wellsley asked if he might call on you, and I told him yes."

Twilight sighed. "You might have asked me first, Harvey."

He looked hurt. "Should I have told him no? After all, you have been widowed some months now. Are you worried about what people will think?"

105

"Yes, well, I don't know." She turned away and picked up a feather duster. She had always worried about what people thought of her. It had made her shy and inhibited because her stepmother had been so critical. "It's just that I'm really not interested in the captain . . ."

"Not interested? Not interested?" Harvey's voice rose. "You're poor as a church mouse and relying on my generosity to eat . . . !"

"I — I reckon you think I'm being too picky, Harvey, but after all, he's a mama's boy and he's younger than I am —"

"So what?" His voice rose. "You expect some Prince Charming to come carry you off on a prancing stallion? You women and your silly fantasies. Marriage is a business arrangement, Twilight, and you should have realized that when I arranged for you to meet Pierre. . . ." His voice trailed off as if he suddenly realized he had said too much.

"I thought when you introduced me to Pierre, you were thinking of my welfare." She stared up at him.

"And so I was." He smiled. "As I am now."

She said nothing. Southern ladies did not contradict men. She swallowed back the spunky reply that came to her lips. Daddy might not approve of such independence, and certainly her stepmother had taught her better. "I'm sure you're right, Harvey," she

106

said, and returned to dusting shelves.

Twilight made one promise to herself as she straightened the counter. After Harvey left tomorrow, if hungry little Indian children came into the store, she intended to slip them some candy or food. Harvey complained that he wasn't making any profit, but having looked at his books, she was certain he was shorting the tribes on their government rations and pocketing the difference. She was afraid of Indians, but she believed in fair play and justice. She might not have much gumption or spunk, but for needy children she could rise to the occasion.

The next day Harvey hitched up the big wagon and pulled out, leaving Twilight in charge. It was a slow day; not many people came into the store. Twilight began to straighten out a drawer of papers under the cash register. Stunned, she flipped through them. Harvey was deeply in debt from gambling with the local soldiers and settlers. She had always suspected that Harvey gambled, but she hadn't realized it was so serious. It crossed her mind now how eager he had been for her to marry Pierre Dumont, who was also a gambler. Could Harvey have owed Pierre money? Surely her own stepbrother wouldn't have stooped so low.

Could he be hoping to use her again, to dip his chubby hands in Captain Wellsley's wealth? Perhaps her stepbrother had not been as generous as she had thought in inviting her to come stay with him. What to do? She had no money unless she robbed his cash register, and she was not a thief. With no resources and no one to turn to, she was pretty much on her own if she decided to pack her bags and leave. She hated herself for not having the courage to do just that. At least she'd have about ten days to make some choices, if she could just get up the nerve to do so.

Her thoughts were interrupted by the ring of the bell, announcing a visitor. A small dark face peered around the door, then another. She gave the children a big smile. "Come in."

The two little girls looked at each other, then at her again. She gestured. "Come in. Mr. Leland is not here."

The children were in rags and barefoot in this cool weather, Twilight noted with dismay as they entered the store.

"Where is your father?" She reached to hand them two candy sticks.

"Smoke hasn't got back —" the younger one began.

"Hush!" the older one warned. "Remember, we don't tell whites nothin'." She took the striped candy with wonder.

"I'm your friend; you can trust me," Twilight said softly, and came around the counter. "Does your daddy know you're here?"

The smaller girl licked the candy. "He's —"

"Don't tell that," the other child said. "Remember, we must not tell."

"Tell what?" Twilight squatted down in front of them.

Now they both looked at her with big, suspicious eyes.

"We must not talk to you," the bigger child said. "You are the enemy."

"Me?" Twilight touched her chest in surprise. "I am no one's enemy."

"You're a rebel." The smaller girl eyed her and licked the candy. "When Daddy and Yellow Jacket get back —"

"Hush!" the older girl commanded. Before the younger one could say anything else, the older girl took her hand and they went out the door, with the little one protesting that she had not told the secret.

Mystified, Twilight went over to shut the door and began to arrange some bolts of cloth on the shelf. Just what were the Indians up to? She wondered if she should mention it to the captain but decided against it. She didn't want to start trouble, especially when she really knew nothing. The captain might laugh if Twilight told him a child had almost blabbed some minor gossip that would turn out to be worthless. More than that, she didn't want to get the children in trouble. Twilight wouldn't admit to even herself that she didn't want to get the big, virile warrior in trouble with the army, either.

The weather turned colder and more miserable. She had few customers that day and the next, so she decided maybe she should clean up the bedroom in the back of the store. Certainly it needed it. Twilight looked with distaste at the cobwebs draped across the wall and the dirty windows. With a will, she began to clean.

She found a broom and dustpan and swept the bare plank floor. When she gathered her skirts and knelt to look under the bed, there were dust balls everywhere. Whatever Harvey was paying the Indian girls to do, she suspected it wasn't cleaning.

What was that in a far corner under the bed? Mystified, Twilight reached with the broom. It took three tries to retrieve the tiny object. It was a blue bead. Harvey sold beads, but how had this one ended up under the bed? She puzzled over it a moment, shrugged, and put it in her dress pocket. Then she picked up Harvey's extra boots. She dropped one, and pebbles rolled out and clattered across the floor. Now, why would he have pebbles in his boot? She remembered him walking without a limp. Now, why would he . . . ?

From the back room, she heard the front door jangle. A customer. She straightened her apron so she would look presentable and started toward the door, but even as she did so, she heard heavy steps striding across the boards. Before she could move, Yellow Jacket came through the bedroom door and stood glaring at her. "What is it you do? Are you a spy?"

"I beg your pardon?" She could only blink up at him in surprise at his anger.

"Don't play innocent with me." He threw two half-eaten candy sticks at her. "You would stoop to learning things from children?"

"I merely gave those children some candy —" Twilight protested.

"We are not beggars, my people," Yellow Jacket said, his rugged face grim with fury.

Twilight backed away until she was stopped by the edge of the bed. She was abruptly aware that she was alone with this hostile man. "The — the children didn't beg," she gulped. "I gave them the candy —"

"And tried to pry information out of them at the same time. You're no better than your robber brother."

"He's not here —" Twilight began, then almost bit her tongue at her own stupidity. Now this big savage knew she was alone. Anything could happen, and there was no one to help her.

"I know he's not here." Yellow Jacket strode across the room and glared down at her. "You think white people are the only ones with spies?"

She looked up at him, hardly daring to breathe. He was standing so close, she could smell the masculine scent of his skin and feel the heat from his muscular body. "I — I don't know what you're talking about." And she didn't.

"Liar!" He reached out and caught her shoulder, pulling her closer.

His hand was so strong, she flinched in his grip. He glanced behind her, and she realized he was looking at the bed. He could throw her down on it, put his hand over her mouth, and . . . The thought terrified her. "Let go of me," she said, "or I will scream and the soldiers will come running."

He smiled without mirth. "I almost think it might be worth it," he murmured, and then took a deep breath and stepped away from her. "I have orders to ask you to come out to see our old leader. He is not well."

Twilight drew a sigh of relief and brushed a stray wisp of hair from her face. "I — I'll do what I can. It will take a few minutes to gather some medicines."

"Good." Yellow Jacket almost smiled. He was handsome when he wasn't scowling. "I'll go harness your buggy."

"I — I don't know whether there's a patrol available to drive me." She licked her dry lips.

He leaned against the doorjamb, evidently enjoying her discomfort. "You don't need soldiers, Mrs. Dumont. I'll drive you myself."

She hesitated, looked away.

"Are you afraid?" he jeered. "Do you think the big savage will scalp you along the road?"

"No," she said, and didn't look at him. What she was really afraid of was the way he was looking at her as if he'd like to pull her into his arms and kiss her. The thought both horrified and excited her. The thought of his hot mouth covering hers, forcing her lips apart while his big, hard hand went down into the front of her bodice . . .

"What's the matter, Mrs. Dumont? Your face has flushed."

"Nothing." She was desperate enough to brush past him as he stood in the doorway. She wanted to get out of that bedroom and into the front of the store. His body was hard and muscular, and she wondered suddenly how he would look naked. Her thought shocked her. Pierre's skin had been as white and soft as any woman's, and his lovemaking had been quick and disappointing.

"Your face is redder still," he said behind her, following her toward the store's front.

She hated him for possibly guessing her thoughts. "Just go hitch up my buggy and I'll get my things together."

He nodded and went outside. Twilight stood there a moment, trying to decide what to do. Should she go alert the captain so he would provide a patrol? She felt uncomfortable doing that, because Yellow Jacket would think her a coward. What the hell did she care what the big savage thought? Her own mental cursing shocked her even more. She never cursed. In the meantime, there was a sick old man out at the Indian camp who needed her care.

Twilight gathered up food and medical supplies and went to the back door. Yellow Jacket waited there with her buggy. He had tied his big pinto horse behind the buggy. "Are you ready?"

"You're going to drive me?"

He nodded.

She'd be sitting next to him on that small seat, his strong, warm thigh against hers. She hesitated. "I — I have some supplies."

"Why didn't you say so?" He got down off the buggy seat, came across the muddy yard to the door, and hefted the sack, looked at her with a question in his dark eyes.

"My brother can spare the stuff," she said. "I'll just put it on the books."

Yellow Jacket took the sack and carried it to the buggy. "Harvey Leland cheats us regularly," he said, "so I guess it is not charity to take these things."

It surprised her that he was so proud. She picked up her medical bag and lifted her skirts to walk across the muddy yard to the buggy.

"Wait!" he commanded. "There's no use

114

getting your shoes ruined."

Before she could protest, he swung her up in his arms. For a split second they looked into each other's eyes, and she was keenly aware of the heat and the strength of his big body. "Put me down!" she protested. "If the captain should see you . . ."

"Are you going to tell him?" He carried her easily to the buggy, sat her on the seat.

She didn't answer. "I don't like your familiarity." She kept her voice cold, attempting to hide her shakiness, thinking about the heat and the strength of the man.

"All right, white girl." His voice was cold, too, as he climbed up on the seat and snapped the reins. "Next time I'll let you ruin those little shoes in the mud."

They started out of the ragged settlement and up a back road. It was a cold day, and there was no one in sight. She really should let someone know she was in the Indian camp. If no one knew . . . She looked about frantically.

"What's wrong?" he growled.

"Nothing," she lied. "I just thought someone should know where I am."

He laughed bitterly. "You're safe enough. I'll see the savages don't scalp you and burn you at the stake."

She felt the hot blood rush to her face and fell silent, too embarrassed to protest again. *You're being a little fool,* she told herself. *These*

Indians are hungry, pitiful, and hemmed in by a large Confederate force. They aren't going to do anything to harm you. Then she remembered Yellow Jacket's hand on her shoulder and how it had trembled almost as if he were fighting to keep from pulling her into his embrace . . . or had she only imagined that because, at that moment, she had wondered how it would feel to be in his arms?

They drove silently and in a few minutes were at the Creek camp.

This time Yellow Jacket reached up to help her out of the buggy, and Twilight said, "I can get down by myself, thank you."

Then she promptly caught her foot in one of her skirt hoops and almost fell. The big Indian caught her arm and assisted her to her feet without speaking. Twilight felt like a fool, but said nothing as she gathered up her doctor bag and was led to the ancient one's tent, where a bunch of stoney-faced warriors stood guard.

"I have come to help," she said. The other warriors looked at her with silent hostility, but Yellow Jacket motioned them away. "She will do well," he insisted.

Twilight relaxed at his good words and almost — but not quite — smiled at him. Then she turned to her patient. The old man seemed weary and listless. She had a bottle of bitters. She didn't know if it would help, but she hadn't much to offer. "Eat better

116

food and stay out of the cold," she told him. He nodded, but she was not sure he was listening.

When she left the tent, accompanied by Yellow Jacket, he caught her arm. "It is well for you to say, 'Eat better food.' You know how shoddy the rations are that your brother gets for us?"

"I — I'm sure Harvey is doing the best he can under the circumstances."

"For himself, maybe," the man grunted. "And it's impossible to stay out of the cold in our flimsy tents and makeshift shelters."

She turned on him. "Don't you people have permanent homes somewhere here in the Territory?"

He laughed without mirth. "Certainly, but they have been overrun by rebel troops. Their officers stay in our warm log cabins and eat our beef."

She suspected that he spoke the truth. "What do you want from me?" she asked in frustration.

Yellow Jacket towered over her. "He is our leader, and if he dies, the people will scatter, uncertain what to do. He must live to get us through . . ."

She waited, but he stumbled to a halt, obviously having said more than he intended.

"Get your people through what?"

"Never mind," he snapped. "Here, I will return you to the white camp."

She didn't argue with him this time as his big hands encased her small waist and he lifted her to the buggy seat. The other Indians were still glaring at her in silent hostility as the pair drove away. She was glad then that she had Yellow Jacket on the seat beside her. She had a feeling that no Indian would challenge her or threaten her with a leading warrior like Yellow Jacket accompanying her.

Back at the fort, Yellow Jacket helped her from the buggy. "Thank you for coming," he said, and his tone was almost warm.

"I'm sorry I can't do more," she answered, looking up at him.

"I will put your buggy away and feed the horse," Yellow Jacket said. He hesitated, then ventured, "You are nicer than most Southerners — very different from your brother."

"You don't understand Harvey," she blurted, not quite certain what to say.

"Mrs. Dumont, you are terribly naive," the Indian snorted. Then he climbed up on the seat and drove the buggy over to the small barn. She stood there in the cold, watching as he put it away, mounted his own great stallion and rode out of the settlement.

Twilight had barely gotten inside when the bell rang, announcing an arrival. She turned to see the captain, red-faced and blinking rapidly. He took off his hat. "Mrs. Dumont, did I just see you return unescorted with that — that savage?"

She winced at the term. Somehow, Yellow Jacket no longer seemed like the war-painted, scalp-lifting demon she had seen in books. "It couldn't be helped. Old Opothleyahola was ailing, and as you well know, my step-brother is out of town."

"You could have called on me for assistance." The muscles worked in the man's pale jaw.

She wanted to say that her goings and comings were none of the captain's business, but she hesitated. "I'm sorry if you were concerned. Next time I'll be more cautious."

That seemed to mollify him. "I apologize if I sounded harsh, Mrs. Dumont; it's just that, well . . ." He hesitated and played with his hat like a small boy. "I've begun to take a more-than-casual interest in you since you've arrived."

She hesitated, uncertain what to say. She tried to picture herself as Mrs. Franklin Wellsley. She would be wealthy, comfortable, and answering to his very bossy mother. On the other hand, she was obligated to Harvey for taking her in and he had implored her to be polite to the young man for Harvey's benefit. "That's very kind of you. Now, if you'll excuse me, Captain, I've got a lot to do."

"Oh." He turned back toward the door but paused as if loath to leave. "Perhaps some time in the next several days before your stepbrother returns, we might get together for a cup of tea. Mother will be leaving soon."

Twilight thought about spending another afternoon with the sour old harridan and winced. But she said, "That might be nice, Captain. I'll see if I can manage it."

The captain blinked again. "Oh, I'm sorry. I just remembered that we are leaving on patrol tomorrow afternoon."

"Perhaps we can have tea when you return." Twilight heaved a sigh of relief.

"We'll be gone for several days. Do you think you will be all right?"

"I think I can manage until you or Harvey return."

He smiled. "Mother liked you. You're the first woman that my mother has thought might be suitable."

What was she expected to say? Mother probably liked her because she was so mild and meek. "That was kind of her. She — she is a lovely lady."

"She was sure that you could fit into our household back in Texas. She's a Forrester, you know, one of the best and most prominent families in Texas. Of course, being from the South, you understand how important that is."

"How nice," Twilight said noncommittally. She had found the social structure of Southern aristocracy a heavy load to carry when she had been an elite belle from Alabama. "Now, if you don't mind, Captain . . ."

"Oh, I'm so sorry, I'm letting in the cold. Well, tah tah." He put his hat back on and stepped out the door, nodding to her as he went.

What kind of man said 'tah tah'? His mother probably said it. Twilight suspected that Captain Wellsley didn't make a move without consulting his mother, and that his mother had liked Twilight because maybe she saw her as a perfect daughter-in-law — a spineless ninny who could be ordered about without complaining. She wished she could be different, one of those spunky, strong women who made their own way in life, but she had been brought up to believe that real Southern ladies were pliant and mild. That was the kind a Southern gentleman preferred.

It was almost dusk. With a sigh of relief, Twilight stepped to the door and locked it behind the departed captain, hung the Closed sign on the window, then began to prepare herself a bite of supper.

Mrs. Franklin Wellsley. She would be respected and comfortable. She would also have a weakling husband and a dragon of a mother-in-law. Her thoughts went to the more intimate part of marriage as she poked up the fire and put a kettle of water on to make coffee. Pierre had been unfeeling and

mechanical in bed. She remembered her dis-
appointment on her wedding night, wondering if there couldn't be more to it. She
thought about sharing a bed with the captain
and winced. It probably wouldn't be any
better than it had been with Pierre. She
didn't mean to, but now her thoughts went
to Yellow Jacket and the way his powerful
arms had lifted her easily to the buggy. He
was all raw, virile power and rippling
muscle — a true stallion of a man. But of
course, he was a savage, and there was no
telling what he would expect from a woman.
Her face burned at the unbidden thoughts.

That night she dreamed he came to her,
took her in his arms, and made passionate
love to her. His hot mouth sought her breasts
as she spread herself for him, and he drove
deep into her most secret place while she
gasped and pulled him deeper still.

Twilight woke suddenly and sat up in bed,
gasping and covered with a sheen of perspiration, even though the room had cooled. She
was horrified at her dream. Never had she
had such thoughts before. But then, neither
had she ever met a man like Yellow Jacket
before. He was both dangerous and forbid-
ding. Like playing with fire, she thought —
and mild, obedient Southern ladies never did
that . . . or did they?

Chapter 6

It was now the middle of Ehole, the frost month that the whites called November. Winter would be fierce this year, Yellow Jacket thought as he joined the council sitting around the fire in the drafty tent. The white rebels seemed to be slowly encircling them, and they dare not meet openly for fear of a rebel patrol arriving unexpectedly.

Yellow Jacket stared into the flames, and his mind went to the white girl with the smoky-colored eyes and the sun-streaked hair. She had a soft, wet mouth. He imagined himself taking her in his arms, holding her close against him while his mouth covered hers, his tongue going deep to explore and excite, his fingers stroking up and down her back as he put his big hand in her bodice . . .

". . . so what do you think, Yellow Jacket?" Opothleyahola asked.

"What?" He came back to reality with a start, ashamed that he had let his mind drift.

The old man frowned at him and broke into a spasm of coughing. "I have almost given up hope that Big Chief Lincoln is

123

going to send us help as he promised. Did the officer in Kansas say he would send him the message over the singing wires?"

Yellow Jacket nodded, then shrugged. "I am past expecting anything from whites, no matter which side."

Smoke, the Seminole leader Alligator, and some of the others sitting in the circle nodded agreement.

"In that case," the withered old leader sighed, "we are going to have to help ourselves. Hundreds of people are gathering, and we don't have the food for them and grass for all their animals. Besides, storms will come soon, and the rebels are tired of my stalling. The Confederate major grows impatient for an answer. They may decide to attack."

"Our people have few weapons and supplies." Yellow Jacket accepted the pipe that was making the rounds, and took a puff of the fragrant tobacco. "If we sit like ducks on a pond and wait for their attack, we will be slaughtered."

"Exactly," the old man nodded, "so I have met with all the tribal leaders. Shall we do the unexpected? Shall we pull out tonight?"

"Tonight?" Smoke exclaimed. "We cannot get six or seven thousand people ready to pull out tonight."

Yellow Jacket considered. "Will they be any more ready tomorrow or the next day?"

"I agree with Yellow Jacket," Billy Bowlegs grunted. "It will be like moving the people of Moses in the white man's Good Book. There is no good way to organize that which is too sprawling to be organized."

Opothleyahola nodded and burst into a spasm of coughing. "We have been waiting many days now, and no messenger has come — nor soldiers — from Chief Lincoln. Perhaps we need to go meet the Union troops that are coming to help us."

Yellow Jacket chewed his lip in thought. "The rebels will try to stop us."

"Not until they realize we are gone," another pointed out. "If we are in luck, it may be days before they know."

"I hate to trust to luck," Yellow Jacket grumbled. "We will lose many if we try to walk the people to this place called Kansas. It is winter."

The ancient one snorted. "It was winter on the Trail of Tears, when the whites forced us to walk hundreds of miles to get here. Many died, but we are a tough people; some will survive."

A murmur of agreement around the fire, and outside, the wind howled as if seconding the thought.

"You are right," Yellow Jacket said finally. "As the whites would say, we are caught between the devil and the deep blue sea."

An elderly chief looked at him, puzzled.

"What does that mean?"

"It means," Yellow Jacket said bitterly, "that if we stay, people will die, and if we go, people will die."

Smoke said, "For us black Indians, we face an even worse fate. If we are captured by the rebels, they will send us into slavery. We would rather die fighting for our freedom than sit here like sheep awaiting our fate."

The old man took a deep breath. "If we leave tonight, perhaps the Master of Breath will look after us and deliver us safely to this promised land called Kansas."

Yellow Jacket looked at the old man with a sinking heart. The white girl had been right. Their leader was old and sick. He might die at any time, and then the people would be leaderless and afraid.

Alligator, the noted Seminole chief, protested. "Maybe we should just wait for the Union troops to come to our aid."

Opothleyahola looked toward Yellow Jacket, and everyone followed his gaze. Everyone knew how much the old man respected Yellow Jacket's judgment. "What say you?"

Yellow Jacket considered. "The weather is turning colder with each passing day, and soon there will be almost no grass to feed our horses and cattle. It is more than three hundred miles, as the white man counts it, to the safety of the Union troops in Kansas."

"Yes," Smoke spoke out, "and it might as

well be three thousand."

Another commented, "More are coming every day from all the loyal tribes. There are people from some twenty tribes gathering, and they expect we will tell them what to do."

"And the rebels surrounding us are getting stronger every day," the ancient one said, and began to cough again. "If we are going to have the element of surprise on our side, we need to leave before the rebels expect it. Yellow Jacket, you have been away to the white man's school and know their thinking. What must we do?"

The others looked toward Yellow Jacket, and he sighed with despair. The white girl had been right. The old man was ill, perhaps ill enough to die. Yet he was the only one who was respected by all as the leader. Surely the old man was too weak to sit a horse. If only they owned a good buggy. The only one he was aware of belonged to Harvey Leland, and he did not think the white girl would give it to them, especially when she found out that the Indians intended to flee the country. Perhaps he could steal it. No, he shook his head. His people were not thieves, no matter what the whites thought of them. Anyway, someone would surely see him driving away and raise an alarm. Within an hour, before the loyal tribes could break camp, that prissy little captain and a patrol would be out at the encampment, nosing around.

There was no other answer, and Yellow Jacket knew it, yet still he searched his heart because of the terrible cost in suffering to his people. "What do the medicine men say about the weather?"

Opothleyahola answered, "They think the storm is coming soon, maybe tomorrow night, with snow and winds that will keep the soft soldiers in their tents, close to their fires."

Yellow Jacket chewed his lip. "Then late to-morrow night we make our attempt."

"Agreed," the frail old leader muttered. "The Master of Breath will be coming for me soon, but I hope to die in a free place where even our black warriors will be safe."

Smoke said, "I vow I will kill my own little girls rather than let them be captured and sent to some vile cotton plantation in Louisiana or Tennessee."

The ancient one stood up and made a dismissing gesture. "Then it's settled. Tomorrow night, if the storm comes in, we will slip away under cover of darkness. All you leaders pass the word to your people to be ready."

The others stood, nodded, and filed out into the night. Yellow Jacket and Smoke paused outside and watched the other men scattering silently.

Smoke said, "It is impossible. We can't

lead six thousand people through rebel lines and walk all the way to Kansas."

Yellow Jacket looked up at the sky. "If we stay here, once the rebels realized we are not going to join up with them, they will attack us and many will die. Is it better to die here, shot down like dogs, or make a try for freedom?"

Smoke gave a short, harsh laugh. "Don't talk to me about freedom. I have scars on my back from cruel masters before I escaped and took one of your women as my own. In a way, old friend, you are lucky. You have no woman or child to worry about on this trip."

"True. But all the women and children in this camp are my responsibility," Yellow Jacket said, thinking of the white girl. He had never felt as lonely as he did at this moment.

"I think she has a better heart than most," Smoke said, "Even though she is from the South that steals our land and would put me and my children back in slavery."

Yellow Jacket scowled. He did not want to think kind thoughts about the girl with smoky lavender eyes. He did not want to think about her at all. All his strength and concentration would be needed the next few weeks as the people made their terrible march toward the northern border. "Let us part, then, and begin gathering our things and telling the people. Late tomorrow night, if the Master of Breath is willing, we will begin our trip."

The next day was cold and gloomy, and there was little business in the store. With the captain and his patrol away on a scouting trip and Harvey still gone, there were few people to talk to, and Twilight was lonely as she cleaned and reorganized things. In one storeroom, she found boxes and crates of food and supplies marked, *U.S. Government. For distribution among the Indian tribes.*

Now, just why were they piled up here in a storeroom when the Indians she'd seen were evidently in such need? Surely Harvey wouldn't stoop to . . . ? Could he intend to sell the goods to whites and pocket the money? Surely he couldn't be that thoughtless and greedy. There had to be a reasonable explanation. She ought to question him when he returned.

The longer she thought about it, the angrier she became. Yes, she decided, she would confront her stepbrother when he returned, and insist the Indian trade goods be parceled out among the needy tribes. That made her think about the ill old leader, Opothleyahola. There was dried soup here, and bacon and sacks of cornmeal. There was also a bundle of good wool blankets, some coffee, sugar, and tea. The old man needed warmth and nourishment. Certainly she couldn't carry enough in her buggy to care for the whole tribe, but she could take out a buggy load and maybe get Yellow Jacket to accompany her back to the store with some wagons for the rest of it.

Harvey would be furious with her. Twilight smiled at the notion. Once she would have quailed at the thought; now she almost welcomed confronting Harvey with her righteous indignation. Twilight realized she was changing. Well, war, a bad marriage, and widowhood would do that to a person. On second thought, the idea of defying her stepbrother made her tremble. As much as she disliked him, at least she had a safe, secure place to live and enough to eat. She imagined being out on her own, facing hunger and cold, and quailed at the thought.

Still, she could do a little that was independent. Putting on a heavy coat and a wool scarf, she put the Closed sign in the window, locked up the store, and went out to harness the bay horse. Then she drove the buggy up to the back door and struggled to load the supplies. She didn't want anyone to question what she was doing, because if confronted, she might not have enough nerve to go through with it. Not that there was anything to worry about — the settlement seemed deserted, with everyone staying by their fires.

Twilight got her medical bag and carried numerous bundles of blankets and boxes of

131

food and medicine out and loaded them in the buggy. When she had put on as much as the rig would hold, she looked around. It was almost dusk. It might be dark before she could return from the Indian camp. Driving alone in a wild place, unescorted, was just not something a Southern lady would chance. Well, if there was any danger, she could ask Yellow Jacket to escort her back. Even though he was a savage, she knew he was a renowned warrior and no one dare cross him, white or Indian. Harvey and Captain Wellsley would be upset or furious, but if she was lucky, neither need ever know about what she had done until Harvey missed the supplies. There would be a fuss then, of course, but what could he do besides shout at her? She almost smiled at the thought. She who had been so timid was becoming braver out of a need for justice.

It was farther to the camp than she remembered. Several times her timidity almost overcame her good resolve, and she was tempted to turn the buggy around and go back to the safety of the settlement. Then she imagined the big eyes of some of those hungry Indian children, gritted her teeth, and kept driving.

It was dusk when she arrived at the outer edge of the camp. Everyone was bustling about; no one paying any attention to her. Something was wrong. With growing apprehension, she tied her buggy to a tree and threaded her way through the woods. Behind the trunk of a big oak, she paused and looked toward the camp circle. Sitting in the middle around the fire were Opothleyahola, Yellow Jacket, the mixed black she knew as Smoke, and a bunch of other important-looking warriors. They were talking and passing a pipe around. She had a distinct feeling that this was important tribal business, because there were no women present. Her instincts warned her that she shouldn't be here, but her curiosity was piqued, and she couldn't bring herself to leave as she eavesdropped.

Mostly they were speaking in their own tongue, but now and then she caught a few words of English.

Yellow Jacket paused in speaking. He had keen eyes, and a slight movement out among the shadows caught his attention. "Say no more," he muttered. "I think we have a spy. Make small talk while I look into this."

The warriors looked up, and Alligator opened his mouth as if to ask something, but Yellow Jacket shook his head in warning. "I will go see about my horse," he announced loudly and got up, stretched, and swept the circle with a warning look. As the others made sudden small talk, he ambled casually away from the circle in the opposite direction from where he'd seen the movement. Once lost in the shadows, he circled around, running light and fleet-footed as a deer to come up behind the one who was eavesdropping on the council.

Now he could see the small figure. By the Master of Breath, it was the white woman, lurking behind a tree. His anger made him grit his teeth as he sneaked through the growing darkness. No doubt her villainous brother or the captain had sent her out to spy on them, thinking the Muskogee were too stupid to suspect a woman. How much had she heard? There was no way to know. That made her dangerous to the success of the mission.

Yellow Jacket hesitated. What to do? They could not allow her to return to the whites with any information that the Indians were planning to move out late tonight, heading north. Success depended on the Indians' traveling as far as possible toward Kansas before the rebel soldiers could organize and attack them. He sighed, knowing what he must do. He had never in his life hurt a woman, but there was no help for it: Yellow Jacket would have to silence her; the council would demand it. That meant he had to kill her. He looked down at his two powerful hands. He could easily break her neck with one quick motion. Her slender throat would be soft and creamy white between his dark brown palms.

He must kill her to save thousands of Indian lives.

Twilight craned her neck, listening to the Indians around the fire. They were mostly speaking in their language, although now and then Smoke said something in English. None of what they were saying seemed intense and important as it had before. More important, where had Yellow Jacket gone? Darkness had settled in around her while she hid behind the tree. What should she do? Perhaps she would leave the goods piled up out here, and the tribe would find them in the morning. She didn't relish driving back to the settlement in the darkness, but she wouldn't have a choice.

A faint sound behind her — so faint, she was not even sure that it might not be her own heart beating. Even so, she half turned. At that moment, she heard footsteps as fast and quiet as a running deer. Before she could react, a big body crashed into her, and they both went down, rolling and struggling in the dirt. Twilight had never known such terror. She opened her mouth to scream, and a hand clapped over her lips. Her fear gave her strength she did not know she had, and she came up fighting, clawing and biting. Her unknown assailant held her down easily, lying on top of her as they struggled. As she fell, her long black skirt had billowed up, and he was lying against her thin pantaloons. She could feel the heat and power and strength of the man. The hard planes of his body pressed hard into her soft curves as they struggled. Now he had one hand on her throat. He was going to kill her — she knew it — and in a flash, she envisioned her long hair hanging from a war lance tomorrow. Why hadn't she listened to Harvey and stayed in the settlement, where she was safe and warm?

She managed to jerk her face free for an instant, and in that brief moment she gasped, "Please . . ."

"Damn you," he growled, "I can't do this!" At this point he scrambled to stand, reached down, and jerked her to her feet.

"Yellow Jacket?" She felt a mixture of surprise and relief.

"Shut up!" he ordered. "What are you doing spying on us?"

"I wasn't spying; I came out to bring the children —"

"I saw you!" he shouted. "You were listening in on the council meeting. How much did you hear?"

She tried to pull out of his grasp. "Not much. Something about leaving, but —"

"Liar. All whites are liars!" He seemed furious as he picked her up, tossed her over his shoulder, and strode toward the council fire.

"Put me down!" She screamed and kicked,

afraid of what the Indians might do to her. "The captain will come out here and —"

He slapped her across the rear as he carried her into the big clearing, then dumped her unceremoniously in a heap by the fire.

Twilight looked around the circle at the closed, hostile faces, then back up to Yellow Jacket. She was terrified, somehow knowing they planned to kill her. "When — when my brother hears how you've manhandled me, he and Captain Wellsley will bring the soldiers out here and you'll be sorry —"

"Silence!" Yellow Jacket towered over her, putting one moccasin on her body and pushing her against the ground. She looked around again at the hostile faces and fell silent, seeing her fate in the savages' eyes.

Yellow Jacket paused and began to speak to the other men in rapid Muskogee. "This is the spy who was watching our meeting." He looked down at the girl lying so submissively by the fire. Her hair had come loose and tumbled in a brown and golden mass over her shoulders, the firelight picking up the shine. Her black dress had slid off one shoulder, and the swell of her pale breasts was visible. Her smoky lavender eyes were big with fear, and she kept licking her lips. He had never seen such a desirable female. He felt his groin swell as he looked at her, wanting to reach down, carry her off to his tent, rip away her dress and take her in a quick, savage mating that would cool the blood that now roared through his ears. After that happened, could he bring himself to kill her?

The ancient one looked the woman over and sighed. "How much did she hear?" He spoke in their language.

Yellow Jacket shook his head and tried not to look at the frightened girl. "There is no way to know."

"You should have killed her to keep our secret," Billy Bowlegs, the Seminole leader, said.

Yellow Jacket glared down at the girl. "Yes, I should have. I — I don't know why I hesitated."

He was aware that all the men were looking at him, and he was angry at his own softness. He had killed more than a dozen men, yet this time something inside him had weakened and he had not snapped her neck, even though everything in him told him the woman could not be trusted.

"We can't turn her loose," Smoke said. "She will tell our secret. . . . But she has been kind to my children."

The others nodded. "She has been kind," several grunted. "Still, we cannot let her alert the whites and the soldiers in the settlement."

Opothleyahola sighed. In Muskogee he said, "Yellow Jacket, she is your captive. It is your responsibility to silence her forever."

He had known it would be his responsibility. Why had he not broken her neck out there in the woods? Because when she got her mouth free, she had whispered, "Please," in a desperate appeal as a helpless woman to a dominant male.

One of the others scowled. "Yellow Jacket, if you are too weak of heart to kill her, I would enjoy doing so."

The others fell silent at this challenge.

The speaker was a coward who had killed other whites, Yellow Jacket knew. Yet if they did not kill this spy, what were they to do with her? He stepped so that he stood with one foot on each side of her as she lay huddled against the ground, and at that moment he knew he would kill any man who hurt her. "She is my captive," he announced loudly in Muskogee, "And I think perhaps she would make a good hostage. The army may not attack us as long as she is with us, fearing to injure her."

There were grunts of agreement and heads nodding around the circle. "A hostage. Yes, that might be a good idea."

The cowardly one frowned. "I say we kill her and be done with it. If we bury her quickly, the whites will never know what happened to her."

The others nodded. "That might also be an answer."

"Do not listen to him," Yellow Jacket snapped. "The whites will find her buggy tracks and come looking for her. If they do not find her, they will attack us. However, if we hold her hostage, they will not attack us as we move north."

He held his breath as the chiefs fell silent, thinking. If they ordered him to kill her, he did not think he could do it. He had a sudden image of grabbing her up and running for his horse to save her life.

Opothleyahola thought a long moment, then spoke. "Yellow Jacket gives wise counsel. I say that her presence among us as a hostage will protect us. Now let us scatter and get our people ready to move out. We will start north at the deepest part of the night. Yellow Jacket, take charge of the prisoner. She is going with us to Kansas, whether she likes it or not!"

Chapter 7

Twilight was too frightened even to struggle as the big savage tied her and lifted her. For a moment he held her, looking down into her face. She could feel the heat and the muscle of the virile male through his buckskins as he glowered down into her face.

"Damn you," he muttered, "why do you have to complicate my life when I have no time for thoughts of you?"

With that, he sat her up on the seat of the buggy and stalked away. Gagged as she was, she couldn't scream for help, and anyway, there was no one around who would help her. Why hadn't she been a dutiful Southern woman and stayed at the settlement, where she belonged?

Around her in the firelight, she could see Indians bustling about, saddling horses, hitching up wagons, bringing down tents. Three warriors unloaded the supplies from her buggy, sharing them around, where the food and blankets were greeted with glad cries. Many had to walk away empty-handed because the things she'd brought were so few and the hungry so many. Around her in the darkness, she heard sounds of confusion, shouted orders, whinnying horses as the Creeks prepared to move out. What was she to do?

She must do something, not sit here like a trussed chicken waiting to be slaughtered. A genteel lady would weep, but she was determined not to do that. Twilight struggled against her bonds, but Yellow Jacket had tied her up expertly as well as stuffing a rag in her mouth. She could only hope the savages didn't kill her before Harvey or Captain Wellsley discovered she was missing and came searching for her. But they were not due back at the settlement for days, and no one would question the fact that the store was closed. By the time anyone discovered she was missing, she might be tortured and ravished or even killed. After all, she was surely going to be a burden to these Indians as they fled north. Somehow, Yellow Jacket didn't seem like that kind of man, but who knew what savages thought?

In less than an hour Yellow Jacket returned, tied his great brown and white stallion behind her buggy, and climbed up on the seat beside her. She felt the heat of his muscular thigh against hers and scooted away from him. He glared at her and frowned. "You flatter yourself, Mrs. Dumont. I don't have time for that right now."

But maybe later you will, she thought with a shudder.

He seemed to notice her trembling. "Cold, are you? Well, it wouldn't do to have our hostage freeze to death before we need you." He reached for a buffalo robe and draped it around her shoulders. For a moment in the moonlight, he looked down into her eyes as his hands gripped the robe about her neck. For just a second he leaned forward ever so slightly, and she thought he might kiss her. She was horrified to realize the thought excited her. Instead, he slid over to his side of the buggy and picked up the reins.

Grateful for the warmth, nevertheless she grunted a protest as he yelled to the horse and the buggy moved out, following hundreds of other Indians as they made a straggly line toward the north.

Yellow Jacket turned on the seat and gave her a warning glare. "You'd better behave yourself, white girl, or you may not last long enough to be ransomed. Some of the others want to kill you and be done with it."

Twilight blinked back tears and fell silent as the buggy bumped along. She was too terrified even to pray. No doubt the Indians intended to kill her anyway as soon as they got a distance away from the camp. Before they killed her, some of these braves would probably . . .

No, she didn't even want to think about that. Twilight tried to keep her balance as the wagon rolled along, but time and time again, when they hit a rut in the dirt trail, she was thrown against Yellow Jacket. He seemed not to notice, his rugged countenance frowning as he watched the ragtag group moving ahead of him. "We'll never get all these people to Kansas with this cold weather," he muttered, "even if the rebels don't come after us — which they will, once they figure out we've got you." He turned his head ever so slightly and glared at her.

This journey was a fool's errand, Twilight thought in silent agreement. Why didn't these tribes accept their fate? Resisting the winds of chance was futile. Even she could see how poorly armed and provisioned these people were. Burdened down with thousands of the old and feeble, not to mention women, children, and livestock, they didn't stand a chance against the hundreds of well-armed, well-fed Confederate troops that would soon be in pursuit.

The cold night seemed endless, tied as she was. The gag kept her mouth dry, and her arms seemed to have no feeling left. Somewhere along the line, livestock mooed and baa-ed; a baby cried, and several dogs barked, but the column did not stop until almost dawn. Then Yellow Jacket climbed down off the buggy and went to confer with a handful of important warriors who had gathered nearby. Twilight tried to pick up their words, but mostly they spoke their native language. In a few minutes, Yellow Jacket returned. "We're going to stop long enough to eat and rest the horses; then we'll move on."

She didn't think she could stand another minute of sitting on this seat with her hands tied. In the cold moonlight, she tried to talk and pleaded with him with her eyes. He reached up and removed the gag.

"Thank you," she gasped.

He shrugged, his face motionless as stone. "I'm not attempting to do you a favor, white girl. There's no one to rescue you around here, so you might as well lose the gag."

"I — I need to . . ." She felt herself color.

"Oh, all right." He tossed aside the buffalo robe, pulled her to him, lifted her to the ground. Then he reached behind her and began to untie her hands. It was almost as if she were in his embrace, the heat of his wide chest against her breasts, his powerful arms around her. "You can go over there in the bushes where some of the other women have gone. Don't try to run away. You can't escape with no horse."

"I know that."

He stepped back, surprise on his rugged face. "Well, the genteel lady is getting a little spunk."

"It's desperation." She pulled her hands in front of her after he untied her, began to rub her wrists to bring feeling back into them.

"Is there any water?"

He nodded and handed her his canteen. "Be careful with it — we may not find another stream for a while."

In her newly found defiance, she turned the canteen up and began to gulp the cold water. It tasted better than any water she had ever tasted.

"You white bitch!" he swore, and grabbed it out of her hand. "I told you we were short on water."

"You've got to keep your hostage alive," she reminded him, and wiped her mouth. She was too tired to be afraid at the moment. Her legs were so stiff, she wasn't sure she could walk. The frost crunched under her small shoes.

"Don't go far," he warned. "You can't get away."

"I know that." She turned and headed for the woods, going deep into the shadows to relieve herself. When she looked around, the other women had already turned and were returning to the column. Twilight took a deep breath and moved so that she could see Yellow Jacket. He stood talking to that big mixed black, Smoke.

Could she get away? Maybe if she could hide deep enough among the walnuts and oaks, Yellow Jacket wouldn't spend much time looking for her. After all, the tribes were on an urgent timetable, and daylight would be here soon. Once the Indians had passed, all she had to do was follow the tracks back to the settlement. Twilight shivered again. It was cold and the wind was blowing harder, but she had to risk it. She ran deeper into the woods. Behind her she heard that deep, angry voice: "White girl, where are you? Damn it, answer me!"

She didn't answer. The fury in his voice caused her to run even faster. Behind her, his voice grew fainter, but she could hear the whips cracking and the shouts as the column started up again. Probably she wasn't important enough now for the Indians to waste time trying to find her. After all, the secret that they had fled would be out soon, and the Confederate army would come in pursuit.

Faintly in the distance, she heard Yellow Jacket shouting and cursing. Twilight found herself a hollow behind a big bush and knelt down, hugging herself to preserve warmth. Too bad she hadn't grabbed that buffalo robe, but if she had, Yellow Jacket would have suspected she wasn't coming back. The wind picked up and brought the sound of the column moving again. Good, he had given up more easily than she had expected. Maybe a hostage was more trouble than she was worth. Even if she froze to death out here, it was better than being raped and tortured by savages.

She did not know how long she crouched

there. It seemed like hours after the sounds of the column had moved on before she dared venture out. She cut through the shadowy woods, still in sight of the muddy trail with its hoof and moccasin prints. She would walk in the shadows until daylight, keeping the trail in sight, then hide until dark and follow the trail in the moonlight back to the white settlement. If she could walk fast, she might reach safety before dark. Somewhere a coyote howled, and Twilight started. If she didn't reach help by nightfall, she might either freeze to death or get attacked by coyotes or hungry wolves. Being Yellow Jacket's captive suddenly seemed not so bad.

What was she thinking? The old Twilight would have returned to the buggy, not struck out on her own, risking everything for freedom. Funny, that's just what the Indians were doing. No, of course it was not the same. The Confederates wouldn't mistreat their captives. Then she remembered how thin and ragged these people were, and a small shadow of doubt crossed her mind as she walked.

Twilight was cold, colder than she had ever been in her life. Daylight came, and the weather warmed a little — a weak sun peaking through the scudding clouds. It looked as though a blizzard might be on the way. She ought to hide, she knew, but she had a feeling that if she stopped for any period of time, she might freeze to death. Her thin clothes were not much comfort against the wind.

She kept walking, realizing that if she were to perish out here in the wilderness, her stepbrother and Captain Wellsley would never know what had happened to her.

Her feet felt like bricks as she walked, her dainty shoes no match for the rough terrain. Once she fell, got up, and stumbled on. At least the walking kept her warm. However, she couldn't walk forever, and when she sat down to rest, would she freeze to death? She wished she had some food or at least some water. Damn that brave for taking her prisoner, and now the Creeks had her buggy. Harvey would be upset about the stolen buggy. The thought of her stepbrother ranting and raving made her smile, where not too long ago she would have trembled at his rage.

The weak sun moved across the horizon as she went to the rutted trail and kept walking, following the tracks home. Once again she tripped and fell, this time landing in a half-frozen mud puddle. She scrambled to her feet, but the damage was done. She could already feel the cold seeping through her wet black skirt. Twilight sat down on a stone to catch her breath and began to shiver again. If she didn't keep moving, she knew she wouldn't make it. The pursuing soldiers would find her tomorrow, lying in the middle of the Indians' escape route, dead and frozen.

The old Twilight would have done just that: given up with a whimper. That thought angered her as much as it scared her. She didn't intend to die until she got revenge on that damned savage for abducting her. Her anger gave her new strength, and she got up, scraped some frost off a tree, and licked it. It numbed her mouth, but it was delicious. She wished she could find more, but she didn't see any. Then she began walking again. The slant of the weak sun told her it was late afternoon, but she had no idea how far she'd come. All she knew to do was keep moving forward, putting one numb foot in front of the other.

It was dusk when she realized that she could walk no farther. Twilight paused, gasping for breath. Maybe she could find shelter from the wind in the nearby grove of trees and rest a few minutes. She turned off the trail, looking desperately for water. She found a small patch of unmelted snow and began to eat handfuls of it, knowing it would only lower her body temperature, but she was too thirsty to stop. As she began to move deeper into the woods, she stumbled again and fell in a little patch of snow, white against the blackness of the earth. For a long moment she lay there, too weary to move, feeling the wet cold seeping through her dress.

You must get up or you will die here. She wasn't sure she cared. It was so much effort to move anymore. She only wanted to close her eyes and drift off to sleep. No, she must not do that. She stumbled to her feet, brushing the wet snow from the front of her dress. Deep in the straggly trees, she found a small hollow out of the wind, but she was shivering violently now, and she had no matches.

Did she hear a horse coming? Maybe she only imagined it. No, it sounded louder now. Hope leaped at the thought the army was coming to rescue her, then died in her throat as she peered out and saw Yellow Jacket on his pinto stallion, coming along the trail. She shrank against the ground as he stopped, dismounted to study the tracks, then turned toward the woods. "Twilight?" he shouted. "White girl, damn it, where are you?"

She almost cried out with relief, then decided she wasn't any better off as a hostage. She might still find her way to a settlers' log cabin. Jumping up, she began to run. Behind her she heard Yellow Jacket's shout of protest. "You! Come back here!"

She didn't answer but kept running, fell, scrambled to her feet, and ran on. Behind her she heard curses of protest and then the sound of running moccasins. She had to

151

outrun him; she had to. The footsteps behind her sounded as swift and light as a deer. "Damn you, white girl, stop!"

She stumbled and kept running. It sounded as if he was gaining on her. She didn't stop or look back, even though she could hear his panting breath now. A big hand reached out and grabbed her shoulder, tearing her dress.

"I told you to stop!" He whirled her around, but she fought him. Better to freeze to death trying to get back to the settlement than be a Creek slave.

He grabbed her and they both went down; he came up on top. "Stop it, Twilight, you're half frozen!"

"Thanks to you!" she shrieked.

He caught her wrist and jerked her to her feet. "You're lucky I found you. You wouldn't make it through the night."

"Better than be your captive!" She fought to keep the scalding tears back, but they came anyway.

"Stop it, woman," he ordered, and turned to whistle to his horse. The big pinto came trotting toward them. "I've got matches and blankets. We'll make it through the night, then join the others in the morning."

Morning. That meant she had to spend the night alone with this big savage. He led her into the shelter of some brush, where he sat her on a rock and wrapped a blanket from his saddle around her. She wiped her eyes and watched him build a small fire.

"Can't get it too big," he cautioned. "The rebels might see it."

She huddled close to the small flame, shivering. "Have you got any food?"

He frowned at her. "As much trouble as you've caused me, I shouldn't give you anything."

She wasn't going to sacrifice her dignity by begging. "All right."

"Here." He tossed her a canteen and a small packet wrapped in oiled paper. "Here's some jerky."

She gulped the water, then unfolded the package and took a bite. It was salty and smoky-tasting. "This is good."

He strode over to a small patch of snow, filled his coffeepot, put it on the fire. "I should have abandoned you. The others wanted me to. They said you'd die of exposure before you ever made it back to the settlement."

"I reckon that was about right," she admitted as she watched him work. "Why didn't you?"

"Oh, hell, I don't know," he growled, not looking at her. The smell of boiling coffee drifted to her nostrils. He handed her a cup, and she wrapped her cold hands around it and sipped the strong, hot brew gratefully.

"Well, thank you for coming," she whispered.

He frowned at her. "Let's get one thing straight. You're nothing but a hostage to me, and the minute you become too much of a burden, the others will insist we kill you, so from now on, don't create trouble."

She looked into his dark, hard face. Was he bluffing?

They finished eating their meager food; then he led his horse behind some bushes out of the wind and unsaddled and hobbled it so it could graze on the dried grass.

"Now," he said, confronting her, "we've each got a blanket and I throw the buffalo robe over both of us."

Twilight hesitated. "We're — we're to share a bed?"

"You fear for your virtue?" he sneered. "How like a Southern belle to worry about that with everything else that's happening. Don't worry, Mrs. Dumont, I've got too much else on my mind right now to think about ripping your clothes off and ravishing you as you expect from a bloodthirsty savage."

She looked away, feeling foolish. Maybe he found her so unattractive that he wouldn't have hungered for her under the best of circumstances. She took her blanket, wrapped up in it, and lay down by the fire. He brought the buffalo robe and the other blanket and lay down next to her. She closed her eyes so she wouldn't have to look into his face as he arranged the blankets and

154

pulled the robe up over them both. She felt the heat of the big man filtering through the covers and instinctively moved a little closer. If he dropped off to sleep, maybe she could steal his horse and ride out.

Twilight waited a few minutes until his breathing became heavy and rhythmic. Then very slowly she slipped out from under the blanket and crept across the clearing to the horse. "Where the hell do you think you're going?" His voice thundered behind her, and he sat bolt upright.

"I — I was going to relieve myself," she stammered.

"Then do so." He glowered at her. "I should remind you, Mrs. Dumont, that sometimes a warrior's life depends on hearing the slightest sound. You're wasting your time trying to escape me. I trusted you to behave last time, but I won't make that mistake again. You try to escape again, and I'll truss you up like a hog and you'll spend a miserable night."

She knew he was watching as she slipped out into the shadows and hiked up her skirts. Should she try taking off through the woods? The wind howled, and she shivered as she stood up. He was right; she had no chance of escape. With a sigh, she returned to the fire and crawled under the blanket.

"Go to sleep," he ordered. "We leave at first light."

She was so tired. She pulled the buffalo robe about her, grateful for the warmth. Her only chance was in staying with this warrior who knew how to survive in life-and-death situations.

His breathing told her he was already asleep. She was still cold. Without meaning to, she huddled closer to his big body. After all, he'd never know she was up against him. Finally warm, she, too, dropped off to sleep.

When she woke near dawn, she was asleep on the curve of his muscular arm, his other arm thrown across her protectively. Her first instinct was to jerk away, but she feared to wake him. Instead, she closed her eyes and pretended to be asleep. He pulled her even closer to him which set her heart hammering in fear. Finally, he awakened, pulled away from her, and got up. She lay there with her eyes shut, listening to him making coffee. Then he nudged her with one moccasin. "Hey, white girl, let's move on."

Was there any way to delay him, hoping the rebels might already be on their way?

She sat up and tried to comb her tangled hair with her fingers. "Uh, maybe you could shoot a rabbit or something," she suggested, "so we'd have food."

He scowled at her. "So the sound could bring a rebel patrol down on us? I think not. Here" — he thrust some jerky at her and a tin cup of coffee — "have a few bites while I saddle the horse."

She grabbed the jerky and ate it greedily as the warmth of the coffee warmed her insides. "Aren't you having any?"

"I'm not hungry." He picked up the saddle blanket and bridle and went to saddle the horse.

She looked at the small bit of jerky in her hand. There wasn't enough for two, she realized, and he had given it to her. For a split second, she felt touched at his unselfish generosity, then remembered. Unselfish? If she died, she wouldn't be much use as a hostage. "Are you going to let my brother ransom me?"

"Shut up and come on." His tone was brusque. "I doubt Harvey has much except what he's stolen from the Indians, and he might not be willing to spend it to get you back."

"I think Captain Wellsley would —"

"He probably would," Yellow Jacket snapped. "Isn't that why you came? Your brother's hoping to get his hands on the rich captain's money if you marry him?"

She felt her face burn. "That's hardly any of your business." She was ashamed to admit the same thought had crossed her own mind.

The big Creek kicked dirt over the fire and packed up the camp. Then he swung up easily onto the fine horse. "Here, give me your hand."

She hesitated.

"Would you rather walk?"

At this, she hurried over to the pinto stallion and held up her hand. Yellow Jacket took it and lifted her easily to the saddle before him, then wrapped the buffalo robe around them both. She tried to stay stiff, but the warmth of his big body was so inviting on this cold morning. He put his arm around her, pulling her closer. She could feel the heat and the muscle of him, and his breath was warm against the top of her head. For a moment, she felt the electricity pass between them, and he cursed softly under his breath.

"Damn you for causing me so much turmoil." He nudged the horse, and they started off at a walk.

"I'll not run away again," she began.

He pulled her closer still, and she could feel the hard manhood of him through her clothing. "That's not what I mean, and you know it."

Twilight was too disturbed to answer. The way his strong arm held her against him possessively told her what he had in mind.

Harvey was in a foul mood as he pulled the wagon up in front of the store and got down. Now why was the Closed sign up? Didn't Twilight know he wanted every penny he could wring out of the Indians and soldiers? He took out his keys and unlocked the door, went inside. The place smelled of dust and mixed spices, but it was neat and orderly since Twilight had taken over. "Twilight? I'm back with fresh supplies. Twilight?"

Quickly he strode through the building, calling her name. She wasn't there. He went out the back door to the stable and began to curse. The horse and buggy were missing. "Where in the hell would she go driving in lousy weather like this?"

Out front he heard hoofbeats and he smiled. So she was back. He'd give her a piece of his mind for closing the store. After all, she was beholden to him for taking her in. "Twilight?"

But when he rounded the corner, what greeted him was the captain leading a patrol down the muddy street. The men looked weary, and the horses were blowing. The patrol reined in before the store. "Ah, Captain Wellsley, been on patrol, I see."

The officer nodded and turned to give orders to his weary men. "Patrol dismissed. Head for the stables, men. I'll be there in a minute."

The other men rode away, and the captain dismounted. "Looks like, from your wagon, you just got in, too." He smiled. "I thought I might clean up and maybe come to call on Mrs. Dumont —"

"So you haven't seen her, either?"

Wellsley pushed his hat back on his light hair. "What do you mean, 'either'? Are you telling me Mrs. Dumont is missing?"

"Maybe she's just gone for a drive," Harvey said, trying to think of a reasonable explanation.

"In this weather?" the captain asked. "How long's she been gone?"

Harvey scratched his bald spot. "To tell you the truth, I don't know. Let's ask around the settlement."

The captain chewed his lip. "A lady doesn't go off unescorted. Maybe she's visiting someone around here."

"She doesn't know anyone," Harvey said. He was growing more and more annoyed with his stepsister.

The officer looked really worried. "I'll get people searching." With that, he rode away. He had been so attracted to the fragile, timid beauty, and felt very protective of her. Or maybe it was guilt, he thought with a twinge. He knew a secret that he was certain neither she nor her questionable brother knew: Twilight Dumont's husband had been a coward and a traitor. To spare her feelings, Franklin was sure she'd been told Pierre Dumont had died a hero. In fact, he had been shot for desertion. Captain Franklin Wellsley had been in charge of the firing squad.

Harvey began his own search. In less than an hour, he had talked to people around the settlement and found out no one had seen her in several days. In fact, the major's wife thought she had gone with Harvey to the railyard to pick up supplies. In the meantime, Harvey had discovered supplies missing. He cursed under his breath. "What the hell could she be up to?"

The captain rode up just then. "No one's seen her. You don't suppose the Indians might have taken her?" His youthful face looked horrified at the thought.

Harvey tried to appear more sympathetic and worried than angry. "A lot of supplies are missing, and Twilight is very softhearted. I'll wager she took some of that stuff out to those damned Injun brats she was so worried about."

"A soft heart is a good thing in a lady," the captain suggested, "but she's too naive to realize how dangerous that can be."

The captain was obviously very worried. Harvey smiled to himself. Maybe he still had a chance of marrying his stepsister into this rich family. "Yes, even now she might be waiting for you to come riding to her rescue."

The younger man hesitated, but only for a moment. "Maybe I need to take some soldiers and go out to the Creek camp to look around."

"I'll ride along. You think I need to bring a gun?"

"By all means. You never know just what

tricks those sneaky savages are liable to pull."

They got a patrol of soldiers and rode out to the Creek camp. Harvey was stunned by the sight that greeted them: a few abandoned tents and saddles, tools, and other heavy things. "Damn, they've pulled out." He could imagine all the business he would lose now with the Creek tribe gone.

"Well," the captain said, "there's no sign Mrs. Dumont was here, but the major will be upset that the Indians have left. We can't let them reach the Yankees, where the able-bodied warriors can join up with them."

Harvey didn't give much of a damn what happened to the Indians or even to the war. He dismounted and studied the ground. "Here's buggy tracks. I reckon she's been here."

The captain dismounted, too, and began to look about. Caught in a bush, a scrap of black fabric fluttered like a tiny flag. "Oh, my God, could this be . . . ?"

Harvey grabbed the scrap and stared at it. "Mother of God," he gasped, "it's part of her dress. They've got her! The savages have got Twilight!"

Chapter 8

Yellow Jacket picked his way along the trail, his big body blocking the cold wind for Twilight. With his buffalo robe wrapped around her and her face against his muscular back, she was warm enough. Once he reached down and patted her hand almost gently, and she jerked away as if touched by a hot coal. When they rejoined the hundreds of weary Indians walking north and Yellow Jacket put her back up on the seat of her buggy and filled it with exhausted children, she gave them her buffalo robe to share among them.

Yellow Jacket frowned at her. "You need that yourself."

"You think I'm going to let children freeze to death, never mind what color they are?"

He almost seemed to smile. "Here, take my blanket." He tossed it into the buggy. "Now stay with the group, Mrs. Dumont. I've got too much to do to chase you down again."

"When Captain Wellsley catches up with us, I'll see that you pay for kidnapping me."

His bronze face turned stony cold. "You'd better hope he doesn't come. The captain knows nothing about fighting Indians; he'll get himself killed trying to play the gallant Southern gentleman." With that, he turned and galloped up the line.

Twilight concentrated on driving her buggy across the frozen ground as the Creeks moved north. As the hours passed, the children said nothing, only looking at her with big, sad eyes. They looked hungry and afraid, but no one cried. In spite of her own fears, her heart bled for the children. She began to sing a soothing lullaby as she drove, and when she looked back, most of them were asleep.

Yellow Jacket rode up just then. "Well, you seem to have a way with children."

She shrugged. "All children are alike, no matter what color they are. This is criminal, to be dragging all these helpless people for hundreds of miles. If you'd just surrender, the Confederates would feed you."

"Would they, or would they wipe us out?" The big Indian frowned. "Better we should die trying to make it to Kansas and freedom than to be captives of the rebels."

A very pregnant woman leading two young children stumbled past the buggy. Twilight recognized the little girls as the ones from the store, Smoke's children. She waved her hand. "Come ride with me; I can make room in my buggy."

The woman stopped, staring at Twilight with evident distrust, then looked to Yellow

164

Jacket. He spoke to the woman in Muskogee and she smiled hesitantly, came over, boosted the children up into the buggy, and got in herself. Twilight smiled at her, but to Yellow Jacket she said, "This woman may be giving birth at any time. She deserves better than this."

"Tell that to your rebels who are trying to stop us from making it to freedom," Yellow Jacket snapped. "The woman understands what she's facing. If her time comes, you'll deliver the baby."

Twilight was aghast. "Out here in the cold with no doctor to help me? I can't —"

"You'll have to," Yellow Jacket said. "I haven't time to worry about one unfortunate woman. We're nearing the river the whites call the Arkansas, and scouts have just brought word that Colonel Cooper's troops are behind us. If we get caught up against the river before we can cross, our people will be slaughtered." He nudged his pinto horse and galloped away.

She was about to be caught in a bloody battle. Cannon fire wouldn't know friend from foe, and she'd be in as much danger from the Confederates as from the Union side. Smiling at the tired Indian woman, Twilight clucked to her horse, and they started north again.

All day they traveled, the walking Indians moving slowly, driving goats and cattle ahead of them. With the hundreds of people and all the wagons and confusion, they seemed to be making little headway, but the people stubbornly kept their faces turned into the north wind and kept trudging. Twilight shivered in spite of herself and cursed Yellow Jacket silently as she drove the buggy.

Late in the afternoon, Twilight noticed that the pregnant woman was in evident distress. She reined in as Yellow Jacket rode past.

"Why are you stopping?" he thundered. "If we can't get across the river before dark, the rebels may catch up to us. We'll be slaughtered if they trap us against the river."

"I think she's going into labor," Twilight snapped. "Where's Smoke?"

Yellow Jacket cursed under his breath. "What a time to have this happen. We may just have to leave her to do the best she can."

"No!" Twilight said. "That's inhumane; I won't do it."

"You've got more spirit than I gave you credit for." Yellow Jacket smiled, almost in admiration. "But there's a platoon of Texas troops with those other rebels, and they'd kill anyone they see, whether it's a woman or not."

"I'll just have to take that chance." She climbed down off the buggy. "Where's their father?"

He gestured with his head. "Smoke? Behind us, making ready to give his life to keep those rebels from overrunning us. I'm going to join him."

"Can you get someone to take care of the children so I can help her?"

Yellow Jacket sighed and yelled, gesturing to an old woman who came, took the children out of the buggy, and hustled them away. The pregnant woman called out something after them.

"What does she say?" Twilight asked.

Yellow Jacket shook his head. "She's telling the old one to get the children across the river and don't look back."

Her bravery overwhelmed Twilight. "Tell her we'll stop here and I'll help deliver her baby. Then you can go on."

Yellow Jacket spoke to the woman, who nodded and then looked at Twilight and said something.

"What did she say?" Twilight took her hand and helped her from the buggy.

"She says even though you are white, you are very brave and have a good heart."

Twilight didn't feel very brave. She and this woman in labor were about to be left behind and might soon be overrun by Confederate troops who would shoot first and ask questions later. Already, Twilight heard distant gunfire echoing through the cold, barren hills. She led the woman over to a hollow out of the wind, then went back to the buggy for her medical bag. She looked up at Yellow Jacket sitting his horse. "I said you could go on. I'll manage somehow."

"Mrs. Dumont," Yellow Jacket said, "I don't think you understand. Between those undisciplined Texas troops and the rebel Indians, you're in danger yourself, especially after it turns dark."

Twilight looked up at the sky. It was late afternoon now. "I'm not going to abandon her. I'll manage somehow."

Yellow Jacket cursed, then dismounted. "I'll stay, too, then."

She frowned at him. "Are you afraid of losing your hostage?"

He hesitated. "Yes," he said, "that's it. Now, stop talking and tell me how I can help."

She hoped the relief she felt didn't show on her face. She wouldn't want the big savage to know how pleased she was not to be left alone out here on this cold, hostile prairie. "Help me set up a shelter of some kind out of blankets and start us a small fire."

"The smell of smoke will be picked up by those rebel scouts."

"Are you afraid?" she challenged.

His face was as hard as his voice. "If you were a man, I'd kill you for that insult."

"Then help me."

The woman, sitting against the trunk of a small scrub oak tree, groaned softly, and Twilight took her medical bag and strode over to her. Behind her, she heard Yellow Jacket dismount and lead the horses over to the hollow. "Maybe here in this brush, the rebels won't spot us."

She looked up at him. "If they capture us, won't they execute you?"

He smiled without mirth. "Only if I'm lucky. Some of those rebel Creeks led by the half-breed McIntosh clan would rather torture me."

Twilight blinked. "And you're still staying?"

He nodded. "I don't want you to fall into their hands," he said. "They'll do worse than kill enemy women."

Twilight had a sudden startling vision of mass rape and saw the fear in the other woman's eyes. Evidently she spoke enough English to understand what danger they all faced.

So he was staying behind to protect them, even though he faced torture if captured by the enemy. Well, maybe it was because the woman was Smoke's wife and Smoke was his friend. Twilight's estimation of the man grew. As she spread blankets and helped the woman, Yellow Jacket built a small fire and set up a lean-to of blankets against the wind.

Twilight knelt by the woman and took her hand. To Yellow Jacket she said, "Do you have any water?"

"Not much."

"Put some of it on to boil," Twilight said.

The woman gasped and bit her lip until it bled.

Twilight said to Yellow Jacket, "Tell her it's okay to cry out."

The woman seemed to understand some of what she said, because she shook her head and said something in their language to Yellow Jacket.

He nodded. "She says she must not cry out, it might alert the enemy if they have scouts out ahead of their troops."

"Oh." Twilight sighed. She was very much afraid with darkness only hours away and the Confederate troops advancing. The firing seemed louder now. She could still get in her buggy and get out of the conflict zone . . . but only if she abandoned this woman. The woman looked up at her with imploring dark eyes, and Twilight wiped the sweat off the woman's brow. "Tell her I'm staying; everything will be all right."

Yellow Jacket nodded and told the woman, who relaxed and smiled. "She understands, but she thinks we should abandon her and go on. She doesn't see why all three of us should risk death or capture."

The girl's bravery impressed Twilight. "You can go on if you want, but in good conscience, I can't leave her."

"I know." His voice was almost gentle. "You're a better person than I thought you were, Mrs. Dumont, unlike most of the whites I've known."

"So when this crisis is over, you'll free me?"

Now he scowled. "So that's what this is about? I should have known. The bad news is, white girl, that even if I freed you now, you're liable to get accidentally shot trying to make it back to the other side. Front-line troops are nervous about strangers approaching at night."

The woman groaned softly.

Twilight reached to mop the girl's forehead. To Yellow Jacket she said, "I can handle this if you'll stand guard."

He nodded, hefted his rifle, and stood up. "I'll keep a lookout."

"Let me know if the troops are getting close."

He nodded and left the hollow.

The next couple of hours crawled past slowly. It would soon be dark, and the sound of gunfire seemed closer. Twilight was scared but tried not to show it to the straining girl. If only she could put her in the buggy and retreat to the Confederate side, there would be safety and a real doctor, but the girl was now in hard labor. "Push!" Twilight said, and made a sign.

Yellow Jacket suddenly appeared. "How much longer? I can see rebel scouts coming through the trees in the distance."

"Any minute now," Twilight answered. "Then we'll get in the buggy and move out."

"I'm good with a rifle," Yellow Jacket said. "I'll try to get up in a tree and buy us a little time."

"Buy us as much time as you can," Twilight said.

He left, and the girl began to push harder. After a moment, a small, dark head appeared. With Twilight assisting her, the girl gave birth to a baby girl. Twilight smiled and smacked its bottom so that it wailed, then wrapped the baby in her shawl. The little mother smiled, too.

Immediately, Yellow Jacket appeared. "Everything all right here?"

The woman said something to Yellow Jacket, and he grinned. "She wants to name the baby for you because you saved its life."

Twilight blinked back tears and laid the baby in the crook of its mother's arm. "Tell her I would be greatly honored."

Yellow Jacket spoke to the woman, then to Twilight. "Can we move on now?"

"In a minute," Twilight said. "There's a little finishing up to do; then you can help me get them into the buggy."

"I'll hold them off as long as I can, but hurry."

Twilight did what she could with the little bit of water, then yelled for Yellow Jacket.

"Can you get her into the buggy if I carry the baby?"

In answer he dismounted, swung the girl up into his arms, and headed for the buggy, with Twilight coming behind with the baby and her medical bag. "Let's get out of here."

Yellow Jacket put the girl in the buggy, and Twilight handed her the baby and climbed up on the seat. Yellow Jacket mounted up, looked behind him. "Those rebs aren't half a mile away."

Twilight snapped the reins, and the horse started off at a trot. She hated the rough ride for the Indian girl, but it couldn't be helped. The late afternoon was shadowy across the frozen prairie as they headed for the river.

They reached the river at sundown. Mass confusion reigned as the fleeing Indians tried to cross the river the whites called the Arkansas. Children cried, and loose dogs ran about barking while sheep baaed and cattle milled. Yellow Jacket shook his head and shouted to Twilight. "We've got to cross the river or be slaughtered right here. Can you take the buggy across?"

Twilight touched her chest in dismay. The river looked deep and dark, with a swift current. As she watched, another light wagon started across. The Indian driving it cracked his whip and yelled at the horses. The horses hesitated, not wanting to brave the current, then plunged in. Immediately, the wagon began to float, then overturned, dumping people into the swift, cold stream. Women screamed and others waded in to rescue them as the driver fought to right the wagon. The horses broke free and headed for the far shore, but the driver and the wagon were swept away and were seen no more.

Yellow Jacket rode up and down the bank, yelling to people, encouraging them to cross. The gunfire of the advancing Confederates grew even louder. The Creeks and the others trapped on the bank looked back toward the sound of the advancing army, then toward the distant shore. To be trapped here on this side, with the river behind them, was a death sentence, and they knew it. More and more of the people drove their cattle and goats into the water or rode horses into the river, fighting to reach the other side. Some of them were swept away and lost.

Twilight looked at the Creek girl next to her. The girl clutched her baby and looked at the water with fearful eyes. Twilight had faced more danger in the past couple of days than she ever had in her whole sheltered life. She drove up to the edge of the water and hesitated. If the buggy overturned, the young mother and her baby didn't stand a chance.

Yellow Jacket galloped up. "Here, I'll help you." He rode out into the water, reached to grab her horse's bridle, led it deeper. "Hang on!" he yelled at Twilight. "The buggy will float if you can stay with it."

Twilight reached over and put her arm around the young Indian woman. "We're ready."

Yellow Jacket nodded and forced her horse deeper into the river. Twilight had a helpless feeling as the buggy began to float. She watched Yellow Jacket's strong arm hanging onto her horse to keep it from panicking and heading back to shore. Now both horses were swimming strongly. The cold water came up in the buggy, around her ankles, and Twilight gasped at the cold. It was numbing and icy. Anyone who was drenched would probably freeze to death before they could be dried out.

It seemed like an eternity that they fought the river, the buggy threatening to overturn or be swept away at any moment, but finally, she felt her horse regain its footing and the buggy wheels hit ground. Then Yellow Jacket was leading it up the other side. He was drenched and shivering.

"Find shelter out of the wind," he gasped. "I think we'll have to fight rebels there at Round Mountain." He nodded toward the low profile of the hill nearby. Now he wheeled his horse and headed back into the water.

"Where are you going?" Twilight called.

"I've got to help hold that bank until we can get all our people across; otherwise, they'll be slaughtered."

"You'll be killed!" Suddenly Twilight was very much afraid of losing him.

He shrugged and plunged back into the racing water. "Get out of sight!" he shouted back.

Twilight watched him reenter the river, her heart in her throat. It was growing dusky dark, and if they didn't get the hundreds of stragglers across soon, they'd have to wait until morning, and by then the Confederates would be here. Women and children would be slaughtered if the rebels overtook them. She looked over at her sleeping namesake with her tiny face and dark hair, and decided she would do whatever it took to aid these helpless people in reaching Kansas and safety.

Behind them, the noise and the echo of gunfire increased. Twilight urged her horse to move faster. Once she would have welcomed being overtaken by her own side, but now she was afraid the gray-clad soldiers might shoot first and ask questions later.

Twilight looked at the weapons the warriors carried as they galloped back across the river to help Yellow Jacket and Smoke. Some of them were well mounted, some afoot. None had warm enough clothing. Few besides Yellow Jacket carried good weapons. Most had old hunting rifles or shotguns; a few were armed only with bows and arrows, knives, and lances.

Twilight stared after them, trying to decide what to do next. Right now, she decided, her main responsibility was to get the woman and baby in her buggy out of the line of fire. The mountain ahead of her was small. Off to one side, the women and children were heading for the safety of the brush and rocks. Twilight slapped her horse with the reins and joined them.

Just before he plunged into the river, Yellow Jacket turned in his saddle to glance back at the white woman and her buggy. She appealed to him as a female, and, too, she might make a good bargaining chip if needed. He must think of her that way, as an object, and stop thinking of her as a desirable woman.

He drew up and addressed his men. "You have your orders from old Opothleyahola. We are badly outnumbered, but perhaps by ambush, we can even the score. Are you ready to die for the good of our people?"

The men set up a shout of defiance, and Yellow Jacket nodded. "We go, then."

With him in the lead, his small war party topped the ridge and saw a line of gray-clad men coming through the brush ahead of them. Yellow Jacket said a small prayer to the Master of Breath and then charged forward, yelling a war cry. Behind him, his men hurled insults and challenges as they rushed forward. The rebels looked startled for a moment, then dropped to one knee and began to fire as their cavalry surged around them, galloping toward the war party.

Yellow Jacket drew in sharply, causing his fine horse to rear. He felt shells whiz past him as the rebels rushed forward. He must not panic and flee. He and his men must wait until the enemy was almost upon them, then turn and lead the unsuspecting gray line back to where the ambush awaited. He could hear the rebels calling to each other as they ran, and behind him he heard a cry as one of his own warriors was shot from his saddle. The smell of gunpowder burned his nose, and the smoke from the weapons made the cold dusk hazy, so that at times he could barely make out the gray-clad men riding toward him.

"Now!" He wheeled his horse as the rebel cavalry rode so close that he could almost make out the color of the white men's eyes. "Now, brave men, make them follow us!" He put the spurs to his horse, as did the others, and turned to ride toward the mountain, forcing the unsuspecting cavalry to chase them. Near him, an old friend cried out and fell from his horse, wounded. Yellow Jacket hesitated. His soul told him to ride back, try to rescue his friend, but there was not time unless he sacrificed his mission. He had been given his orders.

Yelling to his braves to stay just ahead of the rebel cavalry, Yellow Jacket kept riding. When he glanced back, he saw a rebel shoot the helpless brave who had fallen. Yellow Jacket's anger made him give a defiant shout. Now he could feel the bullets whizzing past him, hear the labored breathing of the rebel horses. Were they going to make it or would the cavalry commander realize he was being led into an ambush and pull back?

He looked behind him. The commander was the young Captain Wellsley. The boy would be too green to know what was happening. Only a few more yards, and he and his braves would reach safety, where the warriors hid in ambush on either side of the little gully up ahead. It seemed like a million miles to that draw, and he was not sure any of them was going to make it. Behind him, he heard a rebel rider shout a warning, but when Yellow Jacket looked back, the captain was riding pell-mell ahead, too green to realize that he and his little patrol of cavalry were riding right into the heart of the Indian ambush. He glanced to one side, seeing the last rays of the dying sun glinting off the hidden guns.

"Now!" Yellow Jacket shouted, and wheeled his horse to face the oncoming cavalry even as the guns hidden in the draw opened up with a roar.

Chapter 9

In confusion, Captain Wellsley reined in his rearing bay horse. A moment ago, he and his cavalry unit had been chasing down a ragtag band of savages, led by that big warrior he'd recognized as Yellow Jacket. As he galloped after the fleeing Indians, he imagined the parade back in Austin, his proud, beaming mother watching as he accepted his medal and promotion. Now all hell had broken loose, with rifle fire blazing from behind every shrub and rock. The savages he'd been chasing had disappeared into thin air or had turned their horses, charging him instead of fleeing. Around him, men shouted and screamed as they went down; horses neighed and bolted, dragging riders.

"Ambush!" someone shouted. "Ambush!"

Ambush, yes, that was it. Wellsley hadn't thought the savages would know such battle tactics. "Take cover, men!" he shouted, dismounting his own rearing horse.

Near him, a cavalry mount went down, trapping a rider beneath it. The man screamed as the half ton of horse fell on him. *Oh, God, what to do next?* Captain Wellsley suddenly couldn't remember anything they'd taught him at West Point, and he'd lost his hat. The noise deafened him as his horse neighed and reared and he hung on to the reins. *A man afoot is a dead man.* It took all his strength to hold the horse and tie it to a sturdy bush. The wind felt icy cold against his pale face as the sun sank on the horizon.

Where were the rest of the Texas troops and the rebel Indians? They'd had such superior numbers, but now his men were being shot to pieces after being stupid enough to fall for the oldest trick in the world. *Ambush.* He wouldn't get a medal; he was going to lose his silver bars and be drummed out of the army in disgrace. *What will Mother say?*

At least no one could say he didn't die bravely. Captain Wellsley grabbed the rifle from his saddle and crouched down behind a boulder. He aimed and fired, taking out a warrior who had raised his head too high. What had happened to that escaping group of savages he'd been chasing? They were nowhere in sight, having melted into the landscape, and were now firing back at him. Around him, his Confederate cavalry fell groaning in the bloody snow. In the distant twilight, he saw gray-clad Texas troops coming, but they weren't going to get here in time.

His sergeant grabbed his shoulder, shook him back to reality. "Sir, we're in trouble here; we should retreat."

"Retreat? Gallant Confederates? What will people say?"

The old sergeant blinked. "Better to retreat than to lose all our men, sir."

Wellsley looked about, uncertain. Yes, of course the sergeant was right. Only he wouldn't call it "retreat"; he'd call it regrouping. "Very well, Sergeant," he shouted over the gunfire, "sound recall!"

In a split second, the bugle rang out loud and clear over the gunfire, and the gray-clad men began to retreat. Some of them had lost their horses and were afoot; others, badly wounded, died in a hail of gunfire as they tried to limp away.

Captain Wellsley swung up on his horse, feeling the bullets whiz past him in the dark and the cold. He was terrified. As for Mrs. Dumont, he'd made a gallant effort to rescue her, if indeed she was still alive, and he had failed. With his head hanging in humiliation, he turned his horse to gallop back to the advancing rebels, knowing it was a complete rout. He'd lost most of his command to a clever ambush from a bunch of poorly armed savages.

Behind him, Yellow Jacket watched in satisfaction as the rebels fled. He thought he had seen Captain Wellsley among the rebels and knew the white officer would try to rescue the beautiful white girl. Yellow Jacket didn't intend to give her up. "They run! The first battle of the white man's Civil War in Indian Territory is our victory!"

Around him, warriors set off war whoops and chants, and some ran out to scalp the enemy dead. Yellow Jacket almost stopped them, then shrugged. The civilized tribes had never owned the custom of scalping as the plains tribes did, but he knew some of the rebel Indians and even the Texans were scalping the slain. Twilight. With his heart beating hard with apprehension, he crossed the river and went looking for the white woman. He found her huddled behind a rock, holding Smoke's new baby against her. "Are you all right?"

Twilight was as angry as she was scared, looking up at him. "Is it over?"

"For now." His rugged face was grim and hard. "They'll lick their wounds, and maybe we can sneak away after dark."

She stood up. "Sneak away? Are you joking? You've got a lot of dead and wounded here."

His face in the dusk of the coming night grew stern. "Yes, we have. Get your medical bag and see what you can do. The leaders have to meet with the ancient one to see what he plans next."

Twilight glanced from him to Smoke's woman as she handed her the new baby. "What am I to do with them?"

"I'll see if I can find Smoke. Maybe he can find an abandoned army wagon to transport them." With that, he strode away. She stared after his broad back, thinking he seemed to be a tower of strength among these people. They had little food or weapons, and the odds were against them. All they had in abundance was courage. With all these Confederate forces chasing them, these Indians didn't have a chance of making it the three hundred miles to the Kansas border, and yet, they wouldn't give up. From the smallest child to the frailest old woman, they were teaching Twilight something about bravery and stubborn determination.

Somewhere nearby, she heard a wounded warrior moan. She reached for her medical bag, turned to smile and make comforting gestures to the new little mother, began searching out the wounded around her. Here and there, she found some too mortally injured to be moved, and they seemed to know it. One of them didn't appear to be out of his teens. "I — I'll get a wagon," she promised, but the warrior shook his head.

"No, must not slow the people," he gasped. "The Master of Breath is coming for me. . . . Must — must get the people to the Union soldiers."

She took his hand and nodded, her vision blurring with tears as he breathed once more and then died. Why had she been so terrified of these poor wretches? They were human beings after all, who lived and died and had hopes and dreams just like white "civilized" people. What difference should it make to the Confederates if a few hungry, ragged Indians made it to Kansas? If she could speak to the commander, she'd urge them to let the Indians go in peace.

Around her, people were coming out of the brush, many of them injured, and she had so little medicine to help! Taking a deep breath for courage, she went about ministering to the wounded, doing what she could, which was precious little.

Later that night, as she slumped on a log, shivering, Yellow Jacket found her. "Have you eaten?"

She shook her head wearily. "There doesn't seem to be enough to go around. I'm worried about Smoke's family. . . ."

"He's found an abandoned rebel wagon to carry them. They'll be fine."

"I will be, too, then," she lied.

"Come with me," he ordered.

"But —"

When she protested, he caught her arm and led her, but she tripped and would have fallen if he had not lifted her and carried her to the shelter of a rock, where he had a small fire going. He sat her down and draped a blanket around her shoulders. "I've got a little coffee and some jerky."

Coffee. She was so cold, her hands were shaking. "There's others need it worse than I do."

"Shut up and drink it." He put a tin cup in her hands. It was warm, and instinctively she cupped her hands around it. "Eat a little."

"Is this your food?" She took it. The meat smelled delicious, yet she hesitated.

"What do you care?" He did not smile. "We've got to keep you alive; we need your medical skills."

"Oh, I thought, maybe —"

"Stop thinking and eat." He leaned against the rock and sighed, closed his eyes.

There was no point in protesting, and besides, did she give a damn if her kidnapper went hungry? The thought renewed her defiance, and she ate the meat and drained the coffee. If it weren't for this big savage, she noted, she might have been able to rejoin the Confederate forces and been safe and warm tonight. Could she have slept in that safety, now knowing how these Indians suffered?

For the first time, she noted that he shivered. "What happened to your extra blanket?"

"I lost it." He didn't look at her.

"I don't believe you."

"All right, I gave it to a dying warrior. It eased his suffering until he met the Master of Breath."

"What's going to happen to the severely wounded who can't walk?"

She saw pain cross his face. "We leave them behind. There's no help for it."

"That's horrible. The Confederate troops may kill them when they find them."

"The wounded know that." His face in the firelight seemed to carry the weight of the world. "All that matters is that we get the people to Kansas. Nothing must delay us."

For a moment, there was no sound save the crackle of the fire. Somewhere a wounded one moaned softly, and the sound was carried on the cold wind. In the distance, a newly born baby wailed.

"A life goes; another comes," Twilight said softly.

He nodded. "It is the way of things. A man meets woman; they mate and produce life so that the people prevail. Nothing else matters."

She watched him shiver again and suddenly felt guilty. "I've got your blanket, and you're cold."

"I've been cold before." His voice was brusque. "Did you see your Captain Wellsley out there today, coming to rescue you?"

Captain Wellsley. He seemed like a weak boy beside the warrior next to her. "No, did you kill him?"

He glared at her. "Your rich rebel is safe enough. He fled the battle like a deer running before hunters."

Twilight lowered her eyes, imagining the humiliation of the green, inexperienced officer against a hardened warrior like Yellow Jacket. "Was my stepbrother with him?"

"Hardly!" Yellow Jacket snorted. "At least the captain did his duty. No doubt the craven Indian agent hid far to the back if he came at all. Now shut up and get some rest. We'll be pulling out in the middle of the night, trying to put some distance between us and the rebels."

"Why don't you just surrender?" Twilight urged. "These women and children and old people can't keep walking through the snow —"

"You'd like that, wouldn't you? So you could return to the comfort of the civilized world?"

"I was thinking of the safety of your people," she snapped back.

He stared at her, long and hard. "You are changing, Mrs. Dumont, from when I first saw you as a delicate, fearful Southern belle."

She remembered the first time she had seen him as she stepped from the stage. "Was that what you thought of me?"

His voice was so low, she had to strain to hear him as he stared into the fire. "I thought you were the most beautiful woman I had ever seen, and I wanted you."

She didn't know what to say. What he was

suggesting was not only forbidden, it was un-thinkable. She opened her mouth to speak, and then didn't know what to say.

He turned his head and looked at her, and the expression on his dark, rugged face made her heart beat faster. This virile, powerful man called out to something deep inside her soul, something wild and uncivilized that she hadn't known was there. The thought scared her. It came to her, as they stared into each other's eyes in the flickering firelight, that all she had to do was make the slightest gesture and he would reach for her — and she might not be able to stop herself from responding.

For an eternity, their gazes met and locked in the silence before he broke the spell with a regretful sigh. "Go to sleep, you of the dusky, twilight eyes; I'll wake you when we're ready to move out."

Very slowly she sank to the ground next to him, pulled her blanket close, and closed her eyes. After a moment, she felt his big hand reach out and brush a wisp of hair away from her face ever so gently. Then his hand went to her shoulder in a protective gesture that comforted her. She felt the weight of his hand as she dropped off to sleep.

Before first light, Yellow Jacket was shaking her awake. "It's time," he whispered almost gently.

As she roused, she felt stiff from sleeping

on the cold ground. "Have you been sitting beside me all night?"

"What does it matter?" He did not look at her as he bustled about, stirring up the fire.

"Is there any coffee?"

He shook his head. "We've used the last of it. I've got a little corn bread."

She took it gratefully and gobbled it, then suddenly realized he was only watching her. "You haven't eaten?"

"Stop worrying about me," he snapped. "I've eaten."

She didn't believe him, but there was no point in arguing with him. "I've got room in my buggy to carry a few," she said.

"You might give a lift to some of the wounded if they survived the night," he said, and went off to investigate.

The mortally wounded would have to be left behind to rely on the mercy of the pursuing Confederate soldiers. How many would die before the Union Indians reached Kansas — if they managed to reach Kansas with November soon to be fading into December? She would save those she could, she decided. Maybe sooner or later, she would get the chance to negotiate with the Confederates. After all, what did a few helpless Indians more or less mean to the Southern cause?

It would soon be dawn. Twilight got her medical bag and began to walk the frosty ground, looking for those she might aid. Nearby, she spotted an old woman curled up in the snow like a small, frail bundle of rags. She would offer her a ride to save her life. "Old mother?" She shook the thin body, but there was no answer or movement. With growing alarm, Twilight shook her again.

Behind her, she heard footsteps on the frosty ground and turned to see Yellow Jacket. Twilight blinked back tears. "Help me; I think maybe . . ."

He strode over, bent to look, shook his head. "She's gone; maybe the cold, maybe just willed herself to die so she wouldn't be a burden to her people."

Twilight stared down at the frail body through her tears. "She — she hadn't hurt anyone. It isn't fair."

Yellow Jacket snorted. "Tell that to the noble rebels who are chasing us down like rabbits." He reached and took the old woman's blanket. "Sorry, old mother," he whispered.

"What are you doing? Aren't we even going to bury her?" Twilight was outraged as she faced him.

He glared back at her, and she thought she almost saw his jaw tremble. "Do you think me heartless? I knew this old woman well; in happier times I have supped by her fire. The Master of Breath will understand, as will the dead. We have no time for burials, as the old

191

one has no need for a blanket. Now, get in the buggy."

"This is cruel and outrageous," she protested.

"Mrs. Dumont, will you get in your buggy, or do I have to put you there?"

She tore away a piece of her black long skirt and laid it across the old woman's face, only sorry she couldn't do more. Then, with stiff dignity, she lifted her ragged skirts and walked to her buggy, climbed up, picked up the reins.

"I've got some passengers for you over that next rise," he shouted, then put spurs to his horse and galloped off, throwing up a spray of snow.

Twilight sighed, knowing he was right. In her sheltered life, she had experienced so little hardship compared to what these people were dealing with. She spoke to her horse and moved out through the frozen ground with difficulty, knowing that soon the well-armed and well-fed Confederate troops would be awakening and starting the pursuit again. A long, cold, and miserable day lay ahead, and she knew she was powerless to do anything except help a few individuals. She concentrated on the people waiting over the next rise and didn't look back at the old woman lying curled in the snow.

In the Confederate camp, Colonel Cooper

came awake with a start, grabbing for his pistol.

"Colonel? Colonel Cooper, sir?"

He recognized the voice and relaxed, blinked in the coming daylight as he swung his feet over the side of his cot. "Come in, Rogers. What in the hell's wrong?"

Clem Rogers, the lanky, mixed-blood Cherokee scout came into the tent and saluted. "Something's happened, sir."

"Obviously, or you wouldn't be here." The colonel yawned and scratched, began to search the darkness for his boots.

"Sir, it's Colonel Drew's Cherokee Mounted Rifles, the Keetoowas."

"Troublesome bunch," Colonel Cooper muttered.

The young scout twisted his hat in his hands. "You know they've been grumblin' about this trip, don't like chasin' after the runaway Creeks; think we ought to let them go."

"I know, I know. I don't like it much, either, but ours not to reason why. We just follow orders, that's all."

"Not those traditional Cherokees, the Keetoowa clan," Rogers said. "They've pulled out."

"What?" Colonel Cooper paused in pulling on his boots and stood up. "What do you mean, 'pulled out'?"

Clem Rogers sighed. "What I been tryin'

to tell you, sir, is that almost all the First Cherokee Mounted Rifles deserted in the middle of the night. They're gone!"

Colonel Cooper began to curse. "Damn them anyhow. Where'd they go?"

The lanky boy shrugged. "Not sure. Some may have joined up with old Opothleyahola's warriors; some may have headed to join the Yankee troops; some of them may just be sick of the whole war and gone home."

The colonel rolled his eyes. "Wish I had that option. The other Injuns still with us?"

"Yes, sir. Them McIntosh half-breed Creeks is mortal enemies of Opothleyahola 'cause he assassinated the head of the Mc-Intosh family years ago for signing over their land to Southern whites. It's a Creek law: a death sentence to anyone who sells tribal land. Anyways, the half-breed McIntoshes are itchin' to spill Union Creek blood."

"They'll still get their chance, I reckon." Cooper didn't wait for an answer as he sat on his cot and finished putting on his boots. "Rogers, go alert all my officers that we'll be meeting in a few minutes, and tell the cook to get a pot of coffee going — strong coffee."

"Yes, sir." The Cherokee scout turned to leave.

"Oh, didn't Mrs. Dumont's brother end up coming along?"

"Ridin' far to the rear, sir." Clem Rogers couldn't keep the scorn from his voice.

"Well, you'd better go tell him and Captain Wellsley that we can't go on until we pick up some reinforcements."

"Harvey Leland ain't gonna like that none."

"Can't be helped. I'm not about to move forward with a whole regiment missing. The nearest reinforcements are probably old Stand Watie's Second Cherokee Mounted Rifles; they're loyal to the cause."

"Sir, it'll take a couple of days for them to get here; gives them Yankee Injuns more time to get away."

The colonel swore again. "You think I don't know that? Take one of our best horses and ride for Stand Watie. I've got to have some help here!"

"Yes, sir." Clem Rogers saluted and ran out the door.

"Damn," grumbled the colonel as he reached for his hat. "Damn those Union braves for not being sensible and surrendering." Somewhere inside, he had the slightest bit of admiration for their gritty stubbornness, even though they added to his problems. With a sigh, he grabbed his coat and went out to meet the new dawn's events.

The cold day seemed endless to Twilight. The wind picked up and it began to snow. Yellow Jacket had loaded her buggy with a wounded warrior, a woman, and two young girls. Sometimes her buggy bogged down in the mud, and Yellow Jacket came back to help break trail. The wounded warrior seemed weaker, and when they stopped to rest the horses, he said something to Yellow Jacket, who nodded gravely, dismounted, and helped him from the buggy. He handed the young warrior a rifle. Half supporting, half carrying the man, Yellow Jacket helped him over behind a pile of rocks, then came back alone.

Twilight looked at him. "Isn't he going to ride with me farther?"

The big warrior shook his head. "Twilight," he said softly, "the man is dying, and he knows it. He asks that we leave him behind."

"But he'll die . . ."

"He's already dying. He intends to try to slow the rebel advance, buy our people more time. He said to give his place in the buggy to someone who stands a chance of living."

Twilight's vision blurred. She looked around at the other silent Indians who rode with her. The young woman blinked back tears but said nothing.

Twilight stared at Yellow Jacket, a question in her eyes.

"He's her brother," he said softly.

"Oh, God!" Twilight choked back sobs, "This is all so terrible."

"Tell that to the rebel army pursuing us."

She was tired and cold and miserable. "Why don't you leave me behind?" she said.

"Someone could have my space in the buggy."

"We need your medical skill," he said. "I'll find someone else who can walk no farther to ride with you."

Before she could say anything, he rode away. She looked over at the Indian girl next to her. If this girl could leave a dying brother, Twilight was ashamed to be so weak and complaining. She urged her horse forward, and the buggy lurched on again through the frozen mud. All around her, Indians rode tired, stumbling horses or walked stubbornly forward, bent against the driving north wind.

In minutes, Yellow Jacket rode next to her. "Old Opothleyahola is getting weak, and his horse just died. He's too weak to ride anyway, and we cannot lose him."

Twilight nodded, and in moments, the frail old Indian was led to her buggy. He was bent with age and coughing as Yellow Jacket helped him up. The buggy lurched forward again, slowly.

Yellow Jacket said, "If we don't ease that load, that horse won't make it through the day."

The Indian girl said something in her native language, but Yellow Jacket shook his head. Twilight gave him a questioning look.

"She's offering to walk," he explained.

"Nonsense!" Twilight said. "I'll walk. I'm better able than she is."

"Here," he said, and held out his hand. "We can ride double and let the old one drive the buggy."

Twilight hesitated. She certainly didn't want to ride with Yellow Jacket, but her horse was giving out, and the load in the buggy had to be lessened. With a sigh, she handed over the reins and took Yellow Jacket's hand, letting him swing her up behind him on the saddle. Then they started forward again, following the hundreds of people ahead of them.

Immediately, she was warmer because his big body was blocking the cold north wind. She huddled against him, seeking his warmth and locking her arms around his waist. He reached down and touched her hand, almost gently; then he nodded to the old Muskogee and spurred his horse forward, riding north into the icy blast.

She laid her cold face against the warm back of his buckskin shirt, closed her eyes, and listened to his great heart beat as they rode. She felt more than warm; she felt safe and protected. Then she reminded herself that he was her captor and that if she were lucky, her brother and the captain might catch up to the Creeks in time to rescue her. The thought was not as appealing as it had been yesterday. Like it or not, she was beginning to admire and respect the brave warrior she rode behind.

Chapter 10

Twilight thought the day would never end. She hung onto Yellow Jacket's broad back as they rode into the cold north wind. Around her, people stumbled and fell, got up, and kept walking. Many of the people were without shoes, and now and then she saw bloody footprints in sharp contrast to the white, white snow. Once they passed a dead horse and saw hungry people gathered around, cutting it up for meat.

Finally, it was almost dark, and the people stopped to camp, sharing whatever food they had. Yellow Jacket gathered buffalo and cow chips to start a fire. People crept close to it and warmed their numb hands. Twilight went about with her medicine bag, bandaging minor wounds, handing out what little medicine she had. No longer did she look on these people as savages. They were only people after all attempting to escape the ravages of war.

The big mixed-blood, Smoke, rode up, grinning. "Some good news, finally. Stragglers tell us Colonel Drew's Cherokee Mounted Rifles have deserted. Some of them have joined us, some have ridden over to join the Union forces, and some of them are just tired of the war and have gone home."

"That is good news." Yellow Jacket nodded. "Maybe that'll delay the rebels while they wait for reinforcements. Now we can take some time to rest." He returned to Twilight and the small group who had ridden in her buggy.

She watched him talking to the frail old leader in their native language. The old man bent double with coughing as the pair talked, but he smiled. Twilight caught Yellow Jacket's arm as he turned to go. "What's happened?"

"Some of the rebel Cherokees have deserted, the Keetoowas, the ones we call the 'pins.' That leaves their commanders shorthanded. It's the first good news we've gotten in weeks."

It wasn't good news for her, Twilight realized. If the Confederate troops were delayed, the chances of her escaping were getting smaller. And yet, if she got the chance to escape, how could she go, knowing there was no one to look after the wounded and the sick among these pitiful people? She reminded herself that she was a hostage and these Indians weren't her problem . . . unless she wanted to make them so.

"What are you thinking?" he asked.

"Nothing," she lied. "Can you possibly find

any food for some of the sicker, weaker ones?"

"I'll try hunting," he answered, "but we're short of cartridges."

"We seem to be short of everything except the sick and hungry." Twilight sighed.

The wind blew the tiny fire almost out, and Twilight knelt and began to blow on the embers, fanning the fire to a blaze again while others ran about to gather up twigs and cow chips to fuel it.

Yellow Jacket watched her, nodding with approval. "I'm almost out of matches. When we use them up, we'll be trying to use a flint and steel. That's hard to do with the wind blowing."

She rubbed her numb hands and held them out to the flames. "I wish we had some coffee. If we'd stayed with the Confederates, we'd have some."

Yellow Jacket snorted in derision. "My people aren't likely to trade a chance at freedom for coffee. I'll melt some snow over the fire. I think I have a little parched corn left; we can make a thin soup."

She was too weary to do anything but nod. "If you could shoot a rabbit, maybe I could make a nourishing soup for some of these people." Around her, she could see others stumbling to a halt, trying to build fires. It was starting to snow again as darkness came on. Many of these people would not survive

201

the night, she thought, but she would do what she could. Twilight busied herself getting her soup boiling, and after an hour, Yellow Jacket returned with one thin old jackrabbit, which he skinned, cut up, and added to her soup.

She looked around at the dozens of hungry faces and called out, "Bring your cup or an old hollow gourd and we'll share what we've got."

Immediately, small children came running, but the old hung back. Tears came to Twilight's eyes as she realized why. "There's plenty," she lied, urging the old ones to come forward. "There's enough for everyone."

Within minutes the kettle was empty. "Did you get any?" she asked Yellow Jacket.

"I — I wasn't hungry. Did you eat?"

"Sure," she lied, knowing he would be upset that she had given her share to a frail woman. She couldn't have eaten anyway with all those hungry eyes watching her.

He put his hand on her shoulder. "You have a good heart, Twilight."

She didn't answer and looked away.

"You should have eaten," he scolded gently. "If you're returned in poor shape, Harvey will say we mistreated you."

His words stung her. How could she almost have forgotten that she meant nothing to him except for her medical skills and being a valuable hostage?

Darkness came on, cold and sharp, the wind howling like a wild animal as it blew through their campsite. The fire had dwindled down to glowing coals. The people had scattered, seeking shelter in gullies out of the wind.

Yellow Jacket cut and spread fragrant juniper boughs, then laid his buffalo robe on top of those. "Let's see if we can make it through the night without freezing to death. Bring your blanket." He sat down on the robe and gestured for her to join him.

Twilight reasoned that the whites need never know she had shared blankets with this big savage male. Surviving the night was all that mattered. After a moment's hesitation, she brought her blanket and lay down on the juniper boughs next to the big man. The scent of the fragrant branches reminded her of Christmas. She wondered then how many days had passed and how close to Christmas it was. Did it matter anymore? All that mattered was staying alive and out of the range of the rebel guns until she was rescued.

Yellow Jacket pulled her close to him. She stiffened in protest for a moment; then she lay down on his muscular arm and pulled the blanket over them. They turned toward the fire, spoon-fashion, and he curled protectively around her. The heat and the power of him enveloped her, and she was warm and secure. "How far is it to Kansas?"

His warm breath stirred her hair. "I don't know. We'll just keep moving until we run across Yankee troops."

"Suppose the Confederates catch up to us again?"

"Then we'll fight them again," he answered sleepily. "Now, go to sleep; we'll be on the trail again before dawn, and you'll need all your strength."

"I am so tired of being hungry and cold," she whispered, "and watching people die when there is so little I can do to help them."

"Me, too," he murmured, "but there is no quitting unless we want to be killed or captured by the rebels, so we'll just keep moving north until we either reach safety or the rebels kill us."

She was finally getting warm. She lay on his muscular arm, listening to the crackle of the fire. She didn't want to think about the hardships and the hunger of tomorrow. Tonight it was enough to be warm and safe, to be able to sleep. She began to drift off.

He pulled her closer, and she pretended to be asleep as he stroked her hair. She felt him kiss the side of her face, and then his big hand pulled the blanket closer around her small shoulders. "I'm sorry I got you into this," he whispered, and then he laid his face against hers, his big arm encircling her protectively. In minutes she heard his steady breathing as he dropped off to sleep.

There was no telling what lay ahead of them on the windswept prairie tomorrow — death, or at least pain, hunger, and heartbreak — and a relentless army was coming behind them. She would not think of that. She would think only that she was warm and in the arms of a man who held her as if she were a precious object.

What was she thinking? Of course she was precious to him; she was a hostage and might come in very handy if the Indians needed a bargaining chip with the Confederate army. She must remember that and stop thinking of this big savage as a virile and protective man. She put her cold face against his chest and dropped off to sleep.

In the middle of the night, she awakened to find him propped up on one elbow, looking down into her face.

She blinked. "Is it — is it time to move on?"

"Not yet," he whispered, with a slight shake of his head. "I'm sorry, I didn't mean to wake you. I just like looking at you, that's all." His big hand traced the line of her jaw.

His gentleness touched her. Without thinking, she reached up and caught his hand. "What are you thinking?"

"How much I've wanted to do this." Before she realized what he intended, he bent his head and kissed her gently.

She froze in surprise and then realized she'd been waiting for this moment since the first time she had seen him, since he had claimed her with his eyes so arrogantly and boldly. She let his tongue open her lips, and then she reached up and put her arms around his neck, returning his kiss with an ardor that surprised her. She had not known she was capable of such feeling.

After a moment, he pulled away. "I'm sorry, I should not have done that."

Her heart was hammering. "I'm a captive; I couldn't have stopped you."

"I wouldn't want you that way." He got up and poked up the fire. "I'm going hunting. Maybe I'll get lucky and get something big like a deer. That would save a lot of people from dying today."

She went from the magic of his forbidden embrace to the harsh reality of the coming day. With a sigh, she got up and pulled the blanket around her shoulders. How many miles would they walk today, and how many people would they lose to the cold and hunger?

Yellow Jacket did bring in a deer, and Twilight gathered snow and soon had a big pot of broth going to share around. By dawn, the caravan was winding through the hills, headed north again. However, as she sat behind Yellow Jacket on the big paint horse

with her arms around his waist and her face pressed against the leather on his muscular back, she remembered that kiss time and time again and smiled ever so slowly.

They traveled in peace that day, the rebels behind them evidently waiting for reinforcements. Despite the cold and the lack of food, they kept moving until old Opothleyahola, still riding in her confiscated buggy, called a halt.

Twilight did not want to think about tonight and what might happen. She did what she could to relieve suffering and ate some of the deer meat left from early this morning.

Finally, the pair bedded down near the fire. She did not protest when he pulled her shivering body close to him. Instead, she reveled in the warmth and closed her eyes. Civilization was very far away, and she might not make it through the dangers of tomorrow, but tonight she was finding comfort curled up against this man. She closed her eyes and began to drift off to sleep.

Then she felt him stroke her hair and pull her close. Twilight's heart began to hammer. She wasn't certain if she should protest, or, worse yet, whether she wanted to. Not that it mattered, because she was a captive and he could do with her what he wanted. He stroked her hair. "Twilight?"

She pretended that she was asleep because

she was uncertain how she should or wanted to react.

She felt his lips brush her cheek in the gentlest of kisses. She turned her body slowly so that she lay facing him, her breasts against his powerful chest. In the darkness she felt his hard manhood against her body. She had never felt this way toward any other man before, and tomorrow they might freeze to death or be killed. Her pulse began to beat hard as something deep within her stirred with an emotion that she had never felt. He rose up on one elbow. She could see the hard, rugged planes of his face in the flickering firelight.

"Twilight?" He was asking, and her heart said yes.

Without saying a word, she reached up, put her arms around his neck, and pulled him down to her. He gasped and breathed harder as his mouth covered hers. Never had she been kissed this way before. He claimed her mouth as a prize that he had won, and yet his lips were gentle as a butterfly's wings as they brushed hers. Then his insistent tongue pushed against hers, and she threw back her head and opened her lips in surrender so that his tongue went deep, caressing and tasting hers. His big hands went under her to pull her up against him, and then one of his hands went inside her bodice to stroke there. She, who had never known the ecstasy of a mutual hunger, clung to him now, trembling like a hesitant virgin while he kissed her as if he would never get enough of her. His rugged face was cold as it brushed against hers, and suddenly she wanted to warm him in the most intimate way. She reached to jerk open her bodice and put his face against her breasts. He moaned once, and then his eager lips sought her nipples. Now she was the one who moaned as his hand went to push up her skirt.

His hand stroked her thighs until she trembled with anticipation. Even if she died or were rescued tomorrow, she would have the ecstasy of this night to see what it was that she had missed in the cold, ritual matings with her husband.

"Twilight, are you sure?" He paused and drew back.

"If we were to die tomorrow, I don't want to regret that I missed this," she whispered, and pulled his mouth down to hers.

He hugged her fiercely, his mouth all over her body as he caressed her. She touched him, and he was rigid with need. She opened and enveloped him, her own greedy body pulling him deep within her. She could feel his hard lance pulsating in her as he kissed her deeper still. Then he began to ride her in a rhythm of love, and she had never experienced this soaring emotion before. She dug her nails into his broad back and hips, urging him deeper still in a frenzy of pumping and gasping. Then he began to give up his seed, and in her wonder, her own body responded, locking on to his so that he might not escape the grasp of her long legs until her body had what it craved from him.

For a moment, it was almost as if she were dying, because the firelight, the wind, everything faded but the emotion and the warmth of him riding her deep and hard, and she couldn't get enough of him. Finally, as she came to, she realized he, too, was gasping, limp and satisfied.

"Now the captain won't want you," he whispered. "You've been taken by a savage."

"Is that why you did it?"

He looked down at her. "I wanted to give you my son," he whispered. "If I don't survive this, at least I will have left a son to carry on."

Did he really care about her, or was it only his need to leave his progeny that had driven him? She dare not ask, because she was not sure she wanted the truth.

He leaned over and kissed her again, but he did not whisper words of tenderness.

What on earth had she done? Mating with a savage captor out in the middle of a hostile wilderness with possible death facing her tomorrow? She was greatly troubled, but her body was relaxing in sleep already. She felt Yellow Jacket cradle her in his arms as he rolled over on his side and they both slept.

Before dawn, Yellow Jacket shook her awake, and she blinked, uncertain how to face him this morning after last night's intimacy. She would pretend it never happened. The whole camp was stirring, babies crying, horses neighing. She knew without looking that in this bitter cold, some of the less fortunate had frozen to death last night. She might have, too, but for the warmth of Yellow Jacket's big body. Wordlessly he handed her a cup of hot water, and she looked up at him and said nothing.

Absently she reached into her pocket and touched the blue bead. She had forgotten about that. She brought it out and stared at it in the first light. Immediately, Yellow Jacket grabbed her wrist.

"Where did you get that?"

"Stop it! You're hurting me!" In their struggle, the blue bead flew from her hand and was lost in the white snow. "What's the matter with you?"

He glowered down at her. "My niece, Pretty, had a bracelet made of those. It wasn't found with her body."

"Harvey sells beads of all colors; I picked this one up off the floor of the trading post." She decided not to mention that it was under his bed.

Yellow Jacket's jaw clenched. "They say

Pretty killed herself, but I think she was murdered."

"Murdered?" She backed away, shaking her head.

"Your brother would turn a girl's head with jewelry and ribbons. Pretty was young and foolish. There were boot tracks where she was found, but they weren't those of a man who limped."

She remembered the pebbles in Harvey's boot. Without the pebbles, he did not limp.

"What's the matter with you? You're pale."

"N-Nothing," she lied. "I doubt Harvey has the courage to kill anyone."

"If I was sure, I would track him down and kill him very slowly," he said. "Anyway, it doesn't make any difference now, does it? The Muskogee are on the run, and I've got Harvey Leland's sister as a hostage." His cold tone hinted of revenge. She'd meant nothing to him but a moment's pleasure. What a fool she had been.

"I'll ride in the buggy today," she said coldly.

"No, you won't. It'll be overloaded already with our sick leader and some of the women and children. You'll ride behind me. Now, get a move on; the others are already pulling out and who knows how far the rebels are behind us?"

There was nothing to do but let him pull her up behind him on the big paint horse.

This time, his body felt tense and unrelenting when she put her arms around his waist. At least his body was breaking the cold wind. They started out again heading north, all the people stumbling through the snow, ignoring the dead and dying who lay along the trail.

"Don't look," he muttered. "We can do nothing to help them, and they know it."

She wanted to protest, but she knew he was right. "Maybe the Confederate soldiers will care for them when they catch up."

He laughed, a short, humorless laugh. "You don't really believe that," he scoffed. "Nothing will slow the rebels while they're trying to capture my people."

He spoke the truth, and she knew it. The runaways' only salvation was reaching the Union troops, who would protect them and give them food and shelter. If the migration slowed or halted, they would be overrun and killed by the pursing Confederates.

Yellow Jacket reined in and dismounted, not looking at the white girl. He had almost begun to care for her — and then she had brought out the blue bead. How could he care about the sister of the possible killer of Pretty?

A small boy, perhaps seven or eight years old, stumbled by, half leading, half carrying a toddler girl who cried softly. The boy murmured to the baby as he fell in the snow and got up to walk again. Yellow Jacket spoke to the child in Muskogee. "Boy, where is your family?"

"Dead, all dead, but I can make it to the bluecoats, get myself a gun, and fight the graycoats."

The frail child would never make it to Kansas despite his brave words, and they both knew it.

The little girl looked up at Twilight and whimpered, tears almost freezing on her cheeks.

"Oh, Yellow Jacket," the white woman said, "I'll walk so they can ride."

He made a gesture to halt her. Again to the boy, he said, "Is that your sister?"

The ragged child shook his head and dusted snow off the baby. "I found her by a dead woman who didn't make it through the night. I don't even know her tribe."

"Or her name?" Yellow Jacket's eyes were suddenly moist. The little girl reminded him of his dead niece.

The boy shook his head. "I am Seminole; I do not know her tribe."

Yellow Jacket turned to the white woman. "He's Seminole, they're a branch of the Muskogee. Their name means 'runaways.'"

"Runaways?"

He nodded. "A long time ago, the Seminole went off to Florida, but the government gathered up some of them and sent them to Indian Territory."

"I thought my brother said your people were Creeks."

Yellow Jacket frowned. "That's what whites call us because when they first saw us, we were living on creek banks. We call ourselves Muskogee."

The small boy said, "If we had a little food, we might make it." His big dark eyes were bright with hope.

Yellow Jacket turned to Twilight. "Do you have any food at all?"

"I've got a little corn bread." She reached for it, leaned over to hand it to the child. "We aren't going to leave them, are we?" she begged. "Maybe we could put them in the buggy."

"The buggy is too full already. Any more and the horse won't be able to pull it." He watched the two children wolfing down the cornbread. "Here, she can ride with you and I'll lead the horse." He lifted the baby girl up to Twilight's waiting arms. The white girl looked so natural cuddling a baby. "Her new name is Pretty."

The Seminole boy had finished his corn bread. "A good name," he said gravely, and looked up at the horse with a hopeless wistfulness.

"You shall ride, too." Yellow Jacket lifted him up to the saddle before Twilight.

The boy laughed with relief, and Pretty laughed, too, as Twilight wrapped her buffalo robe around them all. "Thank you," Twilight said.

Yellow Jacket was embarrassed to be seen as sentimental by his captive. "There is no need to thank me; they are, after all, Indian children and we must save those we can."

"All children are the same." Twilight smiled down at him as she held the children close. "What is his name?"

Yellow Jacket took the reins and began to lead the horse through the snow. There were dozens of children who might not survive today, but these two would. "Boy," he called back over his shoulder, "what is your name?"

"Wasko," the child answered. "I thank you for this, Great Warrior."

"It is no matter," Yellow Jacket said gruffly, a little embarrassed by the child's gratitude. Then to Twilight: "The boy's name is Wasko, which means 'Chigger.'"

He looked back at the boy, and the child's eyes were bright with hope. Twilight hugged the pair to her. "Yellow Jacket, can't we keep them?"

"We may not make it ourselves," he muttered, and kept walking. The thought crossed his mind that the white girl looked very natural with a child in her arms, even an Indian one. Now he had a ready-made family. *Careful,* he cautioned himself, *you must not think of her that way. She is a hostage and the sister, maybe, of Pretty's killer. No good can come of that.* Still, it was hard to reason with his heart.

The day was long and cold as they trudged northward. When they stopped to rest, Yellow Jacket went hunting and brought back a rabbit, which fed all four of them. He found a stream and broke the ice to fill the canteens. There was no coffee, but he made a nourishing broth with the rabbit bones. That night, the pitiful procession of thousands finally stumbled to a halt to make camp. Twilight made sure the two children were well fed, then bedded them down wrapped in her buffalo robe.

She felt differently about Yellow Jacket because he had rescued the children, who were not even of his own tribe. He had gone off to confer with the old chief and the other leaders. He came back looking grim.

"What is it?" she asked.

"We gained some time when those Cherokee pin Indians deserted the rebels, but now they've picked up reinforcements and are in hot pursuit again."

"What's a 'pin' Indian?"

He shrugged. "The most traditional clan. They wear crossed feathers or pins to show they are Keetoowa."

"Oh. Well, maybe you can whip them again."

He looked tired. "We'll have to try. I have

a good friend, Jim Eagle, riding with the rebels. He spared my life last time our paths crossed, only a few weeks ago. Now he'll be trying to kill me."

"It makes no sense, but then, war never does."

She watched his gaze go to the sleeping children. "Twilight, it's still a long, long way to Kansas. We don't have much of a chance of making it."

"It can't be that far," she protested.

"With the huge rebel army, including Stand Watie's crack Cherokee Mounted Rifles, chasing us? Ten miles would be too far. I think they'll catch up to us in the next several days. If I'm killed . . ." His voice trailed off, and he did not finish.

She wasn't certain what it was he meant to say. He seemed to be past his anger of this morning. Of course he had been wrong about Harvey. Her stepbrother might be of weak character, but surely he hadn't had anything to do with Pretty's death. She wondered if he was back there somewhere with the pursuing troops. She waited for Yellow Jacket to finish. Instead, he stared into the campfire, and the light flickering on his rugged face told her how concerned and worried he was. If he were killed . . . She realized suddenly that she couldn't bear that thought. Maybe it was only because if he were dead, she wasn't certain what would become of her and these two helpless children. She didn't want to think about what the next several days would bring. At the moment, she and these two children were being well cared for by the big Creek warrior, and she had to be content with that.

When she looked at him, he was sitting cross-legged by the fire, shivering a little in his worn, ragged buckskins. "Here," she said, "I'll share my blanket with you."

He looked at her, hesitated. The fire had died down, and the darkness seemed pitch black except for the snow reflected in the flames.

"I — I want to. We may not be alive tomorrow." She held out her arms to him and he came to her, enveloping her in his powerful embrace, and she felt safe and protected. She was not sure whether he cared for her or was only blocking out tomorrow's possible terrors. As for herself, she didn't ask herself any questions; she only immersed herself in the heat and the power and the passion of the man. If he were going to be killed in battle tomorrow, she wanted to be in his arms tonight.

Chapter 11

December nineteenth. Captain Franklin Wellsley thought wistfully of Christmas as he squatted in front of his campfire and rubbed his cold hands together. Any idea of quick victory against the Yankee Indians, with lots of medals and parades to please Mother, had long since fled. He was also weary of Harvey Leland, whom he had already decided cared not a fig for the kidnapped stepsister but seemed greedy and too eager to know of Franklin's financial affairs.

The young Cherokee scout, Clem Rogers, strode into camp. "Colonel Cooper sent me to fetch you, Captain. He thinks those Yankee Indians have settled in on Bird Creek up ahead. I reckon we'll be attackin' soon."

"I don't see what keeps them going," Franklin muttered, "burdened by women, children, and livestock, and poorly armed and provisioned."

The scout pushed his battered hat back. "Hope, sir — they're runnin' on pure hope."

Captain Wellsley didn't answer. *Hope? Yes. Hope and sheer courage.* He had a soft spot for underdogs. Of course, there was always the matter of the kidnapped Mrs. Dumont, who might not even still be alive. "All right, Rogers," he said, and stood up, "I'll see the colonel and then pass the word to the troops."

Twilight was so weary, she could barely dismount as Yellow Jacket reached up to take the two sleepy children from the saddle. How long had they been on the run? Weeks. It must be at least the middle of December. She thought with longing of Christmas and feasting and elegant balls. "Is there any food?" she asked as she led the children to where the Creek warrior was building a fire. "The children are hungry."

"Maybe I can snare a rabbit or break the ice and catch a fish in the creek," he answered, but he didn't sound too hopeful. He gathered up some rope and a knife and strode away from the fire. She took little Pretty in her lap and held her close to warm her. The boy hunched closer to the fire and looked at Twilight, his face thin and drawn. "Do you think we will reach Kansas soon?"

Frankly, she had long since given up hope of reaching Kansas at all, but hope was all these people had — she must not take that from them. "I'm sure of it," she answered as brightly as she could muster, "and when we get there, the Union soldiers will feed us and give us plenty of blankets and a place to sleep with real wood floors."

Little Wasko smiled. "And what will you do? Will you stay with the white people?"

She hadn't given that a thought. Did Yellow Jacket intend to turn her over to the Union officers? "I don't know," she answered truthfully.

"I thought you were Yellow Jacket's woman," he said.

Was she? She shook her head. "I have a brother among the rebels, and . . ." She did not finish, realizing suddenly that she wasn't sure she wanted to return to the whites. Yet it was absolutely insane to consider staying with the Indians . . . wasn't it?

Pretty had gone to sleep in her arms. "What about you?" Twilight asked. "Will you try to find your folks?"

"I have none left." The child shook his head. "I will join up with Yellow Jacket and go fight the rebels if he will let me."

"Someone has to look after Pretty if I go back to the whites," Twilight said, stroking the toddler's black hair.

The boy looked disappointed. "I thought you would stay and take care of her until Yellow Jacket and I returned from battle."

He was thinking of them as a family. Twilight shook her head. "I don't think I can do that. I'll be expected to return to my own people."

"Do you want to go back?" He nodded toward the south.

She blinked, surprised at herself that she didn't know the answer. "We'll see," she said finally. "Now, you take my blanket and move closer to the fire. Yellow Jacket will be back soon with some food." She said it matter-of-factly, and realized she was confident that the big Creek warrior would take good care of them.

After an hour, Yellow Jacket returned. He had managed to kill two fat squirrels, and they roasted them and ate. Later he helped her bed the children down. Then he sat next to her before the fire and spoke softly. "The rebels are moving up on us. We're going to stage a night attack at the creek — try to take them by surprise. They won't be expecting it." He reached for his extra ammunition.

"Be careful," she blurted without thinking.

He looked at her, surprise in his dark eyes. "You know if they win, you might be freed."

"I know." She nodded. "But if I go, what will happen to young Wasko and Pretty? Harvey wouldn't want them, so I can't take them with me."

The big warrior's expression grew troubled, and she wondered what he was thinking. He reached out and put his hand on her arm very gently. "If I don't come back, turn the children over to one of the women and make

223

your way to the rebels. Use your underskirt for a truce flag so they won't shoot at you. I'm sorry I've put you through this. As for what happened the other night . . ."

"Don't say it." She shook her head. "We were both caught up in the heat of the moment; that's all."

"You regret it, then?"

She looked away. "I don't know. It — it complicates things."

"I always hated whites, especially Southern whites." His voice was low, and he stared into the fire. "And then I met you."

She waited for him to continue, but he did not. Somewhere nearby, Smoke yelled at him to come on. "Take care," she whispered. "I'll pray to the Master of Breath for your safety."

"If I never see you again, remember what I said about making a truce flag and finding your way to the rebels." Then he disappeared into the brush. For a few minutes she listened, hearing the sound of men moving lightly across the prairie — or was it only the harsh wind blowing? She didn't know how far down the stream the warriors were setting up their ambush, attempting to buy more time for their women and children to get away. The small Union force of Indians didn't stand a chance. But neither had they at the battle at Round Mountain. She waited, her heart beating hard as she strained to hear.

The sun moved low on the horizon. Now

there were shouts and the sound of galloping horses, rebel yells and gunshots; lots of gunshots. Both children came awake, the baby crying. All Twilight could do was cuddle them close and pray, knowing now that she was worried about Yellow Jacket — not because of her fate should he be killed, but worried about him because she cared about him. The thought shocked her.

Night came on, and gunfire echoed in the cold darkness; the acrid scent of gunpowder drifted on the icy air. A riderless gray horse galloped past, and in the distance, men screamed faintly in mortal agony. The sounds of battle echoed through the night. She could only hope Yellow Jacket wasn't breathing his last breath somewhere along Bird Creek.

After what seemed like hours, the shooting and the shouting dwindled off, and toward dawn, Yellow Jacket galloped back into camp, his dark face alight with triumph. "We've beaten them off, killed dozens in our ambush. We'll make it to Kansas yet."

He swung down off his horse, and without thinking, Twilight went into his arms, hugging him close. "We were so worried."

"I wasn't!" Little Wasko said proudly. "I knew we would win. Someday I will be big and I will fight the rebels."

Yellow Jacket reached down to pat his head. "By the time you are big, maybe this will all be over. Now, start breaking camp;

we've got to be on the move again before the rebels recover and start after us again."

Around them, she could hear others breaking camp, loading wagons. Old Opothleyahola's badly outnumbered forces were on the move again.

Days blended into days, and their journey north seemed no faster than before, yet still the rebels were on their trail. It was night, and Yellow Jacket sat at the council fire and looked around at the other leaders. The ancient one coughed hard — so hard, he almost bent double. Yellow Jacket exchanged a look with Smoke. They both seemed to know that if the old leader died, their followers would lose heart and the rebels would overrun and slaughter them. Like Moses leading his people to the promised land, Opothleyahola was leading the Muskogee.

The old Creek leader stopped coughing and looked around the circle. "It has been days since we defeated the graycoats at that place they call Bird Creek. Our people are sick, weary, and out of food and ammunition. I now begin to doubt that we can make it."

Smoke protested, "But it is not far now to Kansas. We have come a long, long way."

Another leader grunted, "And that way is strewn with bodies of our dead. It seems Great Chief Lincoln is not sending us help after all."

No one said anything. They had all trusted the Union to keep Lincoln's promise, yet so far, there had been no bluecoat soldiers coming to help them.

"Maybe," Smoke suggested, "maybe they are still coming and are up ahead. It's only a few more miles."

The others glanced about at each other, still hopeful.

Opothleyahola looked to Yellow Jacket. "What think you, great warrior? Do you think they are coming?"

He did not think so, but he could not kill their hope, since hope was all that kept them going. "Perhaps. Anyway, even if they misunderstood and are not coming, what alternative do we have? If we stop, the rebels will overrun and kill us, so we must keep moving north."

The others nodded.

"We have lost many good warriors fighting two battles," Alligator grunted.

"But we have won," Yellow Jacket pointed out. "Even an enemy with plenty of supplies and ammunition is no match for brave men protecting their women and children."

"Hear! Hear!" shouted the others.

"Speaking of women," one of the others said, "Yellow Jacket, you have the white woman with you still?"

He shrugged carelessly, but his heart beat hard. "We need her for her medical help."

"She has no more medicine," one said, "so she's not much help. Would the rebels stop their pursuit if we freed her?"

"I don't know." Yellow Jacket stared into the fire. He did not want to let her go. When he closed his eyes, he could feel her warmth against him on the cold night, the softness of her skin, the scent of her long hair.

Billy Bowlegs said, "Perhaps we could trade her to the enemy for food and supplies."

Smoke snorted. "You would trust the graycoats enough to parley with them? They are sure to betray us, no matter who gives their word."

"That's right," Yellow Jacket said, "we cannot trust them enough to try such a trade."

The Creek leader began to cough again. "Still, Yellow Jacket, she is our last hope. If things get worse, we must try to use her to bargain with."

Yellow Jacket wanted to protest, but he dare not. He knew that the captain might still desire Twilight enough to make any kind of a deal to get her back. He pictured her in the white man's arms, in his bed, and his soul cried out against it. "We'll see," he said, and stood up. "Right now, all we can do is keep moving north."

Days passed as they stumbled forward. Even Twilight had forgotten everything except keeping herself and the two children alive. The cold weather did not let up as they traveled, and always behind them was the threat of pursuing Confederate soldiers. Yellow Jacket looked wearier and grimmer each day, yet he encouraged the others and often rode behind, putting himself in danger to round up the stragglers so the rebels wouldn't capture them. Some of the time, he found enough game to feed their little ready-made family. Sometimes there was nothing but hot water with bones boiling in it to make a thin broth. At night the four of them huddled together under their blankets, attempting to keep from freezing to death.

Every morning, when they arose and started north again, they saw others lying very still in their last, long sleep. For them, the terrible journey north was finished. But they had died free, Twilight thought. A few weeks ago she would have wept like any protected Southern belle to be amid so much misery, but she had changed. All that mattered now was surviving and getting these two young children to the safety of Kansas. She no longer asked to stop and bury the dead they passed; the moving tribe could not spare the energy or the time on those who were past caring for. Always the Indians, under their weakening leader, Opothleyahola, kept their eyes on the north and listened for the sound of the pursuing Confederates.

On December 26, the rebels caught up with the fleeing Indians again, at a place whites called Patriot Hills. Only this time, the Muskogee could not win. They were out of ammunition, their warriors exhausted or wounded and vastly outnumbered. On this, their third major battle as they fought their way north, the Union Indians lost.

No one needed to tell Twilight that the Creeks had lost. All day she had listened to the Confederate cannons booming through the cold air and the screams of the dead and dying. Now Yellow Jacket galloped back into camp, where she and the two children had taken refuge in the bushes.

"They are right behind us," he shouted as he dismounted. "Give me a scrap of your petticoat; then get on my horse and let's move out!"

"My petticoat?" Around them were confusion and cries as women and children fled before the oncoming Confederate forces. Asking no questions, she tore off a scrap and gave it to him. Surely her brave warrior was not going to surrender. His stern face forbade her to question him. Instead, she mounted up and let Yellow Jacket hand her the two children.

"I'll cover the retreat!" he shouted. "Get the children to safety!"

She started to protest but realized she must save the children. Ahead of them, frantic people were running or whipping up tired mounts or thin mules pulling wagons. "Surely we must be within a few miles of the Kansas border."

He nodded, but he did not smile. Like the others, he had finally realized that Great Chief Lincoln was not sending anyone to help them. A handful of starving Union Indians with only the barest of supplies and primitive weapons would have to save themselves. "Get out of here!" he shouted, and whacked the big pinto horse across the rump. It took off at a gallop.

Yellow Jacket watched them ride away before turning back to the fight. He had already made his decision about Twilight. He was going to return her to the rebels because he couldn't stand to see her killed in the massacre that must surely come the next time the graycoats attacked. He held his position until almost dark, giving the slow and the wounded a few precious hours to escape, and then he took the scrap of white fabric, put it on a broken lance, and walked boldly toward the rebel camp.

"Halt! Who goes there?" the guard challenged.

"I come under a flag of truce," Yellow Jacket shouted back. "I must see Captain Wellsley."

"Drop your weapon."

Yellow Jacket raised his free hand slowly.

"You can see, I have none."

The reb looked at him suspiciously. "Got a lotta grit comin' in this way."

He didn't care if they killed him as long as he could save Twilight and the children, maybe slow the attack. "It's a matter of great importance."

"Come ahead, then." The other gestured with his rifle.

Yellow Jacket walked ahead of the sentry into the rebel camp, holding his ragged white flag high. Curious gray-clad soldiers began to gather.

"We should hang him," one of the soldiers muttered, and others took up the cry.

And then Yellow Jacket's old friend, Cherokee Jim Eagle, stepped out of the crowd. "No, and I'll shoot the first man who tries. He's here under a flag of truce. Clem, go get the captain."

Yellow Jacket nodded in gratitude to his old friend and watched the mixed-blood Cherokee scout run for the officer. In moments, Captain Wellsley, followed by Harvey Leland, strode into the crowd. "What's going on here?"

The sentry saluted. "Injun wants to see you, sir."

The three men looked each other over. Yellow Jacket was suddenly jealous of Captain Wellsley, the man who would end up with Twilight, but he must think of her safety. "Can we talk?" Yellow Jacket asked.

Harvey frowned. "Don't trust him, Captain. You know these Injuns — he's probably got a knife hidden and he'll try to kill you."

Yellow Jacket took a deep breath to control his anger. "I gave my word I carried no weapon, and I am not like the whites — a Muskogee warrior keeps his word."

"But —" Harvey began.

"Shut up, Leland," the captain snapped. "We'll talk. Yellow Jacket, let's go into my tent and parley."

Yellow Jacket nodded, and the three went into the tent. Outside, a muttering crowd of rebel soldiers gathered.

The captain frowned at Harvey. "This is a private conversation, Leland. I don't need any civilians."

"But, Captain —"

"I'll call you if I need you."

Leland hesitated, frowned, and went out.

Inside, the two men looked each other over.

"Coffee?" the captain said.

Yellow Jacket hesitated. He had not tasted coffee in several weeks. "If you are having some."

The other nodded, poured two tin cups full, and handed one over. Yellow Jacket wrapped his cold hands around it and sighed at the warmth.

The captain sipped his. He looked older,

more mature somehow than he had when this chase first began. War and bloodshed would do that to a man, Yellow Jacket knew. "Is she all right?" he asked anxiously.

There was no need to ask who the captain was speaking of; it showed in his face.

Yellow Jacket sipped the strong, hot brew and nodded. "She's all right. Do the rebels intend to harry us all the way to the Kansas border? We are out of food and ammunition; it is becoming a terrible slaughter."

The captain played with his cup, not looking at him. "That isn't my decision to make. I'd like to see it end, too. The slaughter of helpless women and children sickens me, and they pose no danger to the Confederacy. But about Mrs. Dumont —"

"That's why I'm here; I want to arrange to exchange her for some food and medicine. Opothleyahola is slowly dying. We are almost to the Kansas border, but I think, if he dies before my people reach it, they will lose all hope, sit down in the snow, and die, too."

"Is Mrs. Dumont all right?" the captain asked, and his love for her shone in his pale eyes.

Yellow Jacket looked away, afraid that his own eyes might betray his love for the girl with the sun-streaked hair. "She's all right."

The captain stared at him. "You care about her, too."

Care about her? She meant more to him than his own life; he realized now what he had been unwilling to admit to himself all these weeks. It would be like tearing his heart out to give her up, but it was for her own good. He tried to shrug carelessly. "We need the food and blankets of the ransom; that's all."

"You're a poor liar," the officer said gently. He opened his mouth, started to ask something, then stopped. The silence hung heavy on the air. Perhaps he did not want to know the answer; perhaps he dare not ask if Yellow Jacket had made love to her. Instead, he cleared his throat. "I can't promise anything," Captain Wellsley said. "I'll have to see what my senior officer says."

"At least you speak with a straight tongue." Yellow Jacket felt growing respect for this officer. He was a good man and a rich one. He would take care of Twilight, and she need never want for anything again. "The fact that you will try is enough for me."

"She wants to return?"

"Of course," Yellow Jacket said, "why would she not?" He did not know whether she did, but of course she would. The captain offered safety and security. Any white girl would want that. "She — she belongs with you, and I know that." He looked away. It hurt him to think of her in this white man's embrace, but he must not think of that now. He would sacrifice his own feelings for her safety.

"I — I thought perhaps you two might have . . . never mind." The captain pushed his hat back and did not look at Yellow Jacket. "Yes, I think my senior officer will be willing to ransom her. I can't offer ammunition," he said, "but I might work out an exchange for food and blankets."

This proud Southerner might not want Twilight if he realized she had been in Yellow Jacket's arms, so now the warrior lied. "She means nothing to me. I kept her because I thought the army wouldn't attack us with her as a hostage."

The captain looked relieved. "I want to marry her, but I was afraid —"

"Your personal feelings for her are nothing to me," Yellow Jacket scoffed, and put down his cup. "You set up the exchange. There's a grove of trees about halfway between the two sides, several miles up ahead, only a little distance from the border. Clem Rogers or Jim Eagle will know where it is. I will bring her there at dawn. Come alone."

"All right." The young officer looked relieved. "You have my word we won't set up an ambush."

"I trust you, Captain, but I don't trust the others. About Mrs. Dumont . . ."

"Yes?"

"Be good to her; she deserves happiness."

"I intend to spend the rest of my life taking care of her, if she'll have me." The captain nodded and hesitantly held out his hand. They shook awkwardly.

Yellow Jacket's eyes blurred suddenly, and he felt as if his heart were being ripped out. He turned to leave.

Behind him the captain said, "I want you to know, if it were up to me, we would let your people go without slaughtering them."

Yellow Jacket paused and looked back. "Thank you for that. I will bring Twilight to the grove in the morning."

"I'll be there, no matter what I have to do to get those supplies," the captain promised.

They went outside, where the curious soldiers had gathered. "Rogers," he ordered, "give this brave as much food as he can carry, and see he gets out of our camp safely. He is under a flag of truce."

There was grumbling, but Yellow Jacket straightened his shoulders and took the supplies the rebel scout gave him. Then he pushed through the crowd, headed out of camp. He had to blink hard to keep his eyes from misting. Tomorrow morning he was going to return his white love to the life she should lead, once again a protected Southern belle who would marry the rich captain and return to an elegant life. It was better this way.

Once he left the camp, he set off for his

own lines at a gallop. It was almost dark, and he had the little bit of food Rogers had given him to share around. In a few precious hours, he would have to give Twilight up, never to see her again. He would not think about that; he would think about the moments she had spent in his arms, and those memories would have to last him a lifetime.

Behind him, Harvey Leland rejoined Captain Wellsley, and they stared after the Indian as he faded into the darkness.

"Damned savage," Harvey muttered, "ought to have shot him in the back."

"We're men of honor, remember?" the captain scolded him. "I gave him my word as a Southern gentleman."

Harvey squelched a smirk. To hell with gentlemen and all that honor crap. Still, he must not anger the officer if Harvey hoped to gain anything. "He still got Twilight?"

The officer nodded and sighed. "I've made a deal with him to ransom her in exchange for food and supplies."

"Now, where you gonna get extra food and supplies?" Harvey groused.

The officer glared at him. "I believe you have a wagonload with you, Mr. Leland, that you thought you'd sell to the Confederate army at big prices when we ran low. I'm confiscating that."

"What?" Harvey squawked, "and payin' me how much?"

"Why, I thought you'd be happy to provide the ransom for your sister."

Harvey hesitated. He must not look greedy, not if he might end up as this man's brother-in-law. "Why, of course, Captain, I never meant anything else."

"Good," the officer said curtly.

"I want to go along on the exchange," Harvey said, thinking he would have his revenge on that damned savage yet. Besides, he wasn't about to hand over a free wagon of goods to Injuns.

"No." Captain Wellsley shook his head. "I promised I'd come alone and there'd be no soldiers. He's afraid of a trap, and I gave him my word."

"I understand," Harvey said. To himself, he said, *I didn't give my word. I'll follow behind and bring some soldiers with me. We'll set a trap and kill that damned savage!*

Chapter 12

Yellow Jacket rode into camp after dark and dismounted.

Twilight came to meet him. "I was getting worried. Where did you go?"

"I went to see if I could steal some rebel supplies," he lied, and began to untie the packages from his saddle. "I got a few things. Here, give some of this bread and meat to the children, and I'll take what's left over to Opothleyahola and some of the other campfires."

She took the package with a nod. "I'll try to ration it so we'll have some for tomorrow."

She wouldn't be here after tomorrow, but he did not tell her that. "I think maybe I can work a bargain with some corrupt rebel to get more."

"I don't like it," she said, looking up at him with those big, dusky lavender eyes. "I'm afraid for you."

He did not answer, merely dismissed her with a curt nod. This was their last night together, he knew, but he did not tell her that. After they shared the food around, they put little Pretty and young Wasko down to sleep

240

in the shelter of some bushes. As the fire dwindled, he watched his white love, thinking she had never looked so beautiful. His heart was so full, it threatened to break, knowing that he must lose her forever tomorrow. "At least we have tonight."

"What?" Twilight looked up.

"Nothing. I am sorry that I forced you to come along and share our hardships."

She put her hand on his broad shoulder. "I am glad I came," she murmured, and rose to kiss his cheek.

"Don't," he said. It would not be right to make love to her tonight, as he yearned to do, and then send her back tomorrow to the white officer who would marry her.

"You're worried."

He nodded, wondering if tomorrow's swap would go off without a hitch. He would have to steel himself not to back out of the bargain. "We need to get some rest." He took his blanket and lay down by the fire.

Twilight was puzzled. He seemed distant tonight, as if he hid something. Well, no doubt after this last terrible defeat at the hands of the Confederates, all the Creeks and their allies were facing the very real and grim possibility that they might not make it to Kansas — and it was only a few miles away. It would be so tragic if they did not, she thought; the Union Indians had fought hard and risked much. They deserved to win.

More than that, she didn't want Yellow Jacket killed or captured by the other side. He deserved to stay free forever.

She took her blanket and curled up next to him, snuggling against his broad back. "I am cold," she whispered.

"I'll give you my blanket."

"Why do you not talk to me? Is it something I've done?"

"Don't ever think that." He turned toward her then, his rugged face grave and serious. "Twilight, if I could arrange to get you back to your people safely, you'd want to go, wouldn't you?"

She blinked in surprise. "Of course." So he did expect that tomorrow there might be another battle and he would be killed and the Creeks defeated. The thought saddened her, and she felt a hot tear make a crooked trail down her face.

"Don't cry; I can't stand it," he murmured, and kissed the tear off her cheek.

She turned her head ever so slightly so that her lips found his. For only a moment he hesitated, and then he was kissing her, while she thought of the uncertainty of their fate. Neither of them might survive through tomorrow. She put her arms around his neck, kissing him with a fervor and a passion that surprised her because she had never been passionate about anything.

"At least we have tonight," she promised

aloud as she kissed him with even more passion, and he gasped and pulled her into his protective embrace.

They made slow, pleasurable, tender love, and again she was struck with the wonder of it, and pitied women who had never known such ecstasy. Afterward they dropped off to sleep in each other's arms, and she dreamed that they were free and warm, that there was plenty of food, and that the four of them had become a family.

It was already past daylight when she awoke and sat up. "I'm sorry." She looked at Yellow Jacket, who squatted by the fire, grim-faced and silent. Funny, he held a flag made of that scrap of her white petticoat. "Where are the children?"

He stared into the fire. "I've gotten an old woman to take charge of them."

"But I want to look after them. I feel like they're my children now." She stood up and ran her hand through her tousled hair. "Do you think we'll make it to Kansas today?"

"You aren't going." He shook his head and stood up slowly. She could read nothing in his rugged, closed face. "Twilight, when I rode away yesterday, I went to the rebels to meet with Captain Wellsley."

"What?"

"He's willing to do anything to get you back."

243

"You're — you're talking about trading me?" She felt both shocked and betrayed.

"Mrs. Dumont," he began, and his voice was cold, "I've made an offer to trade you for food and supplies. I wanted to get ammunition, but they wouldn't give that."

She tried to speak, and for a moment nothing came out. He wasn't taking her with him. He had betrayed her. "Are you telling me that I'm nothing but a hostage after all?"

He nodded, turning his face away so that she could not see his expression. "It's a big ransom. My people need the food and supplies, and he was eager to trade for you."

"Why, you . . . !" She slapped him hard, the sound ringing through the cold dawn.

"If you were a man, I'd kill you for that." He reached up to touch his reddened cheek, his eyes blazing yet sad.

She couldn't stop the flood of angry tears. "You've seduced me, made me think you cared, and it was only —"

"What better trick to keep you from running away?" He turned and began to saddle his horse.

"I hate you for that!" she screamed.

He winced, then continued to saddle up and tied the white flag to his saddle. "We have to leave now. Our rendezvous is for midmorning, and this exchange is all that's keeping the troops from attacking our stragglers this morning."

She had never felt as angry and betrayed as she did at this moment. "All right," she snapped, "at least I know it's not only white men who speak with forked tongues."

He winced and, for a long minute, said nothing. "Here, mount up," he said finally. "They'll be waiting."

She wanted to storm at him, hit him, scratch his face, but there was no point now. With a sigh, she ignored his outstretched hand and climbed up on the horse. He swung up before her. She sat stiff, making sure their two bodies did not touch. In the early morning fog, she could see shadowy shapes as the beaten, hungry Indians took the trail again, heading north. In spite of the misery, she had felt one with them and longed to be with them when they reached the freedom of Kansas, now only a few miles away.

He clucked to his horse, and they started through the brush, headed back south, carrying the ragged white flag made from her tattered petticoat.

She should be thrilled and delighted that she was being rescued to return to the life she had before. That had been no life at all; she realized that now. Yellow Jacket had said the captain wanted her. She could be a rich society lady in Austin, with stylish clothes, a big house, and a fine carriage. More than that, she would have wealth and security.

Somehow, none of that mattered now.

After a while, they rode into a clearing, where Captain Wellsley waited with a big mule loaded with supplies. He looked anxiously at Twilight. "Mrs. Dumont, are you well?"

"I'm fine." She slid from the horse and stepped across the circle.

"You came alone?" Yellow Jacket looked around.

"I told you I would," the officer said, "and I'm a man of honor."

"I know you are," Yellow Jacket said from his horse. "That is the only reason I came."

"Just a minute!" Harvey Leland stepped out suddenly from behind a tree. "I decided to invite myself along."

The captain looked shocked. "Damn you, Leland, you weren't invited to this exchange. Believe me, Yellow Jacket, I didn't —"

"I know." The Indian glared at Harvey. "I've had dealings with the Indian agent before."

Harvey stepped out into the circle and tried to put his arm around Twilight. "Oh, my dear sister, I've been so worried about you." He took off his coat and put it around her shoulders.

She pulled away from him in distaste. "I'm all right, Harvey. I wasn't mistreated."

"Dirty savages," Harvey snarled, and made a signal. Immediately, Clem Rogers and a dozen Confederate soldiers, all well armed, rose up behind every boulder and tree.

Yellow Jacket looked around. "I've been betrayed."

The captain's face paled. "I swear to you, I didn't —"

"Of course you didn't," Harvey grinned. "I went to the colonel, and he gave me the troops to follow you."

"Well," said the captain, "as senior officer here, these troops are under my command. Lower your rifles, men."

The men looked startled but obeyed his order.

Harvey swore loud and long. "Captain, are you loco? Surely you aren't just gonna let this savage ride out of here with this big load of valuable supplies."

The captain nodded. "Yes, I am. I gave him my word, and I think I got the best of the deal." His pale eyes turned to look at Twilight, betraying how he felt about her. Now he walked over and handed Yellow Jacket the lead rope of the mule. "This is enough to get some of your people to Kansas."

"But those are my supplies!" Harvey wailed.

"Oh, shut up, Harvey," Twilight snapped. Her spunk surprised herself almost as much as it surprised her stepbrother. "You've cheated his people out of more than enough to pay for those things."

Yellow Jacket smiled at her as he took the lead rope, but she did not smile back. Instead, she looked away. She had thought he loved her, and he had traded her for a load of blankets and supplies. At that moment, she hated him so bad, she wanted to kill him. She put her cold hands into the pockets of Harvey's coat, touched something, and brought it out with a cry of surprise. A broken bracelet of blue beads. "Where on earth . . . ?"

Yellow Jacket jerked up, stared at the bracelet. "That belonged to my niece. It disappeared the night she died."

Twilight turned to stare at Harvey, and at that moment, the guilty look on his fat face told her the truth. "You murdered her, didn't you?"

"I didn't mean to," he whined. "She was expectin' a baby and wanted me to marry —"

"You rotten . . . !" The big warrior's hand went instinctively for a weapon, but he had come to this meeting unarmed.

Twilight saw Harvey's plump hand go under his vest, and the silver flash of a pistol even as she dove for it. "Yellow Jacket, dear one, look out!"

She caught Harvey's wrist, and they struggled for the gun as Yellow Jacket and the captain watched helplessly. At that moment, she realized it didn't matter what Yellow

Jacket had done — she loved him and would do whatever it took to protect him, even if Harvey killed her.

They struggled for the pistol, and a shot rang out. Harvey's fat face froze in shock. He paused, let go of the weapon, and it tumbled to the ground as he grabbed for his belly and blood ran out between his fingers. She backed away in horror.

"At ease, men," the captain shouted to the soldiers as he ran forward and picked up the pistol.

Yellow Jacket, on his great horse, hesitated. "All right, Captain, you've got me."

"Oh, Captain Wellsley, please," Twilight implored, "let him go. He's done nothing but protect me, and I love him."

"Don't listen to her," Yellow Jacket shouted. "She's out of her mind with shock. Take her away with you."

The captain didn't seem to hear him. He looked from Yellow Jacket to the weeping Twilight. "You — you love him?"

"I love him," she declared, strong and self-reliant now. "Please let him go. I'll go back with you — anything — just let him go."

"No, she doesn't!" Yellow Jacket protested. "She'd make you a good wife, Captain —"

"Mrs. Dumont, do you speak the truth?" Wellsley asked.

She nodded, too overcome with emotion to speak. "Let Yellow Jacket return to his people, and I'll go with you," she said. "I promise I'll make you a good wife."

The captain looked at the pistol in his hand and seemed to consider. If he brought one of the Indian leaders in, he'd be a hero and he'd still get the girl. If he let him go, his troops might talk, and sooner or later he'd be dishonorably discharged for freeing an enemy.

Time seemed to stand still for a heartbeat as the captain made his decision. He looked at her with tears in his eyes. "It's obvious you belong with Yellow Jacket. Now, you two take your supplies and get out of here before I change my mind."

Twilight could hardly believe what she heard. "What — what about Harvey?"

The captain looked at the dead man on the ground. "Since he surely killed Pretty, I reckon justice has been served. And you, Mrs. Dumont — I knew your husband, so I figure you deserve a better man."

She looked at him, a question in her eyes, but he shook his head. "You don't want to know."

With a cry of relief, she ran to her warrior, and he lifted her up on the horse before him. She put her arms around his waist and hugged him as if she would never let go.

The captain sighed and stuck the pistol in his belt. "I know when Colonel Cooper finds out about this, I'll face court-martial —"

"About what?" Clem Rogers grinned. "We didn't see nothin', did we, boys?"

The troops grinned and shook their heads. "Nobody liked Harvey Leland."

The captain looked up at Yellow Jacket. "We may yet meet on the field of battle, but I hope not. Now, take your woman and your supplies and go with the others. If you hurry, you should make the Kansas border this afternoon before the Confederate troops can catch up with you."

Twilight looked down at him. "Thank you, Captain."

He nodded. "I can't say that I didn't wish things hadn't turned out differently, Mrs. Dumont, but everyone in Austin knows me, and if you should ever change your mind —"

"I won't." She said it with stubborn determination, so unlike the pliant, shy woman she had been only weeks before.

Yellow Jacket raised his hand and slowly saluted the officer. "You're a man of honor," he said softly. "It renews my faith that someday our two peoples might live in peace."

The captain returned his salute. "Good luck."

Yellow Jacket took the mule's lead rope and turned toward the north.

Twilight was leaving all the best that white civilization had to offer, but all that mattered to her was the man who rode with her. For him, she would sacrifice everything as long as they could be together. They would rejoin the children as a family. Up ahead lay Kansas and freedom. Up ahead lay a life with Yellow Jacket. It was more than enough. She didn't look back as they rode out.

PART TWO

Jim Eagle's (Wohali's) Story

Chapter 13

Army headquarters, June 6, 1864

"You realize, don't you, Miss Grant, that if you are caught, you may be shot?" The major turned away from his office window and stared at her.

"I — I understand. That's usually what they do to spies, isn't it?" April took a deep breath and reached for a lace handkerchief from the bodice of her pale blue dress. *What had she let herself in for, and was it too late to back out?*

"Yes." The officer ran his fingers through his gray beard. "I'm glad you're so strong for our cause."

Cause? She didn't give a fig for either side's cause. "I was promised there'd be a big reward. . . ."

He frowned at her in evident disapproval. "Reward? Yes, of course. That is, if you get out alive and get the information we need." He paced the small, cluttered office. "As I said before, we're having a lot of bad luck in Indian Territory lately, which makes us suspect we have an informant among our troops."

"A soldier?" She listened to the sounds of men drilling on the parade ground outside.

He shrugged. "We have no way of knowing; that's where you come in. It could be anyone: a soldier, a scout, a trader, even a camp follower — someone is obviously passing vital information to the enemy."

April chewed her lip. This was sounding more and more dangerous. The money was no good if she didn't live to spend it. "When I heard you were looking for a volunteer, I had no idea I might have to go into the Nations."

"We'd rather we had a man, but we didn't find one with your qualifications." He sat down in the chair behind his cluttered desk. "You're Cherokee, aren't you? We wanted someone who knows the landscape and speaks the language."

She didn't like to admit that she had some Indian blood. "Half-breed," they had called her at that snooty Miss Priddy's Female Academy in Boston. "My name is April Grant," she reminded him in an icy tone.

"Have it your way, but our sources tell us your Cherokee name is Kawoni Giyuga and you were born and raised in Indian Territory until five years ago, when your white father took you north. Your parents are now both dead."

Kawoni. "April" in the Cherokee language,

the month of her birth. "That's right," she admitted.

"You're tall and slender for a girl, and you have a deeper voice than most, so maybe you could pass yourself off as a common soldier."

"A soldier!" She stood up, and the hoops swayed under her pale blue dress. "Surely you jest."

"Didn't you learn to ride and shoot in your younger days? And you do speak Cherokee?"

She was almost twenty now. Her youth in the Indian Territory seemed a century away, and she didn't want to be reminded of it. She swallowed back her trepidation, reminding herself that with the reward, she could buy respectability in the white world and turn her back on her Cherokee heritage forever. "All that's true," she admitted grudgingly. She studied the officer, wondering if she could trust him. He might have been handsome except that he had a crooked nose and a big mole on his right cheek.

The major paused to light a cigar. "We'll find a way to sneak you into the Nations and issue you uniforms from both sides. If you do not turn up anything from one, change uniforms, go over to the other, and keep your ears open. The only clue we might have is an X."

"An X?"

He nodded. "It seems to have a special

meaning, but we aren't certain what it is. If you suspect someone, try drawing that letter and see if you get any response. Above all, be careful and trust no one."

April wavered. Did she really need money this badly? Yes, to live like a respectable white girl named April Grant and not be ridiculed for being a half-breed Injun anymore. She went to the window and looked toward the troops drilling outside. The weather was warm, and the scent of the roses beneath the window mingled with the smell of sweating horses and dust from the army barracks. "If I find the spy?"

The officer took a deep puff of his cigar, and the rich scent mingled with the others drifting on the warm air. "Miss Grant, the less you know, the better, in case . . ." His voice trailed off.

"In case what?" She whirled to confront him.

He chewed his cigar and studied her, and seemed to decide she could take the news. "There's always a possibility that you might be exposed, and — and the enemy might do whatever it takes to find out how much you know."

Rape and torture, she thought, and shuddered. "You mean, before they shoot me?"

"I told you it was chancy at best." He didn't meet her gaze, obviously embarrassed to be sending a mere girl into a dangerous situation. "I will sneak into the Territory myself in a few weeks and find a way to contact you. When you think you have vital information, find me and pass it on. Then we'll try to get you out."

"Try?"

"This is war, Miss Grant, and the only thing that matters is winning. The enemy has had bad luck lately. Have you heard about Cold Harbor?"

She shook her head. The name meant nothing to her.

"Cold Harbor, Virginia" — the officer smiled with satisfaction — "happened only a couple of days ago. Big defeat for the enemy; seven thousand causalities in less than ten minutes. A few more battles like that and we'll win this war fast."

Seven thousand causalities. A staggering number. And her death might make it seven thousand and one. No one would care, since she was all alone in the world. "When do I start?"

The officer took a puff and stared at her. "Right away. We'll sneak you into the Union fort first. After a few weeks, I'll be joining you there with further instructions. It's possible we might ask you to desert and go to the Confederate side. General Stand Watie's Confederate Cherokee Mounted Rifles are in southern Indian Territory, and with your background, you can blend in."

She hated to be continually reminded of her shameful Cherokee heritage. When she had her hands on that reward money, she would turn her back on her past and live like a rich, respectable white lady in Boston or New York, with fine clothes and a fancy carriage. The girls who had snubbed her at Miss Priddy's Academy would be begging for invitations to her social events after the war when April was married to a rich businessman. "This whole thing seems so seamy."

He raised one eyebrow at her. "Anyone who would work as a spy, not for a cause, but for money, is pretty seamy."

She whirled on him, dark eyes flashing. "Sir, are you insulting me?"

"Let's say I doubt the character of anyone who thinks only of money."

She looked past his crooked nose and prominent mole to his fine cigar and his custom-made uniform and boots. "That, my dear sir, is because you have obviously never had to do without it. You've always lived as a privileged gentleman."

His expression became glum. "I won't if our side loses this war. Oh, by the way, you'll have to cut that beautiful hair."

"My hair?" April reached to touch her long black locks, pulled into a bun at the nape of her neck.

He nodded. "A soldier would hardly be wearing long hair, now, would he? One last thing: I can't caution you enough — trust no one, even from our side. The one you trust may be the spy and the very one to betray you."

April shuddered. "I understand." She was stubborn and had no intention of cutting her hair. She'd pin it under her hat instead. "Well, Major . . . ?"

He smiled. "Just call me John Smith."

"That's not your real name?"

"Is April Grant yours?" His tone was sarcastic.

"I suppose names don't matter. When I see you again, Major, have the money ready."

"*If* I see you again," he muttered.

"What did you say?" She paused in the doorway.

"I said Godspeed. Another officer will get your uniforms and necessary paperwork. In a few days, you should be deep in Indian Territory."

"Good-bye, sir." April nodded and left his office. What in God's name had she gotten herself into? And what good was all that gold if she didn't live to spend it?

Chapter 14

Eastern Indian Territory, June 15, 1864

Lieutenant Jim Eagle, of the crack Confederate Cherokee Mounted Rifles, swung down off his palomino stallion and handed the reins to his aide. "Here, little brother, hold my horse while I report in."

Tommy frowned, then nodded and accepted the duty. "I should have gone on that patrol with you."

"Maybe next time." He sighed with weariness. The war seemed to go on and on, and he couldn't remember anymore what they were fighting for. Years had passed since Wilson's Creek, when the Confederates had attempted to take Missouri and had failed; the same for Pea Ridge. Then they had planned to keep invading Yankees from taking Texas, but the Yankees hadn't made that move. Now the two sides just seemed to fight up and down the Indian Territory, burning and leveling everything, destroying crops and looting farms with much loss of life among the civilians. Jim frowned as he strode toward the general's tent. He wondered if his widowed mother was still alive, and whether their ranch had been burned to the ground. The Yankees held that area, so he couldn't get home to find out.

Jim knocked the dust from his hat and strode to the general's tent, bending his big frame to enter. "Lieutenant Jim Eagle reporting in, sir."

The legendary Cherokee officer looked up from his small desk. Stand Watie was squat and dark. "Ah, Wohali. At ease, Lieutenant. You know Captain Big Horse?"

For the first time Jim noticed the superior officer standing in the shadows, and saluted him. Jim didn't really like the captain.

The other tossed him an almost condescending salute. "Wohali, you look tired."

Jim straightened his wide shoulders. Wohali. The Cherokee word for "eagle." "I've been out on patrol, sir."

"Got anything worth reporting?" the general asked.

Jim smiled. "Believe it or not, there's a boat coming up the river."

"What?" Now he had both men's undivided attention.

Jim nodded. "I saw it myself or I wouldn't believe it. It's about four miles south of us."

"Headed to Fort Gibson to resupply the Yankees, no doubt." The general frowned. "Our men could sure use some of those supplies."

Jim looked down at his own worn-out boots and thought wistfully of how real coffee would taste, to say nothing of better food. The war hadn't been going well for the Southern side for a long time, and things were getting lean.

Captain Big Horse shook his head. "I don't know, sir; maybe we shouldn't risk it. That boat is probably armed."

"Begging your pardon, sir, but Clem Rogers and I know that area well," Jim argued. "There's a bend in the river up ahead where it narrows and the water's shallow — good place for an ambush."

The arrogant captain shook his head. "Maybe we shouldn't, sir. We could lose too many men."

Jim frowned. He'd always thought Big Horse a coward.

The old Cherokee general paused, considering. "You think we can capture it, Lieutenant?"

Jim tried to control his mounting excitement. "If we take them by surprise, sir. Of course, if we let them get too near Fort Gibson, the Yankees will come to their rescue, and we won't have time to loot the boat."

"It's worth the gamble." General Stand Watie stood up. "All right, we'll give it a try."

"But, sir," Big Horse began, "I don't think —"

"I said we'll attack the boat." Stand Watie glared at the captain.

Big Horse didn't look too happy, but he hushed and glared at Jim.

"Lieutenant," the general said, "this is your project; you can lead the attack."

"Yes, sir." Jim snapped a salute and left the tent at a run, forgetting his exhaustion. Behind him, he heard the old officer come out of his tent, barking orders, and the camp stirring to life.

"What's up?" Younger brother Tommy handed him the reins to his horse.

"We're going on a raid, little brother. How would you like a new pair of boots?" Jim swung into the saddle, and his horse, sensing the excitement, began to dance in circles.

Tommy grinned. "I'd like some good food better."

"You're gonna get it. Tonight Yankee grub is going in Southern bellies."

"What?" Tommy swung up on his own gray horse.

"We're raiding a Yankee supply boat moving upstream."

"Snooty Captain Big Horse in charge?"

"No, I am," Jim said. "He didn't even want to do it."

"Great!" Tommy's handsome dark face gleamed with excitement. "I want to be in the thick of things so I can finally get a promotion and some medals."

Jim shook his head. "Don't take any foolish chances. I promised Mother I'd look out for you."

The boy glared at him. "I'm old enough to look out for myself. Besides, we don't even know if she's still alive."

Jim winced at the thought. His brother was right. They hadn't made it back to the ranch in months since that area was in Yankee hands. For all they knew, Mother might be dead and the home burned and ransacked. That would be the most devastating thing to happen since their middle brother, Will, had deserted and gone over to the Yankees back in '61.

Around them, men grabbed up weapons and ran for horses as the bugle blew. With any luck, Jim thought, they'd surprise that Yankee boat, kill or capture the crew, and help themselves to supplies. He spurred the palomino stallion and led his gray-clad cavalry toward the river.

Aboard the Union supply boat *J. R. Williams*, Private A. G. Grant watched the muddy river swirl past as the boat headed north. So far, April had managed to pull off her masquerade. She spoke little and did not mingle with the other soldiers. Always she was aware of the danger, but the lure of the reward was strong. She concentrated on the money and how it would buy her the respect-

266

able white life she craved. If she kept her wits about her, maybe she'd uncover the spy . . . if indeed it was a Yankee.

The day was sultry warm, and she felt perspiration running down between her small breasts under the blue uniform. There was no breeze, but she pulled her hat farther down around her ears. It wouldn't do to have her black hair cascade down. She should have taken the major's suggestion about cutting it. April watched the riverbank with its forest of oaks, willows, and cottonwoods. She had left this country more than five years ago and had never intended to return south, but her mother's death had brought her.

She was shocked at what she'd seen so far. The war had wreaked havoc on the landscape and especially the Five Civilized tribes. As she'd come up the river, she had seen burned crops and destroyed farms as both armies fought up and down the eastern Indian Territory while bushwhackers roamed at will, raiding both sides.

Was that a glimpse of gray she saw through the trees? April blinked in the blinding sun and looked again. Maybe she had only imagined that movement. Up ahead the Arkansas River narrowed and she'd get a better look. She leaned on the railing and watched the muddy bank as the boat chugged upriver. Maybe she was imagining things. They were only a few miles from Union-held Fort

Gibson, and there were no Southern troops reported this close.

Suddenly, she caught the sound of running horses and saw more gray moving through the brush a few hundred yards away, and her heart went to her throat.

Frantically, she glanced around. The other Yankee soldiers were gathered about a man playing a mouth organ while they clapped and sang, ". . . *de camptown ladies sing dis song, doo dah, doo dah . . .*"

The captain. She had to alert the captain. She ran, shouting. Even as she did so, a small cannon opened up from the thicket, laying a shot across the boat's bow.

Acrid black smoke boiled through the sultry hot air and now rifle fire opened up along the bank. Aboard the ship, the surprised soldier dropped his mouth organ as other blue-clad soldiers ran up and down the deck in confusion. The commanding officer came out of his cabin, looking about wildly. "What the hell . . . ?"

"We're being attacked! Rebels!" April yelled. She found her knapsack and her rifle and tried to decide what to do. The cannon boomed again and, this time, found its target. The *J. R. Williams* shuddered as it took a hit. The officer in charge was yelling something, but April couldn't hear him, and the small escort of soldiers seemed too panicked to respond.

Rifle fire was pouring down on them from both sides of the river now as they neared the narrow bend, and the boat was listing as if taking on water.

The officer waved his arms wildly. "If we can make it a couple more miles upriver, men, our troops at Fort Gibson will hear the battle and come to the rescue!"

They'd sink before they made it that far, April thought in a panic. She hurried to the steps and looked down into the engine room. Water was coming up from below. Men ran up and down the deck, shouting to each other while, from the riverbank, gray-clad troops poured rifle fire at them.

She'd never live to collect that reward, she thought; she was going to be shot down in this Confederate ambush and buried as a common Union soldier. Worse yet, if she were captured by this bunch of rebels, there was no telling what they'd do when they discovered she was a woman. Out here in the wild, these men probably hadn't seen a woman in months. That thought galvanized her into checking her pistol. She didn't care which side they were on — she'd kill the man who tried to rape her.

Another cannonball found its mark, and there was no doubt now that the *J. R. Williams* was sinking.

The Union officer yelled to his bugler to blow retreat. "The water's shallow here, men!" he shouted. "This cargo isn't worth dying for!"

The soldiers needed no urging. They began going over the far side, swimming away from the deadly-accurate rifle fire. April hesitated. She couldn't swim.

"Come on, young fellow," a grizzled old sergeant gestured as he jumped.

April paused by the railing, considering what to do. Not much choice. Either she drowned trying to get away or stayed here and got captured and maybe raped. She'd have to take her chances in the water.

Her knapsack. It lay forgotten on the burning deck, and inside was the Confederate uniform she'd need later when she tried to sneak through Southern lines. The roar of cannon and screams of dying men deafened her. The sooty smoke from the shells and burning boat made her choke. She ran back for her knapsack as the last Yankee soldier went over the side, swimming for the far shore. She had the knapsack now; all she had to do was get off the boat. If the water was shallow enough, maybe she could flounder to the opposite bank.

Even as she thought that, a rifle bullet grazed her, cutting into her arm, and she screamed out and went to her knees. Her flesh felt as if it were on fire. Numbly she reached out and clasped her arm, noting the scarlet blood on the torn blue fabric. Well, at

least she wouldn't have to chance the water now. Around her the boat foundered and burned as screaming gray-clad soldiers dismounted, charged down the riverbank and onto the bloody decks.

Even in her pain, April tried to keep a clear head. If she was going to be captured, she'd better get rid of that telltale gray uniform before the rebels found it. Her arm seemed to be on fire, but she staggered across the deck. If she could drop the knapsack in the river where it would float away, the damning evidence would be lost.

"What the hell you doing?" A big, dark Confederate lieutenant raced onto the deck. "What you got there?"

She didn't answer. She must get rid of the evidence so her captors would think her only a common Union soldier and treat her as a prisoner of war rather than as a spy. She clutched the knapsack and staggered toward the railing, leaving a trail of blood behind. However, the big Indian caught up to her, grabbed her wounded arm. "What the hell you got there?"

April gasped in pain and dropped the knapsack. It went sliding across the deck but not into the water.

"Answer me, you Union scum!" He pulled her close to his face, and she realized just how big he was. The pain in her wounded arm made her so giddy, she thought she would black out, but she knew she had to get rid of that evidence. She gritted her teeth and pulled out of his grasp, tottering toward the knapsack, but he moved fast as a striking snake and scooped it up. "What's in here that's so important?"

"N-nothing," she gasped, and sank down on the deck.

"You're lying, Yank." He hung on to the knapsack, knelt next to her, pulled a knife from his belt.

He was going to finish the job, and she was too weak to stop him. She stared up into his rugged, handsome face, too proud to beg for her life. He looked Cherokee. Cherokee had never gone in for scalping, but she'd heard terrible stories of atrocities during this bloody war. Around her, rifle fire dwindled as the rebels seemed to realize that most of the Union soldiers had gone over the side, swimming for the far riverbank, where they ran like rabbits.

April held up a restraining hand. "Don't — don't kill prisoners," she gasped.

He slapped her hand away. "I ought to," the lieutenant snarled, "but you might have some information for us." He turned and yelled to his men. "Clem, you and some of the others see if you can force the captain to run her aground before she sinks, and then start looting her."

"Thieves!" April spit at him.

"Shut up, Yank!" he ordered, then turned back to a younger boy, who ran to his side. "Tommy, tell the others to hurry up. The Yanks who escaped will be heading for Fort Gibson. We'll only have maybe an hour to unload her cargo before reinforcements show up."

The Indian boy peered down at her with curiosity on his handsome face. "Jim, we got no wagons."

"Then we'll take what we can carry on horses. Now, get a move on."

"What you gonna do with the prisoner? Kill him?"

April sank back against the bloody deck. Having her throat cut might be more merciful than being gang-raped when they found out she was a woman.

"Hell, no, I won't kill him," the big one snapped. "What's the matter with you, little brother? We don't kill prisoners. Besides, he might be able to give us valuable information."

The younger soldier nodded. "You might have to torture him to get it."

"Go do what I told you," the officer growled. "I'll deal with him."

The young soldier turned and left.

Torture. Now she knew why the mysterious officer had been so hesitant to tell her anything. But would the rebels believe that, or would they think she was just being stub-

273

born? She was in so much pain, she wished she could pass out, but then he might kill her rather than bother with her. So instead, she gritted her teeth and glared at her captor. If he found out she was a woman, it might save her, but he probably wouldn't believe she knew nothing. Besides, the rugged lieutenant kneeling on the deck might be the very spy she was supposed to ferret out. She remembered the major's caution: *trust no one.*

The rebel lieutenant took his knife. "You're bleeding pretty bad, Yank. I'll use strips of your uniform to staunch the flow."

She could only nod. "Water. You got water?"

"I ought to let you go thirsty for trying to outwit me." Even as he said that, he handed her his canteen and began to cut her blue uniform, tearing off strips and examining her arm. The blue cloth was sodden with scarlet blood. His big hands were gentle as he took the canteen and poured water over the wound. She flinched. "You're a stubborn one. Don't know how you managed to stay conscious with this wound."

She wasn't sure she wouldn't faint from the pain, but she said nothing, frantic about what to do next. Her telltale knapsack lay by his side.

He reached in his pocket and retrieved a small bottle of liquor. "Damn, I hate to waste good whiskey to clean a Yankee wound. This is gonna hurt, soldier."

She bit her lip. "Can I — can I have a drink first?"

He paused, glaring at her. "Oh, hell, yes. It ain't your fault you're here any more than it is mine." He put his muscular arm under her shoulders and helped her to a half-sitting position, held the bottle to her lips. She gulped it, choking and coughing on the strong spirits.

"Why, you're just a boy, about the age of my brother." His voice sounded almost sympathetic.

A ray of hope kindled in April's heart. Maybe if he took a liking to her, he might help her escape and never realize he was dealing with a woman. Escape? Not much chance of that until her arm was better and she might steal a horse and ride on to Fort Gibson. On the other hand, wasn't she supposed to eventually infiltrate the Confederate lines if she didn't find her spy among the Yankees?

He took the bottle from her hand. "This will sting."

April gritted her teeth and closed her eyes as he poured the whiskey on the wound. It felt like liquid fire. By biting her lip bloody, she managed only to groan, not shriek, which might alert him to the fact that she was female. She kept her eyes closed as he ministered to her. His hands were gentle as they patted a strange-smelling herb over the wound and bandaged it expertly. Evidently, he'd had a lot of experience dealing with wounded men.

"What's your name, soldier?"

She kept her voice low. "Uh, A. G. Grant."

He laughed without mirth. "Any kin to General Grant?"

"If so, you think I'd be here?"

"And smart aleck, too," the lieutenant snapped as he pulled a bandanna from his pocket and made a sling for her arm.

April didn't answer, watching past his shoulder as Confederate soldiers moved about the deck, unloading boxes and bales.

Her captor turned to watch the progress. "Hurry up, men!" he shouted. "The Yankees will be coming soon."

"We won't be able to take it all with no wagons, Lieutenant," a lanky half-breed yelled.

"Well, then, Clem, tell the boys to take what they can carry, and we'll just have to burn the rest. We ain't leaving nothing for the Yankees."

The young soldier named Tommy returned. "He die yet?"

Her captor shook his head. "I stopped the bleeding. We'll keep him, but I doubt a common soldier knows much."

Tommy reached for her knapsack. "What's this?"

"That's mine!" April panicked, and struggled to crawl toward him. If she could just throw it over the side . . .

"Tommy" — the officer caught her arm — "see what the Yank's so eager to keep us from getting."

"No!" she said.

Tommy grinned as he began to open it. "Maybe the Yank's got some extra food, maybe even some coffee. You don't want to share your coffee, Yank? We ain't had any in months."

She didn't answer, only watched helplessly. April felt perspiration break out on her clammy skin.

"Just bring it along, Tommy." Her captor swung her up in his arms. "You can check it out later. Let's get off this tub before she sinks."

However, the younger soldier paid no heed, continuing to dig in her knapsack.

"I said forget it, little brother, and let's get the hell out of here." She laid her face against the Lieutenant's muscular chest as he began to stride away.

But behind them, Tommy cried out in surprise. "Well, I'll be damned! Look, Jim."

She could only gulp, heart beating hard. Now they would know she was a spy and shoot her.

"What is it?" The big Cherokee carrying her paused and whirled around.

The private held up the telltale gray clothing. "One of our uniforms. Big brother, what's a damned Yankee doing with a Confederate uniform?"

The lieutenant glared down at her. "Answer that."

"I — I took it as a souvenir off a rebel captive."

Tommy scratched his head and stared at the uniform. "It's new, Jim. He didn't take it off no prisoner."

The handsome Cherokee glared down into her face. "Bring it along, Tommy, and we'll get some answers later. Let's get out of here before the Yankees send reinforcements. Tell Clem to set fire to the whole boat; we'll not leave any supplies for the Yankees to recapture." He strode off the deck, still carrying her, and headed for a palomino stallion on the bank.

She was in so much pain, she was barely aware when the big Cherokee lifted her to his horse and mounted up behind her. "Yank, you've got some explaining to do," he snarled as he spurred his horse and they rode out. "Otherwise . . ."

"Otherwise, what?" she gasped.

He glared down at her. "Otherwise, dawn tomorrow, we'll be shooting you as a spy!"

Chapter 15

The Confederate raiding party galloped away from the burning wreck. April was in pain, but more worried about what would happen to her now that the soldiers had found the uniform in her knapsack. Union reinforcements might arrive at any time, but it would be too late to rescue her.

They rode into the rebel camp, and other soldiers began to gather, curious. "You get any food?"

The younger brother dismounted, swaggering a little. "We got food and supplies, but better than that, we got a prisoner."

Her captor swung down from his palomino, reached to pull her from his horse, and led her through the gathering crowd. "Somebody tell the general we're back."

The scout called Clem took off at a run. At this point April staggered, and the big man caught her and lifted her in his arms. "Don't you die on me, Yank; you've got some questions to answer."

And when she couldn't or wouldn't answer them, then what? She glanced around at the curious soldiers. What a ragtag bunch. Her heart almost went out to them because they were ragged and thin. Some of them didn't even have boots. The looted supplies were already being distributed, and the men grinned like kids at Christmas as they dug through the boxes, searching for things they could use.

The scout returned. "General Watie says bring the prisoner to his tent."

The man who carried her turned to his brother. "Tommy, come along and bring that knapsack."

What would happen to her when the general saw the Confederate uniform in her knapsack? Union reinforcements might arrive at any time, but it would be too late for her. She hadn't even had a chance to look for a spy before she was captured and unmasked. Maybe she should tell her captors the truth. Even as she considered it, April shook her head. They wouldn't believe her.

The lieutenant and his brother stopped before a tent, and her captor tossed her on the ground as a squat, dark, white-haired Indian in a gray uniform came out, accompanied by a handsome Indian captain.

The lieutenant and his brother saluted.

"At ease," the old man said. "The mission was a success?"

"Yes, sir, we came back with lots of supplies."

"The Yankees might try to recapture

them," the captain grumbled.

"I doubt that, Captain Big Horse," the lieutenant snapped. "Of course, you weren't along to see them run like rabbits."

"I had other duties," the captain said coldly.

"Stop it, you two," the old general said. "Lieutenant Wohali, you've got a prisoner?"

Wohali, she thought. "Eagle" in the Cherokee language. Well, it fit the big man.

Her captor nudged her with his boot. "Yes, sir, just a private. Took him off that Yankee boat we plundered."

"A private?" The old man scowled. "Why do you bother me with a common soldier?"

"Because he was carrying this, sir." Lieutenant Eagle leaned over, took the gray uniform from the knapsack Tommy carried, and held it up.

The old man reached out and took it. "He had this?"

The other nodded.

"Fought like hell to get rid of it," Jim Eagle said.

"Hmm. He know anything?"

Jim Eagle shrugged. "Haven't asked him much yet, sir. We were eager to get out of there before the Yankees got word and came down from Fort Gibson to recapture the boat."

"Get much food?"

"All we could carry without wagons. We'll eat good for a while anyway."

The old general sighed. "We can sure use them. Not much getting through enemy lines anymore. They seem to know our every move."

The captain shoved her roughly with his boot. "Because of spies like this one, I reckon. We should shoot him, General." He kicked at her again, but the lieutenant blocked the captain's motion.

"There's no need for that," the lieutenant snapped. "The Yank's wounded and helpless."

April took a deep breath. If only the general would believe her, she might tell him . . .

"Yank, what are you doing with a Confederate uniform?" The old Cherokee glared down at her.

Oh, dear God, she wished she'd never let herself in for this. "I — I found it."

"That's not what he said first, sir," Tommy piped up, obviously wanting some attention and adding to his own importance. "First he said he took it off a prisoner."

"That doesn't sound unusual." The general seemed to stifle a yawn.

"Sir," the lieutenant protested, "it's a new uniform. How long's it been since we've had any new uniforms out here in Indian Territory?"

The general looked around at the ragged gray uniforms of his men, then at the new uniform and glared down at her. "Something strange here. Soldier, where'd you get this?"

He'd never believe her if she told him the truth. "I — I took it off a dead reb."

The captain snorted. "Now he's got a third story. This is a new uniform, sir, and there's no blood on it."

"Hmm." The general looked at her, then at the curious soldiers clustered around. To the lieutenant, he asked, "A spy, you think?"

"Sir, I don't know what else to think."

Captain Big Horse laughed. "I say we shoot him."

She was so frightened, she forgot about how much pain she was in. "I — I'm a prisoner of war," she gasped. "There's certain rules —"

"Not if you're a spy," Jim Eagle snapped.

As she watched, the general strode away, motioning for the lieutenant and the captain to follow him. They walked over to stand under the shade of a tree and began to talk.

"Well," the younger brother muttered, "he could have asked me to take part; I was in on this."

Strain as she might, April couldn't hear what they were saying, but she knew it couldn't be good. In the meantime, her heavy blue uniform felt sweltering in the hot June weather. Curious soldiers gathered to gape at her, so now all she could see were worn and ragged boots.

In a moment, the big Cherokee pushed his

way through the crowd. "All right, men, dismissed."

"Jim, what you gonna do with the prisoner?" his younger brother asked.

The rugged officer paused, looking down at her. "We've decided the Yank's right; he's got rights as a prisoner of war, although Captain Big Horse was eager to execute him. I'll look after the Yank, and maybe later we'll do a swap."

Tommy seemed to turn sullen. "But what about the Confederate uniform?"

"For now, forget about the damned uniform."

April heaved a sigh of relief. Good, they weren't going to kill her after all. Maybe they'd let her go without ever finding out she was a woman.

"In the meantime, Tommy," the lieutenant ordered, "go enjoy the booty. Everyone else get back to your posts. I'll take charge of this prisoner."

He picked her up, and the crowd began to melt away reluctantly.

Tommy peered at her. "Where you takin' him, big brother?"

"I've got to keep him away from our troops. Some of them might be itching for revenge for some of our losses these past few weeks. Bring me some food down by the river."

The river. Was he going to drown her? No, he'd said he was going to treat her as a prisoner, trade her to the other side later. Maybe, in an unguarded moment, she might escape. Why had she been crazy enough to think she could be a spy and collect that reward money?

The big Cherokee carried her easily, striding through the camp. It was almost dusk, and around her the soldiers were celebrating, laughing and singing.

Behind her, she heard Tommy yell, "Jim, I think there's even a stash of good whiskey."

"Good. Bring it, too. I could use a drink."

She could use some food and a sip of whiskey, too, she thought as he carried her toward the river. He might not even give her a hunk of bread, and she was too proud to beg.

Damn, he hated being a wet-nurse to this damned Yankee. His burden was little more than a boy and very slender, Jim thought as he carried the wounded enemy down to a protected grove of trees near the water. He wanted to be out of sight of the troops. General Watie had ordered him to find out if this Yank was really a spy, and if so, discover what the man knew.

Then the general had paused. "Do whatever it takes to get the information you need, Lieutenant. We've got a leak somewhere, and we're losing too many men. Dismissed." The old man saluted and returned to his tent, leaving the pair.

"The general's right," Big Horse echoed. "After you get your information, you know what to do with him."

"But I thought, by the rules of war —"

"The rules don't apply to spies," the captain snapped. "There's only one way to deal with a spy, Lieutenant Wohali. Once we know what he knows, there's no reason to keep him alive, and we can't take a chance on him escaping and letting the enemy know we've found out."

"He's just a boy, sir," Jim had protested.

"So are the soldiers we've lost because of information leaks," the captain reminded him. "It may be regrettable, but it can't be helped."

"Yes, sir." Jim Eagle saluted. He wasn't about to execute a prisoner on Captain Big Horse's say-so. He wasn't sure the general would okay that, and even if he did, Jim wasn't sure he could carry it out.

The other officer started to walk away, then paused. "Oh, and by the way, Lieutenant, I don't know how you will get that information as long as you get it."

"Sir?"

"You know what I mean."

Jim nodded and saluted. Then they had walked back to where the wounded Yankee lay on the ground. He was to get any information this prisoner might have, no matter what he had to do to get it — meaning torture, terror, beatings or threats. Confederate lives might depend on finding out what, if anything, this mysterious Yankee knew. As he picked up the slight enemy and carried him down to the river, Jim wasn't looking forward to forcing information out of this mere boy. He hoped Tommy brought him a full bottle of whiskey. He might have to get a little drunk to make himself do what he knew needed to be done.

April tried to remain calm as the officer carried her. It would be dark soon. In the distance, she heard the Confederate troops celebrating. Her arm throbbed, but she could stand the pain. What worried her was not knowing exactly what the Confederate officer planned to do with her.

"What — why are you taking me so far away from camp?" she protested.

"None of your business." Her captor sat her on the ground against the trunk of a tree. "You tell me about that uniform in your knapsack, maybe I'll give you some food."

"Can I have some water?" She pulled her cap down tighter, wishing she had followed orders and cut her hair.

He paused, then scowled as he tossed her his canteen. "You'll make it easier on yourself if you'll tell me what I want to know."

She couldn't get the stopper out of the canteen.

He knelt and took it from her, then put one muscular arm behind her shoulders and held her. She caught his big hand with her small one and guided the canteen to her lips.

"Just a boy," he muttered. "Why is this my assignment?"

She was afraid to ask what he was talking about, so she gulped the water and wiped her mouth, saying nothing. If she told him the truth, he wouldn't believe her. Besides, he might be the very spy she was looking for. As long as he thought she held important information, he might take care of her wounds and keep her alive. If he figured out that she knew little and was waiting to be contacted herself, he might let her die. Maybe, in the darkness, she might slip away and make it to Fort Gibson. They'd believe her that she had been captured with the supply boat, because the survivors would back up her story.

"You look awful young to be a soldier," he said.

"No younger than your brother."

"You hurtin'? I've got some laudanum if you want it."

April hesitated, then shook her head. That was so tempting, but she might spill what little she knew while she was semiconscious.

"You afraid you'll say something under the drug?"

She didn't look him in the eye, afraid he'd

288

see the fear in hers. "Got nothing to tell."

He poured water from his canteen onto a bandanna and wiped the smoke and sweat from her face. "Tommy's bringing us some food and whiskey. You tell me what I want to know, and I'll give you some."

And if she told him what he wanted to know, he'd never believe her, even if she told him the truth. "Not hungry."

"I doubt that." He began to gather sticks, got a campfire going, and put on a kettle of water.

In the distance, she heard the faint sounds of soldiers moving about and horses neighing as the camp settled down for the night. No doubt the Union troops had found the abandoned burning boat by now, but they wouldn't dare attack this big Confederate camp. She'd have to devise a plan.

His younger brother came through the woods with a box of things. "Hey, Jim, here's some supplies, new blankets, too, and some coffee — real coffee."

"Good. Now, go back to camp." He took the box and set it on the ground.

The boy watched her with curiosity. He was probably younger than she was. "Jim, what you gonna do with him?"

"Feed him."

"Then what?"

The officer sighed, hesitated. "Go back to camp, Tommy. That's an order."

He didn't want to talk in front of her. That scared her. She gave the boy a beseeching look.

"Tommy, I said go back to camp."

The boy hesitated. "You think because you're the oldest, you always get to give the orders."

"I give the orders because I'm an officer."

"I'll be important, too, someday; you'll see." He turned and left.

Now she and the lieutenant were alone again. She watched the big, muscular Cherokee moving around the fire, opening the sacks Tommy had brought. Soon she could smell soup cooking. It smelled delicious, as did the biscuits that came out of the cast-iron Dutch oven. He put an old tin coffeepot on the fire. "You want some of this?"

In the darkness, she watched his face and tried not to think about food. She was so hungry.

"Tell me what I want to know and you can have some."

The bastard. She should have known he wasn't being kind. "Got nothing to tell."

"Have it your way." He got himself a bowl of soup and a biscuit and settled down to eat nearby. It occurred to her he was making sure she saw every bite.

It looked so good. She tried not to watch him eat. "Why — why are we camped so far from the others?"

He hesitated, didn't look at her. "Wanted you to have quiet; that's all."

"Liar." She was afraid to guess why they were alone.

"You sure you don't want some of this?"

"I might talk if you'd feed me."

He paused. "Talk first."

"Food first."

"You're stubborn, Yank. All right." He looked relieved as he got up, poured another bowl, laid a biscuit in it, and brought it over.

"I — I'm not sure I can hold a spoon. My arm —"

"Here." He had to put his arm behind her shoulders as he began to feed her. "You're awful small for a soldier."

"Big enough to hold a rifle." She kept gobbling in case he changed his mind and took the bowl away.

When she had finished the soup, he set the bowl aside, staring down into her eyes. "Want some coffee?"

She nodded, and he got her a cup. She held that in her good hand, grateful for the warmth of the cup now that the darkness was turning cool. It tasted so good. "Sugar?"

He shook his head. "Haven't seen sugar in months."

"You rebs don't seem to have much of anything."

"We got guts, Yank. We're runnin' on sheer guts."

"You can't win a war with that."

"You damned Yankees are invading our land, stealing our livestock, killing our people, raping our women." His voice was bitter.

"You own slaves?"

He shook his head. "Never had that kind of money; don't believe in it anyway. Enough questions, Yank. You talk."

"Tomorrow," she whispered, and closed her eyes.

He began to curse, but she ignored him. Time was what she needed, time to gain strength so she could escape.

"I've got my orders, Yank. Make it easy on yourself and tell me what I want to know."

She just looked up at him.

"All right, then, I don't want to do this, but I'm under orders." He grabbed her good arm, dragged her to her feet, and turned her face against the tree. He took a length of rawhide from his belt and tied her wrists together around the tree trunk. Before she could protest, he reached up and caught the collar of her shirt and jerked hard, ripping it down the back. She felt her shirt falling away to her waist, and she pressed her bare breasts against the rough bark so he wouldn't see them. She glanced back over her shoulder and saw him pull the quirt from his belt.

Oh, my God, he was going to whip her. She gritted her teeth stubbornly and concentrated on her throbbing arm. Maybe if she thought about something else, she could bear the pain without shrieking and giving away her sex.

Damn the Yank anyhow. Jim stared at the naked, slender back and brought his quirt up. He didn't want to whip the slight boy, but he was under orders to find out what, if anything, this prisoner knew. He snapped the quirt back and brought it down lightly on the boy's bare flesh, leaving a livid pink streak. The boy cried out and hung on to the tree. "Damn it, kid, tell me what I want to know and spare yourself this pain."

The boy only shook his head. In anger Jim reached out and jerked off the boy's cap. Instantly, a cascade of long black hair tumbled down the bare shoulders, almost hiding the red streak the quirt had inflicted. "What the . . . ?"

He cut the rawhide, grabbed the boy's shoulder, whirled him around. First he saw the eyes, dark and defiant, and then . . .

The small, taut breasts thrust from the remnants of the torn blue shirt. "A girl! Oh, my God!"

Chapter 16

He stared down at her in disbelief. There were tears in her eyes, but she did not scream, although blood dripped from her bitten lip. He caught her as she staggered away from the tree, and for an instant he was acutely aware of the feel of her bare breasts against him; then he swung her up in his arms. "What the hell's going on here?"

She only shook her head at him, tears in her dark eyes. He carried her over and laid her gently on his blankets. She winced, and he rolled her over on her belly, staring down with distaste at the whip mark he had put there. "Damn it," he muttered, "why didn't you tell me?"

She seemed to be fighting not to cry. "Not gonna tell you anything."

"We'll deal with that later." He got some ointment out of his saddle bags and smeared it slowly down the wound. Her skin was smooth as dark cream. It had been a long time since he had a woman, and just putting his hands on her flesh made his groin ache. It crossed his mind that she was helpless and his prisoner. No one would know or care if he used her for his pleasure here in the darkness. What the hell was he thinking? He couldn't resort to rape, not even of a damned Yankee spy. "Tell me what you were doing on that boat. Did the Yankees know they had a girl aboard?"

She sighed, enjoying the gentle feel of his hands on her bare flesh as he ministered to her. "No. I — I was trying to reach my lover at the fort, that's all."

"You must really love the guy to take the risk," he muttered. "Damned crazy thing to do."

He believed her. A sense of relief swept over her. "I — I hadn't seen him in a long time."

"So where'd you get the gray uniform?" He kept smearing ointment on her bare back, his hands moving lower and lower.

She thought fast. "I was taking it to him as a souvenir."

"You little liar." He turned her over and stared down into her face. "That's a new uniform." His gaze dropped to her bare breasts, and she was acutely aware of the hunger in his dark eyes. Evidently, he had been a long time without a woman. She tried to shake her black hair so that it fell across her chest, but his hand reached out and cupped her breast.

She attempted to push him away as she shrank back. "Don't touch me."

His thumb raked gently across her nipple, and she felt it swell at his caress. "I'll do more than touch you if you don't tell me what I want to know."

She looked up at the need in his rugged face, now shadowed by the darkness. She knew now what she might use to buy her freedom. "If I let you make love to me, will you let me go?"

He hesitated, his thumb stroking her nipple until a warmth like she'd never known stirred her blood. He shook his head, then paused. "You little bitch, that's the devil's own bargain."

Before she was aware of his intent, he pulled her to him and kissed her, his hands circling her back so that he pressed her naked breasts against the brass buttons of his uniform. His mouth covered hers, forcing her lips open so that his hot tongue could invade inside. For a moment, the unexpected feelings that swept over her caused her to freeze in place. She tasted the heat of his eager mouth as his hand came around her back very slowly to touch and stroke her.

"Would you like to make love to me?" she whispered.

He pulled away from her with an oath. "You little tart, you'd do anything to make me forget my duty, wouldn't you?"

"I — I just want you to set me free." She began to sob now, unable to stop herself.

"That isn't going to happen." He went to his saddlebags, dug around, returned with one of his gray shirts, and tossed it to her. "Put this on."

It was much too big, but she put it on, making sure he saw the movement of her breasts as she did so.

He cursed again and began to roll a cigarette with shaking hands. "Damn you for flaunting yourself like that. I've got a good mind to take you right here in the dirt."

She paused, seeing the mental picture of this big savage ripping her clothes away, shoving her down in the grass. He'd put that hot, wet mouth on her breasts, sucking them until she was writhing with her own need, then force himself between her thighs. No doubt he was built like a stallion and knew how to please a woman. In her innocence, she was both fascinated and afraid of losing her virginity.

He paused, the tip of his smoke glowing red as he inhaled deeply. "Now, damn it, now tell me the truth."

What would he believe? Certainly not the truth. Besides, he might be the very spy she was seeking.

"All right." She shrugged as if in defeat. "I'm just a common whore."

"Common? With your body, I'd say you're not too common. I'd say you were a toy for officers and rich men."

She smiled. "That's right. I figured to make plenty of money off the officers at Fort Gibson."

"And the Confederate uniform?" He was staring at her in a way that made her uneasy, as if he could see into her very soul and know the truth.

She didn't look at him. "I — I bought it on the black market. You can buy anything if you've got enough money."

"Including you?" He sounded annoyed and angry.

She shrugged. "I told you so. I figured I'd get all the money the Union officers had to spend on entertainment, then move over to the rebel side."

"You have no loyalties to either?"

April shook her head and laughed. "Only to gold. If you hadn't taken me off that boat, I'd be in some Yankee officer's bed right now, taking as much money as I could get from him."

"You shameless little slut." His disgusted tone told her he finally believed her. Yet his eyes still betrayed how much he wanted her. "How much do you get for a night?"

She tried to figure out how much he had. What would she do if he took her up on it? She'd never bedded a man in her innocent life. She smiled archly. "Whatever the market will bear. I'll do you for a cartwheel."

"Twenty dollars?" His voice rose. "I hear

the best whores in New Orleans don't get but five or ten."

She winked at him. "But you're not in New Orleans. I told you, whatever the market will bear."

He ground out his cigarette. "Suppose I just take me a free sample?"

She gasped, then decided to bluff, although she might be playing with fire. Somehow, he didn't seem like the kind of man who would rape a woman. "You'd like it a lot better if I were willing."

"You win, you bitch. It's a shame an Indian girl has lowered herself to become a plaything for rich white men."

"I'm not Indian," she protested.

"And ashamed of your blood, too — that's worse. What's your real name?"

"None of your business," she snapped.

He stared at her. Then, very slowly in his Cherokee language, he said, "I think I'll just cut your throat and throw you in the river."

"Don't you dare!" She came up alert and ready to fight.

He smiled without mirth. "So you're Cherokee, are you?"

"I'm not." She stumbled to her feet, backed away against a tree.

"What's your real name?"

"April. April Grant."

"Kawoni." He said it slowly, then said it again, rolling it across his tongue as if he liked the taste of it. "Kawoni. I think I knew a girl by that name once, a half-blood girl who was born in the month of April. My younger brother, Will, was in love with her." He turned and stared at her as if puzzled, then a light broke across his face. "Well, I'll be damned."

"Of — of course it's not me. Same name, maybe. I'm from Boston." She shook her head, but she didn't look into his eyes, because he might read the truth. She recognized him now. When she was not old enough to marry, Will Wohali had wanted her to be his wife, but she had had eyes only for his older brother, who didn't seem to know she was alive. Then her father had taken her away north.

The officer shrugged. "Well, I reckon I was mistaken. The girl I remember wouldn't sell herself for money; no Cherokee girl would."

"I am white, I tell you," she fired back.

"And she'd be proud of her heritage, not ashamed."

When had she become ashamed? When the snooty white girls at Miss Priddy's fancy school had taunted her and made her life miserable. Money might make the difference in being accepted. "So now that you know I'm nothing but a whore, you going to let me go?"

He shook his head. "Not without talking to the general. Sometimes camp followers are used to carry messages."

He was staring at her again as if he'd give anything to possess her.

She ran her tongue over her lips very slowly, looking at him. "If you'd let me go, I'll make love to you."

For a moment, he said nothing, just stared into her eyes as if he were attempting to see into her very soul. "You slut. You're beneath contempt."

"But you still want me?"

"Shut up." He stood up, turned away as if ashamed of his need. He strode over to his saddle bags and came back with a fresh length of rawhide.

"What are you going to do?"

"Tie you to a tree so you can't run away. I'll figure out what to do with you in the morning." He grabbed her good arm and wrapped the rawhide around her wrist.

She'd never escape if he tied her. "You can't sleep with me if you tie me up."

"I'm not sleeping with you," he growled.

"But you want to."

"I didn't say I didn't." He began to tie her. She looked down at the knot and knew she couldn't untie it. There was only one way to escape. Tonight she'd have to sacrifice her innocence by seducing this lieutenant into setting her free. She wasn't quite certain how to seduce a virile rogue like this one. She'd only flirted with a few green boys.

"Before you get me trussed up like a hog for the night," she said, "I need to go into the bushes."

He frowned. "Why didn't you say so before?"

She didn't answer, and he sighed and began untying her. She made sure she brushed her bare breast against his hand as she turned away and started into the brush.

"You slut, don't try to run away. Besides the fact that you won't get very far, there's no telling what's out there in the woods."

She paused and looked back at him over her shoulder. "Am I in any more danger out there than I am with you?"

He scowled at her. "I was an honored Lighthorseman before the war. You know what the Lighthorse do to rapists?"

She remembered then. The Lighthorse was the law enforcement for all the Five Civilized Tribes. Their courts were swift, and their justice merciless, the sentences carried out by public lashings or a firing squad of warriors. "Don't worry, I'm not going far." She watched him settle down before the fire with a hand-rolled smoke and a cup of coffee. He looked exhausted.

Once out of sight in the woods, April took off at a run. Her arm and her wounded back throbbed, but she had to escape. She knew now that this tough soldier would do whatever it took to get the information he needed, and she wasn't sure that she had convinced him she was merely a whore.

In the darkness she ran into a low limb and fell, got up, and took off again. After a few yards, she tripped over a tree root and fell again. She wasn't even sure which direction she was moving, but it didn't matter as long as she escaped from this grim rebel. She had to put distance between them.

Behind her, she heard the lieutenant shout, "Yank, where are you?"

She didn't answer but kept running. Behind her, she heard him call again, and this time he was cursing. There was no telling what he would do if he caught her. She was breathing hard, but there was no time to stop and rest. He probably knew these woods well, and being a former Lighthorseman, he was surely also a skilled tracker. Well, he couldn't track her in the dark, and she'd take her chances at daylight.

She didn't hear him calling anymore. Good, maybe he'd decided it wasn't worth it to come looking. After all, if she managed to get anywhere near Fort Gibson, a Yankee sentry might pick him off.

She wasn't sure how far she'd run or how far she was away from the camp. All that mattered was escaping that rugged Cherokee and his hungry eyes.

A shadow suddenly appeared in the path before her — a big, wide-shouldered shadow.

She cried out and tried to dodge him, but she was moving too fast to stop.

"Gotcha!" He reached out and grabbed her, and they struggled, but she was no match for his strength. They went down in the soft leaves, and she came up biting and scratching.

"Stop it; you'll hurt your arm!" his deep voice ordered as he pinned her to the ground with his muscular body.

"You don't give a damn about my arm." She was trying not to cry as she struggled to get out from under him. She could feel every inch of his hard, aroused body along the length of hers. Her gray shirt had come open, and his brass buttons pressed into the flesh of her breasts.

"You little liar," he swore, and she felt the warmth of his breath on her neck, "I ought to turn you over my knee for running away."

"Why not whip me to death!" she screamed in defiance.

"Don't tempt me, Yank." One of his big hands went to cover her bare breast.

"You're going to rape me. I knew it." She gritted her teeth and glared up at him.

He shook his head and sighed regretfully as he stood up. "Unlike you, my little Yankee whore, I'm not a liar."

She reached to jerk her shirt closed because in the moonlight, she could see the way he was staring down at her with hot desire in his dark eyes. "I — I was afraid."

He snorted with derision. "A whore afraid of men? I doubt it, slut." He reached down, caught her hand, and pulled her to her feet. "So why did you run?"

She didn't look at him. "I — I figured the Yanks would pay better than a bunch of poor crackers who can't even afford new boots."

"Now, that I can believe, you greedy little tart. Our troops haven't been paid in a while. Come here." He held out one hand.

She backed away. "Why?"

"You want to walk back to camp?"

"I'm perfectly capable of walking." She didn't want those hot hands on her body again.

"Oh, hell, I'm tired of fooling with you, girl." Before she realized what he was about to do, he caught her wrist and swung her up in his strong arms, turned, and strode back through the darkness. She was exhausted, and he probably was, too. She sighed and laid her face against his wide chest, wondering what might happen next.

Jim Eagle tried not to look down at the slender girl he carried. Her flesh was soft, and her tumble of hair smelled of scented soap. She was no common camp follower, this one, yet he still wasn't certain she was nothing more than a high-priced whore. If she knew anything, he was going to find it out, and one thing was certain: if he got a chance, he was going to bed her and see if she was as skilled as she was beautiful. It was time the Confederates shared a few of the delicacies Yankee officers were enjoying!

In silence now, he carried her back to his fire and sat her on the ground. The camp had grown quiet except for an occasional horse whinnying and, somewhere, a dog barking.

She studied him, trying to decide what to do next. Maybe she could make a friend of him and gain his trust. As a last resort, the way he stared at her told her she still might seduce him. "I'm cold; is there any more coffee?" She put her arms around herself, letting her unbuttoned shirt hang open so he could see her breasts.

"Help yourself." He seemed to be attempting not to look at her nakedness as he squatted on the ground by the fire.

As she poured herself a cup, she considered splashing him with the boiling liquid and making a run for it again, but decided against it. "You want some?"

He shook his head. "Look, I've been on patrol all day. What I need is sleep, not coffee."

She sat down on the log next to him. "I'm sorry I'm so much trouble, but thank you for bandaging my arm."

He didn't move. "I'd do it for any prisoner."

"You really hate me, don't you?" She sipped her coffee.

"You disgust me," he snapped. "To think a Cherokee girl would work as a whore —"

"Might as well be a Cherokee as any other. I'll wager you never give a thought to the hundreds of women working soldier camps in this war."

"The Cherokee are a proud people with a long heritage," he said. "I'm ashamed for you."

Tears came to her eyes, and she blinked them away. "I hate my Indian blood. Up north, the white girls made fun of me. They called me a 'savage,' 'redskin,' and 'half-breed.'"

"The Cherokee are one of the Five Civilized Tribes," he said, "and we had a high civilization, fine homes, even black slaves before greedy white people found gold on our lands in Georgia."

"Then why do you support the South?" she asked. "Did your family own slaves?"

He shook his head. "I support the Confederacy as the lesser of two evils. I've never trusted the Union after President Jackson forced our people to walk the Trail of Tears in the chill of winter. I lost many relatives on that long, deadly trek, as did your mother, I'm sure."

She didn't answer.

He sighed. "We were betrayed by the

Union after we were their allies and friends, fighting on their side against the British in the War of 1812."

Again April said nothing, only sipped her coffee. She knew the Creek tribe had fought on the side of the British in that war until they were defeated in the bloody Battle of Horseshoe Bend. The Cherokees had been treated no better than the Union's enemies. No wonder Jim Eagle was bitter.

"Besides," her captor said, "the Confederates have hinted that if they win, they will let the Indians have their own separate state with no white people invading it."

She thought about it. "Maybe they lie, too."

"Maybe, but we already know the Union lies to us, so I'm willing to take the chance." He picked up a stick and began to scratch in the dirt.

April looked at his worn boots and faded uniform. "It doesn't seem to be going very well."

"I don't need a Yankee whore to tell me the obvious." He continued to scratch in the dirt with his stick.

In the firelight, she watched him and almost felt sorry for this weary, bitter warrior. Then she took a good look at the marks he was making in the dirt. A row of X's. What was it the major had said to her — something about their only clue? She took a deep breath and stared. Was Jim Eagle sending her a signal or was he fishing to see what she knew? There was no doubt she'd found either her contact or the spy she sought.

Chapter 17

"What's the matter with you?" He paused and looked directly at her.

"Nothing." She was afraid to comment on his marks in the dirt. Was he the spy she sought, or was he attempting to trap her? *Trust no one.* If she made the wrong choice . . . ? She feigned a yawn. "I'm tired, too. If I gave you my word of honor that I won't run off, would you not tie me?"

"The word of honor of a whore?" He raised one eyebrow.

She hesitated. "What about the word of honor of a half-Cherokee girl?"

Now he threw back his head and laughed. "You just got through denying you were Cherokee. You can't have it both ways, you little —"

"All right; I can see you'd never believe me, no matter what I told you." She held out her wrists, and when he began tying her, she looked up at him and ran her tongue across her lips. "I won't charge you for kissing me," she whispered.

"You think pretty highly of yourself, don't you?"

"Men tell me I'm skilled at what I do." Before he could react, April slipped her arms around his neck and kissed him. She didn't know much about kissing, but she followed her own emotions, putting her warm, wet mouth over his, her lips half open, her tongue tracing a path across his until he opened his lips and took the tip of her tongue inside. Then he took over the kiss with a deep, sharp breath and pulled her so close that her breasts were crushed against his chest.

She had never been kissed before, but she was bedazzled by the sensation and never wanted it to end. She put all her pent-up passion into her kiss.

He seemed to pull away with great difficulty, breathing hard. "Damn, you are skilled. If you kiss every man like that, no wonder they're willing to pay so much."

She smiled up at him. "That was just a free sample. Maybe when I get to know you better, there'll be more."

"Tonight?"

If she gave him her virginity tonight, he'd realize that her whole story about being a whore was a lie, and then he might figure out she was a spy. On the other hand, if he was the agent she sought . . . "Some other time. Looking forward to a treat is half the fun."

He cursed under his breath. "Maybe for

311

you, you little tart. You get men to pay more that way?"

"I told you I'd give you a free sample. That was it. I don't reckon you have the gold cartwheel I charge."

"Twenty dollars? You are joking." He looked shocked and angry.

April drew a sigh of relief. She had figured correctly that he didn't have that much money.

"You conniving slut, I could just help myself."

She smiled a little too sweetly. "But it'll only be enjoyable if I'm willing, and the more I'm paid, the more willing I become."

He swore under his breath. "And to think that long ago, I once thought . . ."

"Thought what?" She settled herself on her blanket.

"Nothing. I reckon there's not much left of the girl I once knew."

His harsh words stung, but she would not cry even though she blinked rapidly. Once she had been in love with this man, once when she was too young and she had been pledged to his brother. "You're wasting my time, reb. Let's get some sleep, shall we?"

He smiled without mirth while reaching into his jacket. "I never thought I'd do something like this, but I just happen to have the money." Almost triumphantly he held up a handful of silver dollars, and the campfire made them gleam in the darkness.

April's mouth went dry. He was calling her bluff. "Maybe you should think it over, reb. I'll wager you have better use for the money."

A shadow crossed his rugged, handsome face. "I planned to spend it on things for the ranch, but I may not live to see the end of the war, so maybe I should take some pleasure while I can." With a contemptuous nod, he tossed the coins into her lap.

Oh, God, now what was she going to do?

"I — I really am tired. Why don't we put this off until another night?"

"A whore turning down hard cash?" His tone was faintly mocking and dripping with contempt.

She had to make him believe she was a whore, for her own safety. "All right, we'll do it, but at least give me a chance to wash up a little."

"Sure. I've got some soap, and the river is close by."

She tucked the money into her shirt and stood up. Maybe when she got to the river, she could escape. "Now, you just wait here —"

"You think I'm that naive?" He glared at her. "I'll go with you to make sure you get back."

"I'm not going to let you watch me wash," she protested.

"Whores let men see them naked all the time; why are you suddenly so modest?"

"All right, if you must. Bring the soap and a towel."

Her heart was beating with trepidation as she started for the river with the big Cherokee following along behind. Was there any place along the way that she could dart into the woods and lose him? It didn't seem likely. She walked slowly, but in only moments they were standing by the water.

Now what? Slowly she began to unbutton her shirt.

Behind her, Jim Eagle complained, "At this rate, we'll still be standing here at noon tomorrow. Hurry it up."

"The anticipation is half the pleasure," she said, not looking at him.

"I thought whores are like any business — time is money."

There was nothing to do but keep undressing. She could only hope for some interruption. She turned her back to him and slipped off the shirt.

"Don't I get a look at what I'm buying?"

"Don't be in such a rush." She tried to sound coy, but her mouth was so dry, she could hardly swallow. She sat down on a rock, took off her boots, then stood up. Her hands went to her belt. What kind of mess had she gotten herself into? Was all that money she'd been promised worth losing her virginity? It might be a choice between that and her life.

"Stop stalling," he demanded. "If there's any kind of action back at the camp, I might get called away."

She'd been counting on that, but it didn't seem to be happening. To be believable, she was going to have to let this man use her body for the evening or risk being shot as a spy. Ever so slowly she took off her trousers and stood with her back to him.

She heard a deep intake of breath. "You're worth the money, all right."

"Toss me the soap and towel."

"Come and get them."

There was nothing to do but turn around and walk toward him in the moonlight, feeling his hungry eyes devouring every inch of her. April forced herself not to cross her arms over her body. She smiled archly. "So you like what you see, reb?"

"You know I do. Forget the bath. I'll have you right here and now." He reached for her, but she slipped away from him, grabbed the soap and towel, and hurried into the water.

"I choose the time and place," she answered. "Now, why don't you go back to camp and give me some privacy?"

He shook his head. "You're too desirable. I could watch you all night."

"Then we'd never get to the best part, would we?" She grinned at him and began to bathe, feeling his hot gaze sweeping her body even as she moved deeper into the water.

She washed with one hand, keeping the bandaged arm out of the water, while he leaned against a tree and watched her silently. How on earth could she get out of this? She spent a long time washing until finally, Jim Eagle seemed out of patience. "Hell, you washed every inch of yourself twice. Come on out."

There was nothing to do but come out of the water and reach for the towel she'd left hanging over a tree limb.

Jim Eagle watched her emerge, wet and naked. Her beautiful, lush body shone in the moonlight, and he had never wanted a woman so badly. Without a word he reached and caught her, pulled her into his embrace. She was stiff and wooden as he tried to kiss her.

"Not here," she protested. "Let's go back to camp."

He was loath to let her go, but grudgingly he turned her loose. "No wonder you command so much money — you really know how to make a man lust for you."

She smiled up at him with those full lips half parted as she wrapped the towel around her body. "Part of the job."

He took a deep breath, needing her so badly, his hands trembled. "And to think, I doubted you were a whore. Here, let me carry you back to camp. You're wounded and barefooted, and there's stickers in the grass."

She hesitated, then nodded. "All right."

He had never had such pleasure as he felt now, reaching for her. Her lithe body was wrapped in a towel, but the bare skin of her shoulders and arms was wet and warm. He grabbed up her clothes and held her close as he turned to walk back to camp, then bent his head and kissed the wetness of her throat. "You are really something," he murmured.

"You'll find out," she promised.

He strode toward camp, carrying her. She weighed hardly anything and fit into his arms as if she belonged there. She seemed to be trembling, which puzzled him. Maybe it was part of her act — exciting men by pretending to be reluctant.

He carried her back to camp and laid her gently on his blanket near the fire, then tossed her clothes nearby. Her skin was still wet, and her hair had come loose and hung around her shoulders. Now he stood looking down at her and very slowly unbuckled his belt. "Take off the towel."

She ran her tongue over her lips and looked around as if searching for escape. "Wouldn't — wouldn't you rather take it off me?"

He reached down and jerked the towel away, tossed it on the grass. He never took his eyes off her as he peeled off his shirt and

317

then his pants. He was wearing nothing un-
derneath.

April looked up at him, her heart hammering. She had never felt so vulnerable as
she did at this moment with his hot gaze
sweeping over her. His dark, naked body bore
several battle scars, and the taut muscles rip-
pled as he came toward her and dropped to
his knees. She leaned back on her elbows
and tried to smile at him. The poultice on
her arm was working — she barely felt any
pain. "I — I'm about to prove to you I'm
the best whore you ever topped."

"It'll be my pleasure."

Again she managed to quell the reflex to
cover herself with her hands. "You like what
you see?"

His eyes were dark with desire. "You know
I do. The question is, will your performance
be as good as you look?"

Would it? She barely knew anything about
sex, much less how fancy whores pleased
men. If she couldn't fool him, he'd know she
had been lying and start asking questions
that she didn't want to answer. "I'll prove it,
and then you can tell the others. Some of
them might be willing to pay plenty to enjoy
me."

He frowned as if he didn't like that
thought, even as he reached out and caught
her bare shoulder, jerking her to him. He
kissed her then, deeply, his tongue going into

her mouth as he pulled her against him so roughly, she could feel the hard muscles of his chest against her bare breasts. One of his big hands went to explore her breasts, and in spite of herself, she felt her own excitement rising.

She put her small hands on his wide shoulders, feeling the sinewy strength there as he shifted her so that his hot mouth was on her breast, kissing and caressing. She gasped at the sensation and couldn't hold back a moan of pleasure.

Now they lay together naked on the blanket, his strong hands roaming her body while her soft ones explored his. He was narrow-waisted, small-hipped, and steel-muscled. She imagined what it was going to be like when he put his manhood inside her, and the thought scared her, but she knew she must not protest or he would know she had lied.

"You really know how to excite a man," he gasped against her breast, and she felt the heat of his breath on her bare flesh. "I never should have doubted you were a whore."

She was scared, but she knew she'd have to go through with it. His hands stroked her skin until she had goosebumps all over and was clinging to him, wanting this union as his fingers went to stroke between her thighs, making her shudder with pleasure.

"I never believed I could want a woman

like I want you," he whispered, his voice thick with desire. "You may get my entire paycheck for the next few months."

She didn't intend to be here any longer than it took to search out the spy and receive the reward, but at this moment, she didn't want to think about anything past loving this savage, virile man.

"Now," he whispered, "I'm going to do what I've wanted to do since the first moment I saw you the day my brother brought you home to the ranch."

He had wanted her then? How much time had they lost by not admitting their attraction to each other? And now he thought she was a whore, and she dare not tell him the truth. Nothing mattered now except that she wanted to mesh with this man for a few wild moments of passion in the moonlight.

Abruptly, she heard running feet, and Tommy ran into the camp site. "Jim, the general wants . . . What's going on here?"

She grabbed for her towel as Jim Eagle came up off the blanket, cursing. "What the hell does it look like?"

The boy turned, flushed and embarrassed. "A girl? Gosh, I'm sorry, Jim, I didn't know I was interrupting —"

"What is it you want?" The big Cherokee got up off the blanket and reached for his pants.

She pulled her towel around her, but she

noted that the young boy's gaze never left her body.

Tommy blurted, "Our prisoner's a girl?"

"It's a long story." Jim sounded frustrated and angry.

"Uh, the general needs an officer to take charge of a patrol, and they can't find Captain Big Horse."

"He's always disappearing," Jim Eagle grumbled as he dressed. "It's a wonder he doesn't get busted in rank. Why the patrol?"

Tommy shrugged. "Something about someone thinking they saw a bushwhacker on the perimeters of the camp. I think the old man's afraid of being infiltrated by Yankees."

Jim Eagle finished buttoning his shirt. "He sees spies everywhere. He even thought she was one." He jerked his head in April's direction.

"I told you that was ridiculous." She tried to appear nonchalant. "I told you I'm just a whore."

"Shameful for a Cherokee girl," he muttered. "Well, I can't have you roaming the camp while I'm gone." He strode over and caught her arm.

"What are you doing?"

"I'm gonna tie you back up until I return. You owe me some pleasure, remember?"

How could she forget? She'd come close to losing her virginity to this man only moments ago. "I'm not in the mood anymore. I'll give you your money back."

He shook his head. "Uh-uh. I'll take it out in trade when I return."

"At least let me get dressed." She grabbed up the shirt and pants as he led her back to the tree.

Tommy watched with big eyes. "Aw, Jim," he protested, "there's no need for that; she's not going to run away."

"And I'm making sure of it," Jim said as he continued tying her. "Now, Tommy, you stay away from this whore, you hear me?"

"Why?"

"Because I said so. Come on, little brother." He put his hand on the boy's shoulder, and they walked away, although Tommy looked back over his shoulder at her.

April heaved a sigh of relief as she dressed. It was difficult with one arm tied to the tree, but she managed. What was she going to do when Jim Eagle returned? If she let him make love to her, he'd find out she was a virgin, and then he'd know she was a spy and maybe execute her or, at the very least, do whatever was necessary to find out what she knew. Why had she been stupid enough to get herself into this mess, and more important, how did she get out?

After an hour or so, she heard someone coming. Her mouth went dry, but it was Tommy who walked into the camp. "Oh, it's you. You didn't go on patrol with your brother?"

He shook his head. "I was on guard duty." He watched her. "Is it — is it true what Jim said about you being a . . . well, you know."

She knew from the hunger in his young face what he was thinking. "Tommy, I'm sure you don't have that much money."

Tommy's face flushed, and he turned sullen. "Someday I'll have plenty of money and be important, and no one will boss me anymore."

April nodded. "It must be terrible to be the younger brother and always have Jim ordering you around."

"I get damned tired of it. He treats me like a baby, and I'm a man."

Could she possibly persuade him to free her? She smiled at him. "You sure are. What happened to your other brother?"

"Jim mention him? He usually never talks about Will, but I reckon he thinks about him a lot."

She indicated he should sit down by the fire. "What happened to Will?"

Tommy sat down close to her. "Will's one of the Keetoowa, the traditional members of the tribe. His unit of the Cherokee Rifles deserted back in 'sixty-one and went over to the Union. I think Jim felt betrayed."

"Will must have had his reasons."

Tommy shrugged. "I don't know much

about it except the Keetoowa cling to traditional ways and think the tribe will do better going with the Union than the rebels."

She favored him with a smile. "What do you think?"

He grinned at her. "Nobody ever asks me what I think. Frankly, I'm not sure it makes any difference. You been in a big city?"

She nodded. "I'm going back there first chance I get."

"That's what I dream of." The young Cherokee's face was eager. "Will and Jim, they might want to go back to sweating on that ranch, but me, I want to go north and live in a big city. I want a nice house and a fine carriage, maybe a job in an office."

April wondered if she could enlist his help. She reached out and put her hand on his arm. "Everyone ought to be able to follow a dream; that's what I did. I was tired of being a traditional Cherokee girl."

"Maybe we'd end up in the same city." His voice was eager. "I wish this war would hurry up and end."

"I do, too, Tommy." She sighed and gave him her most winsome smile. "You know, Jim thinks I'm a spy, and when he gets back, he's determined to get information out of me, no matter what he has to do to me."

Tommy frowned. "That doesn't sound like Jim."

"I think maybe he feels the end justifies

the means, and he'll do whatever it takes."

He stared at her. "Will said that, too. Are you really a spy?"

She touched his arm again and laughed. "Of course not. I'm just a girl who got caught in the middle of this war."

"That's too bad, miss." He shook his head.

She let tears pool in her dark eyes. "I — I'm so afraid of what your brother will do to me."

"Don't worry, miss, I won't let him hurt you."

She had to try; she was desperate. "I don't know how you can stop him, unless — unless maybe you turned me loose."

Tommy appeared shocked. "I — I don't think I could do that. Jim would be real mad."

She dabbed at her eyes. "I know. I'll just have to wait and take my chances. You saw what he was about to do when you showed up while ago."

There was a long pause as the boy seemed to think all this over. "That doesn't seem like Jim."

"War does strange things to men." April shook his head. "Being his little brother, you wouldn't want to rile him."

He frowned. "I get damned tired of being the little brother. It's time people started treating me like a man; I'm almost nineteen, you know."

April sighed. "I'm scared, Tommy, scared of what the rebs will do to me trying to get information."

"If I turned you loose, I could get in big trouble."

He was weakening.

"Tommy, please. You could make it look like I escaped by myself."

He was visibly wavering. "I don't know . . ."

She cried some more. "If you don't help me, who knows what will happen?"

He thought a minute, then sighed. "I'll do it."

"Oh, thanks." She put her arms around his neck and hugged him.

In turn, he grabbed her and kissed her clumsily. "I'm gonna be rich someday. I got big plans, and I'll need a wife. Maybe we can meet in Boston after the war."

"I — I can't promise that, Tommy."

"I'll take that chance." He took a knife from his belt and cut the rawhide that bound her. "I'll get you some supplies, too." He hurried out of the camp.

April breathed a sigh of relief. She suspected that Jim might be the informant, but she wasn't sure she could tell that to the major when he sought her out. He'd think she'd be at the Union fort, so maybe that's where she'd better go when she left here. Or maybe she should just forget the whole thing as too risky and clear out. All that money wouldn't do her any good if she were dead.

Tommy was back in minutes with a knapsack of supplies. "Captain Big Horse is back in camp and asking about the prisoner."

She felt a chill go up her back, remembering how the captain had looked at her. "Where'd he been?"

Tommy shook his head. "Who knows? He gambles, so maybe he's meeting with some soldiers to play cards or shoot dice. Jim says he's not a very good officer."

Could Captain Big Horse be the informant she was looking for? There was no way to find out unless she stayed in this camp, and that was too dangerous. The reward wasn't worth her life. "Thanks, Tommy. I hope you don't get in any trouble over this."

He grinned. "The war isn't going to last much longer, and then, when I've got money, I'll find you in Boston."

Hopeless daydreams for a young boy, she thought. Tommy would probably end up back on that ranch he hated, sweating over branding horses and cattle.

There was no way she could take a horse without it being missed, so she nodded goodbye to Tommy, took the knapsack of supplies, and slipped away into the forest. By the time Jim Eagle discovered she was gone, she would be miles away.

Jim rode into camp and dismounted in

front of the general's tent. Captain Big Horse stuck his head out, and Jim saluted. "Lieutenant Eagle reporting in, sir."

"At ease. Come on in, Lieutenant. The general has been waiting for your report."

Jim stooped his tall frame and went in, aching to ask where the captain had been when they needed him, but knowing he dare not. The captain was not much of a soldier, no better than Tommy. They both disappeared every chance they got, especially when there was work to do.

"Ah, Lieutenant." The old Cherokee smiled and motioned to him. "Like a drink?"

Jim accepted it gratefully. "Sorry, sir, didn't find any bushwhackers lurking anywhere near the camp. Must have been a false alarm or we scared them off."

The general nodded. "That's good. How are you doing getting information out of your mysterious lady?"

"How did you know . . . ?"

"Your little brother told half the camp."

Damn Tommy. Now all the men would want a chance at her. Jim's groin tightened when he thought of April. He'd been within seconds of taking her when his brother had interrupted everything. He still had plans for her tonight. "Haven't learned anything yet, sir."

Captain Big Horse laughed. "Maybe she's just what everyone says she is: a whore who was trying to get to Fort Gibson. Our money ought to be as good as the Yankees'." He rubbed his hands together and grinned.

The fact that the arrogant captain was picturing making love to her rankled Jim, and he frowned at the other man. "I'm not sure that's all she is, sir."

The general leaned back in his camp chair and sighed, then picked up a pen. "If she's just a whore, we ought to turn her loose. A woman in camp will cause a lot of trouble among the men."

He realized then that he didn't want to let her go. Maybe once he'd had his fill of her, he wouldn't care. "Begging your pardon, sir, I feel she might have vital information she was trying to take to Fort Gibson. If I keep her a few days, maybe I can get her to lower her guard and tell me something."

The senior officer didn't look convinced. "You realize, Lieutenant, that it's a lot more likely she's just a common whore than a spy?"

Common? Kawoni would never be common. She was too special, too beautiful.

Jim said, "If I could hold her captive awhile and gain her trust, maybe she'd tell me what she knows, if anything."

"Are you saying make her fall in love with you so you could betray her?" the general asked.

"All's fair in love and war." Jim smiled.

"I'd be willing to volunteer for that duty," the captain said.

Jim gritted his teeth, imagining her in the other man's arms, then remembered that the other was a captain and his superior officer.

For a long moment the general said nothing. "I don't need the extra trouble this girl is causing me, especially if she's just a common whore."

The captain shook his head. "Doesn't seem very common to me, sir, but then, of course, I haven't tried her out." He favored Jim with a curious stare.

Jim almost rushed in to save her reputation but then realized that if she wasn't a whore, she was certainly a spy and could be shot.

"I say we ought to let the officers enjoy her and then get rid of her," Captain Big Horse said.

Jim gritted his teeth to hold back his anger at the thought of her being passed around the officers' tents. "Captain, I'd think better of that remark if I were you."

Before the other could answer, the old man threw down his pen. "Enough. See what I mean? She's already causing trouble between my officers, and I don't need that. I'm wishing you had never captured her."

"Give me a chance, sir," Captain Big Horse said. "If she knows anything, I'll find it out if I have to —"

"Enough, Captain." The old man held up his hand for silence. "Somehow, the Yankees seem to know all our maneuvers, and I'm desperate enough to try anything to solve this leak. Give it a shot, Lieutenant Eagle. Do whatever it takes to find out what she knows . . . if anything. You're both dismissed."

Jim saluted, turned smartly on his heel, and started to leave the tent, followed by the captain.

"Oh, Lieutenant, one more thing," Big Horse said.

"Yes, sir?"

"If she is a spy, you know what you'll have to do. We can't have her carrying information about our troops back to the enemy."

Jim glared at him. "With all due respect, sir, I don't think I could kill a woman."

The other glared at him. "Remember, a lot of Confederate lives might be at stake if that pretty little tart manages to carry information back to the Union."

"I reckon you're right, sir." Jim nodded.

"Good." The other smiled without mirth. "Then we understand each other, don't we?"

Jim didn't answer. He saluted and strode away, his mind in turmoil. What in the hell had he gotten himself into? He had no idea if the sultry beauty was truly a whore or a spy; he'd only been intent on keeping her to satisfy the hunger she'd built in him. He

331

didn't want to think any further ahead than tonight.

General Stand Watie stared after the two young officers long after they had left his tent. There had been bad blood between the two for a long time, and now it was obvious they both lusted after the girl, which only added to the general's problems. He didn't need disharmony in the ranks over a woman when the Confederates were having such bad luck.

He stood up and paced his tent, deep in thought. Things hadn't been going well for his troops for weeks. They always seemed to be riding into ambushes or being outflanked at every turn. It was almost as if there were a spy in the Confederate camp. Stand Watie shook his head. It was unthinkable that one of his own men might be a traitor.

Then he remembered that only four years ago, as his troops chased the Union Creek tribe that was fleeing toward Kansas, a whole regiment of the traditional Keetoowa Cherokee troops had deserted and gone over to the other side. In fact, one of them had been Jim Eagle's own brother. The general paused and rolled an unwelcome idea over in his mind, then shook his head. No, he'd stake his life that Jim Eagle was as loyal as he was brave. On the other hand . . .

He shook his head to clear it. He was old

and tired and didn't know what to believe anymore. Besides, half his soldiers had relatives who were members of the so-called pin Indians, who were now fighting for the Union.

Well, there were many others in the camp coming and going all the time: troops, traders, scouts, and even an occasional camp follower. It wouldn't be that difficult to sneak out and meet with a Yankee informant.

Stand Watie paced some more. The capture of that Yankee boat had been the only good luck his men had had in weeks. Maybe the Cherokee Mounted Rifles were just unlucky, or maybe they were being betrayed. Could this mysterious girl shed some light on this? If there was a spy in his ranks, General Stand Watie vowed silently that he would personally pick the firing squad.

Chapter 18

Jim Eagle strode through the darkness toward his tent, his mind on the beauty that awaited him there. Yes, he'd try to get information out of her, but that wasn't the main thing on his mind. He longed to finish what had begun hours ago. He wondered where Tommy was. His younger brother had seemed too interested in the girl, and she was smart enough to try to take advantage of him.

He detoured and checked Tommy's tent. With a growing uneasiness, he realized Tommy's blankets hadn't been slept in. The girl. Would Tommy try to . . . ? Well, she was beautiful. Jim hastened his step as he went to his own camp.

"Tommy, are you here?"

No answer.

"Tommy?"

The girl was gone, and he found Tommy just pulling himself into a sitting position and groaning.

"Tommy" — he knelt — "what in the hell happened?"

Tommy put his hand to his head. "She —

she was afraid of you, begged me to free her —"

"And when you weren't looking, she hit you in the head and escaped," Jim guessed.

"Uh, yes, that's right."

Jim Eagle began to curse. "She's smarter than I thought. Why would she be in such a rush to get away?"

Tommy grinned sheepishly. "She said she feared what she thought you might do to her —"

"The little bitch will be twice as afraid when I catch up with her. Are you all right?"

His brother nodded.

Jim swore and stood up, looking around. "How long's she been gone?"

Tommy's youthful face furrowed in thought. "It must have been just after dark."

"That means she got a big head start. I've got to find her before word gets out I've lost the prisoner."

Tommy looked down, shamefaced. "I'm sorry, Jim, I didn't mean to cause you any trouble."

"That's okay, little brother." He patted Tommy's shoulder. "She could make a man forget his duty, forget everything but her."

Tommy stared up at him. "I never saw you act this way about a woman before."

Jim realized it, too, and it angered him. "There's just some women that affect men that way, and she's taken advantage of it.

There's no telling where she's headed."

Tommy rubbed his head. "She said something about Fort Gibson — asked a lot of questions about Will."

Jim blinked, trying to block out the twinge of jealousy that flooded his soul. "Will? You suppose he's at Fort Gibson and she was trying to reach him?"

"She didn't say. What you intend to do, Jim?"

"Hell, what can I do? I'm going to find her and bring her back."

"She may be a long way off by now. You're risking Yankee patrols if you follow her toward Fort Gibson."

"You think I don't know that?"

"I'll go with you." Tommy scrambled to his feet, swaying a little.

Jim shook his head. "You're in no shape to ride."

"I wish you'd stop treating me like a baby," Tommy snarled. "I'm a grown man and can take care of myself. Someday I'll show you. I'll be rich and important."

"Sure, kid." Absently he patted Tommy's shoulder.

"Why don't you let her go, Jim? Does General Watie really care if she gets away?"

Jim faced the truth. He didn't know whether it made any difference to the Confederacy what happened to the girl, but it did to him. He wanted her, desired her with an urgency that almost scared him. "Try to keep anyone from finding out I'm gone until I find her."

"Suppose you don't?"

Jim began to gather supplies. "I reckon I'll deal with that when I get there." He strode toward his horse, thinking: she'd probably follow the river if she was trying to reach Fort Gibson. Was Will there, and was she attempting to rendezvous with him? Was it something as simple as love, or was it something more? He didn't know which thought gave him the most discomfort. Jim mounted up and rode out, avoiding the sentries in the darkness as he headed the palomino toward the river.

It was a bright moonlit night, so he might be able to track her. Here and there, he got off his horse to look at a faint track or a broken weed where someone had passed. She was traveling along the river, all right. Maybe she hoped to find a canoe or an old raft there. Jim rode through the night, remembering his naive little brother's words. Maybe she wasn't a spy; maybe she was just a camp follower who intended to work both sides of the line, making money off the sexual appetites of Union and Confederate. He was getting farther and farther away from the Confederate forces. If he had any sense, he'd turn around and go back, get a patrol to accompany him. Jim thought about it a moment, then shook his head. He'd be in trouble for letting her get away, but worse, so would Tommy — and Tommy had plenty of demerits now.

Jim Eagle had been riding for hours when he dismounted to rest his horse. Leading it, he moved silent as a shadow through the trees along the river.

April had paused to rest at the riverbank, trying to decide what to do next. She was wearing ragged Union pants and an oversized Confederate shirt. That would make it impossible to sneak into Fort Gibson as a common soldier. She'd gotten herself into a big, dangerous mess without finding a single clue that she could trade to her mysterious Major Smith for gold. Maybe she should try to cross the river and keep walking until she found a town, and forget this whole adventure. April opened the little cache of supplies Tommy had given her, and began to eat.

She heard a noise in the brush and froze. In eastern Indian territory there were brown bears, an occasional bobcat, some wild tusker hogs, snakes, and prowling bushwhackers from both armies. She didn't have a weapon, so she was on her own. "Who — who's there?"

No answer. Maybe she'd imagined the sound. After a moment, she was satisfied that it was only the wind or some small creature like an owl. She finished her smoked jerky and hardtack and washed it down with water from the canteen. She wished she had some coffee, but even if she had some, she wouldn't dare chance a fire. Some sniper from either side might pick her off and ask questions later.

For a split second, she thought she heard a sound, and then a big form came running out of the shadows and collided with her. She fought back instinctively, and they rolled in the dirt as her assailant grappled with her. She made no sound, biting and clawing, but her attacker was bigger.

The moon came out suddenly, and she realized with horror that she looked into the wild face of a bushwhacker.

She screamed instinctively, and the man hit her, knocking her backward. April tasted blood as she fell, half stunned. She half heard, half felt him ripping at her clothes. He was going to rape her. The horrid realization gave her renewed strength, and she began to fight, but she was no match against his lust-starved strength.

"Stop it, bitch," he growled, "or I'll kill you. I aim to have you, so save yourself the trouble."

Not without a fight, she thought, and screamed again. With a curse, he hit her across the face as she fought to get away from him. He might rape her, but he'd have to kill her first. She had never been so terrified in her life.

At that moment, another big shadow darted out of the woods. Oh, my God, he had a partner. She didn't stand a chance, but she fought anyway. Then in the moonlight she recognized the second man. "Jim! Oh, Jim!"

He didn't answer as he attacked her assailant, but she saw the fury in his dark face as he hit the man hard, sending him stumbling backward over a log. With a roar like a crazed beast, the man clambered to his feet and attacked Jim Eagle. He picked up the Cherokee in a terrible bear hug and held him off the ground.

From her spot on the edge of the clearing, she saw the pain and desperation in Jim's face as he struggled. She had to do something. April grabbed up a rock and attacked the crazed giant. He dropped Jim with a muttered curse and turned toward her. "You bitch, I'll kill you for that!"

Jim staggered to his feet, breathing hard. "Not unless you kill me first!"

The giant turned toward Jim, blinking and muttering.

"Look out, Jim," she shrieked, "he's got a knife!"

She saw the sudden gleam of a pistol barrel as Jim pulled it from its holster, and the sudden flash as he fired.

The bushwhacker grabbed his big belly with one hand, lurching toward Jim with his blade. The moonlight flashed on the steel as he cut at the empty air. The Cherokee dodged away skillfully.

April took a deep breath and held it. The hot summer air smelled of gunpowder and warm blood as the giant lurched toward Jim and then collapsed and lay still.

"April, are you all right?"

With a sob, she ran into his arms without thinking, and he held her close. "It — it was terrible. He was going to . . ."

"I know." He held her close and patted her hair. "Don't think about it; you're safe now."

She looked up at him, and he kissed the tears from her face. Then she was returning his kiss while he murmured reassurances to her. "It's okay, Kawoni, I won't let anyone hurt you."

Nothing mattered at this moment — not the war, not the spying, not the reward money. Nothing mattered but being safe in this man's embrace while he kissed and caressed her.

The kiss deepened, and Jim Eagle drew a sharp, shuddery breath. She clung to him, letting his tongue probe along her lips until she opened them in surrender so that he could explore the velvet depths of her mouth. "Oh, Jim, Jim . . ."

Her bare breasts were pressed against him

in her torn shirt, but she was oblivious to everything except his hands stroking her flesh, and then he lifted her in his arms and kissed her nipples, so that she gasped and wanted more.

"I've dreamed of doing this a thousand times since the first time I saw you," he murmured, and his breath was warm against the valley between her breasts.

She put her arms around his neck and urged him to taste and caress more with his mouth. Nothing counted to her anymore — nothing except finally meshing with this man she had loved since she was a young girl. "Take me, Jim," she whispered. "Oh, I can't stand it any longer; take me!"

He seemed to need no further urging as he carried her deeper into the forest and laid her down on the soft grass. "I want you like I've never wanted another woman."

She didn't even worry about what he would think when he realized she was a virgin. Her pulse pounded in her head, making a roaring sound that drowned out everything else but their mutual need. Then they were both naked in the moonlight and kissing and caressing as their heat built.

April arched her back, offering him her breasts as he came down on her, pushing her thighs apart. He hesitated just a moment, and she felt his big manhood rigid and pulsing with need. Then he plunged into her, deep and hard. The sudden pain almost made her cry out, but then his mouth covered hers in a deep kiss that muted her voice. He began to ride her hard, stroking deep into her velvet softness. She could feel the heat pulsating from him, and her own need rose. She wanted him deeper and deeper still. "More," she whispered, "and faster . . ."

She put her hands on his lean hips and felt the power there as he drove into her rhythmically. She couldn't get enough of him. They were both covered with a fine sheen of perspiration as they locked in the eternal ritual of mating. He was panting and grinding down hard on her as her emotions built. She didn't know what was happening or what to expect; she only knew she never wanted this moment to end.

And at that instant, it built to a climax, and he paused, straining against her even as her own passion raced out of control like a prairie fire. She held him close, digging her nails into his back as they locked and strained together. It seemed like an eternity of pleasure, but it wasn't enough, she thought; she could never get enough of this virile man's arms. Then it was over, both of them still locked together in a passionate embrace, breathing hard and shiny with sweat.

"Oh, my God," he gasped, "no wonder you charge so much. I never had a woman love me like this before."

He still thought she was a whore. Anger and hurt flooded her soul, even though she knew she should feel relief that her secret was safe. She wanted to scratch his face and beat him on the chest, scream and bite. *I hate you,* she thought. *I hate you for thinking I'd do this with anyone else, especially for money.*

Then the realization flooded over her. She'd just given her virginity to her captor out in the woods. In this bright moonlight, he would soon see the evidence of her virginity, and then she'd have to answer tough questions.

"Be quiet." Jim Eagle tensed, still lying on her.

"What?"

"Listen. I think I hear horses." His voice was low, urgent. "We've got to clear out; there's no telling how far the sound of that gunshot carried, and we may run across a Yankee patrol."

For her, was that good or bad? Then her anxiety was for Jim because he might be killed rather than taken prisoner. "Let's go," she whispered.

Now she could hear the horses coming, too. She scrambled up, grabbing for her clothes. "What'll we do?"

"No time to make a run for it. Toss your clothes over here in the shadows, and we'll go into the river. Maybe they won't find that body."

The horses sounded closer now.

April was suddenly afraid for him. If it was a Yankee patrol, they'd kill or capture him. "What about your horse?"

"Left him deep in the woods. With any luck, no one will see him. Come on, let's hide in the water."

He took her hand and led her naked into the stream.

"Maybe it's a Confederate patrol," she whispered.

"We'll find out; here they come."

They both grabbed reeds and went under, watching the riverbank as they stayed submerged all but their eyes. The current was strong, and she felt Jim grab her hand to keep her with him as they crouched in the dark water.

In minutes, a cavalry patrol galloped into view and reined in near the river. The moonlight gleamed on their brass buttons. The uniforms were blue.

"Sergeant," one of the men yelled, "are you sure you heard a shot?"

The grizzled old sergeant looked around. "I would have sworn I did. Maybe it came from another direction."

April held her breath and did not move, breathing through the straw. She felt Jim's arm reach out and pull her naked body close to his. *All I've got to do,* she thought, *is stand up and raise the alarm. The Yanks will capture*

Jim Eagle, and I'll be taken to Fort Gibson to continue my search. That's where the major will be expecting to find me. As she thought it, she knew she couldn't betray him.

After a moment and some discussion, the Yankee patrol rode away. She raised her head up out of the water, gasping for air, and listened to the hoofbeats fade into the distance. "That was close."

"More than you know," he muttered. "I recognized a couple of old friends riding with that patrol: Yellow Jacket and Smoke. We were Lighthorsemen together before the war." He took her hand and looked down into her face. "Thanks for not giving me away."

She shrugged, both of them still standing in the shallow water. "I told you I wasn't a spy; I was just a whore trying to make a living."

"And you are good at what you do," he murmured, and pulled her close, kissing her deeply. They clung together, naked in the river as his hands explored her body. "I'm sorry I ever doubted you."

At least the evidence was washed away, and he'd never know the difference. "So now you gonna let me go on to Fort Gibson? I figure those Yanks have more gold than rebels."

He put his hands on her shoulders, scowling down at her. "I haven't had my fill of you yet. Why should I let damned Yankees have any entertainment?"

Entertainment. Yes, that's all it had been to him. She had just given this warrior the precious gift of her virginity, and he was treating it as a moment's pleasure. Well, what had she expected? Even if she told him the truth, he surely wouldn't believe her any more than he would believe the truth about who had sent her and why. If she got out of this intrigue alive, she was going to go back north and never try spying again.

"Let's get dressed," he said.

She nodded, and they came up out of the water and began to dress. April's mind was busy. She wasn't learning anything of value in the rebel camp, and if she didn't get to Fort Gibson, she would miss rendezvousing with the major. If she didn't get further instructions, she wouldn't know what to do next.

A thought occurred to her as she finished dressing. Jim had his back to her, putting on his boots. She still had the money he had given her earlier in camp. All she needed was a horse. Jim Eagle had a horse. He was putting on his boots now, oblivious to her, his pistol still in its holster in the nearby shadows. Did she have the courage to do this? She thought about the money that would give her the respectability of a white girl. It was worth the chance.

April stepped noiselessly across the grass and took the pistol from its holster.

Jim turned and half rose at the sound. "What the — ?"

He never got a chance to finish, because April brought the butt of the Colt down across his head. He swayed just a moment and then collapsed and lay still.

Oh, dear God, she hoped she hadn't hurt him. No, he was breathing. When he came to, he'd come after her, she thought, and he'd be furious and dangerous. If she was smart, she'd shoot him and rid herself of that threat. Even as that thought crossed her mind, she knew she couldn't do it. For a moment she stood looking down at him, resisting the urge to touch his face and make sure she hadn't hurt him too much. He'd only be unconscious so long, and if she was still here when he woke up . . . The thought of his anger galvanized her into action. She took the pistol and tucked it into her waistband, then ran through the woods until she found his fine palomino tied in the shadows.

Would the great stallion even let her mount up?

"Steady, boy, steady," she crooned, and the horse started and snorted. She put her hand on its velvet muzzle, and it quieted so she could mount. She urged the horse forward and took off at a lope through the woods. She knew she could follow the river and find Fort Gibson, but riding a horse with a Confederate saddle and blanket and wearing a

348

ragged, mismatched uniform, she'd face a lot of questions she didn't want to answer. Well, she had Jim Eagle's silver dollars. Out here in the Territory, real money would buy almost anything. She'd figure it out as she went. It wasn't long until dawn. The main thing now was to clear out before Jim Eagle regained consciousness.

For a split second, she worried about the man. Jim Eagle would awaken only slightly worse for wear and walk back to the Confederate camp. That might take a while, so no one would set up a hue and cry after her for a few hours. That thought cheered her as she rode. Somewhere up ahead was the fort, and she had some planning to do before she got there.

Chapter 19

Jim came back to consciousness, his head throbbing. Where in the hell was he? Gingerly he reached to touch his head, then remembered what had happened. Why, that little . . .

He stumbled to his feet in the darkness and looked around. She was gone, as were his horse and pistol. She'd knocked him in the head and fled, leaving him here in the woods. He was only lucky he hadn't been found by an enemy patrol. There was nothing to do but start walking back to camp and hope he didn't run into trouble along the way.

He had only walked a few hundred yards when he heard the sound of horses coming. For a split second he was cheered, thinking Tommy had sent a patrol out looking for him; then he realized it might also be Yankees. Quickly he crept behind some brush. If he only had a weapon . . . Jim flattened himself against the dirt, watching the trail in the moonlight. His heart hammered, thinking how much danger he might be in with no way to defend himself. The sound of drumming hooves grew louder. Now in the distance, he could see a patrol coming, the moon throwing distorted shadows ahead of the horses. Then the light caught the flash of brass buttons, and he saw the blue uniforms.

He didn't want to spend the rest of the war in a miserable prison camp. He could only hope the patrol rode on. Jim held his breath as the horses passed so near, he could have reached out and touched the nearest one.

"Lieutenant, I would have sworn I saw a track back there," a soldier said.

"We'll spread out and look around. Be careful, men." A familiar voice, Jim thought — an old friend from the Lighthorsemen: Yellow Jacket. He hadn't seen or heard of the Muskogee warrior since that long ago snowy day in '61.

"Smoke," the familiar voice ordered, "take the men and spread out along the river. See if you can find anything."

A murmur of assent, and then the horses scattered, moving away from where he crouched in the brush.

Only Yellow Jacket paused and dismounted, looking around. He was so close, Jim Eagle could almost have reached out and touched him as the warrior walked up and down the trail, looking about with keen eyes. Jim held his breath. Any moment now, his old friend would discover him hiding here and shout the alarm. The others were some distance away, searching along the river.

At that moment, Yellow Jacket turned and paused, looking straight at Jim. Jim tensed, ready to fight or run when the other called to his patrol. For a moment, the only sound was both of them breathing. At that precise instant, Yellow Jacket stared straight at Jim, seeming to recognize him. He hesitated only a moment; then he smiled very slowly.

In the distance, one of the Yankees yelled, "Hey, Lieutenant, there's nothing here. You see anything?"

For a heartbeat, the Muskogee officer looked at Jim, and then he made a gesture. He saluted Jim, and, stunned, Jim returned the gesture.

"No," Yellow Jacket yelled back, "don't see a thing. I think we'd better be getting back to the fort." He smiled at Jim, then mounted up and rode off down toward the river to join his patrol.

Jim lay there, finally taking a deep breath, and realized his clothes were plastered to him with cold sweat. He lay there a moment longer, listening to the fading hoofbeats as the patrol rode away. Finally, he got up and began to walk. With any luck, he'd be back at camp before dawn. If he ever caught up with that Cherokee whore again, he'd make her wish she'd never been born. The bitterest part was that he'd found himself attracted to her in a way he'd never felt before. Damn her anyway.

April rode though the forest toward Fort Gibson, not daring to look behind her in case Jim Eagle had come to, found another horse, and was in hot pursuit. She wasn't sure of the time except that she knew it was near dawn. What was she to do? She dare not ride into the fort in this ragged uniform on a horse with a Confederate saddle and bridle. There'd be too many questions asked.

Up ahead on a ridge, she saw the faint outline of a log cabin. Maybe she could get help here. April felt in her shirt pocket. Good. She still had the silver dollars Jim Eagle had given her. She hoped he felt he'd gotten his money's worth. Tears came to her eyes as she thought of him. She was torn between attraction and hatred that he had taken her virginity and hadn't even appreciated her sacrifice. She hoped a Yankee patrol caught him and threw him in some awful prison camp. She had left him without weapons or a horse — he was defenseless if a Union patrol should find him. She didn't care; he deserved it, she thought defiantly, angry at herself because she was having misgivings about what she'd done.

A dog at the cabin began to bark, and the faint light of a lantern flickered inside. Quickly April dismounted. Suppose these settlers were Yankees? She didn't want to be caught with a Confederate horse or weapons. There would be too many questions to answer. Instead, she turned the horse back toward the Confederate camp and whacked it across the rump. "Go, boy. Go find Jim." The horse took off at a gallop. April watched it leave and then walked up on the cabin's porch and pounded on the door.

"Who's there?" A quavery old woman's voice. "Go away. I've got a gun."

"It's just me and I'm alone. I'm lost and hungry; can you help me?"

Very slowly the door opened, and a tiny Indian woman peered around the door, holding a shotgun. "Who are you?"

"I've lost my horse," April said, "and I'm stranded and afraid of bushwhackers."

"Me, too." The elderly woman smiled as she opened the door and gestured April in. "Come in. I don't have much, but you're welcome to share."

With a sigh of relief, April went inside, and the old woman closed the door, asking, "Girl, why are you dressed like that?"

April held up her hands to show they were empty. "It's a long story. I'm lost, was captured, and this old uniform is all they gave me to wear." She looked about in the dim light and realized how poor the woman was. "Have you got anything to eat? I've got money."

"Real money or worthless Confederate dollars?"

"Real silver." April reached in her pocket and brought out the silver dollars. "If you've got some clothes I can change into, I'll pay for those, too."

The old woman put down her shotgun. "I haven't seen real money in a long time. I've been hoping to find a way to buy supplies. I'm almost out of salt and flour, too."

"Coffee?" April asked.

The old woman shook her head. "Just a little bit, but I can make it do." She began to bustle around the kitchen.

April sat down on a stool before the fire, abruptly realizing how exhausted she was. "You support the North or the South?"

The old Indian woman paused, looked at her, and laughed. "What difference does it make to me who wins? One son has died on each side. I only hope to survive till it's over."

She dished up corn pone with sorghum syrup poured over it, and a pot of weak coffee. April found herself wolfing it down. "Don't you want to know what I'm doing out here in the middle of the woods?" April asked.

The old lady shook her head. "The less I know, the better. When you finish, I'll fill a tub and let you wash up. I might be able to find you an old calico dress."

"I'd be so grateful," April said, "and a little sleep would be nice, too." She laid most of the silver on the table, and the old lady's eyes got big and round.

"I'll be able to buy enough for months at the sutler's store at the fort."

April looked out the window. The sun would be coming up soon. If she could get a little rest, she'd go on to the fort. The mysterious major might be waiting for her there. With all her needs met, she curled up on a small bed in a corner of the cabin and dropped off to sleep. Jim Eagle might come searching for her, but right now April was too weary to care.

The dawn light was just breaking in the east at Fort Gibson when Will Eagle swung into the saddle. "Sergeant, mount your patrol."

"Yes, sir." The short, hairy man saluted in an almost arrogant way. It was evident that this white man felt he was too good to serve under an Indian officer.

The patrol rode out just as last night's patrol rode in, headed up by Yellow Jacket. Will paused and saluted him. "Run across anything out there?"

Yellow Jacket hesitated. He didn't like the younger brother as well as he liked the elder. Will was shorter and not as handsome as Jim, and there was something ruthless about

Will, as if he didn't care whom he stepped on to achieve his ends. Yellow Jacket didn't regret not killing or capturing Jim Eagle last night. After all, he owed Jim his life from an earlier time, in '61.

So now he shook his head. "If there's any rebs in those woods, they're all back in camp asleep, which is where I mean to be in a few minutes."

Will nodded and grinned. "Haven't had a chance to talk to you, really, since you were shipped in last week. "How are things in Kansas?"

Yellow Jacket sighed. "The Union troops didn't treat us that good when we arrived in 'sixty-one. I reckon so many refugees overwhelmed them."

Smoke said, "I'm afraid the Union cares no more about us than the rebels."

"We're Indians." Will shrugged. "I only hope the Union treats us better in the long run than the Confederacy, because we know how the rebels treated all our tribes when they ran us out of the South."

Yellow Jacket nodded as he wiped the sweat from his brow. The blue uniforms were hot in the late June dawn. "Let's hope the Union keeps its word."

"Me, too," Will said with a nod. "I only wish I could convince my stubborn brothers of that. I reckon Jim is still clinging to that forlorn hope that the Confederates will give

357

the Indians their own state. We disagreed on that."

Yellow Jacket watched the other's angry face, thinking of his old friend, Jim Eagle, who was now the enemy. "You seen Jim since the Keetoowa came over to our side in 'sixty-one?"

"No, but I know he and Tommy are alive."

Yellow Jacket glanced at him. "How can you know that for sure?"

The other hesitated. "I — I just hope so, that's all."

Smoke glanced toward the fort. "Maybe you brothers can make up after the war finally ends."

Will laughed without mirth. "I doubt it. I think Jim feels I'm a deserter because I crossed over. I'd do anything to shorten this war, end it before any more people are killed. The South can't win, so it's foolish for them to keep fighting."

"I want it to end," Yellow Jacket said, "so I can get back to my woman and family. Twilight's in Kansas waiting for me to return. We've got a baby boy and two other little kids we saved on the trip to Kansas."

Will Eagle grew quiet, his eyes wistful. "There was a girl I fancied once, but she was ashamed of being Indian. She went up north to go to school and never came back. I don't even know if she's still alive. For that matter, I'm not even sure if Mother's alive, what with all the fighting and bushwhackers roaming the Indian Territory."

Yellow Jacket didn't say anything, but he saw the pain in the other's eyes. "Things will work out with your brothers; you'll see."

The other shook his head regretfully. "I doubt it. Jim was your friend, too; now he'd kill you on sight because you wear a blue uniform."

"I doubt that," Yellow Jacket said, remembering. "In the early days of the war, he found me cornered without a horse or weapons."

"And?" Will asked.

"He pretended he didn't see me and let me go."

"Jim was always the one with principles," Will agreed. "Me, I've decided the end justifies the means; whatever it takes to end this war, I'm going to do."

Yellow Jacket frowned. "That's not a moral choice."

"Don't talk to me about morality and war in the same breath," Will snapped.

"You've changed, Will."

"Have I?" the other said. "Hell, this war would change anybody. All that matters now is ending it."

"In an honorable way," Yellow Jacket said.

"In any way I can," Will snapped. "Whatever it takes."

Will realized suddenly that the black Indian

and the Muskogee officer were staring at him. He'd said too much. "I've got a scouting mission to ride. Sergeant, see to your men." He saluted the other officer and rode out into the summer dawn while Yellow Jacket's patrol rode into the fort.

Next to Will, Sergeant Henley's voice was contemptuous. "If you want my opinion —"

"I didn't ask for it," Will snapped, and looked straight ahead as he rode. He didn't like the squat sergeant, because Henley was a toady who shirked work and responsibility and drank and gambled too much. Besides that, he was aware the white man hated serving with Indians.

They rode for several hours, seeing nothing unusual. It was the last days of June, and the blue uniforms were hot. Will ordered his men to spread out along the river miles ahead, searching for anything unusual while he and Henley rode together into a small valley.

For a mile they saw nothing, and then a shot whizzed past his head, and his horse reared and whinnied. "Damn, Sergeant, we've got a sniper in the brush. Come on!"

They galloped to where Will thought the shot might have come from, and dismounted as the firing continued. "See if you can get behind them," Will ordered as he pulled his rifle from his scabbard.

"Sir, the patrol will be coming now that

they've heard the shots," Henley whined. "Shouldn't we wait until —"

"And have the snipers get away?"

"But we can't be sure how many of them there are, or anything else."

"Sergeant, are you disobeying my order?"

"No, sir. I'll go." Henley rode out.

Now Will smelled the faint scent of smoke. What the . . . ? Was the rebel setting the woods on fire? Will crept through the dense brush. In the distance, he heard Henley yelling that he was behind the snipers. The cornered men would surely realize they were trapped and surrender. Instead, the unseen enemy continued to fire at them. Will had now surmised it was only one man and that he wasn't going to surrender without a fight. It might be easier to wait him out, but Will was hot and tired and didn't want to take any chances. "Come out with your hands up!" Will yelled.

Instead, there was another volley of shots. In the distance now, he could hear the patrol coming. They'd soon surround the rebel sniper. Will crept closer. Now he could see just a partial view of the sniper's head. He could yell at him again to surrender, but Will was angry that the man had ignored his first offer. Will aimed and fired. The man fell. He waited for a moment to make sure there was no more danger, then stood and waved to Sergeant Henley. "I got him. Come on in."

The two of them ran into the clearing.

Henley paused, his eyes wide. "Oh, God, Lieutenant, you've made a big mistake."

Will gasped as he got a good look at the dead man lying crumpled near a small fire. A dead officer in a blue uniform. Will cursed. "We've killed one of our own."

"Not me," the sergeant corrected, "you."

Will Eagle cursed again and bent to turn the dead man over. The sunlight reflected off the blue uniform and brass buttons of the cavalry major. His eyes stared sightlessly into eternity. "Why in the hell was he shooting at us?"

Henley grinned as he stared at the dead man. "Maybe he couldn't see we were Yanks and panicked, started shooting."

Will Eagle looked around. "There'll be hell to pay back at the fort for this. Funny, I don't recognize this man, and I thought I knew all the officers."

Henley picked up a small scrap of paper smoldering by the fire. "What's this? Looks like he was trying to burn something when we closed in."

Will Eagle grabbed it up and examined it. There was not enough left to know what it had been. "Maybe he thought we were Johnny Rebs and he was carrying important dispatches."

In the distance, they could hear the rest of the patrol coming. Henley grinned. "Looks like you're in big trouble."

The body lay on the edge of a gully. Will felt sweat breaking out on his dark forehead. He had killed a Union officer, and Sergeant Henley knew it. At the very least, there'd be an investigation. As an Indian, he couldn't count on a fair trial if he went to court-martial. "Maybe," he thought aloud, "we could throw him in the gully and forget we ever saw him."

"Well, Injun, I believe I could help you out of your pickle — for a price." The white man's tone was contemptuous and conde-scending.

"That's no way to speak to an officer," Will snapped. "I'll have your stripes for that."

"Sure, Lieutenant, and I'll testify at your court-martial. But for a price —"

"Okay." Will conceded defeat. "I've got a little money put away. Now, help me roll him into the gully."

"I knew you'd see it my way, Injun." The squat sergeant strode over and helped him roll the body off the edge and into the deep ravine. With all the vines and brush, no one would ever find the missing major.

"Hey." The sergeant turned back toward the fire. "The major left a knapsack." He walked over and picked it up.

Will Eagle watched him. He knew Sergeant Henley had the means now to make his life miserable, forever blackmailing him. He couldn't allow that. "What's in the knap-sack?"

The squat white man was bending over it, opening it. Will Eagle pulled his pistol, clicked back the hammer.

The sergeant glanced up at the sound. Terror filled his ugly face in that split second before Will fired. Henley raised his hand in a silent plea as he fell dead.

Will ran over, grabbed the knapsack, and looked inside. *A Confederate major's uniform?* What in the hell was a Yankee officer doing with that? Was the dead man a Yank or a rebel spy? There was no way to know without questioning him, and it was too late for that. "I might have been a hero who captured a spy instead of being drummed out of the service for killing a Union major by mistake."

It was too late now that he'd just murdered his own sergeant to cover up the killing. Cursing, Will strode over to the ravine and tossed the knapsack down the hill and into the brush. He heard the drumming of the patrol's hoofbeats. Quickly Will walked back to bend over the sergeant as his patrol rode into the clearing.

"Lieutenant, what's happened?" The lanky corporal yelled as he dismounted.

"Bad news." Will answered somberly. "The sniper got away, but before he did, he killed Sergeant Henley."

The soldiers dismounted and gathered around, muttering about bad luck and damned rebels.

"Well," Will sighed, "it happens. Let's take him back to camp, boys. We'll see that he gets a hero's burial."

They threw Sergeant Henley across his saddle and rode back toward the fort. Will Eagle breathed a sigh of relief. He could only wonder about the major with the two uniforms. He would see that face in his mind forever: the crooked nose and the big mole on the major's cheek. If he were a Union officer, eventually someone would miss him, but they'd never find him now, and there was no way to trace his death to Will.

The end justifies the means, he thought as they rode back toward the fort. *Anything I can do to end this war sooner, I'm willing to do.* He had never been his mother's favorite; she loved her oldest and youngest best, but Will would show her he could be the most successful of her sons. What Will wanted was to have an important career as an army officer at a prestigious post, such as guarding the White House. Tommy had dreams about getting rich and moving to a city, but in the end, his spoiled little brother would stay on the ranch, where Jim could look after the kid and Mother, too. Maybe Will should be ashamed of what he'd been doing to hurry the Union's victory, but he wasn't. He'd do whatever was necessary to achieve his goal.

As he rode, Lieutenant Will Eagle reached up to touch the two crossed straight pins on the collar of his jacket. The crossed pins were the sign of the Keetoowa, the traditional branch of the Cherokee that were loyal to the Union. The hot summer sun reflected off the little X of steel the crossed pins made on his blue uniform.

Chapter 20

April slept until the middle of the afternoon at the old woman's cabin. After getting directions to Fort Gibson, she bought the old woman's mule and started out. She wasn't quite sure what she was going to do next, but she had to get away from Jim Eagle before he tracked her down and she weakened and told him everything. She was helpless against her attraction for the man. Then she remembered that she'd given Jim her virginity and she was nothing more than a plaything to him, and she gritted her teeth with anger.

It was late afternoon when the log buildings of the fort came in sight.

"Hallo the fort!" She reined in and waved to the sentry, who seemed to come awake.

"Halt! Who goes there?" The very young soldier aimed his rifle at her, the hot sun gleaming off the barrel and his bright brass buttons.

"Don't shoot! I'm April Grant."

"Advance and be recognized." He lowered his rifle. Now she noted movement as soldiers came out of the stockade or reined in if they were riding past, staring in disbelief.

She rode up.

The curious Yankee soldiers crowded around her. "A girl. A pretty girl. What's she doing out in the middle of this war?"

"Can someone direct me to your commanding officer?" She hadn't figured out what she'd say, but if she were lucky, soon the major would find her and tell her what to do next.

The young soldier motioned with his weapon. "Come on, miss, I'll take you to the colonel. You fellows stop gawkin' and get out of the lady's way."

She was aware of the hungry stares of the men as she rode into the stockade. Soldiers were coming out of barracks all over the grounds as word spread about the visitor. The sentry helped her from the mule in front of a log building. "This is the colonel's office," he said. "I'll tie your mule, ma'am."

"Much obliged." She went up the steps and into the crude log cabin.

The colonel looked up from his desk, where he was conferring with a lieutenant over a map. "Yes?" He had a big mustache and looked annoyed at being disturbed. "How can I help you, miss?"

What could she tell them that might be believable? "I — I'm April Grant," she stammered, "and I've come —"

"Kawoni?" The younger officer looked up

from the map and smiled almost as if he couldn't believe his eyes.

"Why, Will Eagle, so good to see you again."

He came around the desk and took both her hands in his, shaking his head, still smiling. "I thought I'd lost you forever. What are you doing in this area?"

"Uh, I came back to bury my mother." That was partially true. Will was as handsome as she remembered, but lacked the virility and the rugged masculinity of his older brother.

"I'm so sorry; I hadn't heard."

Now the colonel stood and smiled. "Well, Lieutenant, I didn't know you had a sweetheart."

She started to correct him, then realized that a woman riding into the fort unescorted might be under suspicion. "I — I heard Will might be here at Fort Gibson, so I couldn't leave the Nations without seeing him."

The Cherokee smiled warmly at her as she pulled her hands from his. "I don't know whether you could get out of the Nations anyway, Kawoni, without great risk. Why, those rebs are getting so sassy, they captured our supply boat a few days ago."

"Really?" She feigned surprise.

The colonel nodded to her. "I'm sure you two have a million things to talk about so I'll dismiss you, Lieutenant. We'll talk later."

"Thank you, sir." Will saluted smartly, took her elbow, and escorted her out of the hot, dusty office. "Oh, Kawoni, you don't know how glad I am to see you. When you went north, I thought we wouldn't see you again."

She felt rotten for getting his hopes up. "Will, I'm really not staying. I'll be headed back to Boston as soon as there's enough break in the hostilities for me to travel without danger."

He frowned as they walked across the parade grounds. "Oh, I had hoped . . . never mind." He spoke now in Cherokee, and she frowned at him.

"Will, I'm sorry, but I've turned my back on life as a half-breed Cherokee. I call myself April Grant now."

His dark eyes told her he understood. "It gets to be a burden, being Indian. I feel like I'm always trying to live that down."

"Your big brother always thought we should be proud to be Cherokee."

"Jim, yes, he was foolish that way." Will frowned.

She sighed. "If I have enough money, I can live as a white girl back east and no one will laugh at me."

"I know. I'm aiming to be a top army officer, maybe on a general's staff so I can live down my brown face."

"My white father said that was why he took me north."

"Jim never saw it that way." His handsome face mirrored pain and conflict as he paused in the shade of a tree. "Oh, I reckon you haven't heard. Jim and Tommy are both fighting for the Confederacy."

She averted her eyes. "I hope this hasn't made enemies of you three."

"It tore the family apart, but then, there's hundreds of families all over the country in the same fix." He shrugged and leaned against a tree trunk. "You remember, Tommy and I never got along, but he's easily led. Jim and I were close, but you remember how stubborn he was."

She thought about Jim with a pang of sorrow. "Yes, he was, wasn't he?"

"Always had to be the leader because he was the oldest," Will said in a bitter tone. "I tried to convince him the Cherokee would be better off sticking with the Union, but he wouldn't believe it."

She picked a wildflower and twirled it in her fingers. "You think you might still be enemies when this war's over?"

"I wish I knew." Will sighed. "The Union is bound to win. If Jim weren't so stubborn, he'd realize that. He'll probably want to return to the ranch, but I'm not sure the place will be still standing at war's end."

"Is your mother all right?"

He nodded. "Last time I heard, she was still trying to hold the ranch together for her sons, not realizing that two of us hate the ranch."

She remembered and said, "It's over east of Tahlequah, isn't it?"

"Yes. Everyone in the area knows the Eagle spread and brand. I don't know what will happen to Jim and Tommy when the Union wins."

She twirled her flower, probing for information. "Are you that sure the Union will win?"

"Of course. They've got the money, factories, and everything else they need to win a big war. Anything I can do to bring the war to a close sooner, I'm prepared to do."

Now she looked up at him and frowned. "Anything?"

His dark, handsome face furrowed. "I reckon. The sooner the rebels are defeated, the better. But enough about the war. You certainly put yourself in danger riding in here from your old home place."

She didn't want to talk about that — too many questions she didn't want to answer. "I — I thought so, too. That's the reason I sought refuge here at the fort. Does Jim know you're stationed here?"

He shook his head. "I have nightmares about having to finally face him in battle." His face saddened. "I don't think I could kill him, Kawoni — I mean, April."

"Nor could he kill you," she said.

"I don't know about that. He was very

angry that I deserted and went over to the Union. I wanted to be on the winning side. Jim just wants to do what's noble, even if it's hopeless."

She put her hand on his arm in a comforting gesture. "You don't give yourself enough credit," she said gently.

He sighed and looked away. "In times of war, men do things they regret later. They make mistakes."

She waited for him to elaborate, but he did not.

"But enough about this terrible war." He seemed to brighten as he smiled at her. "Do you think you might stay awhile now that we've finally found each other again?"

She'd have to stay until the major contacted her and told her what to do next. "I'm a little short of money, so I really need to find a way to earn the price of a stagecoach ticket when things get a little more quiet in the Territory."

"Why didn't you say you needed money? Why, Kawoni — I mean, April — I'd be glad to —"

"No, I wouldn't think of it." She didn't want to feel obligated to Will.

"Well, I heard they were looking for a part-time clerk at the sutler's store. You'd bring in some business from all these lonely soldiers."

"Will, you flatter me, but I'd be interested."

"Good." He offered her his arm. "Let's go see about it, shall we? By the way, there's going to be a big Fourth of July dance for the officers. I'd love to escort you."

She took his arm, relieved that she'd be able to wait for days, or even weeks if necessary, for the major to contact her. As she looked up at Will and took a really good look, she noted for the first time that the sunlight gleamed on a pair of straight pins in his collar, stuck in such a way that they made a perfect X. "What — why do you wear those?"

He grinned at her as they began to walk toward the sutler's store. "These? The crossed pins are the sign of the Keetoowa clan. All my Cherokee soldiers wear them."

She only nodded, too stunned to say more as she remembered what the major had said to her about the X clue. Then she remembered Jim Eagle drawing that mark in the dirt. Were these two in some kind of spy network together? No, what a crazy idea. Well, when the major showed up, she'd tell him and let him deal with the information.

The elderly sutler and his wife were only too happy to offer her a clerking job and a bed in the loft of the store. The big Fourth of July dance was several days away. Perhaps there she could pick up bits and pieces of military gossip that would let her know what was going on with the war. Certainly she hadn't learned much among the rebels.

Later that night, April lay sleepless, trying to puzzle things out. All the Keetoowa were wearing crossed pins on their collars, so maybe that clue meant nothing. She could not believe that Will, her old sweetheart, could be a spy, and certainly not Jim Eagle, with his dedication to the Southern cause. As she lay there, April decided that the only logical thing to do was keep her ears open, listening for information, as she'd meant to do before she was kidnapped off that ambushed Yankee boat. Sooner or later, the major would ride into the fort, and she would tell him whatever she had found out and collect the reward. A couple of months from now, she could be living comfortably back in Boston, and no white girl would dare look down her nose at April ever again.

The next morning, April began her job as a clerk. The few ladies at the fort were eager to hear news of events back east. They may have been a little superior in their attitudes toward a half-breed clerk, April thought, but their curiosity brought them into the store in twos and threes.

"What are the fashions now back east?"

April smiled. "Hoops are getting even larger, if possible. Mrs. Lincoln is said to be spending a fortune on clothes and even gloves, and the president can't do a thing with her."

The colonel's wife paused and frowned. "You know, I heard she was a sesesh. Her brothers are fighting for the Confederacy."

The other ladies looked aghast.

April did not comment as she totaled up the purchases.

"And what else is new?" another prompted.

"There was an uprising in New York City. Irish immigrants fought being drafted into our army, and some of the city was burned and a bunch of people killed in the riot."

The ladies paused and made disapproving sounds.

The colonel's wife looked at her. "Tell me, Miss Grant, are you related to the general?"

April hesitated. "I — I don't know for sure." She wanted their approval, and if the white women knew she had chosen the name because it was close to "Giyuga," they would not approve.

Now all the ladies seemed to warm to her. She felt guilty, and yet it was good to be accepted.

One of the ladies peered at her over her spectacles. "You are coming to the dance, aren't you, Miss Grant? Our young men are so handsome, and you'll enjoy the celebration."

"I'm looking forward to it." April smiled and nodded, thinking about the one man she really cared for. Things could never work out between her and Jim Eagle. Once she reported to the major and collected the reward, she never expected to see Jim again. "I'm afraid I don't have a suitable dress. . . ."

"Oh, we'll remake something for you, dear." The elderly colonel's wife seemed to have warmed considerably since she thought April might be related to General Grant. "Someone will have a ball gown we can cut down for you."

"You're so kind." April's mind was busy. She had a job and a place to stay, but she'd have to be very careful because she could trust no one. The next several weeks were going to be both dangerous and important.

Every night now, she woke up drenched with sweat, and it wasn't just the summer heat. She was having nightmares about being stood up in front of a firing squad, but she was never quite sure what the color of the uniform was. However, there was no doubt who the officer leading the execution squad was. She saw his grim, handsome face glaring at her as he gave the order to fire. It was Jim Eagle.

The colonel's wife dug in her closet to come up with an old ball gown, and some of the other ladies offered pieces of ribbon and lace. April, being clever with a needle, managed to transform the old dress into a beautiful pink fashion by the afternoon of the dance.

As she dressed for the event in the July heat, she decided she would listen to all the gossip and see if there was any hint of a traitor in their midst or any information that might bring her that reward.

Lieutenant Will Eagle called for her that evening. "I had forgotten how beautiful you are, Kawoni."

"April," she corrected him firmly, and took his arm. In her other hand, she carried a lace fan.

"It's just across the parade ground," he said as they walked into the dusk of evening. "The band has been practicing all week. We haven't had a dance or anything much except fighting the last few months."

She fanned herself as they walked along through the hot July evening. "I'm looking forward to it, Will."

He smiled at her. "And the men will look forward to dancing with you. I'll have to fight to get my name once on your dance card, but I intend to monopolize you."

She remembered now how sweet and gentle he had always been, not at all like his fiery older brother. "I'll be sure to save you plenty of dances, Will."

"You know, Kawoni — I mean April" — he glanced sideways at her — "when your father took you away north, I was thinking of proposing marriage, except that you were too young."

She didn't want to get in any deeper with him emotionally, because she did have some scruples about leading him on when it could never be. "Will, let's not talk about the old days. I've closed the door on my past. I'm living like a white girl in Boston now."

He smiled at her as they strolled across the fort's grounds. "Maybe you'd like being one of those society ladies with a husband on the president's staff. No one would laugh or be snooty to you then."

She thought about being Will's wife, then remembered the heated passion of Jim's kisses. "Let's talk about something else, shall we?"

He sighed. "All right. Let's talk about the future. The Union is going to win this war, and I'm doing everything I can to help them. Maybe when this is over, I'll be a highly placed officer, with a lot of traveling and mingling with important people. It sounds as if we want the same things."

"I suppose so." She focused on the path as she walked. "I'm just not the type to be an old-fashioned Cherokee wife on a ranch out in this wilderness."

"So for the right man —"

"It is a lovely night for the dance." She changed the subject. *For the right man.* She wondered if the right man for her was Jim Eagle, but of course, that could never be.

He glanced sideways at her and patted the

hand that was gripping his arm. "All I'm asking is that you consider it."

"I will. Oh, look," she said brightly, "it looks like there's going to be a big crowd."

Up ahead of them, in the mess hall, lights streamed, and music floated on the hot air from the open windows. A few buggies were tied up outside, and a handful of officers gathered in small groups, talking and smoking before going inside. She noted that many of them were Indians — mostly Cherokee, no doubt. They quickly snuffed their smokes and hurried to greet Will Eagle. "Lieutenant Eagle, we had no idea you knew such a lovely lady; do introduce us."

Will frowned. "I'll introduce you inside, but be warned, I intend to hog her dance card."

A white officer grinned. "We'll see about that."

Another made a bow. "We will be awaiting the pleasure of the lady's company."

April nodded and fluttered her fan, acknowledging them.

Inside, the room was crowded and heavy with the scent of wildflowers that had been picked and put in vases around the few tables. Faded red, white, and blue banners hung from the rafters. At the front of the hall, a perspiring group of musicians in blue uniforms and gleaming brass buttons was playing loudly but not too well.

Were the ladies ever so slightly hesitant because she was Indian, or was it only her imagination? Some of them greeted her.

"Well," the colonel's wife said, "it's amazing what can be done with a hand-me-down dress and a skillful needle."

April felt a flush rise to her face. She wasn't sure whether she was being complimented or insulted. Perhaps she was being too sensitive.

One of the plump, older ladies gushed, "I do hope you get a chance to meet my nephew."

"I hope so, too," April said.

The band broke into the old army song "The Girl I Left Behind Me."

Will nodded to April. "Appropriate, or vice versa."

She pretended she hadn't heard that.

When the band finished, the fat little corporal who led the band announced, "Let's have a Virginia reel, folks."

There weren't many women, but the officers' wives and grown daughters danced with as many men as possible. There didn't seem to be many single women in this war zone. Of course, there might be a few Indian girls around the fort, but they wouldn't have been invited to an officers' dance. April was only too aware that if she weren't a polished person from back east, and if no one thought she might be related to General Grant, she wouldn't have been welcome, either.

She and Will danced the reel, and when it ended, they were both panting. She fanned herself with her dainty fan.

He smiled down at her. "That was wonderful. May I get you some punch?"

"I'd love some." She fanned herself and looked around. Officers were gathered in small groups talking, and here and there she heard gossip about troop maneuvers and the latest news from the eastern front. She edged closer, wondering if she might pick up enough to find that leak her mysterious major had sent her to search out. If she did find out anything, just who would she report to, and where? Well, her contact was bound to show up soon.

Will came back with the punch. "I had to search for you; I didn't expect you to move."

She thought quickly as she accepted the punch. "I — I wanted to get near a window; it's so hot in here."

"We could go outside," he said.

That was the last thing in the world she wanted to do. All the tidbits of important information would be found in here. Besides, she didn't want to encourage Will. "I think your fellow officers would be so disappointed if we did that; there's so few ladies for them to dance with."

"I suppose you're right." He looked glum.

A handsome captain strode over to them

and bowed. "I do hope, Miss Grant, you've saved this next dance for me?"

"Certainly."

The band began to play a favorite of the time, "Lorena," and the captain put his white-gloved hand on her small waist, took her hand in his other, and they danced away, leaving Will frowning behind them. "I can't tell you, Miss Grant, how pleased we are to have you on the post."

She gave him her most fetching smile. "I suppose your men have seen a lot of action lately, Captain?"

He nodded. "No one knows exactly what the rebs are up to, but we've got many more troops than they do."

"Oh, really?"

He was so pleased that she was interested, he told her how many soldiers were on the post and how many horses they had under saddle.

When the dance ended, it was evident he was reluctant to return her to Will Eagle, but immediately the colonel came over for a dance. "Miss Grant, will you do me the honor?"

"I'd be delighted, sir."

But about that time, the band struck up a polka, and the old officer looked disappointed. "I'm afraid I don't polka."

"Well, why don't we have some punch and visit?"

The old man's face lit up, and he led her over to the refreshments, talking all the way about how the war was going. "Oh, but I'm probably boring you, Miss Grant."

She batted her eyes at him. "Why, not a bit of it, Colonel. I love hearing military men talk."

"Well, in that case . . ." He began to talk of the war, what his role was, where the troops expected to be sent next.

April was rather startled by how much information she was picking up at the dance. Evidently, it never occurred to any of these big strong men that a pretty girl might be rooting out a spy or gathering information.

The colonel leaned closer as they sipped their punch. "Something big happening in a few weeks," he whispered.

"Oh?" She leaned closer.

"Oh, I'm not to discuss it; neither are my officers."

She giggled. "Why, sir, I don't know what harm there could be in talking about it. Who around here, especially a mere girl, would have any use for military information?"

"That's true." He puffed up with his own importance. "Still, I don't know much yet. I'm waiting to hear more details from headquarters."

She nodded. "I'm sure headquarters has chosen well in entrusting you with this endeavor, Colonel."

Now he colored modestly. "Well, if I do say so myself, it's about time. I've been feeling forgotten out here in the Territory, with the major part of the war happening in places like Virginia and Georgia."

She looked over and saw Will watching her. "If you don't mind, Colonel, I really must forgo such fascinating company. I promised Lieutenant Eagle the next dance."

"Oh." He seemed loath to let her go. "I do hope you are going to stay a few days, Miss Grant?"

"Well, I hadn't originally planned to, but I hear travel across the Territory is growing increasingly dangerous, so it looks like I might be here several more weeks." *Or at least until that major shows up to give me directions.*

"Good." The officer's gray mustache wiggled as he talked. "I'll look forward to more conversations with you."

"And I shall, too. I'm working at the sutler's store, you know."

He laughed. "How could I not know? The whole post is abuzz with the coming of a pretty and eligible young lady."

She fanned herself and fluttered her eyelashes. "Colonel, you flatter me too much."

The senior officer smiled, evidently pleased, as he walked her back to the younger officer. "My apologies, Lieutenant, for keeping her so long. She's delightful."

"The feeling is mutual." She curtsied, and

the colonel left as Will frowned and took her out on the dance floor, where he held her a little too closely as they danced. "Please, Will," she murmured, "people will talk."

"I don't want other men to get the idea that you're available." His tone was possessive and jealous — a side she hadn't expected from him.

She pulled away from him a little and looked longingly at the groups of blue-coated officers gathered around the punch bowl, laughing and sharing conversation. Was there a spy picking up valuable information there? Were there strategic bits that would help her get that reward?

As they danced near a French door, Will unexpectedly whirled her out onto the veranda, into the darkness. "It's hot in there," he complained, "and I thought you'd like a breath of fresh air."

"People will talk." She looked toward the crowd inside.

"What difference does that make? You make too much of what people think about Indians, April."

"Perhaps I do, but the more I act like a very high-class white girl, the more accepted I can become."

He took both her hands in his. "You know I wanted to marry you years ago, and I still do."

"Will, this isn't the time or place," she protested, "at least, until we see what this war holds."

"You're right, my darling." He brought her hands to his lips and kissed them. "It wouldn't be fair to leave you as a widow. However, this war won't last much longer, and then we can make plans."

She tried to disengage from him. "We'll talk about that some other time. In the meantime, the war rages on. What do you know about this big event the colonel's talking about?"

He looked puzzled and shook his head. "The younger officers aren't always privy to top information — at least, not until it's time for action. Why?"

"Just making conversation," she said lightly. "Now, let's go back inside before people start gossiping. Then I'd like to leave early. I'm very tired, and tomorrow will probably be a busy day at the store."

As July passed, April enjoyed working at the sutler's store. The fort was a safe place to be, and certainly her living quarters were more comfortable than the primitive conditions at the Confederate camp. She picked up a lot of useful information from soldiers and passing traders, but nothing that would indicate a spy at the fort.

Will Eagle came by the store as often as he could and seemed determined to court her, although she was cool to him unless he was talking about post business. Many days, he was gone from the fort on scouting patrols and minor skirmishes. To April, it seemed the war was indeed slowing down, at least in Indian Territory.

She was saving her small salary so she could afford a stage ticket when the need arose. Two things kept her here: awaiting the arrival of the mysterious major, and hoping for more news of the big event the colonel had hinted at the night of the dance.

One evening in late July, she was sitting in the swing out back of the store when Will Eagle showed up. "Are you all right? You look tired, Kaw— I mean, April."

"We've had some busy days at the store," she admitted, "and maybe I've been working too hard."

"You need to marry me and quit that job." He sat down in the swing and took her hand.

"Remember?" She looked up at him and tried to keep things light, "we're not to discuss that until the war ends."

He grinned. "In that case, anything I can do to hurry that up, I'd better do."

She shook her head. "I wish you could. I'm so tired of the killing and destruction."

"I'll take you far away, back east like you wanted."

April didn't answer. She couldn't marry Will and let him make love to her while thinking of the man with whom she'd shared such passion, his older brother.

"You need to stop working so hard," Will said.

"I'm not feeling terribly well," she admitted.

"You see?" He looked her over anxiously. "In the summertime, we always have outbreaks of malaria and yellow fever. There's no telling what else these new recruits bring in. You've got to be careful."

"I'll be careful," she promised, and pulled her hands away from his. "Maybe I just have a delicate constitution."

He took her hand again. "April, you need someone to look after you. The war can't last forever, and maybe —"

"The war doesn't seem to ever end," she sighed.

"The Union will win," he promised her, "and I'm doing everything in my power to help make that come true. So someday, you might think about —"

"Oh, Will" — she pulled her hand away again — "I wish you wouldn't —"

"Maybe if I did something big, got a promotion, maybe we could afford to live back east." He would not be dissuaded.

She shook her head. "I can't honestly encourage you."

"Then I'll keep trying until I change your mind." His voice was so earnest, she felt ashamed and didn't look at him. She was embarrassed that her mind was on his big brother, and she was afraid Will might see that in her eyes. The swing creaked loudly in the silence.

"April," he tried again, "I've picked up information that the rebs have been called to Arkansas to fight, but I don't think it will go well for them, no more troops and cavalry than they've got. Especially since our troops at Fort Smith have been tipped off that the rebs are coming."

"How do you know that?" She looked up at him, puzzled.

He hesitated. "Everyone says so. When we capture rebel soldiers, they're always hungry and ragged. They're getting almost no supplies from the east because everything's going to the war efforts in places like Virginia and Georgia. It's only a matter of time before they'll be forced to surrender."

She sighed and thought of Jim Eagle. "Some soldiers may never surrender as long as they think they've got a chance."

"But they haven't, don't you see that? Maybe I can get myself a big promotion. We could live pretty well back east on a major's or colonel's salary, maybe."

She didn't answer, thinking of his brothers. Yes, Jim and Tommy were probably going hungry, and the supplies from the captured Yankee supply boat couldn't have gone very far. "What of your brothers?"

Will sighed. "Sooner or later, they'll see that they can't win. They'd both be better off back on the ranch raising cattle and horses — at least, Jim would; he loves the place. Tommy never cared for the hard work of ranching. If he could get enough money, he'd probably move to a city and look for an easy life."

Yes, that was what Tommy had told her, she thought. She looked into Will's eyes and smiled. "Tell me about this big thing that's about to happen."

Will shrugged. "Don't know much right now. We're waiting to find out more about what the other side's doing before we go into action."

"Now, how would you learn that?"

Will hesitated, then kissed the tip of her nose. "Never mind, dear. The less you know, the better."

Chapter 21

"What are you telling me?" April sat bolt upright, causing the swing to creak loudly.

He seemed taken aback. "Don't look so shocked. I'm sure it's something both sides do, but so far, the rebels haven't been very successful. Why, there was a major . . ." He stopped suddenly, and April held her breath, waiting for him to say more, but the expression on his dark face told her he was certain he'd said too much already.

She took his hand and smiled up at him. "Of course, I'm just a silly, naive girl who doesn't know much about war. What was that about a major?"

He shook his head, his eyes guarded. "Forget I said that; forget everything except that I love you, April."

She didn't answer, her mind busy. He'd almost told her something that she might need to know. Was the major he spoke of John Smith? There was no way to know, and if she pressed the issue, Will might become suspicious — too suspicious. There was nothing to do but wait and hope that he'd slip and drop more information. She looked at the small X of steel pins on Will's collar and thought of Jim scratching that symbol in the dirt. Was Jim Eagle the spy among the Confederate forces, and Will his contact? She didn't want to believe that. "I — I'm suddenly not feeling very well; it's so hot," she said. "I believe I'll go in."

"I told you, you looked pale." Will took her hands in his and kissed her fingertips. "I'll be leaving on a scouting patrol tomorrow and may be gone a few days. You take care of yourself while I'm gone."

"I will." She extracted her hands from his and fled into the store, up the stairs, and threw herself across the bed, sobbing. Was Jim Eagle a spy and not a highly principled officer? If so, he was a low-life scoundrel. But was he any worse than she was, spying for cold, hard cash? Jim did not fit into her plans of returning to the east, rich and respectable. Somehow, her goal was not as appealing as before. She didn't want to think about that. In the meantime, all she could do was wait and hope that Will would tell her more or that the major would show up at the fort with further instructions . . . if he ever showed up.

She dropped off to sleep, and when she did, she dreamed Jim Eagle came to her and they made frenzied love on the soft grass, and she never, never wanted the dream to end.

It had been almost a month since the Cherokee girl had knocked Jim in the head and escaped with his horse. The horse had returned, and Jim wondered if it had gotten away from the girl or thrown her. When he pictured her lying out in the woods somewhere, helpless and slowly dying, he almost went crazy. Then he reminded himself that she'd attacked him, not caring what happened to him when she left him out there unconscious and defenseless. He tried to be angry with the little chit, but at night, when he closed his eyes, he saw her as she had been in his embrace, passionate and giving. He didn't want to think of April at all, and yet he couldn't stop remembering her kisses and the moments of ecstasy she had given him.

As days passed, things were not looking good for the Southern cause. The Confederate troops were ragged and often hungry. Some of his men deserted, and he couldn't blame them — the war news from farther east was so discouraging. He knew some of them probably went over to the Union side, where there was food aplenty. Others probably just went home to neglected and ravaged farms. Yet Jim Eagle fought on because of a forlorn hope that the Confederates would treat the Five Civilized Tribes better than the Union had. It would be good to have their own state. Already, the Cherokees were talking of calling it Sequoya, after their hero who had created the Cherokee alphabet so that now most of the tribe could read.

One hot summer day, word came that the Cherokee Mounted Rifles were being sent to Arkansas on a raid.

Another officer brought the news. "Why the hell do you think they're doing that?"

Jim shook his head. "Fort Smith, just across the border, is strategic. Besides, there's probably plenty of supplies and fresh horses there if we can take it."

"I reckon we'd better be gathering our troops and passing the word." The officer started to walk away.

"Who brought us that news?" Jim yelled after him.

"Clem Rogers. You know he always knows what's going on since he's a scout."

Jim thought about the other officers; particularly Captain Big Horse. The captain wasn't a very good officer and didn't inspire much confidence in his men. Besides being a goldbricker, he disappeared a lot. Jim wondered if Big Horse was like Tommy, slipping off into the woods to gamble, or if he was simply hiding out from his duties.

Tommy sauntered up just then, distracting Jim from his thoughts. "What's going on?"

"Where have you been? I've been looking everywhere."

Tommy grinned. "You know we got a little pay, and some of the men wanted to shoot dice."

"No wonder you always have money," Jim snapped. "I wish you'd spend more time on soldiering and less time gambling."

"I hate the army," Tommy reminded him. "I wouldn't even be here if Mother hadn't insisted I enlist with you."

"We've had this discussion before," Jim said.

"When the war is over, I'm not going back to that miserable ranch. I'm moving to a big city and marry a pretty girl who wouldn't look at me if I was just a poor rancher."

Jim didn't answer. His mind went to the girl he'd fallen in love with, and he hated her for it. What future was there with a whore who might also be a spy?

Tommy shook his head. "Jim, can't you see the South is losing? We ought to desert and go over to the Union side like Will did."

Will. His beloved brother. Absently Jim began to scratch the sign of the Keetoowa in the dirt. "I'm sure Will did it out of principle."

Tommy snorted. "You'd never believe anything bad about him, even if you end up shooting at each other. Just because you're guided by principle doesn't mean anybody else is. Money and power are what make the world go around."

"Amen to that." Captain Big Horse joined them.

Tommy snapped to attention and saluted, but Big Horse motioned him down. "At ease, soldier." He looked at Jim. "The kid may be right, Jim. We don't own any slaves, so we've got no stake in this war. Have you given any thought to going over to the Yankees?"

"Never," Jim said. "I believe General Lee and his cabinet. If we can't trust they'll set up an all-Indian state, the tribes are doomed."

The mixed-blood Cherokee, Clem Rogers, sauntered up just then. "Who's doomed?"

"Anyone who doesn't support the Union, I fear," Captain Big Horse laughed.

Clem frowned. "That may well be."

Jim shook his head. "I disagree. My brother Will is a fool to trust the Yankees. That doesn't matter now. I reckon we'd all better get ready to move out."

Clem nodded. "Orders are that we leave at dawn."

General Stand Watie and General Douglas Cooper led their ragged, motley troops east toward Fort Smith, Arkansas. On July 27, a little group of Choctaws and Texans under Colonel Gano forged ahead and attacked a small force of Yankees at Massard Prairie, a few miles from the fort.

Waiting in the distance for the main attack

397

as the surprised Yankees retreated toward Fort Smith, Jim Eagle watched impatiently. "We should have hit them with everything we've got," he muttered to Tommy, sitting his horse at Jim's elbow. "Now they'll know we're coming."

"They might anyway," Tommy said.

Jim looked at him sharply. "Why do you say that?"

The younger man shrugged. "Captain Big Horse seems to think they might be tipped off."

Jim frowned. "I don't know who would do that unless . . ." He didn't finish. One did not accuse a superior officer of treason lightly. "Never mind. Be careful, Tommy, when we go in. You've never been in a big battle before, and —"

"I know," the other snapped. "I can take care of myself without any help from you."

"I'll forget you're being arrogant to a superior officer," Jim warned. "That's a major offense, you know."

Tommy said, "We won't always be in the army, and someday you and Will will treat me with more respect."

"Sure, kid. Now, fall back in the ranks. The troops are getting ready to move out. Unfortunately, those Yanks that got away will alert them at the fort."

"Then why are we bothering to attack?"

Jim sighed. "Because there's supplies and

plenty of horses there, and we need both."

As Jim had warned, when the combined Southern forces finally attacked Fort Smith on July 30, the Union troops were well prepared. It was a pitched, fierce battle with shells whistling and men screaming as they were hit by cannon fire. Horses whinnied and bolted, throwing riders to the ground. Gunsmoke hung black on the hot air, so that dying men choked on the acrid scent. Sometimes in the heat of this battle, Jim was not sure where the enemy was. He was fearful of getting cut off from his men and trapped behind enemy lines, but he was more afraid that his younger brother might be killed or badly wounded.

Jim made sure he kept Tommy close, to protect him, but Tommy was too terrified to fight. He seemed to panic and, with some of the others, turned his horse as the battle intensified. It was clear now the Southern forces were being slaughtered, driven back. Jim yelled at his sergeant to sound recall, and then he reined in his horse, fighting a rear-guard action so that his men could retreat. They left a trail of dead and wounded, even though they fought valiantly. In the end, the weary and defeated Confederate forces straggled back toward Indian Territory.

Jim had a minor head wound that had dripped blood down his face, but his spirit was even more wounded as his tired stallion stumbled along the road away from the fort. "We're beaten," he said to his younger brother, "and that was our last chance to lay our hands on Yankee supplies. I don't know what we'll do now."

Tommy looked very young and scared. "Will the Yanks come after us?"

"I don't know; I doubt it. There's plenty of Yankees left in Indian Territory for us to fight, and they know it."

Tommy wiped gunpowder smudges from his face. "You think this will end the war so we can all go home?"

Jim shook his head. "We'll do what brave men do; we'll keep fighting as long as we are able."

"That's plain stupid," Tommy said.

"I agree with your brother." Captain Big Horse rode up and fell into pace with them. "There's no hope left."

Jim glared at both of them. "I'll pretend this conversation never happened. We fight as long as there's hope. God only knows what will happen to the Five Civilized Tribes if the Union wins."

The defeated troops straggled back west into Indian Territory. It was a long, discouraging ride without the supplies and fresh horses they'd been counting on. Jim Eagle distracted himself by remembering the Cherokee girl and the minutes of ecstasy he'd spent in her arms. April Grant. He hated that uppity white name. Kawoni. Now, there was a musical name that rolled easily on the tongue. He thought about her as he rode, and wondered idly how she would look with her hair in braids and wearing a traditional Cherokee dress of bright calico. For a moment he imagined her weaving baskets, or in the kitchen of the cabin, making fry bread and succotash for the evening meal.

Jim Eagle, he said to himself, *have you gone loco? She's gone, probably back east, and you'll never see her again. Anyway, that uppity would-be white girl would never be a Cherokee wife and live on a poor, small ranch. She craves the wealth and fine living of a big city.*

He remembered her with a sigh. Kawoni was pretty. No doubt, if she played her cards right, after the war some rich white man would marry her and buy her that big house back east, give her fine clothes and lots of jewels — all things that Jim Eagle could never give.

They returned to their old camp, and now the military action was only desperate guerrilla raids as August passed. Jim Eagle stubbornly led his patrols and tried not to think of the beautiful girl who was gone forever.

As the heat of August made working in the store almost unbearable, April grew frantic.

The major had never shown up, and she was without orders. What to do? One wrong step and she might be shot as a spy. In the meantime, the only clue she had was that small slip of the tongue from Will, which might be meaningless. She wasn't feeling well, either, which she confided to Will as they sat in the swing one hot August night.

He looked concerned as he took her hand. "Be careful," he warned. "The water sometimes gets polluted, and people die from dysentery. There's also yellow fever and malaria every summer, but no one knows exactly why it happens then. Many think it's caused by stagnant water."

"I'll be all right," she assured him.

"April, as soon as this war is over, why don't you marry me? I'd spend my life making you happy."

"On the ranch?"

He shook his head. "Jim's the only one who cares about the ranch. I'm thinking of being a career officer. You'd like being posted to the excitement of Washington, with all its balls and parties."

"That does sound tempting, almost as good as Boston." Then she thought of sleeping with Will while the man she really desired slept with another woman at the ranch. "I — I'd have to think about that, Will. To be honest, I'm not in love with you."

He seemed to brush aside her comment. "Oh, I'd be so good to you, I could make you love me. I'll persist until I wear you down and you marry me."

She didn't answer, her mind busy. She was saving her small salary to buy a stage ticket, but most of the time, the stagecoaches weren't even running to the Indian Territory. She might have to wait until the war ended to get out. It would be easy to marry Will rather than struggle on her own. "Will, do you have any clues about when the war might end?"

He shook his head. "It can't be long, but the rebels are more stubborn than expected. They attacked Fort Smith several weeks ago but were beaten back."

He must have seen the alarm in her face, because he hastened to say, "Don't worry, my brothers are okay, but Stand Watie's troops are getting desperate for food and supplies. Even Jim must realize that it would be best for all if the rebels would give up their arms and surrender."

"Jim never seemed like the type to surrender," she said.

"Yes, he's stubborn, but he's not stupid." He kissed her fingertips, and she smiled at him. She must learn more if possible, so she would have something to report if the major ever showed up.

"What's the matter, dear? You're frowning."

"Nothing." She shrugged. "I've been worried about you, Will. Some weeks ago, you acted quite undone — something about a major."

He hesitated, looking down into her face. "It doesn't matter. I think I was upset for nothing."

She persisted. "You acted as if it was important."

He fidgeted, as if trying to decide whether to trust her with his secret. "April, something awful happened." He lowered his voice and looked around as if to see if there was anyone nearby. The post was quiet in the August evening.

"Oh, Will, you can tell me."

He hesitated. "I — I killed an officer by mistake."

"What?" She started, and the swing creaked loudly.

"I didn't mean to." He looked frantic and apologetic. "He was shooting at me from the brush, and I shot back. When I killed him, I discovered he was a Union major."

"Oh, my God." She felt her face go ashen.

"But I'm not sure he was one of ours." Will seemed to be attempting to reassure her. "Here's the funny thing; he also had a Confederate uniform in his things."

She had a terrible sinking feeling. "Who — who do you think he was?"

"I don't honestly know if he was a Yank

404

who'd been spying on the rebels or vice versa."

"But when you told the colonel, didn't he question . . . ?"

"April . . ." Sweat broke out on his face now. "I — I didn't tell anyone. I was so afraid I'd get in trouble, I rolled the body off in a ravine and pretended it never happened." He paused and looked at her anxiously. "Are you all right? You look faint."

She felt faint. She knew now why Major John Smith had never contacted her. She'd waited for weeks, and all this time, was he lying dead in a gully somewhere near the fort? "What — what did he look like?"

"What difference does that make?"

She took a deep breath, knowing she must not betray her emotions. "I don't know; just curious, I suppose."

Will shrugged. "I don't really remember, it happened so fast. Middle-aged, maybe. I think he had a big mole on his cheek, and his nose was crooked."

She didn't say anything for a long moment. She hadn't counted on this. She didn't know what to do now.

"April, say something."

"I — I don't know what to say, Will. You probably should have told your superior officers."

Sweat broke out on his dark face. "I didn't know what to do. I was afraid of being court-martialed. But anyway, there's been no official questioning about a missing officer, so my guess is, he was a rebel spy."

"A rebel spy? Surely you're joking, Will. Why would a rebel spy be sneaking into Fort Gibson?"

"We don't know he was headed to Fort Gibson," Will said. "He might have been going anywhere. He must have been carrying some important dispatches, because when we rode up, he'd burned them before I killed him."

"We?"

In the dusk, his face turned ashen. "I — I meant me."

Somehow, she knew he was lying about being alone, and wondered who else was in on this cover-up with him.

"April, you won't tell anyone, will you? It might get me in big trouble, and I'm trying to move up in rank."

She blinked in disbelief. "You're saying that getting a promotion is a good excuse to keep this secret?"

"April, I swear I never meant to kill him. If I'm to have a career in the army, this can't come out. Promise me you won't tell."

She patted his hand, her mind busy. "I promise I won't get you in trouble."

"Oh, good. I knew you had to care about me, even though you keep putting me off. We're going to have a wonderful life together,

April." Before she could react, he gathered her into his arms and kissed her. She was too stunned to do anything but submit, but as he kissed her, her mind went to Jim and the ecstasy of his kisses.

She managed to pull away, wondering what she should do. The dispatches the major had burned were probably meant for her — so she'd know what to do next. Now she was on her own. She patted Will's arm. "Everything will be all right."

"I feel better now that I've told you. I've been about to go crazy worrying about getting caught."

Not guilt, she thought, *not even pity for the dead man; only worries for himself and his career.*

"It's war," she murmured, "and you said you didn't see him when you shot at him, so it's just a terrible mistake."

"That's right, isn't it?" He brightened considerably.

What to do? "If you don't mind, Will, I'm feeling poorly again. I think I'll go in."

Now his face mirrored concern. "I'm afraid I've given you a shock. I never meant to, April."

"It's all right," she murmured. "I think I must have gotten some bad food; I've been sick at my stomach a lot lately, especially in the mornings."

"That bacon we get is moldy," he said,

nodding, "and sometimes, the eggs are almost rotten. Be more careful what you eat."

"I will." She stood up and turned toward the store, but he caught her hand.

"April, I forgot to tell you: I'm being sent to Fort Scott on an assignment soon."

"Fort Scott, Kansas?"

"Don't worry, I won't be gone but a few days."

"Oh, what for?" This information might be important.

"I don't know much yet, but it's nothing that would interest your pretty little ears." He leaned over and gave her a quick kiss on the forehead. "Now, go in, dear, and get some rest; you look pale."

"I won't be getting much rest," she answered. "The owners are gone over to the nearest town, trying to get supplies for the store, so I'm in charge. Good night, Will."

She went in to bed, but she didn't sleep. This expedition to Kansas sounded important. She'd have to keep her ears open and see what she could learn. Then she thought of the dead major. She was in a tight spot already and didn't know what she should do next. The Yankees would shoot a spy as quickly as the Confederates would, and she knew it.

The next evening, right before closing time, she was on her knees behind a counter, straightening a shelf, when she heard the bell tinkle as the door opened.

"April, dear, are you here?"

Will. She sighed and started to get up, but about that time, she heard other footsteps.

"Oh, Lieutenant Eagle, glad to have caught you; we need to talk." The colonel's voice.

"Yes sir. Talk right here?"

"This is good enough; there's obviously no one around, although we can't be too careful about spies these days."

"Whatever you say, sir."

"I want to give you final details about your trip to Fort Scott. I've got maps for you over at my office."

"Oh? I've been wondering what this was about, sir."

"Big news. There's a huge wagon train of supplies waiting at Fort Scott: three hundred wagons and hundreds of fresh horses and mules."

"Three hundred wagons coming here?"

The colonel cleared his throat. "Yes. Enough supplies to get us through the winter. Good thing the rebels don't know about it. They need supplies worse than we do. I'm sending you to escort that supply train."

Will made a sound of exclamation. "Thank you for the honor, sir."

"You deserve it, Lieutenant Eagle. If this campaign is a success, I've got my eye on you for a captain's bars, and after that, who knows?"

"I won't disappoint you, sir."

"Good. Let's go over to my office and get those maps."

April heard the door close, then silence. Very slowly she stood up and looked out the window at the two disappearing across the parade grounds. She realized she'd been holding her breath as she exhaled, and went over to lock the door and leaned against it, breathless. This was the big event the colonel had talked about that night of the July Fourth dance: thousands of dollars' worth of food, ammunition, boots, and blankets — items the Confederates needed desperately. If the rebels only knew the wagon train was coming, they could intercept it.

She could take the word to Jim Eagle. Even as she thought that, April shook her head. He wouldn't trust or believe her. She pictured Jim's hungry, ragged troops. This might be their last chance to get enough supplies to carry them through the winter — the difference between winning this war and losing it. She didn't really care who won the war; she never had. Her only interest had been the money she would be paid as a spy, but now the major was dead. She wondered if the dispatches he'd been carrying were to tell her about the wagon train?

What to do? The safest thing was to do nothing. Why should she stick her neck out? Jim would never believe her if she went to him and told him. In fact, he might have her shot if she returned to the Confederate camp, or she might end up in a miserable Southern prison like Andersonville.

She wrestled with her decision all night and through the next day as the ladies gathered to give the troops a send-off. She waved and smiled as Will rode out, and he turned in his saddle and blew her a kiss. After the troops had left the fort, she returned to the store, still attempting to make a choice. By nightfall, she knew what her decision had to be, even if it cost her her freedom or her life.

She waited until darkness; then she sneaked away, stole an army horse grazing in a field outside the fort, and rode out, searching for the Confederate camp and Jim Eagle.

Chapter 22

April had some misgivings as she rode toward the Confederate camp. Now that she was finally going to tell Jim the truth, she had no hope that he would believe or even listen to what she had to say. And if he was indeed Will's accomplice, would Jim try to silence her? Self-preservation warned her that now that things had gone awry with the dead major, she should try to get as far from here as possible and, using her pay from the store, head back east.

Then she thought of those hungry Confederate soldiers and those big Yankee supply wagons and knew she had to make the sacrifice, no matter the personal consequences.

It was late night when she arrived at the perimeter of the Confederate camp and reined in.

"Halt! Who goes there?" The sentry aimed his rifle at her. The voice was familiar.

"Tommy, is that you?" She held her hands up so he could see them. "It's April, and I'm unarmed."

"April?" He came closer, peering up at her. "You've got a lot of nerve coming back here after what you did."

"I know, but it's important. Take me to Jim."

"Jim?" His voice was as surprised as his face. "Oh, April, I don't know whether you want to see him; he's furious with you. There's no telling what he's liable to do. He thinks you're a spy."

And there was a possibility that Jim was, too. In that case, she was in danger. Tommy's advice was good, but she made her decision based on love. Love meant trust, and she was willing to wager her life that the man she loved could not possibly be a spy. "I know," she answered patiently, "but I've got to see him."

"April, I don't think he's forgiven you. You know, this war can't last forever, and I've got big plans. We could meet in Boston."

She sighed. He was so young and naive with his great ambitions. "Tommy, I've got to talk to Jim."

"All right, but don't say I didn't warn you." Taking her bay horse's bridle, he led her through the dark camp and its rows and rows of tents.

Jim came out of his tent as she rode up, and Tommy said, "Jim, she insisted on seeing you and —"

"Never mind." Jim dismissed his younger brother with a disgusted wave of his hand. He peered up at April, and in the moonlight she could see the anger on his rugged face. "You've got a hell of a lot of nerve coming back here."

"Now, Jim," Tommy said, "I'll protect her if you're thinking of —"

"Shut up, Tommy, and return to your post."

The boy looked uncertainly at April.

"Go on, Tommy," she said gently. "I'll be all right."

"Are you sure? You need me, April, you just yell."

"Tommy," Jim thundered, "get back to your post!"

The younger brother fled, looking back over his shoulder.

"Well," Jim snarled, looking up at her, "I see my younger brother is so smitten with you, he's forgotten what you did."

She sat her horse, fidgeting under his cold glare. "Aren't you even going to ask me to dismount?"

His frown deepened. "What the hell are you doing here?"

" 'Hello' might have been a good starting point." She tried to smile, but his expression stayed stormy. "I — I don't blame you for being angry."

"That's nice of you. Knock me and Tommy in the head, steal my horse and weapons, then leave me out for the Yanks to kill."

"Tommy?" She hadn't hit Tommy, but

maybe the boy had been afraid to tell Jim he'd helped her escape.

"As you can see, he's all right, no thanks to you."

She wouldn't call Tommy a liar. "As for yourself, you seemed to have made it all right."

"No thanks to you, you little tart."

She winced at his words. "Look, Jim, be mad at me if you want to, but I've got important news for General Watie."

"Then why didn't you go to him?" He folded his arms, but his face was furious.

"I — I didn't think he'd listen to a girl, but he'd listen to you."

"Okay, talk." His hostile expression didn't change.

"With what I've got to say, we'd better have some privacy." She looked around at the other tents, wondering who was listening. If Jim was the spy, she would be putting her life in danger, yet she had to take that chance. She knew deep in her heart that Jim Eagle could never be a traitor to his cause.

He gestured. "All right, get down. I'll give you five minutes."

"Aren't you going to help me?"

Without a word, he came to the side of the horse, and she slid off to the ground with his arms around her. They stood that way a moment as their eyes locked.

"Oh, Jim," she whispered, "I've missed you so."

He didn't mean to do it, but he couldn't stop himself from abruptly pulling her closer and kissing her as if all his pent-up passion was being channeled into this moment. No matter if she was a spy, no matter what she might have done, he loved her; he couldn't stop himself. "Damn you for the hold you have on me."

This was where she belonged, held tightly in Jim's arms. She laid her face against his broad shoulder and wept.

He stroked her hair. "Are you all right?"

She nodded, unable to speak for a moment. Should she tell him everything? "I — I've seen Will."

"Will?" He took her by the shoulders and stared down into her face.

"He's at Fort Gibson."

"And you've been with him?" he guessed, and pulled away from her. "How much information did you give him about our operations here?"

"Let's go in and talk." She tried to lead him into his tent, but he resisted.

"You sneaking little spy, what . . . ?"

"I'll tell you, but you may not believe me." She took his hand and led him into his tent, where a lantern burned feebly.

"Damned right," he snarled. "You won't take advantage of my feelings for you again. I'll turn you over to General Watie and —"

"At least listen to what I have to say first

416

before you put me in front of a firing squad."

"Don't tempt me, missy."

She took a deep breath. "All right, Jim, I am a spy, just like you suspected."

"I knew it, damn it; I knew it, but I was so taken by you, I let it blind me —"

"Hear me out," she snapped. "I'm a spy, but for the Confederacy."

"What?" His eyes widened. "If that isn't the biggest lie I ever —"

"I met with a certain major who said the Confederate upper echelon thought they had a spy here in Indian Territory, and they wanted me to help ferret him out."

Now he simply stared at her, and then his expression grew cynical. "And what was this major's name?"

"I don't know his real name; he called himself John Smith."

"Uh-huh. Makes it pretty hard to check, doesn't it? There must be thousands of John Smiths in both armies."

She shook her head. "Wouldn't do any good — he's dead."

"How convenient for you. So I'm to believe that some mysterious officer with a fictitious name who is now conveniently dead sent you to spy for our side?"

"I know it sounds ridiculous, but all I can ask you to do is trust me."

At this, he threw back his head and

laughed. "It's great to have a little humor after all our losses lately."

How could she convince him? "Look, Jim, you've got good reason not to trust me, but I've got vital information to take to General Watie. I'll tell you and you can decide whether you want to give it to him or not."

"You risked your life to come here; you realize that?"

She nodded. "It was important enough to take that risk. Trust me or not; believe this: The Yankees have a big wagon train of supplies coming from Fort Scott, Kansas, headed to Fort Gibson. If you can convince General Watie to intercept it, I understand there's enough food, boots, and blankets to last your men through the winter."

For a moment he only stared at her; then he chuckled as he shook his head. "You really had me going for a moment there, April. I thought I might be mistaken about your being a Yankee spy, but I see what you're up to now. The Yanks want you to lure us into an ambush, and they'll be waiting to wipe us out. How much are the Yanks paying you?"

She was not going to be able to convince him, and she was getting desperate. "Jim, I swear I am sent by the Confederate higher office. Yes, I'm sure the Yankees would be willing to pay me more, but now the money doesn't matter."

"I thought money was what you wanted so

you could live like a rich white girl in Boston?"

In her frustration she began to cry. "I've changed, Jim; all that matters now is telling you the truth so you won't hate me, helping the Confederates get those supplies so the men can survive. I love you, Jim; please believe me."

He paused, watching her weep. His heart was in turmoil over this girl whom he had loved for so long but whom he did not, could not, trust. Dare he take a chance on leading soldiers into an ambush based on what this beauty told him? He tried to think, but his heart wouldn't allow him to be rational. He made his decision then, based on love. "All right," he admitted defeat, "I'll take you to the general and let him listen to your story."

She wiped her eyes. "Thank you."

"Don't thank me," he snapped. "General Watie may still put you up in front of a firing squad."

They left the tent together and walked to the old Cherokee's tent, where Jim quickly told the Cherokee leader the story.

Stand Watie questioned April at length. "You say a big wagon train of supplies?"

She nodded. "At least three hundred wagons — enough to keep your troops provisioned for months, General."

He clasped his hands behind his back and

paced up and down. "Well, Lieutenant, what do you think?"

He hesitated, looking at April, loving her as he had never loved another woman. He couldn't love her without trusting her; he realized that now. "I'm willing to gamble that she's telling the truth, sir."

"We're taking a mighty big chance," the general muttered. "It might be an ambush."

"General," April said, "I swear I'm telling the truth."

The old man paused and peered at her keenly. "How did you get this information?"

April hesitated. She couldn't bear to let Jim Eagle know she suspected his brother was involved in an espionage operation. "I — I overheard officers talking. Jim's brother Will is one of those assigned to bring the supply train in."

"Will?" Jim asked.

She nodded. "I know that complicates things for you."

Jim sighed. "It's war; things happen that we can't control."

"Hmm." The old man paced some more. "Lieutenant, if you'd rather not go on this mission —"

"No." Jim shook his head. "Begging your pardon, sir, but our men are hungry and ragged. If I can help bring in supplies, I'll do whatever's necessary."

The old man looked at him a moment.

"Let me confer with General Gano before I decide. You two are dismissed."

Jim Eagle saluted smartly, and he and April left.

"Well," he said, "I've gone out on a limb with this, missy. I've staked my career and a great many men's lives on believing that you're telling the truth."

April hesitated. Should she tell Jim that Will had hinted there was a spy in the Confederate camp? Suppose he had been lying. Suppose it was Jim. "I'm telling the truth, Jim. Eventually, you can check it with Confederate headquarters."

He paused in front of his tent and took both her hands in his. "It'll be weeks before I could get a message through, and you know it. Right now all I can do is trust you."

"Oh, Jim . . ." She went into his arms.

He held her, kissing her eyes, her face, very gently. "I know I shouldn't want you, but I do. However, if you're leading us into a trap —"

"I wouldn't do that, Jim. I — I love you. And something else: When I told you I was a whore, that was a lie because I knew you wouldn't believe the truth. You're the first and only man I've ever been with."

He only stared down into her face in the darkness. "Somehow, I think I knew that," he whispered; then, silently, he took her hand and led her into his tent. "It will be a while

421

before the general makes his decision," he whispered.

They made slow, gentle love, each knowing that with the impending raid, they might not be alive tomorrow. As he kissed her and held her close, April wondered if she should tell him her other secret. No, she decided, that would only complicate things right now.

They were lying in each other's arms on Jim's cot when the assembly bugle began to blow outside.

Jim stood up, grabbing for his boots. "The old man must have decided to make the raid," he said with excitement.

From outside drifted the noise of men coming awake, yells and shouts, the sounds of neighing horses as men reached for saddles.

About that time, a sentry yelled outside Jim's tent. "Lieutenant Eagle, sir, the general wants to see you."

"Shall I go with you?" April asked.

He shook his head. "Stay here until I get back." Then he disappeared.

Outside, the racket built as men came awake and dressed; officers shouted orders. There was plenty of confusion as the troops made ready to move out before dawn.

Jim was back in moments, his face grim. "The general insists you accompany us in case it's a trap. I tried to argue against it, because it's so dangerous, but —"

"Oh?" She had wanted to go but hadn't expected she'd be allowed on a dangerous raid such as this. She wanted to stay by Jim's side.

He bustled about, getting saddlebags and weapons. "Come on."

They went out, and April mounted up as Jim looked about. "Now, where in the hell is Tommy?"

Tommy appeared just then, sleepy and disheveled. He'd probably been asleep on guard duty, April thought. "What's happening?"

"We're going on a raid after a wagon train," Jim snapped. "Where have you been?"

Tommy grinned and ran his hand through his rumpled hair. "It doesn't matter; I'm here now." He looked at April with longing, but she looked away. Jim Eagle was the man she loved, no matter what happened now.

"Oh, hell," Jim grumbled, "and I haven't been able to find Captain Big Horse or Clem, either. Try to make yourself presentable, Tommy."

"A raid?" Tommy yawned. "What wagon train?"

"Never mind," Jim said, "just get yourself ready and saddled up."

Tommy looked up at April. "Is April going with us?"

She nodded. "I'm the one who brought the news."

Tommy looked askance. "We're planning a

major raid based on what she says? Excuse me, Miss April, but if you happen to be mistaken —"

"I'm not mistaken, Tommy."

The boy hesitated.

"Tommy," Jim snapped, "we don't have time for this."

"But we're going on a big raid based on what a girl told us? Maybe you should try to talk to the general about taking a few days to think it over."

"We don't have time, little brother. If they can make it to Fort Gibson with those wagons, they're safe. They're only vulnerable on the trail between the two forts."

"But if we'd wait a little while to check her sources —"

"Tommy, shut up and get your gear. We'll be leaving in a few minutes."

"Oh, all right." Tommy scowled and sauntered away.

"Damn that kid," Jim grumbled.

"You can't blame him," April said gently. "You're going out on a limb to trust me, and he thinks you're a fool."

He looked at her in the moonlight for a moment. "I may well be, but somehow, I can't believe it. If so, it's a firing squad for you and a dishonorable discharge or worse for me."

Hundreds of horses and men were falling into formation as the Cherokee Mounted Rifles made ready to ride on their surprise raid.

They were delayed a few minutes while waiting for Captain Big Horse and Clem to be found, although Tommy finally arrived to join his troop, riding a gray gelding.

Could the captain or Clem be the spy who was passing information to the Yankees? April wondered. There was no way to know. At least, going into battle on such short notice, the informant wouldn't have time to alert the enemy.

In half an hour, the Confederates were on the march, April riding next to Jim Eagle and General Stand Watie as they headed north in the darkness.

Tommy scowled as he rode, wishing he was back in his cot asleep instead of eating dust back in the ranks while Jim and that beautiful girl rode up front with General Stand Watie. Jim had always treated his younger brother like a baby, but Tommy would soon show him he was a grown man. Maybe when April Grant realized how important Tommy was, she'd change her mind about going north with him when this war ended. She'd show him around Boston or New York, and they would have wonderful, exciting times together. Let Jim have his damned old ranch. Tommy didn't intend to spend the rest of his life breaking horses and herding cattle.

September 16, as they rode north, the

Confederate forces attacked a haying operation in the fields near Flat Rock Creek, and the Yankees took heavy losses. The Southern troops burned thousands of tons of hay the Yankees had planned to use to keep their cavalry horses fat through the next winter. Then the Confederate troops rode on up the old Texas Road through the valley of the Grand River, planning to intercept the Yankee wagon train.

Will Eagle was very pleased with himself. Here he was, accompanying Major Henry Hopkins in charge of the big supply train moving toward Fort Gibson, and everything had gone without a hitch so far. He had at least three hundred wagons loaded with supplies to keep Fort Gibson comfortable through the coming winter, while the Confederate troops were already in desperate condition. He knew from his spy that the rebs and their horses would starve when the weather turned cold.

As he rode, Major Hopkins, of the Second Kansas, joined him. "Lieutenant, I've just received a dispatch saying the rebels are coming up the Texas Road with many Indian and Texas troops. Do you think it's accurate?"

Will reined in and considered. "I've got an informant among the rebs and haven't been alerted to anything new."

"Maybe he's in a situation where he's not able to get a message to you," Major Hopkins suggested.

"Could be. I don't know how the rebs would know about this. I never told my spy — just to be cautious."

"Nevertheless" — the major wiped his sweating face — "maybe it would be smart to stop at that little post we have at Cabin Creek until we're joined by additional troops. It'd be easier to defend."

"Yes, sir." Will saluted. He didn't think it was necessary, because his insider would certainly have alerted him if anything was afoot. However, the major was being extra cautious with this much food and supplies at stake. Will yelled to his sergeant to turn the wagons toward the Union post at Cabin Creek.

September 18, additional Union troops arrived to back up the Indian Home Guard and protect the big supply train in case the rebels were planning an attack. They now had over six hundred soldiers to defend their prize, but Will's informant hadn't sent him any warning. Will felt very secure as he took to his blankets that night.

Chapter 23

Lieutenant Jim Eagle had had misgivings about this whole campaign. If it weren't for the girl, he would never have believed this wild story about a gigantic wagon train. It was turning dusk, and the early autumn evening turned cool, with an occasional yellow leaf whirling from a tree. He glanced over at the girl riding beside him. "So far, you've taken us on a wild-goose chase. If it's an ambush . . ." He left the sentence unfinished. He loved her too much, no matter what.

"I told you the truth," she repeated stubbornly.

Tommy rode up just then. "I tell you, Jim, she doesn't know what she's talking about. You're gonna lose your officer's bars over this. You ought to convince the general to turn around and head back south."

"Tommy, you just stick close and don't be wandering away where some Yankee sniper might pick you off."

Tommy looked as if he might argue, then fell silent.

April didn't say anything. She knew that Tommy hated her now because she knew he

428

had lied about how she escaped, and because she had spurned his advances. She dare not tell Jim that. She had been keeping a close eye on Captain Big Horse and Clem Rogers on this campaign, in case one of them was the spy taking information to Will. *Or could it be Jim?* No, her heart refused to believe that, no matter the cost.

"Stay here," Jim ordered. "I've got to report in."

"Can I go with you?" Tommy sounded eager. "I never get in on the action."

Jim shook his head. "Stay with the lady."

April looked at him. "You afraid I'll escape and go over to the Yankees?"

Jim grinned without mirth. "Just try it. Remember, April, I'll be in big trouble if you disappear."

"I'll be here when you get back."

Tommy said, "I'll see to that."

Jim nodded and rode off to find the two generals, Stand Watie and Gano, sitting their horses in the shadows, discussing strategy. Even as he saluted, Clem Rogers galloped onto the scene. "General, the little lady was right. There must be at least three hundred wagons camped up ahead at Cabin Creek, and several hundred mules. Plenty of Yankees with them, though."

The two generals both grinned.

"Best news we've had in months, right, Lieutenant?" General Stand Watie asked.

"I'd say so, sir." Jim smiled in sheer relief. He'd been right to follow his heart and trust her.

The white general rubbed his chin thoughtfully. "You suppose camping at Cabin Creek is a deliberate trap to lure us into an ambush?"

General Stand Watie looked at Jim. "What do you think?"

Jim took a deep breath. He loved April; therefore, he must trust her. "Maybe we could surprise them. Even if they've got more troops, surprise might turn the trick."

Clem nodded. "Sounds smart to me, General."

"If I might suggest it, sirs," Jim said, "there's a full moon tonight, and we might be able to get close to the Yankees before they realize we're here."

"Attack in the dark?" The white general looked doubtful.

However, the old Cherokee nodded. "Sounds like a good plan to me, Lieutenant. We've got artillery to surprise the Yanks with, too. If we mount a sudden night attack, we might capture the wagons before they have time to destroy them."

They talked a minute more while Jim waited patiently.

"All right, Lieutenant Eagle," General Watie said, "pass the word to maintain silence, and we'll wait a couple of hours until

their camp is bedded down for the night. Then we'll sneak as close to those sleeping Yanks as possible before we attack. Clem, you do some more scouting; get us some more details. Where's Captain Big Horse?"

Clem and Jim looked at each other and shrugged.

"Damn him," General Watie grumbled, "he's probably off shooting dice again. Remind me to break him in rank and throw him in the guardhouse when we get back. He's never around when we need him."

"I'll look for him, General," Clem said.

Jim said, "I'll start passing the word to the troops."

"Dismissed." The general nodded.

Jim saluted and rode back, his mind preoccupied with April's and his little brother's welfare in this coming fight. He wished he had a safe place to send them until this was over, but Tommy was a soldier and duty-bound to take part.

He rejoined them. "We're going to try to take the Yankees by surprise in about an hour."

"Tonight?" Tommy sounded horrified.

Jim nodded. "I said we were going to try to take them by surprise."

Tommy started to ride away.

Jim reached out and grabbed Tommy's bridle. "Where the hell do you think you're going?"

"I — I thought I might get a little sleep in the meantime."

"I reckon that's all right," Jim agreed, "but don't stray too far from our lines. They may have snipers on the perimeter of their camp. You might get yourself killed if you aren't careful."

"I'm a grown man," Tommy snapped, "and I'm damned tired of you treating me like a baby, especially in front of her."

"Sorry, kid," Jim said. He hadn't meant to humiliate him. "I swore to Mother I'd look out for you."

"I'm tired of that, too. I'm a hell of a lot smarter than you give me credit for."

April said gently, "Tommy, I'm sure Jim didn't mean —"

"I know what he meant. I'll see you two later." He wheeled his horse and rode off into the darkness.

"You embarrassed him," April said.

Jim sighed. "I know. I have a hard time thinking of him as a man. To me, he'll always be my baby brother."

April watched him in the moonlight. "You worry about both your brothers, don't you?"

Jim nodded. "I wish Will weren't with that supply train. I told Mother I'd bring them both home safe and sound, and now I'm leading one into battle and attempting to kill the other one."

"You take too much responsibility on your-self."

"It comes from being the oldest." He frowned.

"You look like you could use a little rest yourself," she suggested.

"I don't have time; I've got to meet with the other junior officers and discuss strategy. You might want to find a sheltered place, though, away from the fighting."

He wheeled his horse and started to ride away.

"Jim," she called after him, then hesitated.

"What?"

This was neither the time nor the place for what she had to tell him. There was so much she wanted to say to him about how she loved him and how she would give up all her dreams of returning east if he would just ask her to stay. "I — I just wanted to tell you to take care of yourself."

He looked at her in the moonlight, her hair blowing in the cool September air, her lips parted. There was a lot he wanted to say to her, but he couldn't commit to anything. He might not be alive after tonight's attack. Well, Will loved her, too. If he didn't survive and Will did, she'd be taken care of. Jim wouldn't let himself think of his brother making love to her. He had to put all his energy and emotion into the coming battle. There was so much depending on it. "Try to find yourself

433

a safe place out of the line of fire."

"I'll pray for you."

"Thanks. Do me a favor and make sure Tommy doesn't get too far from our lines. He's pretty irresponsible." He nodded and rode away.

Still looking out for his kid brother, who resented it. Well, if it would make Jim happy, she'd check on Tommy. April nudged her horse forward in the growing darkness, looking for the boy as she went.

She passed Clem Rogers. "Clem, you seen Tommy Eagle?"

He scratched his head. "Come to think of it, I did, miss, he was heading north, far ahead of our lines. I yelled at him, but he didn't answer me. I reckoned maybe the kid was carrying dispatches for his brother. Anything wrong?"

"N-no, of course not." She started to ride on.

"Miss," said the scout, "it ain't my business, but you're loco to ride any farther north. There's gonna be a hell of a battle up there in about an hour."

The thought scared her to her very core. "I know, but I promised Lieutenant Eagle I'd keep an eye on his little brother." Then she nudged her horse and rode out.

"But, miss . . . !" he protested.

April ignored his shouts and didn't look back as she rode on north into the darkness.

There was a big, full moon tonight, and she remembered Tommy rode a pale gray horse that should be easy to spot.

Behind her, Clem took off his hat and brushed his hair back. "Damn silly female," he grumbled, and then turned his horse, headed to look for Lieutenant Jim Eagle. He hoped little Tommy wasn't deserting, terrified of the coming fight. Or could the pair be escaping together? Nevertheless, Clem figured the lieutenant ought to know that the girl and his brother were riding into danger.

He found the young officer and told him.

"What? Are you sure, Clem?"

The other nodded. "Both of them at different times, headed north, right into the battle zone."

Jim began to curse. "What in the devil . . . ?"

"Maybe you should just leave 'em be, Lieutenant. They're either loco or . . ." He didn't finish. "Well, I've done my duty." He put spurs to his bay gelding and loped away, leaving Jim struggling with the news.

What in the hell was going on? He'd thought Tommy too cowardly to get right in the middle of a battle, but maybe the boy was trying to prove something to Jim. Maybe the girl was confused about directions and didn't realize where she was going. Another horrible suspicion crossed his mind: Could April be leading the Confederate forces into a trap, and want to clear out now while the

getting was good? One other thought occurred to him; then he shook his head. No,
he could never believe that April and Tommy
might be running away together. One thing
was certain: He had to find them both and
get them out of the area between the two armies and quickly. He didn't have much time
before he'd be caught in the middle of a terrible battle, but he had to rescue the pair.
Jim put spurs to his palomino and started off
through the woods to the north.

He was acutely aware of time ticking away
as he rode, but he did not turn back. Any
minute now the big Confederate cannons
would open up, and cavalries would go at
each other in full gallop. The landscape between the two sides would be littered with
dead and dying horses and men. Jim had deserted his post to look for the pair, which
meant he might be shot as a deserter, but he
didn't care what happened to him — he was
only worried about the welfare of the two
people he loved.

Will came suddenly awake as a sentry
shook him. "Sorry to disturb you, sir, but
we've captured a young reb attempting to
breach our lines. He says he has to see you."

"What? There's no rebs near —"

"This one is, sir. He won't talk to nobody
else."

Will reached for his boots, sleepy and baffled. "Bring him in and then you can leave, Corporal."

Tommy rushed into the tent, breathless and evidently terrified. "Will, General Stand Watie is about to launch a surprise attack on your wagon train."

"Here?" Will grabbed his brother by his sleeve, cursing. "Damn, Tommy, we pay you to report such things."

The boy shook his head. "I know, but I haven't had a chance to get a message out."

"Damn it, I don't know how the rebs found out about this campaign." He put his hand on Tommy's shoulder, and together they walked out into the night.

"The girl told them."

"What girl?" He was baffled.

"April. She's riding with Jim."

Will paused in the moonlight, thunder-struck. "Jim and April are with the attack force?"

Tommy nodded.

The end justified the means, and now it had boomeranged on him. Will threw back his head and laughed without mirth to keep from crying out in anguish. "Why, that ornery little rebel. Here I had a spy in their army; I never imagined they'd put one in ours. I was crazy about her."

"So is Jim."

Will sighed. It all came suddenly clear: why April had been so hesitant about marrying him. She was not only a spy, she was in love with his big brother. Mother had loved Jim best, and now the girl Will adored loved Jim best, too. No matter if he climbed in rank to become an important general, he would always be second-best to the two women who meant the most to him. "Thanks for alerting us, Tommy. Now, you'd better get to safety before the shooting starts."

"Can I keep riding north and skip this fight?"

Tommy was a coward, but that couldn't be helped. The family had always spoiled and protected him.

Will shook his head. "You couldn't get through our lines to the north in that gray uniform."

The boy hesitated. "I think I'll wait to get paid."

"You greedy rascal. You'd better forget about money and get the hell out of here. We'll pay you later."

Tommy started to walk away. "Remind them about the money."

"Have we ever neglected to pay you in the past? Get on your horse and vamoose before Jim misses you."

Tommy hesitated again, looking very young and scared. "I'm afraid to ride back south, Will. The fighting might start at any minute, and either side might kill me by mistake."

"I'll ride with you to the edge of our lines." Will yelled to his orderly for a horse. "You see that April is safely behind the lines, too, you hear me?"

"You don't hate her?"

Will shook his head as he swung up on the horse. "She can't help it if she loves him best, and I reckon she's no worse than I am; her loyalties are just different." He watched Tommy mount up. Will's first duty was to ride to Major Hopkins and warn him about the impending attack, but he was out of time, and his little brother and the girl Will loved might be in immediate danger. He'd get Tommy safely through the Union lines, and then he'd take care of his duty.

April reined in, in the darkness of the woods and warned herself not to panic. She'd lost track of Tommy and wasn't sure if she had crossed enemy lines or was still somewhere in the landscape between the two sides. Any minute now, the cannons would open up and hundreds of Confederate soldiers and cavalry would attack. For Tommy and her to be caught between the two forces was surely a death sentence.

Jim Eagle was sweating now, although the night was cool. Where in the hell had that pair gotten off to, and why? He could believe that irresponsible Tommy might have wandered away from the Confederate troops by mistake, but what was April doing out here in this shadowy land between two opposing armies? Could he have been mistaken about her? Had she led his troops into an ambush, and was she now making her escape?

Jim paused, considering. No, he'd stake his life that she was telling the truth. He had no hard evidence to support that theory except that she had taken a big risk bringing him her information, and because he loved her, he had to trust her. All he could do was try to find the pair before the firing started. For him to be caught between the two forces, especially if he had crossed into Yankee lines, was like signing his own death sentence. The pair's welfare was more important to him than his own life, so he kept riding.

April came to a clearing and reined in, trying to decide where she was. There was a full moon, but that didn't help much. She had no idea how much time had passed, but she realized that any time now, the battle would start. Every instinct told her to turn back and let the irresponsible boy take the consequences of his actions. Why would Tommy be headed north? No doubt, he was afraid and deserting. If she didn't bring him back, the Confederates would execute him when they caught him. That would devastate Jim, who doted on his little brother. She sat her horse, trying to decide which way to go now.

And at that moment, cannons broke the silence as the Confederates mounted their attack on the surprised Yankees. Behind her was noise and the echo of shouting men as they galloped to the attack. Her horse neighed in panic as April breathed the acrid scent of cannon fire. Her head rang with the roar of gunfire as she fought to control her terrified horse. The horse took off at a gallop, and a low-hanging limb caught April and knocked her from her saddle. The horse galloped away, leaving her lying stunned and breathless on the dirt.

She was in mortal danger here with both sides shooting at every shadow. She must get out before troops rode into her clearing. Her head ached, but she stumbled to her feet. If she could only catch a riderless horse that she heard galloping nearby . . . Then she realized the beast would be too panicked to stop and she'd be trampled. She was afoot near a battle zone, and any minute she might be caught in a charge. What to do? She ran to the edge of the clearing, paused in the bright moonlight.

Two riders galloped toward her, and she froze, expecting to be shot down.

"April!" Will suddenly galloped out of the darkness, the brass buttons on his blue uniform shining in the moonlight. Next to him,

Tommy's face was pasty pale in terror.

Will yelled, "What in blazes are you doing here?"

"I — I was following Tommy."

His youthful face frowned. "You suspected me all along, didn't you?"

She shook her head in confusion. She had no idea what Tommy was talking about.

Will reached for her. "Come on, you'll be safe enough with me."

"But, Will —"

"I won't take no for an answer." He reached down, grabbed her hand, and lifted her to the saddle before him. "Let's get out of here before we get killed."

She looked over at Tommy's face, and suddenly, she knew who the spy was. He stared back at her with guilty eyes.

Will reined in, looking about. "I don't know which way to go. Either way, we're liable to get shot. "Why aren't you at Fort Gibson, April?"

She couldn't tell him that she had ridden to warn Jim and that she was a Confederate spy. Maybe he knew already.

"Never mind," Will shouted. "Let's get out of here, and when this is over, I'm going to marry you."

Marry her? No, her heart belonged to Jim for now and always. Nothing else mattered but him.

Even as they paused, a shell exploded

nearby, and without meaning to, April shrieked in terror.

Jim paused, his horse rearing. Was that a woman's scream? *April.* All he could think of now was that she was in danger. He forgot his duty and his own safety, thought of nothing but the girl. In the clearing up ahead, the gunsmoke cleared momentarily, and he saw two horses, one carrying two riders. In the moonlight he saw the girl's terrified face. "April?" he yelled.

Her heart was in her throat now as she recognized Jim galloping toward her. "Jim, go back!" she shouted.

"What the . . . ?" Will seemed taken by surprise at her outburst as he held on to her.

"Will" — she turned her face up to his — "let me go!"

"No!" Will fought to hang on to her. "No, April, it makes no sense to choose him. Stay with the winning side; stay with me."

She wanted Jim, win or lose. In that split second, she attacked Will with teeth and nails while Jim ran over and pulled them both from the rearing, neighing horse. The two men grappled as April stumbled against a tree, sobbing. All she could do was watch as the two brothers fought. She looked up as Tommy cursed and struggled to control his gray horse. In that moment, April knew what the boy intended to do; she could see it in his eyes. If Jim were dead, the two spies would be safe.

"Look out, Jim!" she screamed.

Both older brothers paused for a split second, looking toward the boy on the horse, and in that split second, Jim froze in disbelief, then tried to shove Will out of the way. Tommy's horse shied, and April saw the flash of fire as Tommy pulled the trigger. Will grabbed at his chest and fell.

"Tommy, are you crazy?" Jim ran across the clearing and dragged the boy from the horse, attempting to take the gun from him. They fought and rolled, but Tommy hung on to the pistol, striking Jim hard with the butt.

April had run to gather Will into her arms as she watched the two brothers fighting. Blood ran out of his mouth, but he smiled up at her. "I — I was wrong . . . didn't deserve you . . . Jim does. Help him. . . ."

What to do? She stumbled to her feet, watching the two men fighting. Jim had Tommy down and was winning — it was clear — and then Tommy went to the ground, came up with a big rock, and hit Jim across the head. Jim went to one knee, clearly stunned as Tommy staggered over, picked up his pistol, and aimed it at Jim. "I'm damned tired of always being the baby brother, always having to take orders —"

"No!" April grabbed a stick, and he whirled, leveling the pistol at her.

And in that heartbeat, she saw the flash of gunfire in the moonlight, heard the blast. What — ?

Tommy dropped his pistol, staring at her almost in disbelief as he clutched at his chest. Blood ran out between his fingers as he staggered, staring past her. "You — you shot me."

She whirled. Behind her, Will had made it to his knees, and his pistol was smoking. Will threw away his pistol with a sob. "I — I'm sorry, Tommy; I couldn't let you kill either of them . . ." Then he tumbled over on his face.

April ran to Tommy's side even as Jim gathered the dying boy into his arms. "Little brother," he wept. "Oh, my little brother. Don't go, Tommy, please! I'll get a doctor."

"Too late . . . wanted money," Tommy gasped, and blood trickled scarlet out of his mouth. "Tired of always being the unimportant one . . . wanted to go to a big city . . . Yankees paid me well. . . ."

"Tommy?"

There was no answer. The boy lay still. Jim hugged his brother to him, trying to shake life back into the limp form. It took a moment to realize that the little boy who had followed him around the ranch all those years was dead. Numbly he stood up and looked into April's stunned face as the cannon boomed and echoed and the noise of battle grew closer. He was only dimly aware that his uniform was dark with Tommy's blood. "Dead," he gasped. "They're both dead."

"Oh, Jim, I'm so sorry. It's my fault. If I hadn't gotten involved, they'd both be alive."

What would he tell his mother? He had failed in his duty to look after his brothers, failed in his duty to the Confederacy, and now the cavalry was thundering toward this very spot. His agony became an unreasonable rage. "Get out of here," he gasped, and motioned her toward Will's horse. "Get the hell out of here!"

"But, Jim —"

"Go, damn it, go! Haven't you caused me enough grief? Get out while you still can. I've got a battle to fight."

She looked into his dazed face and realized there was no reasoning with him. He was in shock with grief, but his eyes told her he blamed her for his terrible loss. She could hear the cavalry now, thundering closer as the battle built around them. She caught Will's horse and mounted. "Jim, please —"

"Leave me alone!" he shouted at her. "My brothers are both dead, do you hear me? Go back north where you belong!"

She saw the agony on his features and realized he was in a state of shock. "All right, Jim, I'll go, but I need to tell you —"

"Damn it, just go!" He was sobbing now as

he waved her away and stood with shoulders bowed in grief. "Go away and leave me with my dead."

How she wanted to gather him into her arms and comfort him, but she knew he hated her now and blamed her for his brothers' deaths. She did not speak another word, and she would not allow herself to cry lest she become hysterical as she nudged the horse into a lope and rode away. Behind her, she heard Jim weeping and victorious rebel yells ringing out. The Confederates were winning, she thought; they were capturing the wagon train.

Her vision blurred as she rode away in the moonlight. She would save her weeping until she was away from this place, so that Jim would not see her. April was not sure where she was going now or what she was going to do. The money she'd been promised for spying no longer mattered; nothing mattered when the man she loved hated her and wanted her out of his sight.

No, there was one thing that mattered, she thought as she raised her chin stubbornly and rode away from the battle. She had something to live for, something that made it all worthwhile if she never again saw the man she loved. Jim Eagle would never know she was carrying his child.

Epilogue

June 1865

Capturing the Yankee wagon train had been the biggest Confederate victory in Indian Territory. However, there had been little action the past nine months, and everyone seemed to know it was only a matter of time before the Union forces triumphed. Things would not go well for the defeated, Jim Eagle knew.

Not that it mattered. Nothing much mattered to him anymore since the tragedies of early autumn and since the woman he loved had ridden out of his life forever. He had not realized how much he had cared for the mixed-blood Cherokee girl until she was gone. He had been too distraught over the deaths of his brothers to think clearly when he sent her away. Now it was too late, and she was gone forever.

Finally, one day a rider brought word that the war had ended two months ago in a faraway place called Appomattox, Virginia. On April 9, General Robert E. Lee had signed the official papers. Now all that was left was for General Stand Watie, the last Confederate general, to surrender his troops to the Yankees near the little town of Doaksville.

"Well," the old man said to Jim, "we have fought the good fight, and now there is nothing else to do but surrender. Gather my officers and tell the men to put on their best uniforms and polish their buttons and bridles. The Cherokee Mounted Rifles will go out proudly. We will not look defeated, with our heads hanging."

So on June 23, 1865, the weary, gaunt Cherokee soldiers made sure they looked as good as they could in their worn, faded uniforms, and rode to the former Choctaw capital to surrender.

When it was over, old Stand Watie shook hands with his men and told them to return to their homes and get on with their lives.

Home? Jim wasn't even sure if there was anything left of his ranch after four years of fighting back and forth across it, nor could he hope that his mother was still alive. He'd not managed to get word from anyone. The only merciful thing was that if she was dead, she would be spared the heartache of learning that her two younger sons, Will and Tommy, were both dead and that they had been traitors, selling their loyalties for gold. She need not know that terrible truth.

Jim rode next to the old Cherokee commander as they left the town. "What will you do now, sir?"

"You don't need to call me 'sir' anymore, Jim," Stand Watie sighed. "I am no longer a Confederate officer, I am a tired, defeated old man."

Jim smiled at him. "Sir, to me you will always be an officer, and a gallant one."

"Well, I'm going home, if there's anything left of my farm. Between Southern bushwhackers and damned Yankees, they've probably burned the place and stolen all my livestock. What about you, son?"

Jim shrugged. "Probably the same story."

The other raised his chin stubbornly. "We're Cherokee, a proud people; we survived the Trail of Tears, and now we'll survive whatever the Union does to the vanquished."

Jim nodded, but his heart wasn't in it. What he needed to give him the strength to begin again was a beloved woman, and she was gone forever. If she ever thought of Jim at all, it would no doubt be with amusement or maybe a little sadness at the memory of everything they had endured together. He couldn't blame her. With his ranch needing to be rebuilt, there'd be lots of hard work and little money, no fine clothes and elegant carriages such as those the girl who called herself April Grant had hungered for.

He and the old Cherokee rode north

through burned farms and devastated villages. Indian Territory seemed destroyed, its people dead or defeated. Only the bravest dared hope enough to begin rebuilding.

"What happened to that girl you favored?" Stand Watie asked.

Jim swallowed hard, remembering the warmth and the passion of her, the taste of her mouth. "She's in Boston now, I reckon, married to some rich white man."

"Nice Cherokee girl needs a good Cherokee warrior," the old man grunted.

"I was a fool, and maybe I didn't have much to offer."

"Did you ever tell her you loved her and wanted her to stay?"

Jim shook his head. "I sent her away, but maybe it wouldn't have mattered. A broken-down ranch in the middle of a war-torn territory can't compare with a fancy back-east city."

The old man smiled. "It would if she loved you."

Jim didn't answer, remembering. He hadn't realized how much he loved her until she was gone, and now he would not get another chance to tell her.

They came to a crossroads and reined in.

The old general said, "I'll be heading east from here."

"I'm going over past Tahlequah," Jim said.

"Good luck to you, son." The old man

held out his hand, and they shook solemnly. Then he turned his bay horse and started east.

Jim watched him go, knowing that the door was closing on his life as a Confederate soldier. They had lost the war, and there was no telling what punishment the federal government would inflict on the tribes for daring to support the Southern cause. It didn't matter; nothing mattered much without the girl he loved by his side. He had never felt so lonely and bereft in his life as he rode toward his ranch. Perhaps he would return to being a Lighthorseman. He wondered if his old friends, Yellow Jacket and Talako, had survived the war, and whether he would run across them again. One thing was certain: From now on, he would be a true Cherokee; no more white man's name for him.

It was almost dusk two days later as he topped the hill and looked down into the valley of his ranch. He breathed a sigh of relief as he saw that the log cabin and the barn were still standing and appeared to be in good repair. A few horses and cattle grazed in an adjacent field. Down below him, a small figure in a poke bonnet and a faded calico dress labored in a garden. She was old and stooped, but hoeing stubbornly.

Mother. His eyes teared up as the hot June breeze carried the scent of wildflowers to him. Now the woman paused and turned to look in his direction, shielding her dark face from the sun with one hand.

"Hey, Ma!" He galloped his horse down the hill and across the green landscape, hardly reining the palomino in as he dismounted, and they ran into each other's arms. "Ma! Oh, Ma, I thought you were dead!"

"Jim, boy, oh, Jimmy!" The old woman threw her arms around him, sobbing as she did so. "I thought you'd never come."

They hugged each other.

"I'm home now, Ma, and I'll never leave again." The time he dreaded had come. "Ma" — he pulled away from her — "about Will and Tommy —"

"I know." Her wrinkled old face grew somber, and she nodded. "Your woman brought me the news that they'd both died heroes in the war."

"My woman?" What on earth was she talking about?

His mother gestured toward the house, and for the first time, Jim noted a young woman with long black braids sitting in a rocker on the porch of the cabin. She had her head down, but she wore a traditional Cherokee dress, and she was nursing a baby. He could only stand and stare as the girl got up out of the chair hesitantly and put the baby in a cradle on the porch. She came down off the porch, slowly walking toward him as if she was not quite certain of her reception.

He stared at her, not believing his eyes. He had dreamed too long of her, and now he must be dreaming again. "April?" And then his arms came up, naturally, as they had a million times when he dreamed of holding her.

She had sat on the porch, hardly daring to believe what her eyes told her as the big, dark man on a palomino horse had come riding out of the dusk, silhouetted against the setting sun. She had pictured this reunion a million times, but she was not sure if he could ever forgive the part she had played in his brothers' deaths, or even if he had ever loved and wanted her. Then, very slowly, he had held out his arms to her, and she was running, running. It seemed like a thousand miles across that yard, and she saw nothing but his beloved face and those outstretched arms reaching for her. Then she was in his embrace, and he held her as if he would never let her go, while they both wept. "Jim! Oh, Jim!"

"Oh, April, I never expected you would come here —"

"I am not April," she said softly, looking up into his rugged face, blurring through her tears. "I am Kawoni, a proud Cherokee, and I am Jim Eagle's woman if he wants me."

"Wants you? Oh, Kawoni, I've been such a fool for mistrusting you, for sending you away."

"It doesn't matter anymore," she whispered, and kissed his dear face. Then his lips found hers, and they clung together as if this embrace would never end.

"And I am no longer Jim Eagle," he said. "I will be a traditional Cherokee. I am Wohali, and I am home forever."

She smiled up at him through her tears. "It is good, Wohali. Your mother and I have held the ranch together, awaiting your return."

He held her close, and there was no need for words. She loved him like she could never love another.

"Kawoni, I don't know what the future will bring now that the Confederate Indians have been defeated."

"It doesn't matter; we've got each other; we'll manage somehow."

The baby began to wail from his cradle, and Jim looked toward the house and then down at her, his eyes full of surprise and questions.

Behind him, the old woman laughed. "We go in to supper. You will want to meet your son."

"My son?" Jim looked toward the house again, then back into Kawoni's eyes.

"Your son," she nodded, her heart too full to speak. "I knew when I rode out that night, but never got a chance to tell you."

"My son," he whispered. "Oh, Kawoni, until a few moments ago, I thought I was just a defeated soldier with nothing to my name, and now I have everything."

"We are a very, very rich Cherokee family." Kawoni smiled up at him, and then the three of them walked toward the cabin, where little Jim wailed lustily.

Tonight, she thought as Jim picked up his chubby son and kissed him, *tonight, we have much to make up for, and a long night of passion awaits us.* "I love you," she whispered.

Still holding the baby, he put his arm around her and hugged her to him, kissing her again and again. "And I love you, my Cherokee woman, more than you'll ever know!"

TO MY READERS

The general public is unaware that Indian Territory became a bloody battleground as the Union forces in Kansas and the Confederates in Texas met in the middle to fight over it. The Civil War did indeed pit brother against brother, friend against friend, and split tribes down the middle. While the Choctaws and Chickasaws mostly went for the Southern cause, the other three of the Civilized Tribes split more evenly. When it was over, farms were destroyed, villages burned, and 14 percent of the Indian children in the area were orphans, and 33 percent of the women widows.

In the end, none of it mattered. Greedy whites waited on the sidelines, looking for any excuse to steal the Indian lands — and they found one. Their excuse was that since many from the Five Civilized Tribes had fought for the South, they deserved to be punished by having their land confiscated.

It is a true but little-known story of the Civil War that Old Opothleyahola, the elderly

Creek leader, led his people valiantly as they battled their way through three hundred miles of winter snow and Confederate troops to reach Union Kansas. We do not know much about him or even have a good translation of the meaning of his name. Unfortunately, he did not live until the end of the war. He died an exile in Kansas and is buried near the town of Belmont. He holds a place of honor in the Indian Hall of Fame in Anadarko, Oklahoma, but otherwise, he has been pretty much overlooked and forgotten.

When the many fleeing Union Indians finally reached Kansas, sadly, they were not much better off than they had been under Confederate rule. The Union forces were not expecting almost six thousand Indians to arrive, could not deal with their numbers, and surely did not want them. Many of these unfortunate Indians starved or froze to death in the miserable temporary camps, among them the valiant old Creek leader. In all, the Creek had lost almost two thousand of their people dead along the way as they fought their way north. It is surely one of the most poignant, untold stories of the Civil War.

If the subject interests you, I'll suggest two books that you might find at your public library: *Now the Wolf Has Come: The Creek Nation in the Civil War*, by Christine Schultz White and Benton R. White, Texas A&M University Press, College Station, TX, 1996;

also *Opothleyaholo and the Loyal Muskogee: Their Flight to Kansas in the Civil War*, by Lela J. McBride, McFarland & Co., 2000.

For further information on the Creeks, you might enjoy a book by Oklahoma's own beloved historian, Angie Debo. The book is *The Road to Disappearance: A History of the Creek Indians*, U of Oklahoma Press, Norman, OK, 1941.

The Creek had fought on the side of the British in the War of 1812, and the Cherokee fought on the side of the United States. The bloody battle of Horseshoe Bend, led by future President Andrew Jackson, defeated the Creek. In the long run, our government treated loyal Indians no better than they did the others.

The sinking of the *J. R. Williams*, and the Confederate capture of the big Union wagon train, known as the Second Battle of Cabin Creek, were the two greatest Confederate victories in the Indian Territory.

Some of you may be astounded to hear of the black Indians. Yes, they do still exist and have voting rights as members of at least two of the Five Civilized Tribes. I've already told you about the famed Seminole Negro scouts who rode with the U.S. Cavalry after the Civil War, in an earlier book, *Bandit's Embrace*. There are other tribes besides those in Oklahoma that have mixed-blood members. For more information, I suggest *The Black*

Indians: A Hidden Heritage, by William Loren Katz, published by Aladdin Paperbacks (Simon & Schuster), 1986.

There are numerous books on the Cherokee. Among them are *Cherokee Tragedy: The Ridge Family and the Decimation of a People*, by Thurman Wilkins, U of Oklahoma Press, 1970; and *The Cherokees*, by Grace S. Woodward, U of Oklahoma Press, 1963.

Yes, Stand Watie, a Cherokee, was the only Indian general of the Civil War and the very last Confederate general to surrender. He died in 1871 and is buried in Polson Cemetery, about fourteen miles northeast of Jay, Oklahoma, in Delaware County.

Ironically, on the Union side, a Seneca Indian, Colonel Ely S. Parker, wrote the surrender document and was present as one of General Grant's aides as Lee signed it.

I included the young Cherokee scout Clem Rogers in this story for a reason. Clem was an actual person who survived the Civil War and became a prominent rancher. Rogers County, in northeast Oklahoma, is named for him. However, here in my home state, Clem is best known as the father of Oklahoma's most beloved son the entertainer, Will Rogers, who was killed in a 1935 plane crash.

The McIntoshes, the half-breeds who had signed away the Creek lands in Alabama, became even more prominent after the Civil

War. McIntosh County, in southeast Oklahoma, is named for this family. There are also a Cherokee County and a Creek County. The town of Doaksville, where Stand Watie surrendered, no longer exists. The town of Bowlegs is named for the Seminole chief, and of course, the Creeks' Tulsey Town survived to become the city of Tulsa. The Western Cherokee capitol is Tahlequah, where there's a good museum, and a pageant every summer reenacting the Trail of Tears. The Creek capitol and museum is in Okmulgee, if you'd like to visit.

The Creek warriors in the early years carried red-painted war clubs and were called the Red Sticks. In French, the words are Baton Rouge. So now you know how the capital city of Louisiana got its name.

For general information on American Indians fighting in the Civil War, I recommend *General Stand Watie's Confederate Indians*, by Frank Cunningham, U of Oklahoma Press, Norman, OK, 1998; *The American Indian in the Civil War, 1862–1865*, by Annie Heloise Abel, U of Nebraska Press, 1992; *Between Two Fires: American Indians in the Civil War*, by Laurence M. Hauptman, The Free Press (Simon & Schuster), 1995; and *The American Indian and the End of the Confederacy, 1863–1866*, by Annie Heloise Abel, U of Nebraska Press, 1993.

For those who scoff at the possibility of a

woman fighting in the Civil War disguised as a soldier, historians have documented at least one hundred women who did just that. It is estimated that as many as five hundred to a thousand women may have joined the two armies. A book on the subject is *All the Daring of the Soldier: Women of the Civil War Armies*, by Elizabeth D. Leonard, W. W. Norton, 1999.

All my stories connect in some way in a long, long saga that covers some fifty years of our country's Western history. Both Yellow Jacket and Jim Eagle had been members of the Lighthorsemen, the law enforcement arm of their tribes. They are both friends of another Lighthorseman, Talako of the Choctaw tribe, the hero of my earlier book, *Warrior's Honor*. Many of these stories are written out of sequence. The clue to following the saga is the date each story begins, which is always in the first several pages of each book. Some of my earlier books are still available from Zebra's mail order or your local bookstore.

I am always glad to hear from readers. For an autographed bookmark explaining how all the stories fit together, and a personal reply, please send a stamped, self-addressed #10 envelope to: Georgina Gentry, PO Box 162, Edmond, OK 73083-0162, or check my Web site at: www.nettrends.com/georginagentry.

So what story will I tell next? I received an

enormous amount of mail from readers who loved my last book, *To Tame a Texan*. They all wanted me to continue writing more humorous stories about Texans and the Durango family, and I'm pleased to do so.

Lacey Van Schuyler Durango has been reared by her aunt and uncle, Cimarron and Trace Durango, down in the Texas Hill Country around Austin and San Antonio. Prim, uptight Lacey is an ambitious Texas newspaper woman who has no time and no use for men. She's also the national president of the Ladies' Temperance Association. Lacey's riding a train to the Oklahoma Land Rush with plans to stake a claim and start her own newspaper. She and her L.T.A. ladies intend to mount a crusade to keep this new town dry, figuring if there's no saloons, their ideal city won't attract disreputable rogues.

Speaking of disreputable rogues, enter Blackie O'Neal. Blackie is a charming Texas rascal who could talk a dog off a meat wagon. This handsome scoundrel has been run out of half the towns in the Lone Star State. Think Rhett Butler, only more so. On a fine chestnut stallion, Blackie is galloping into this new town with plans to build the world's fanciest saloon and bordello, Blackie's Black Garter. He's got his eye on a choice piece of real estate right downtown. Unfortunately, it's the same land that our Texas temperance leader, Lacey, wants for her newspaper office. Uh-oh.

If you like feisty heroines and sexy heroes caught in humorous conflicts, come along for the adventure as this staid liquor-hating lady and the whiskey-peddling rascal clash. And maybe, just maybe, there might be a Texas-size romance in this story I call *To Tempt a Texan.*

Adios till next time,
Georgina Gentry

Swell